CW00570906

3.2.1.

by

Rebecca Xibalba and Tim Greaves

(from an original idea by Rebecca Xibalba)

In memory of HRH Queen Elizabeth II.
Our one true constant.

3.2.1.
Copyright © 2022 Rebecca Xibalba and Tim Greaves
TimBex Productions

All rights reserved.

This is a work of fiction. None of it is real. All names and events (and some places) are the products of the authors' imagination. Any relation to any real persons, organisations or events within the story are purely coincidental, and should not be construed as being real.

No part of this work may be used or reproduced in any form, except as allowable under "fair use" with the express written permission of the authors.

INTRODUCTION

Sebastian sat on the unforgivingly hard wooden chair waiting for his turn to be called up. Endeavouring to quell an uncharacteristic outbreak of nerves, he watched in silence as his classmates, along with students from other forms, scurried around the vast assembly hall, moving from their own row of chairs to the desks where the purveyors of countless bright futures sat awaiting their next conscript.

'Sebastian Matthews.' A voice called out from the desk in front of him.

Sebastian leapt to his feet and hurried forward.

'Take a seat, lad,' the bespectacled career advisor with a kindly face said. 'So, Mr Matthews, do you have an idea of what sort of career you might be interested in pursuing?'

The man's eyes twinkled and Sebastian felt his nervousness ebb a little. He looked down and shuffled his feet awkwardly. 'Not really, sir,' he replied.

'Well, that's why we're here,' the man said cheerfully. 'Now then. Have you given any thought to what you might like to do when you leave school?'

Sebastian shook his head.

'Not at all?'

Sebastian shook his head again.

'What about something you're keen on. When I was a young lad I wanted to be an astronaut.' He grinned.

'Why didn't you?' Sebastian asked.

It was a genuine question, but the man didn't quite seem to take it that way. His smile waned a little and he cleared his throat. 'Yes, well, we have to be realistic, not everyone is made for hopping around the galaxy like Flash Gordon.' His spectacles had slipped down his nose and he pushed them back into place. 'Most boys and girls at least have an inkling of something they'd like to do,' he continued. 'What about you?'

Sebastian shrugged.

The man's smile disappeared completely. 'Come on, lad, there must be something you're good at that you think might work for you as a profession. Something that can be cultivated.' A small note of irritability had crept into his voice. 'Do you have any special skills, for example? Something you can do that gives you a real sense of achievement?'

'I can hypnotise my cat!' Sebastian answered enthusiastically.

Momentarily unsure whether the boy was being facetious, the advisor looked at him over the rim of his glasses. 'Yes, well, unless you're aspiring to be the next Paul McKenna, I don't think that particular skill will be of much use to you career-wise, do you?'

'Paul who?' Sebastian asked.

'Paul McK...' The man paused. He opened the beige folder in front of him. 'Never mind. Let's just see if we can find something in here that might capture your interest.' He leafed through the paperwork in the folder. 'Now then, what have we got here?' he muttered to himself. His spectacles were slipping again. He righted them. 'Aha!' he exclaimed, withdrawing a sheet of paper from the folder.

Sebastian sat forward expectantly.

The man's smile had returned in force. 'Book-keeping and finance control! What about that then, eh?'

Sebastian's shoulders dropped, his face fell and he sagged back in his chair.

2

Fifteen years on, Sebastian was not only aware of who Paul McKenna was, he absolutely detested him. The man's books were everywhere and Sebastian felt that he really knocked the razzmatazz out of the mystical art of hypnosis, especially with his outrageous and boring claims that he could turn fat women into supermodels and cure addictions.

Sebastian's parents were forever nagging him and he had fought them for as long as he could to pursue his dream of becoming a stage hypnotist. But they resolutely refused to support his "fantasies", as they referred to them, and they weren't at all happy with their pet cat, Nala walking around in a daze most of the time either; especially when she fell off the garden fence and broke her tail. The extortionate vet's bill for prescription pain relief that ensued added ire to injury and resulted in Sebastian being grounded for a month and forced to hand over half of his weekly paper round money until his father had been fully remunerated.

Now, working for an app development company in a small, dual-aspect workspace on the 14th floor of an office block in Canary Wharf was Sebastian's reality. Although it paid well and he didn't have far to travel from home to get there, it wasn't really how he'd envisaged making a name for himself.

He gazed out across the expanse of grey water; it was stormy out and the tinted glass of his office window made it appear even darker. It was only two o'clock in the afternoon on a mid-September day, but it looked more like early evening outside.

His eyes followed a pigeon as it crash-landed on a narrow window ledge on the block opposite and tried fruitlessly to mount another pigeon before tumbling off and cascading downwards until a clumsy flap of its wings

3

took it airborne again. It soared away over the rooftops and out of sight.

'Sebastian!'

The voice made him jump. 'Yes, Ryan?' he replied, spinning in his chair to face his manager.

'Have you completed that design yet?' Ryan asked irritably.

'Nearly.'

Ryan scowled. 'Nearly doesn't cut it. Stop bloody daydreaming and crack on with it. You're holding up the rest of the team.'

'Sorry,' Sebastian replied. 'Don't worry, I'll have it done by close of play,' he added, trying to sound enthused.

Ryan strolled off and Sebastian turned back to face his computer. The screen displayed a selection of ladies heads, all missing their vital features. Beneath the blank faces were several rows of eyes, noses and lips. Sebastian stared at the screen with disinterest as he manipulated various noses onto the faces with his mouse.

The app, created to allow women to see how they would look after cosmetic surgery procedures, was possibly the most tiresome assignment Sebastian had been given since he'd started at the company 12 years earlier and only enforced the fact that this was certainly not how he'd foreseen his destiny. He sighed and tried his hardest to focus on the job at hand, but his mind was elsewhere.

CHAPTER 1

The Cauliflower public house in Seven Kings, just outside Ilford, was already getting busy. A popular gin palace that had been in situ since the late 1800s, it now attracted mostly beer drinkers and fans of live music. On alternate Friday nights the venue hosted karaoke and it always proved popular, drawing in scores of wannabe Gloria Gaynors and aspiring Neil Diamonds.

Joshua Hunter and his girlfriend, Maisie Peters, were sitting at a stained, circular wooden table right beside the stage, feasting on rather anaemic-looking chicken nuggets and chips from a plastic basket.

Joshua picked up a bottle of ketchup. Scowling, he picked off the crusty residue that had formed around the nozzle and then squeezed the contents liberally all over his chips.

'Do want some chips with that red sauce?' a voice behind them said.

Joshua turned his head and smiled. 'Alright Jordan, mate?'

Jordan King and Joshua had been friends since primary school, and were affectionately referred to by everyone who knew them as "JJ" in response to their joined-at-the-hip friendship. That friendship had been put under strain recently by the arrival of Maisie in Joshua's life, who, despite her protestations as to otherwise, was more than a little jealous; she would never have thought herself to be of that nature, yet there was no denying she found it difficult sharing her new-found love with his ever-present best mate.

Jordan smiled at Maisie and with undisguised reluctance she forced a smile in return.

'What you lovebirds drinking?' Jordan asked, gesturing to the empty glasses on the table.

'I'll have a pint of Carlsberg, mate.' Joshua looked at Maisie. 'Another Coke?'

'Nah. I'm good,' she replied, very obviously avoiding making eye contact with Jordan. She popped a bent chip into her mouth and chewed on it.

'Back in two.' Unphased by the girl's aloofness towards him, Jordan turned and strolled over to the bar.

Detecting her change in mood, Joshua eyed Maisie with slight concern. 'You alright babe?'

'Yeah, fine,' she replied curtly.

Joshua frowned. 'You sure?'

'I said yes, didn't I?!' Maisie snapped. Flicking back her long blonde hair, she picked up her phone and opened WhatsApp.

Joshua sat staring blankly at the stage, concluding – but not daring to raise the subject – that it was probably Maisie's time of the month.

A movement to the right of the stage caught his eye and he saw a man struggling to bring in equipment through the side door.

'I might see if Frank needs a hand,' Joshua said as he stood up. He looked across towards the bar, where he could see Jordan holding a £20 note aloft amid a throng of other waiting customers. Popping his last chicken nugget into his mouth, he walked over to the stage. 'Need a hand, mate?'

Frank Henderson, who was bending to set down a silver flight case on the stage, looked up. 'That would be great,' he said with the familiar Mancunian twang. 'Cheers, lad.' He stood upright, put a hand to the small of his back and winced. 'I'm not the man I never was.' He winked at Joshua.

Maisie was still glued to her phone, but had switched from WhatsApp to her Instagram page. Scrolling through the recent images, she tutted at the sight of the selfie she'd taken earlier in the toilets at work. Beneath the photo there was a tiny heart emblem with the words **2 LIKES** alongside it. She typed a name into the search field and grimaced as her eyes fell upon a photo of Karlie Samuels pouting at the screen. The photo had attracted **65 LIKES**.

Karlie and Maisie both worked in sales at a package holiday company. Karlie always smashed her targets, leaving Maisie well behind and often the subject of ridicule at the end of week catch-up meeting.

Maisie closed down her phone and sighed. She rolled her eyes as she watched Joshua effortlessly carrying in a large speaker.

Jordan appeared behind her and set two pint glasses down on the table. 'Where's Joshy?'

Maisie inwardly shuddered; she hated it when he called him Joshy. 'Over there helping the karaoke guy,' she said.

Jordan beamed. 'Legit? What a teacher's pet!'

Maisie threw him a dismissive look. 'I actually think it's nice of him to help,' she said, slightly haughtily.

Jordan snapped his fingers in the air. 'Yeah. S'pose it is really.' He swaggered over to the stage and chipped in.

Maisie rolled her eyes again. Her phone started buzzing and skimmed around the table in a rhythmic circle. She grabbed it up and tapped **Accept**. 'Katie, where are you?'

'In the pub, where are you?' Katie's voice replied.

Maisie looked round the room, but she couldn't see any sign of her friend. 'We're near the stage,' she replied.

'Ah, okay, I'm over by the pool tables,' Katie said. 'Mark is playing. We'll be over when he's been thrashed!'

7

Maisie laughed. 'Yeah okay,' she said. 'Can you bring me a Coke when...' She trailed off as she realised Katie had hung up. 'Charming!' she muttered under her breath.

Jordan and Joshua returned to the table and sat down. Jordan picked up his pint and almost downed it in one, leaving less than a quarter in the bottom of the glass.

'Thirsty?' Joshua asked.

'Thanks to the impromptu roadying I am,' Jordan replied, licking the line of froth from his top lip.

'You only carried one box!' Joshua said sarcastically

'It was heavy, bruv!'

Joshua laughed. 'You're getting weak mate. It's all that hanging round old folk.'

The pair of them burst out laughing.

Maisie looked at them both contemptuously.

Joshua raised his right arm and clenched his fist, posing like a body builder. 'Check out these guns!'

Suddenly a hand appeared and fingers closed around Joshua's bicep making him jump.

'Showing off for the ladies again?'

Maisie's face changed to an uncharacteristically happy one at the sight of Mark gripping Joshua's bicep with his huge hand. She burst out laughing.

'Alright, babe,' Joshua said, a note of embarrassment in his voice. 'It wasn't *that* funny.'

Mark chuckled. 'It was a bit.' He pulled out a chair and collapsed onto it. 'All ready for a bit of a sing-song then, peeps?' Scratching at his unshaven chin, he turned to face Katie, who was standing behind him. 'Pass us the book, doll.'

Katie handed him a large ring binder and sat down beside him.

Mark had latched himself onto the circle of friends the previous summer. They had all been attending an outdoor festival in Chelmsford and someone had stolen Mark's wallet and clothes whilst he was lying face down in the mud, completely wasted, just six feet away from the sanctuary of his tent. The friends had taken pity on him and given him a lift back to his home in Romford. Ever since then, he'd followed them around and despite the 20-years age gap he'd fitted in rather well. Katie was his long-suffering girlfriend and despite Mark's evident problematic relationship with alcohol – not to mention his often all too apparent aversion to soap and water – she loved him.

'Where's Seb?' Katie asked.

'Probably still at work,' Jordan replied.

As if he'd been summoned, Sebastian suddenly stepped up to the table. 'Whatchya!' He put his glass down on the table and walked across the dance floor to grab a spare chair. 'Busy in here tonight,' he said as Mark and Katie moved their chairs to give him enough space to wedge himself between them.

'Yeah. End of the month, innit, mate?' Mark replied. 'Payday!'

'And karaoke!' Katie added enthusiastically.

Sebastian sighed. 'Oh, God, *really*?!'

Katie grinned. 'Yeah. And you're up tonight!'

Sebastian shook his head. 'Not a chance!'

Katie put an arm round his shoulders. 'Aww, don't be shy. Katie wants Sebby to sing her a song.'

'Not happening.' Sebastian took a sip of his drink.

'Here,' Mark said. 'What do you call a group of singing terrorists?' He looked around the assembled faces, eagerly waiting to reveal the punchline.

'I don't know,' Maisie said. 'What *do* you call a group of singing terrorists?'

9

Mark opened his mouth to reply, but Katie cut in. 'A taliband.'

Everyone burst out laughing except Mark, who looked a little crestfallen.

Katie saw his expression. 'Oh, sorry, did I steal the glory, sweetie? I'll make it up to you later.' She pursed her lips and blew him a kiss.

A look of annoyance on his face, Mark slapped the ring binder down hard on the table in front of Sebastian, sending the now empty chicken baskets flying. '*Sebastian*!' he exclaimed.

'What?' Sebastian said wearily.

'Not you, sunshine. The Cockney Rebel song. *Sebastian*. I reckon you should indulge us.'

'Who's Cockney Rebel?' Joshua said, frowning.

Mark looked at him in disbelief. 'You're kidding me. Steve Harley was a legend!'

Joshua shook his head. 'Never heard of him.'

'I know the song,' Sebastian said. 'My Mum used to sing it to me. But I'm not a performing seal.'

Mark laughed. 'Chicken. Thought you might like a bit of Cock...' – he paused just long enough for effect – '...ney Rebel. Jordan does, don't you mate?' He puckered his lips at the dark-skinned man and made little kissing noises. 'Likes a bit of Cock...' – he paused again – '...ney Rebel, does our Jordan.'

Rolling her eyes, Katie looked apologetically at Jordan. 'Pay no attention to him, lovely.'

Jordan grinned broadly, displaying a mouthful of perfect white teeth. 'Pay no attention to who?'

Katie turned her attention back to Sebastian. 'You don't have to do it if you really don't want to. But why not just have a look through for something you like and think about it. It's good fun, we're all gonna do one and nobody will be judging you.'

Sebastian surveyed the list of songs in the binder, hoping that if he at least feigned interest he could surreptitiously avoid actually getting up on stage.

'We could do a duet if you like,' Jordan chipped in. 'Moral support and all that.' He drained his glass and looked at Joshua, mouthing 'Another?'

Pouting, Joshua shook his head. 'I thought you and me were the duet kings, mate?'

Maisie shot him a disdainful look.

Joshua was beginning to think it had been a mistake bringing her along. She had been very reluctant to come.

Katie turned to Jordan. 'How do you fancy duetting with me on *Islands in the Stream*?'

'I knew I should have brought my blonde wig,' Jordan said, running a hand through his tight braids. He grinned at her. 'But I'm game. *You* can be Dolly and I'll be Kenny. You got a pen?'

Katie ferreted around in her bag and handed him a biro with the end all chewed.

Jordan pulled the folder towards him and removed one of the pages of perforated request slips from the back. 'I'll wait till we've all chosen something, then I'll take them all up,' he said.

'Well, I'm doing *Money for Nothing*,' Mark said.

Katie laughed. 'Apt.' She grinned at Maisie. 'He's always in dire straits.'

Maisie forced an unconvincing smile.

'Come on then,' Mark said, elbowing Sebastian and almost making him spill his lager. 'What ya singing, sunshine?'

'I still haven't made my mind up.'

11

'Bucks Fizz!' Katie exclaimed. '*Making My Mind Up*, that's a really good one.'

"It's *Making* Your *Mind Up*,' Maisie said irritably. 'Oh, for God's sake, just take the request slips up and let's get this nonsense over with,' she snapped. 'We'll be here all night at this rate.'

Katie looked at Jordan. '*Islands in the Stream* then?"

Jordan nodded. He filled out a slip and handed it to Joshua. 'Thanks.'

Mark handed him his request too and Joshua took the slips of paper over to the stage where he handed them to Frank.

'He ain't chickening out,' Mark said, elbowing Sebastian again. 'Here…' – he leant in close – '…if you won't pick one I'll do it for you. What about *24 Karat Magic*?'

'Ooh, that's a good one,' Katie said. 'It would be perfect for you, Seb. You can do magic!'

Sebastian shook his head. 'Hypnosis isn't magic. It's an art and not many people possess the skill to do it.'

'Hark at him,' Mark scoffed. 'An art, my arse. Utter bollocks is what it is.'

Sebastian smiled thinly. He'd learned not to rise to Mark's bait. 'If you say so.'

Mark grinned. 'Don't get all riled up, I'm only pulling your plonker.' He nudged Sebastian playfully. 'You know that, right mate?'

'Sure.'

'So, come on then. Are you going to sing something or are you just gonna be a chicken?' He nudged Sebastian again. 'A great big fat chicken. Buk-buk-buk ba-gawk.'

Sebastian opened his mouth to respond, but his words were lost behind the high-pitched squealing sound of the microphone as Frank Henderson, wearing a pork pie hat, took to the stage behind them.

Frank was Manchester-born and proud of it. But whenever he got behind a microphone he adopted a weird American accent that sounded like… well, a Mancunian doing an American accent. Badly. He evidently did it to make himself appear cool, but unbeknownst to him it had the opposite effect.

'Good evening ladies and jellyspoons,' he drawled. 'And welcome to Frank's Friday Night Frolics.' He winked. 'And it's the lad himself speaking, by the by.'

'The *prat* himself,' Mark muttered under his breath.

Katie shot him a look. 'Shoosh, you!'

'Now then,' Frank was saying. 'I've already got some requests in, so don't be shy, everyone's welcome. But I'd like to get you all in the mood with a favourite – I'm always asked to do it, y'know – so start thinking about a new career, Olly Murs, cos Frankie's in town! And here's *Dance With Me*!'

He pressed a button on the rig and the music blared out. As Frank began to sing, with the exception of the regulars who knew him, the mood of the crowd changed from the mild amusement born of low expectation to astonished appreciation; Frank was surprisingly rather good. People began to clap along.

Even Mark looked impressed. 'He's actually not that bad.'

'He's probably got the mic on autotune,' Sebastian said. 'He'll turn it off as soon as the plebs go up to sing.'

'Cynic,' Katie said.

'Guilty,' Sebastian replied.

Frank's performance came to an end and the pub erupted in a cacophony of applause, cheers and whistling.

13

'Right then,' Frank said. He held up one of the request slips. 'Please welcome to the stage Dolly Parton and Kenny Rogers, ay-kay-ay...' – he glanced at the paper – '...Katie and Jordan.'

Katie and Jordan got up and hurried up to the stage. Frank handed them a mic. 'Only got the one tonight, the other one packed up. Hope you two lovebirds don't mind sharing.'

'Oh, we're not...' Katie began.

Jordan interjected: 'We don't mind one bit.' He took her hand. 'Do we, baby?'

Katie had always had a thing for Jordan but, even had he not been gay, she would probably never have summoned up the courage to tell him so. She looked him in the eyes and smiled. 'I guess we don't.'

Mark, who was all too aware of her feelings about the younger man, had been watching as they mounted the stage. He saw the expression on her face and tutted. Getting up he waggled his empty glass in the air and snapped, 'Anyone for another?' He ignored Sebastian as he reached for his empty glass. As Jordan and Katie started to sing, Mark turned and walked off to the bar without giving anyone else a chance to respond.

'What's up with him?' Joshua mused aloud.

'Are you really that blind?' Maisie said, tutting. 'It's obvious Katie fancies Jordan.'

Joshua looked confused. 'She does? Since when?'

'Pretty much since forever. Haven't you noticed how she is around him?'

'Nope. But she's old enough to be his mother.'

Maisie scowled. 'Actually, she's only five years older than him.'

'Whatevs,' Joshua scoffed. 'She knows he's gay. And so does Mark.'

14

Sebastian stood up. 'I actually thought Mark was going to put his hand in his pocket for a moment. That would have been a first. How naïve am I? Come on, I'll get them in. What are you having?'

Joshua held out his glass to Sebastian. 'Cheers, bruv. Another Carlsberg please.'

Sebastian took the glass from him. 'When are you going to graduate to a man's drink?'

Joshua laughed. 'It *is* a man's drink. And you can talk, drinking Foster's. It's like gnat's piss.'

Maisie handed her empty glass to Sebastian. 'Diet Coke, please. Thanks, Seb.'

Sebastian made his way over to the bar where Mark was still waiting to be served.

Joshua leant over to Maisie. 'Can't you at least try to appear like you're enjoying yourself? You've got a face on you like a bulldog chewing a wasp.'

Maisie suddenly felt bad. She put a hand on Joshua's knee. 'Sorry, baby. I'm just not in a very good mood tonight.'

'What's up?' Joshua said, imbuing the words with just the right level of concern.

'I just don't want to be here. I'd rather be home watching *Love Island*. I thought it would have been nice for just the two of us to go somewhere for a change.'

'Friday night is the only night we can all get together. We can go out just us another night.'

'But we never do!'

'We will. I promise.' Joshua kissed her cheek. *Definitely time of the month*, he thought.

Katie and Jordan finished their passable rendition of *Islands in the Stream* and Frank stepped over and patted them both on the shoulder. 'Nice job, guys.' He looked out

15

across the pub. 'Come on, ladles and jellyspoons, let's hear it for…' He faltered.

'Katie and Jordan,' Jordan said.

'Katie and John!' Frank shouted.

As the crowd responded enthusiastically, Mark and Sebastian returned to the table. With a sulky expression on his face, Mark slumped into his chair and downed half of the contents of his pint glass in one. He belched. 'Well that was decidedly underwhelming.'

Sebastian handed Maisie her Coke and set down Joshua's drink in front of him. 'One pint of Carlsberg for the big man.'

Joshua smiled at him sarcastically. 'Cheers, bruv. I just gotta go take a leak.'

As he got up and made his way to the toilets, Katie and Jordan stepped off the stage. Behind them, Frank was holding another request slip aloft. 'Will our budding Robbie Williams come on up. Yes folks, it's one of our regulars, one of The Cauliflower's favourites and mine. It's Adrian! And this evening he's treating us to *Angels*.' He glanced at the lanky lad who bounded up on the stage and put a hand over the microphone. 'Getting like a stuck record with this one aren't you, kid?'

A man sitting on his own at the table next to the group of friends made a note on a piece of paper in front of him.

Laughing, Katie and Jordan arrived back at the table.

Katie's smile faded. 'Didn't you get me another?' she said, eyeing the glass in Mark's hand.

'Didn't know what you wanted,' Mark mumbled, avoiding eye contact.

'I'll get you one,' Jordan said. 'What d'ya fancy, hun?'

Mark banged down his glass and jumped to his feet. 'I said I didn't know what she wanted, not I wasn't getting her one!'

16

Everyone sat looking at him.

Jordan had crossed swords with Mark needlessly in the past and he wasn't about to instigate another absurd confrontation. He raised a hand of silent surrender and sat down. 'No problem.'

As the Robbie Williams wannabe launched into an excruciatingly off-key take on *Angels*, Mark fumbled around in his pocket and pulled out a folded £5 note that looked so tattered and torn it probably ought to have been withdrawn from circulation. He unfolded it and held it out to Katie. 'Get whatever you want.'

Batting it away, she sat down. 'I'm not thirsty. I'll have something later.'

'Suit yourself.' Mark stuffed the money back in his pocket and sat back down.

Sebastian, who had been watching the little drama unfold with mild amusement, was suddenly distracted by the sight of a young woman who'd just come into the pub and joined her friends at a table nearby. Their eyes met for a moment and then she turned away. Had there been the fleeting trace of a smile on her lips? Sebastian wasn't sure.

Katie noticed Sebastian looking and nudged him. 'Ahh, so it all becomes clear.'

Sebastian frowned. 'What does?'

'Why the man who detests karaoke shows up on karaoke night. Are you ever going to pluck up the courage to ask Tilly out?' Katie nudged him again.

'No idea what you're talking about.' Sebastian buried his face in his glass.

'You think I haven't noticed you eyeing her up before? Everyone has. She's a really nice girl, she works at the Co-Op. I know her mum. Hey, why don't you get up and sing her a song?' She winked at him.

Mark had been listening and, never one to miss an opportunity to wind up Sebastian, he started to get up. 'If chicken here won't talk to her, I'll do it for him.'

Sebastian's eyes widened and he nearly choked on his drink. 'No!'

Mark chuckled. 'I don't mind helping out a chicken.' He waggled his elbows and made a little buk-buk noise. 'Or better still, why don't you put one of your spells on her, make her fall madly in love with you?'

'Tell you what,' Sebastian started, desperate to stop Mark ruining any chance he might have of ever speaking to the woman himself. 'You're always taking the piss out of me about hypnosis. Let's make a deal.'

Mark sat down again. 'Go on.'

'If I can hypnotise one of you here and now, you leave me to talk to her in my own good time. And if I fail I'll go talk to her right now.'

Mark grinned. 'This should be worth seeing.'

Maisie suddenly perked up. 'Do Joshua!'

Sebastian nodded. 'Okay.' He thought for a moment, then looked at Joshua's untouched pint of Carlsberg. 'I'll make him think he's drinking piss.'

'Too easy,' Mark said. 'It *is* piss.'

'He loves it,' Jordan said. He looked across the room and saw Joshua appear in the doorway to the toilets. 'Here he comes. Go on then, Seb do it.'

As the wince-inducing noise that could barely be identified as *Angels* came to a finish, Joshua dropped himself back into his chair. 'That's better,' he said, picking up his glass.

'Just a moment before you drink that,' Sebastian said, leaning forward.

Joshua paused, the glass at his lips. 'What?'

As Frank summoned the next performer onto the stage – a rotund man in his 50s wearing a football shirt that barely covered an unsightly beer belly – Sebastian locked eyes with Joshua.

'You are very thirsty.'

'Too right I am, mate. I...' Joshua suddenly stopped speaking and his expression went blank.

'You are very, *very* thirsty,' Sebastian continued. 'But all you have to drink is a glass full of gnat's piss.'

Up on stage, Beer Belly Man started to warble the unlikeliest of songs: *I Will Survive*. He was surprisingly good.

Joshua continued to stare blankly at Sebastian.

'It will taste vile,' Sebastian went on. 'Because that's what gnat's piss tastes like. Vile. How will it taste?'

'Vile,' Joshua said quietly.

'That's right.' Sebastian nodded, his eyes remaining fixed upon Joshua's. 'Vile. You *know* it will taste vile. And yet you are so thirsty you have no choice but to drink it anyway.'

'I have to drink it anyway,' Joshua intoned.

Everyone was watching Joshua, waiting to see what was going to happen. Even Mark looked interested.

'Your lips are getting drier,' Sebastian said softly. 'And your mouth. And your throat. Your thirst is becoming unbearable. You just *have* to quench it or you will die. Yet all you have is the gnat's piss. What is it you have?'

'Gnat's piss.'

'That's right. Vile, stinking gnat's piss. It's no good. You have tried to resist, but you know you have no choice but to drink it.'

Joshua's eyes fell upon the glass in his hand. 'I have no choice but to drink it,' he said, almost inaudibly.

Sebastian nodded gently at Joshua. 'That's right. You know it's going to taste vile, but you must now drink. Go ahead.'

Joshua licked his lips and took a large mouthful of lager. In an instant he screwed up his face and a spray of liquid and foam erupted from his mouth and splashed all over the table. 'Fuck's sake!' he exclaimed. 'That's vile.'

Maisie scowled. 'Ewwwww!'

Everyone else roared with laughter.

Sebastian leant forward and snapped his fingers in front of Joshua's face as the laughter continued.

'What's so funny?' Joshua said, wiping his mouth on his sleeve. He glared at Mark. 'Did you put something in it you bastard?'

Mark held up his hands. 'Don't look at me, pal.'

Sebastian sat back in his seat with a satisfied smile on his face. 'Told you it was gnat's piss, mate.' He looked at Mark. 'I win.' He glanced to his right and to his surprise he saw that Tilly was looking directly at him. This time she definitely smiled at him. He felt his cheeks burning and quickly turned away. 'Sorry, mate,' he said to Joshua. 'It was just a silly joke. They wanted me to hypnotise you. I'll buy you another one.'

'You wanker,' Joshua exclaimed. He looked distinctly unimpressed. 'What a waste of a pint!' He looked at Jordan. 'Here, mate, do you remember when Seb got you doing that ballet dance?'

Jordan gave him a sarcastic smile. 'I'm hardly likely to forget it. And even if I did you're always gonna be right there ready to remind me.'

Joshua cackled. 'I nearly pissed myself. You could have given Darcey Bussell a run for her money. It was bloody hilarious!'

20

'Again – as you like to remind me.' Jordan rolled his eyes.

'Do Mark!' Katie suddenly cried enthusiastically.

Jordan laughed. 'Yeah, go on, Seb.'

Mark grinned and shook his head. 'Not possible,' he said. 'I'm immune to that shit.'

Sebastian smiled. 'Really?'

'Yep.'

'Then you won't mind me trying.'

'Waste of time,' Mark said. He glanced round the table and saw that everyone was looking at him expectantly. His grin faded a little. 'Alright then.' He got up, spun his chair round and sat down again with his legs astride it. 'Come on then, magic man. Bet ya can't!' The cocky tone was still there, but the expression on his face wasn't quite so assured.

Beer Belly Man reached a crescendo and was greeted by a loud round of applause. Frank stepped over and relieved him of the microphone. 'Nice one, sir.' He looked out across the pub. 'Okay then,' he said, inspecting another request slip. 'Next up is Stuart.'

A man at the back waved a hand in the air – 'That's me!' – and made his way to the stage.

Frank pushed a button and the music started.

Sebastian stood up and stepped over to Mark who was jigging about in the chair like an excited schoolboy.

'This is gonna be a breeze. Drinks on Seb when he fails,' Mark said confidently.

'Sit still,' Sebastian said sternly.

Mark sat bolt upright. Sebastian leant forward and stared into his eyes. For a moment it looked as if Mark was taking it seriously, but then he burst out laughing. Sebastian sighed and turned away.

21

'Alright, alright. Sorry. I'll sit still,' Mark said, grinning broadly.

Sebastian turned back and fixed him with his gaze. 'I'm going to count backwards from three to one, and when I reach one you will fall instantly under my control. I will bring you back to this world by saying "stop" and snapping my fingers. Do you understand?' Mark nodded. 'Three... Two... *One.*' Mark's grin disappeared completely and his face went blank.

Katie, Jordan, Maisie and Joshua watched in silence as Sebastian leant forward and spoke softly. 'Every time somebody says the word chicken you will *behave* like a chicken.'

Mark said nothing.

'You will walk like a chicken. You will flap your wings. You will make noises like a chicken. You will feed like a chicken. Nod if you understand.'

Still Mark said nothing, but he nodded.

The man at the next table who had been watching the singers all evening and making notes put down his pen and turned his attention to the group of friends.

'You will become a chicken,' Sebastian continued. 'A fat, feathery chicken. What will you become?'

Mark remained silent.

'What will you become?' Sebastian repeated.

'A chicken,' Mark said.

'Very well. The next time you hear the word chicken, you will *become* one.' Sebastian smiled and stepped back. He suddenly became aware that not only were his friends watching, so was the man at the next table. And – his heart skipped a beat – so too was the woman of his dreams. Adopting a showman-like stance, he raised his hands theatrically. 'Ladies and gentlemen, I give you Mark the human *chicken*!'

Upon hearing the trigger word, Mark leapt up out of his seat. 'Buk-buk!' He jerked his head quizzically to one side, then the other. 'Buk-buk!' he said again, more loudly this time, as he strutted around the table with his hands tucked up under his armpits.

The group of friends burst out laughing. Except Maisie, who simply rolled her eyes.

'Nice one, bruv!' Jordan said, rocking with laughter.

People sitting around the pub turned their attention away from Stuart, who had his eyes tightly shut as he belted out *Careless Whisper* for all he was worth, completely oblivious to the charade that was unfolding in front of the stage.

Everyone was now captivated by Mark's antics and laughing along with Sebastian's friends.

Sebastian glanced at Tilly and was delighted to see she too was in hysterics.

Stuart suddenly became aware of the laughter and opened his eyes. He saw Mark circling the tables and abruptly stopped singing.

The whole room was filled with uproarious laughter as Mark flapped his makeshift wings, making clucking noises at the top of his voice.

Katie was wiping the tears of laughter from her eyes.

Mark started to move away from their table and strutted over to where Tilly and her friends were sitting. Each of them was holding a glass of wine and there was a bowl of tortilla chips in the centre of the table. They watched with amusement as Mark approached. He stopped beside the table and his eyes fell upon the triangular snacks. 'Buk-buk-buk ba-gawk,' he said loudly, cocking his head sideways.

One of the women held out a tortilla chip towards him. She smiled. 'Here chick-chick,' she said.

Mark stepped towards her and with his mouth open wide lurched forward and took the chip. The three women burst out laughing. Mark crowed out loud and scraped the floor with his feet as he stepped even closer to the table. In one swift movement he sunk his face into the bowl.

'Hey!' one of the women snapped. 'That's just taking the piss!'

Sebastian, realising that he had let things go too far, rushed over. He stopped in front of Mark and stared into a face that was dappled with tortilla-crumbs. 'Stop!' he commanded and snapped his fingers.

Mark stood upright and stopped still, with tiny pieces of tortilla chip dropping off his stubble dotted chin. 'What the...?!' he muttered.

'Return to the table and sit down,' Sebastian said calmly. 'You're making a complete twat of yourself.'

Without a word, Mark turned and obediently plodded back to the table.

'I am *so* sorry!' Sebastian said. He was addressing all the women seated at the table, but he was looking at Tilly.

She smiled. 'Did you make him do that?'

Sebastian looked a little awkward. 'Well, I, er...'

'It looked to me like you did,' Tilly said, still smiling.

Sebastian looked contrite. 'Yeah, I suppose I did. Just a silly little game between me and my mates.'

The woman beamed up at him. '*Silly*? I think it's incredible!'

Sebastian could feel himself beginning to blush. 'Well, thank you. I'm really sorry about your tortillas though. Can I get you another bowl?'

Tilly smiled. 'No, it's fine, they weren't very nice anyway.'

'Well, Mark seemed to enjoy them,' Sebastian replied with a cheeky twinkle in his eyes.

24

Tilly giggled.

'I'm Sebastian by the way.'

Tilly held out her hand. 'Tilly,' she said.

Sebastian took her cool hand in his. 'I've seen you in here before, I think.' *I think*? Did that sound as phoney as Sebastian thought it did. 'Do you like karaoke?' he continued.

'She can't stand it,' one of the other women said. 'She comes with us on the promise we won't cajole her into getting up on stage.'

As Sebastian smiled, the music started up again and he looked to see *Careless Whisper* guy marching back to his table looking distinctly miffed, and Jordan and Joshua had taken to stage. 'I'd better go re-join my friends,' he said. 'Once again, I'm sorry about the chips.'

'See ya,' Tilly said, as Sebastian walked away.

He paused and looked back at her. She was smiling at him warmly. His heart beating hard, he said, 'Yeah. See ya.'

As Sebastian reached the table, Katie jumped up and grabbed his shoulders. 'So?'

'So what?' Sebastian replied innocently.

'Did you ask her out?'

Sebastian shook his head. 'I was too busy apologising for...' – he lowered his voice – '...chicken boy over there.'

Mark was sitting with a faraway look on his face.

'You alright, mate?' Sebastian said.

Mark shook his head and blinked a couple of times. Then, as his eyes focussed on Sebastian, he burst out laughing. 'See!' he exclaimed triumphantly. 'Told you I'm impervious to that shit.'

Sebastian winked at Katie. 'As we found out.'

25

Joshua and Jordan finished their very respectable version of Pharrell Williams's *Happy* and bounded down from the stage.

Katie got up to greet them and threw her arms around Jordan. 'That was pumpin'!' she exclaimed.

Mark looked suitably nettled at the sight of Katie and Jordan embracing, but kept his thoughts to himself.

Maisie stood up. 'I'm going to the ladies room.' She looked at Joshua. 'When I come back can we get going please? I've got a headache.'

Joshua was about to offer up a reason why they should stay, but he saw the expression on her face. In Maisie-speak, a question prefixed with the words "can we" seldom translated as anything other than a statement: "we *are*".

'Sure,' Joshua said resignedly.

Maisie stepped away from the table, a young girl took to the stage and Frank handed her the microphone.

Katie watched as Maisie pushed her way between the tables. She sniggered. 'She ain't gonna like the toilets here. They're scummy.'

'Ladies can't be any worse than the Gents!' Jordan exclaimed.

'Wanna bet?' Katie replied, pulling a face. 'I refuse to go in there ever again.'

Jordan downed the last of his pint. 'Where we off to then, Joshy?'

'I think I'd better take her home,' Joshua said, looking – and sounding – rather dejected. 'We'll go via the chip shop. That'll cheer her up a bit.'

'You old romantic,' Katie said, chuckling.

'Chips aren't gonna help you, sunshine,' Mark chimed in. 'She said she's got a headache. Someone ain't getting any tonight.'

A minute later Maisie reappeared in the doorway to the toilets and beckoned to Joshua urgently. He got up and made his way through the tables to meet her.

'What's up?'

'Those toilets are bloody rank. They stink of pee and there's toilet paper strewn all over the floor. And as for the pans...' – she faltered, struggling to stop herself from gagging – '...I thought I was going to be sick.'

'Okay, come on, let's go to the chippy.'

Maisie shook her head. 'I don't want to go to the chippy, I want you to take me home. I still need to go and I sure as hell couldn't go in *there*.' She gestured at the toilet door.

'Okay.' Joshua turned and looked back at his friends. He gave them a half-hearted wave.

They all raised a hand in acknowledgement.

As Maisie made her way to the door, Joshua glanced down and noticed a piece of toilet paper stuck to the heel of her shoe. He decided against drawing her attention to it; all being well it would fall off as they walked up the street.

Frank thanked the girl – whose voice had been so quiet that her song was barely audible – and inspected the next request slip. 'Next up is Mark!'

Mark got to his feet. 'Time for a proper singer to show 'em how it's done.'

Katie rolled her eyes. When he was out of earshot, she leant over to Sebastian. 'I think we've already seen him at his best tonight.' She gave Sebastian a little kiss on the cheek. 'Buk-buk!'

CHAPTER 2

As Joshua parked up outside the gym where he worked as a personal trainer he checked his reflection in the rear-view mirror. One of the things he was always telling his clients was that in order to maintain a healthy routine you must get plenty of sleep. Yet here he was, puffy-eyed and running on empty after a three-hour heated argument on the phone with Maisie, which had gone on into the early hours. Subsequently unable to sleep, he'd tossed and turned as jumbled flashes of the argument spun relentlessly around his mind. To add insult to injury, no sooner had he at last managed to drift off than the six-thirty alarm rudely woke him.

Rubbing a crumb of sleepy dust out of the corner of one eye, he looked over towards the main entrance where he could see some of his regular clients filtering in. Quickly retrieving his hold-all from the passenger seat, he got out of the car and strolled over towards the doors, adopting a carefree stride and his signature warm smile.

He signed in at the reception desk, but as he turned to walk away, Linda, the pretentious and somewhat annoying receptionist called him back. 'Oh, Mr Hunter! You forgot to fill in your arrival time on the sheet.'

Joshua turned back to her and smiled. 'Could you do it please, Lin? I'm in a bit of a hurry.' He tapped his wristwatch. 'Eight a.m., yeah?' Without waiting for her to reply, he hurried off towards the sports hall.

Linda looked up at the clock on the wall. 'Eight-seventeen,' she mumbled to herself irritably as she jotted the digits down on the sign-in sheet.

As Joshua entered the hall, a few of his 8:30 clients were already changed and waiting for him. He respected eagerness, but just for today he couldn't help wishing they had turned up on time. 'Morning guys,' he called out, endeavouring to sound chirpier than he felt. They returned his greeting in garbled unison. Joshua's phone started to buzz in his pocket. He let out an exasperated sigh. 'Oh, jeez, not now!' He turned to face the assembled fitness fanatics. 'If you want to start your warm up, I'll be with you in two ticks.' He swiftly ducked through the doorway into the changing room area and as he pulled out the phone he breathed out another huge sigh; this time it was one of relief. He tapped **Accept**.

'Hey. Jordan. What's up?'

'Just a quick one bruv,' Jordan replied. 'I know you're at work, but I've just seen Katie, innit. She said you and Maisie have split up.'

A puzzled look crossed Joshua's face. 'Really?! First I've heard of it!'

'What's goin' on, bruv?' Jordan asked with a note of genuine concern.

Joshua sighed. 'Oh, I dunno mate. She spent most of last night shouting at me down the phone and then crying and then shouting some more. To be honest, I lost track of what the row was even about. She's proper high maintenance.'

'That's harsh, man! Listen, do you wanna meet up for lunch? Come round the home, I'll smuggle you out a sandwich.'

'Yeah, that sounds good. Not egg and cress this time though.' He made a jokey gagging noise. 'See if one of the old girls will part with something a bit less 1960s, eh?'

Jordan laughed. 'Sure thing, bro. See ya round about one, yeah?'

29

'Yep,' Joshua replied and ended the call.

He returned to the sports hall to find the remaining members of his class had arrived and they were all chatting amongst themselves. 'Come on, you lot,' he said, switching into instructor mode. 'You've gotta warm up your whole body, not just your tongues!'

*

Mark was having a belter of a day. Sitting at the bus stop waiting for the number 86 to take him to work his eyes were drawn to what appeared to be a curled piece of plastic lying in the curb. He stepped over to investigate and his eyes lit up as he realised it was a £10 note.

As soon as he got off the bus he skipped to the off licence cum newsagents on the corner and invested his find on a try-your-luck scratchcard and two cans of beer. He eagerly scratched off the silver coating with the edge of a 20p coin to reveal a £10 win.

'Wow!' he said out loud. 'Must be my lucky day.' He hesitated, wondering whether to return to the shop to claim his winnings, then decided to do it on his way home instead. He crossed the road and, as he arrived at the garage where he worked, the shutters were just opening.

'Morning, John,' he called out as a face appeared from under the rolling steel.

'Mark,' the man replied, with a bare minimum response that was typical of him.

Mark strutted inside and pulled a set of overalls down from a hook on the wall. Stepping into the grease-stained outfit, he clapped his hands together.

Another man who had been immersed in a tabloid newspaper looked up. 'Morning, Mark.'

'Alright, Fred,' Mark replied. 'What's first this morning?'

Fred returned his attention to the newspaper. 'The Picanto over there. Clutch is sticking.'

Mark looked over towards a dusky pink car. 'That a bird's motor?' he asked.

'What do *you* think?' Fred grunted. 'Blokes don't tend to drive pink cars, not in my experience anyway.'

Mark grinned. 'Not unless they're queers. So it *is* a bird's then?'

Fred lowered the newspaper and glared at him. 'Yes. It belongs to a lady.'

Mark sniggered. 'No surprise the clutch has gone then, eh boss?'

Fred set down his paper and stood up. 'Listen you, what have I told you about making remarks like that? I don't want the equal opportunities mob sniffing around here.'

Mark scoffed. 'Bloody snowflakes. What do they know?'

Fred stepped up close to him and lowered his voice. 'Just keep the caveman quips under wraps, son. Especially when the shutters are up. Understood?'

'Yeah, alright boss,' Mark replied unconvincingly. He strolled over to the Picanto, opened the driver's door and reached down to release the bonnet. Stepping round to the front of the car, he lifted the hood. 'Fuck's sake!' he exclaimed. 'Look at the state of this!'

John stepped up behind him and peered down at the engine. 'Good luck with that,' he said, chuckling. Landing a hearty slap across Mark's shoulders, he retreated to the rear of the service area, leaving him to it.

Fred came over and looked inside. 'Looks like the head gasket has blown. I'll give Miss Grant a call before we go any further.'

Mark walked over to the desk. Wiping his hands down the side of his overalls, he opened the appointment book and smiled. 'Sweet. I'll take the Morgan when it comes in.'

John shouted across the garage, 'Too late, my son, I've already bagged me that.'

Mark's lip curled. 'Wanker,' he muttered under his breath.

John stepped over to him. 'There's a Honda out back that needs a cage welding over the cat. Nice easy job for you.'

Suddenly Fred called out, 'Cat! Well done, John, I would have clean forgot!' He approached his colleagues, who were both looking confused. 'My wife asked me to ask you if Katie's got any kittens in at the moment.'

Mark shrugged his shoulders. 'I've no idea, mate, but I can ask her tonight. If there's none at her shelter, she might know somewhere that has.'

Fred patted Mark on the back. 'Cheers, my son. We lost our old girl a few months ago and Joan says she misses having a cat around the house.'

The three men stood for a moment and an unusual air of emotion lingered in the air for a few seconds. Every one of them had experienced the loss of a beloved pet in their lives.

'Anyway,' Fred said, breaking the silence. 'Back to it. Bring that Accord in, Mark, and I'll ring the Picanto lassie.'

*

Sebastian was finding it difficult to concentrate. He had spent most of the weekend in a bit of a daze. He'd fancied Tilly Shaw for months. He'd not reacted on Friday night when Katie mentioned that Tilly worked in the Co-Op, because the fact was, he already knew and didn't want it to become common knowledge. There were several supermarkets that were a lot closer to where he lived, and yet even though it was a good three miles from home, he often made a beeline for the Co-Op. Of course, he was far too shy to even think about introducing himself to Tilly. And even if he did manage to summon up the courage, what would he say? Luckily, with the compulsory wearing of facemasks in shops over the last year or so, he could covertly navigate the aisles and even stand in the queue watching without her noticing him. Sometimes he felt a bit guilty, creepy even, but he had never been that confident around girls. Once, the perfect moment of opportunity had presented itself and he'd stepped up to the checkout... and then, true to form, crumbled.

Last night, in a dream, he *had* made that long overdue move. He'd taken a large bunch of roses and some Thornton's chocolates up to the checkout and made sure he was served by Tilly. She'd commented on them being beautiful and questioned him about who the lucky lady was. With a spark of self-assurance only the dream-world version of Sebastian could muster, he'd flashed a winning smile and declared, 'You.' Tilly had swooned – yes *actually* swooned – and Sebastian had taken her hand in his, leading her out from behind the checkout and into his arms. But as the dream was approaching the moment where their lips would meet, the bedside alarm clock had cruelly wrenched him out of his little bit of heaven and back to the reality of his single bed in a small flat above the shops in Chadwell Heath High Street.

33

Suddenly a loud bang on his desk startled him out of his thoughts. With his heart pounding, he looked up to see his manager, Ryan glaring at him. He looked back down at the desk to see the source of the bang; it was a pile of ring binders, which were now slowly slipping towards the edge of his workspace. Sebastian reached out to stop them cascading to the floor. He looked back up at Ryan. The man was almost seven foot tall and he had a face like thunder.

'Is everything okay?' Sebastian felt stupid as the words left his lips. Clearly everything *wasn't* okay.

'Okay?' Ryan replied, his thick South African accent tinged with anger. 'Let me see.' He reached for the binder on top of the pile and flung it open. 'Here we have "Changing Faces", our revolutionary new beauty app, which we hoped would win us this year's app developers' top prize.' He put the binder down and reached for the next one. 'And here we have "Pretty Pooches", our app for 5-10 year olds with a passion for small fluffy dogs.' He forced the binder under Sebastian's nose. 'You see the little doggies here, prat?'

Sebastian pushed the folder away from his face. 'Yes, I see the dogs,' he replied calmly.

Ryan dropped the folder down on the desk and picked up the final one from the pile. 'This morning. In a boardroom, with 20 of my peers, I opened the Microsoft presentation to show them our fantastic new facial enhancement app.' He irritably flicked the pages in the folder. 'Some very average-looking women in here. I might go so far as to say they're a bit rough. Wouldn't you?' He glared at Sebastian, who offered no response. 'Anyway. I proceeded with my presentation until the penultimate moment came – the million-pound software we'd bought with *their* money was about to be revealed.

34

And what did we get?' He was still glaring at Sebastian, his face crimson with a prominent vein pulsing in his forehead. Sebastian remained silent. 'Fucking dog-faced women! That's what! Women with long fucking ears and studded collars!'

Sebastian's face changed to one of bemusement. Ryan thrust the folder at him and he flicked the pages in disbelief. 'I... I must have got the artwork mixed up,' he stammered apologetically.

'No shit, Sherlock!' Ryan blazed, showering the desk with little droplets of spittle.

'It's an easy fix,' Sebastian said. 'Leave it with me, I'll have it sorted by lunch time.' There was a note of pleading in his voice.

'You've had your last chance here, fuckwit. You sit there staring out the window all day when you should be working, and it would be over-generous to say everything you've submitted recently has been substandard.' Sebastian opened his mouth to apologise again, but Ryan held up a hand. 'I don't want to hear it. Pack up your stuff and get the fuck out of here before I do something you're gonna regret!'

'But...'

'Just do it!'

All the other people in the office watched in shocked silence as Sebastian picked up his satchel and emptied the top drawer of his desk. One of them gave Sebastian a conciliatory look, but he didn't notice.

Ryan, standing impatiently with his hands on his hips, glared at his staff. 'What are you lot gawking at? Get on with your work or you'll all be lining up behind this soppy bastard outside the job centre!'

Everyone else in the room shuffled round in their seats and buried their faces in their computers.

35

*

Joshua had been counting the hours until lunch time. Fortunately he only had three morning sessions scheduled on a Monday, which left the afternoons free to handle the ever increasing pile of paperwork he loathed beyond words. The accounts and health and safety admin bore, which had doubled since Covid, could wait though; meeting Jordan for lunch held far greater appeal.

As he pulled into the car park of Wisteria Heights, a private care home situated down a country lane in Shooters Hill, South East London, he could see his friend standing at the entrance, where he appeared to be deep in conversation with a middle-aged couple.

Joshua turned off the engine and sat in his car until Jordan had finished talking.

As the couple walked away, Jordan glanced over towards the car park and when he saw his friend he beamed from ear to ear.

Joshua climbed out of the car as Jordan approached him.

'Alright bruv? You're early!' He reached out his hand and pulled Joshua forward into a shoulder bump.

'Yeah, I couldn't wait to get outta there,' Joshua said with a smile. 'I really wasn't feeling it today.'

'You hungry?'

Joshua smiled. 'Depends what's on offer. If it's egg and cress, I might have to give it a swerve.'

'It's your lucky day, Joshy. The canteen was fresh outta cress today so I stashed a couple of chicken and bacon paninis for us.'

Joshua rubbed his stomach enthusiastically. 'Mmm. Now you're talking!'

The two men walked up the steps into the care home and Jordan led the way along the hallway – bedecked with tired-looking flocked floral wallpaper – and into the dining room.

'Find a table, sir. I'll go and alert the kitchen of your arrival,' Jordan said, mimicking the posture of an overly-attentive waiter.

'You knob!' Joshua quipped back as his friend sashayed out through the swing doors into the kitchen.

There were a dozen circular tables in the ornate dining room, which was swathed in light from the vast floor to ceiling windows that formed a perfect semi-circle around the outside of the room. Across the far side there was an elderly lady sat dozing in the sunlight, a half-eaten plate of sandwiches in front of her. Joshua pulled out a chair quietly so as not to wake her and sat down at the table nearest the kitchen.

A few moments later, Jordan burst through the swing doors backwards, a tray in each hand. 'We have chicken and bacon in an overpriced Italian bread roll and some of the chef's finest deep-fried, thinly sliced potato for your delectation, sir.'

Putting a finger to his lips, Joshua made a little *sssh* sound. Jordan looked confused and set down the trays. Joshua pointed to the old lady in the corner.

'Oh don't worry about old Peggy, bruv,' Jordan chuckled. 'She'd sleep through an explosion, that one.' He took the plates off the tray and handed Joshua a drink. 'Orange juice okay?'

'Yeah, great thanks,' Joshua replied taking a large slug from the glass of chilled juice.

Jordan moved the trays across the table and pushed Joshua's plate towards him.

'That looks lush,' Joshua exclaimed. He picked up a crisp and popped it into his mouth. 'Prawn cocktail. My favourite!'

Jordan smiled at him. 'Since forever.'

Joshua smiled back warmly and took another crisp. 'Yeah.'

'So, come on. What's going on with you and Maisie?'

Joshua swallowed the crisp and washed it down with a mouthful of juice. 'I dunno, mate. She's hard work.' Jordan studied Joshua's face as he continued. 'She was banging on about commitment and I freaked. I'm too young for all that shit, you know?'

Jordan said nothing. Nodding, he took a bite from his panini.

'We've only been together for a few months and she's already talking about moving in together.' Joshua scowled. 'It's all too heavy for me. I kinda like my own space.'

'So, where did you leave it? Katie said you'd broken up. At least that's what Maisie told her anyways.'

Joshua sighed. 'Yeah, well, that was news to me. But maybe it's for the best. She's proper mental sometimes and I'm not sure I really wanna be bothered with all that.' He looked up at the ceiling and let out a big sigh. 'Jeez! Why does everything have to be such a mission? My last bird was a right head case too. I seem to attract them!' Jordan laughed. 'It's not funny. I dunno what goes on in their heads. I wish it could be like us, you know? We don't have all that shit, do we?'

Jordan's smile faded. His eyes fell and he could feel his stomach knot a little. He looked back up at Joshua and as their eyes met, his insides flipped. He stood up and walked towards his friend. He rested both his hands gently on Joshua's shoulders. Joshua looked up at him and smiled.

38

Just as Jordan opened his mouth to speak, a voice called out from across the room. 'Jordan, my darling,' Peggy said. She sounded tired. 'Could you get me a cup of tea please, sweetheart?'

CHAPTER 3

Following his dismissal from work on Monday, Sebastian was half-heartedly searching the job sites online for something suitable. He'd hated working there anyway and job satisfaction had been nil, but it was convenient and the pay was good so he'd made no real effort to put feelers out or consider looking for employment elsewhere. Now his hand had been forced and, as much as it irked him, he had to find a new position quickly. He was scrolling through the listings and hadn't spotted a single job that inspired him.

He glanced over to his book shelf. Sitting amongst the Marvel annuals and various Japanese comics was a small section of much older books, most of which centred around the age-old art of hypnotism. He reached out and withdrew a large navy-blue book with a tattered cover: *The History of Stage Hypnosis*.

Sebastian let the book fall open in his hands and looked down at an old photograph of an eccentric-looking man with golden hair curled over his ears. It was one of Sebastian's heroes, Franz Mesmer, a German physician cited as the first man to discover and practice hypnotism in the late 18th century.

Sebastian sighed. At this point in his life, did he really want to end up a slave to the grind in a job he despised? Closing the book with a loud thud, which sent dust particles drifting into the air, he leant back in his chair and stared out of the window. All he'd ever wanted was to be on stage. Stage... It suddenly dawned on him: *The Stage*, a magazine that had been running for well over 100 years and was a go-to for performers looking for recruitment.

Sebastian jumped up out of his seat and hurriedly threw on his jacket. Five minutes later, as he strolled along the high street, he felt more energised than he had for some time. Reaching the newsagents on the corner, he pushed open the door and stepped inside.

At the tinkle of the bell, the man behind the counter looked up.

'Alright, Derek?' Sebastian said cheerfully.

Derek nodded. 'Yep. Mustn't grumble,' he replied with a distinctly grumbly tone.

Sebastian scanned the row of magazine shelves. The newspapers at the bottom were all mixed up and he bent down to rearrange them to see what might be buried underneath. He stood up again and turned to face the counter. 'Have you got *The Stage* by any chance?' he asked.

'Nah, don't do that one,' Derek replied with disinterest. 'No call for it.'

'Bugger!' Sebastian muttered as he walked out of the shop. He stood on the pavement and considered his options. WH Smith would have it for sure, but the nearest one was in Romford and he wasn't really sure he fancied going in to town. As he stood pondering what to do, he caught sight of a Number 86 bus on the horizon. The bus stop was only a matter of yards away too. 'Ah, sod it,' he said out loud, making up his mind to go into town after all.

The Number 86 stopped at the kerb and Sebastian's face fell as he saw it was absolutely packed. The driver opened the doors and a few people got off, leaving just a small amount of room at the foot of the stairs. *Standing room only again*, Sebastian thought. He squeezed aboard behind a rather robust lady who was eating chips from a polystyrene tray – the smell of vinegar was almost overwhelming – and the doors hissed shut behind him.

Thankfully it was only a short journey. Most of the passengers got off at the market, leaving Sebastian and a handful of others still aboard. It was too late to worry about taking one of the now vacant seats – his stop was next – so he remained standing for the last couple of minutes. Something caught his nostrils and Sebastian gingerly sniffed the sleeve of his jacket, recoiling with revulsion and retching at the acrid smell; it stank of vinegar. He scowled. That damned woman must have brushed her tray of chips against him when she elbowed her way past to get off. As the bus rounded the corner, Sebastian pushed the bell. He couldn't wait to get out into the fresh air.

Alighting, he headed straight into the Liberty shopping centre and walked through to WH Smith. Making a bee line for the magazines, he failed to spot Tilly stood beside the rack of greetings cards. She noticed him as he whizzed past though, and she kept one eye on him while she continued to peruse the selection of birthday cards. Sebastian let out an audible 'Yes!' as he found what he was looking for, held the copy of *The Stage* aloft and spun jubilantly on the spot. As he turned to face the front of the shop, his eyes fell upon Tilly, who was looking right at him and clearly trying to stifle a giggle.

'Oh… er… Hi Tilly. Fancy seeing you here.' *Fancy seeing you here?* Sebabstian thought. Had that sounded as lame to Tilly as it had to him? Composing himself, he walked over to her.

'What have you found that's got you so excited then?' she enquired.

'Oh, this?' He held out the magazine. 'It's *The Stage*. I was hoping I might find a job in there.'

'*The Stage*?' Tilly replied. 'Isn't that a magazine for theatre actors and musicals and stuff?'

42

'Yeah. There's loads of that in there, but the situations vacant section is for all sorts of performers.'

'Well, your victory dance was quite impressive.' Tilly giggled. 'You'll be in with a good chance if you're looking for a dancer's job.'

Her dainty laugh was like music to Sebastian's ears. He smiled. 'Yes... well... Billy Elliot eat your heart out!' He was trying his hardest to match her with humour, but the truth of the matter was that he was almost dying from embarrassment.

Tilly laughed again.

'Er, look... do you fancy going for a coffee?' Sebastian asked nervously. 'Er, if you're not busy I mean.'

'Yeah, sure. I just need to try and pick a birthday card for my Mum. You go pay for your magazine and I'll see you outside.'

Sebastian smiled. 'Brilliant! I mean, great. I mean, er, yes, I'll see you outside. I'll wait on the bench. Don't rush.' He strolled off to the till to pay for his magazine, then feeling like he was walking on air he left the shop and found a bench outside to sit on and wait for Tilly. He took the only empty space he could find on the end of a row of metal benches. He sat back and without any real interest watched as shoppers bustled back and forth, going about their day.

There was a young woman sat next to him, rhythmically nodding her head along to music in her earphones. Suddenly she stopped nodding and turned her head towards Sebastian. She frowned and wrinkled her nose. Out of the corner of his eye, Sebastian caught her staring and as he turned to face her she stood up and quickly walked away with her hand up to her nose. Baffled for a moment, Sebastian looked at the empty place on the bench, then down at his shoes, turning them to

43

examine the soles. As he leant to get a better look at his left foot, the smell hit him. *Vinegar!* He sniffed the sleeve of his jacket. In all the excitement of finding the magazine and bumping into Tilly, he'd forgotten the dowsing he'd received on the bus. Anxiously he glanced up and saw Tilly coming out of WH Smith. As she approached him, he stood up and quickly whipped off his jacket. He retrieved his wallet and phone from the inside pocket and screwed the jacket into a ball, pushing it into a waste bin conveniently positioned beside the bench.

Tilly stepped up to him. She was frowning. 'Why are you binning your jacket?'

Sebastian's face had the look of a guilty child. 'Oh, er, well it's very warm today and er… I've had that jacket for years, so…'

Tilly's usual expression of placid sweetness changed momentarily to one of disdain. 'Seems a terrible waste. Couldn't you give it to a charity shop or something?'

Sebastian blushed. 'Of course. I'm sorry, how thoughtless of me!' He reached in and pulled out the jacket, brushing it down with his left hand. 'There's a Hospice shop around the corner, I'll drop it in there.'

Tilly smiled. 'That's much better than just throwing it away.'

'Actually,' Sebastian began, silently praying that Tilly wouldn't notice the pungent aroma of vinegar, 'there's a nice little café across the road from the charity shop. Perhaps we can have a coffee there?'

'Perfect,' Tilly replied, hooking her left arm through Sebastian's right.

Sebastian looked down and beamed. 'Yeah. Perfect.'

As Tilly was taking a seat in the café, Sebastian found himself standing at the end of a very long queue in the charity shop.

The volunteer at the till was talking to the woman she was serving, seemingly oblivious to the increasingly impatient customers waiting to be served. The man third in line decided to give up and dumped a pair of trousers on the shelf beside him, almost knocking off a crystal decanter.

The volunteer continued chatting and although Sebastian was a good 20 feet from the till point, he could hear every word as clear as a bell.

'Yeah, it's not too bad,' the woman was saying. 'But if I'm on me feet too long, it really starts to throb and the smell is unbearable.' She pulled a face and wafted her hand in front of her face.

Sebastian resisted the urge to call out 'Too much information!', deciding to let that particular thought stay well-cached in his head. All he had wanted to do was drop off his jacket as quickly as possible and join Tilly across the road, but everyone in front of him was holding an armful of goods. Making the decision to jump the queue, leave his donation and run, he sidestepped the large man in front of him and snuck round the side of a display of knitting wool. Dropping the jacket beside the counter, he dashed off back behind the wool stand and made for the door.

As he got there the volunteer called out to him. 'Excuse me, sir. This jacket stinks. We can't take that!'

Sebastian could feel his cheeks burning red hot as all the people in the queue turned to look at him. Without turning back, he pulled the door wide open and dashed outside.

The volunteer tutted, then continued discussing her leg with the woman in front of the counter.

There was no doubt that in most aspects of his life Sebastian was a confident man. But if there was one thing that was guaranteed to leave him in a state of befuddlement it was the opposite sex. Although he could be relaxed in the company of women in general, the problem would invariably arise if there was someone around for whom he felt an attraction. Yes, he could bluff the necessary self-assurance if the moment called for it, but inside he would seldom be less than a gelatinous blob and he'd inevitably end up saying or doing the wrong thing and making a complete fool of himself. Which made it even harder to calm his nerves the next time.

It had been this way for him since he was a boy and he knew only too well the reason why.

Sebastian had been just weeks short of fourteen years old when he first met Kylie Heath. Always smiling and laughing, she was one of the most popular girls in school and he had fallen head over heels for her. Never really believing she'd entertain the likes of him, when he'd finally plucked up the courage at the school Christmas party to ask her if she'd like to dance, no-one was more surprised than Sebastian when she said yes. They became an item and there followed three happy months as they got to know each other, spending as much time together as they could and relishing the thrill of stolen kisses behind the gymnasium at break time. But in matters of romance Kylie wasn't one to let the grass grow under her feet and she eventually broke it off. Although Sebastian had been heartbroken, it could only have been expected really. After all, they were fourteen years old, it was puppy love, and they were only just setting out on life's path.

It was what happened next that left Sebastian's confidence with women irreparably scarred.

At the height of their relationship he had written a number of starry-eyed notes to Kylie – as indeed had she to him – which were passed back and forth between lessons; silly little scraps of paper declaring their eternal love for one another; "eternity" back then translated as *until I get bored and move on*. When they split up, the obvious thing for Kylie to have done was simply throw his notes away. Instead, weirdly, she asked Sebastian if he would like them back. Why on earth would he? He understood she'd not want to keep them, but it still upset him that she was so quick to be clearing house of his memory. It hurt. He told her she could keep them, but he knew full well they would end up in the bin.

Except they didn't.

He never did understand whether it was an act of calculated cruelty on Kylie's part – he couldn't quite believe it was, for she had no reason to bear him malice – or simply a spontaneous moment of thoughtlessness. But instead of disposing of those missives in which he'd poured out his feelings for her, she distributed them among her friends, who the next day assembled around him just before class and, through fits of giggles, read aloud his most intimate proclamations of love. Much to the hilarity of everyone in the room. The humiliation was overwhelming and poor Sebastian had been left with no choice but to sit there, cheeks burning as he'd fought back the tears. Although for everyone else it was nothing more than a fleeting moment of spiteful fun and soon forgotten, for Sebastian it had been an ordeal that would hobble his confidence with women forever.

47

Since then his track record with the opposite sex hadn't been much to speak of. Some while back, on a night out with friends, someone had remarked to Sebastian – purely in jest – that he should employ his "magic" to hoodwink girls to go out with him. Amidst much laughter and ribbing he'd naturally dismissed the suggestion as preposterous. Yet a few weeks later, alone in his bed in the small hours of a sleepless night, he actually caught himself giving it serious consideration. How easy it would be to make April Moore – the pretty young secretary from the office next door who he'd had his eye on – fall for him. Fortunately common sense prevailed. He'd just as quickly dispelled the notion and vowed to never stoop so low. He was desperate to be with someone, but it was also important that, whoever it was, they genuinely wanted be with him. And if it took a while, so be it.

He never did get together with April – he'd fumbled his way through an invite to the cinema and, with a discernible trace of amusement playing at the corner of her mouth, she had politely declined – but patience and a little bit of good fortune had finally paid off. For here he was about to embark on his first date with the girl of his dreams. Could it *actually* be called "a date"? *Of course it can*, he told himself.

It was true, things hadn't got off to the most auspicious start, but as he left the embarrassment of the charity shop incident in his wake and hurried towards the café where Tilly was waiting for him, he was determined not to blow it.

Sebastian burst through the glass door into the café, almost sending an elderly man who was standing on the other side flying. The man raised his walking stick and

48

waved it angrily at Sebastian. 'Watch where you're going, son. You nearly knocked me over!'

Sebastian put his hands together as if he was about to break into a prayer. 'I'm so sorry, I didn't see you there,' he said, thinking that people who stood idly in front of swing doors deserved to suffer the consequences.

'Obviously,' the old man muttered. 'Your generation has no respect.'

'Really, I'm genuinely sorry,' Sebastian repeated.

Unconvinced by Sebastian's sincerity, the man shuffled past him and out onto the street.

Catching his breath, Sebastian scanned the café and smiled as he spotted Tilly sitting over in the far corner. From the expression on her face it was apparent she'd witnessed his unintentional assault on an old age pensioner, and as he stepped over to the table Sebastian smiled sheepishly. 'What would you like to drink?'

Tilly pointed to a sign beside a condiments rack which read *Table Service*.

'Ah, okay.' Sebastian took a seat opposite Tilly. She was staring at him with a cheeky knowing smile. 'What?!' Sebastian asked in a high-pitched voice.

'Nothing. Just wondering if you make a habit of mowing down old folk?'

Sebastian could feel his cheeks glowing again. 'Only the ones with walking sticks,' he replied with a grin, immediately regretting it and hoping it sounded as humorous as he'd intended it to. He was relieved when Tilly giggled.

A man appeared at the table holding a small notepad and a pencil. 'Are you ready to order?'

Sebastian held out his hand towards Tilly. 'Ladies first.'

Tilly looked up at the waiter. 'I'd like a coffee please.'

49

The waiter frowned and let out a little sigh. 'Latte? Cappuccino? Macchiato?'

'No. Just a normal coffee please,' Tilly replied.

The waiter scribbled on his pad and turned to Sebastian. 'And for you, sir?'

'The same please. With one sugar.'

They both heard the waiter tut to himself as he returned to the counter.

'Lattes, macichinos... I ask you, what's wrong with a good old fashioned coffee?' Tilly said.

Sebastian smiled. The way she had innocently mispronounced macchiato made him feel all warm and fuzzy inside. He adored everything about this girl and he doubled his resolve not to do anything else to embarrass himself. 'It's all a pretentious and overpriced load of old nonsense,' he replied, picking up the folded menu from the table. 'I mean, look at this: Eight different types of coffee, various different teas and three kinds of hot chocolate. Surely chocolate is chocolate, right?'

Tilly leant towards him and Sebastian caught a trace of her scent. She smelt wonderful.

'Apparently not,' Tilly said, peering at the menu. 'You have salted caramel chocolate, velvety milk chocolate and intense dark.' She smiled at Sebastian. 'Oooh, I guess we're a bit boring, eh?' she said with mock concern. 'Having a plain old coffee, I mean.'

'Nah. Sensible, but definitely not boring.'

The waiter reappeared carrying a tray. He lifted the coffees and placed them on the table along with two small round biscuits in a plastic wrapping. 'Would sir or madam like anything else?'

Sebastian glanced enquiringly at Tilly. She shook her head. He looked up at the waiter and smiled. 'No thank you. We're fine.'

The waiter afforded them a forced smile and walked away.

'So. Tell me about this job you're looking for,' Tilly said, resting her chin on her hands.

'Well. Don't laugh, but I'd really like to be a stage hypnotist.' Tilly smiled. Sebastian looked at her. 'I said *don't* laugh!'

'I'm not laughing.' She averted her eyes from his and with a wave of her hand encouraged him to continue.

'I lost my job on Monday.'

Tilly lifted her head. 'Oh. I'm really sorry to hear that.'

'Nah, don't be. I hated it there anyway. I've always wanted to work on the stage and maybe this was the sign I needed to kick me in the right direction.'

Tilly smiled. 'From what little I saw in The Cauliflower last week, you're really good.'

Sebastian's eyes lit up and he beamed from ear to ear. 'Thank you. I've always had a bit of a talent for it, right from when I was a kid. I'd just like to move it up a level. You know, something a bit more showbiz than making a spectacle of my mates in the pub.'

Tilly reached for the magazine. 'Well, shall we have a look to see what's on offer in here?'

Sebastian sat up straight. 'Yes. I feel like today might just be my lucky day!'

*

As the words left Sebastian's mouth, back in Stratford someone else's luck was running out.

'Bollocks!' Mark yelled, the sound reverberating across the garage.

The other three mechanics looked up and a pigeon fluttered out from the roof beams and clumsily tumbled in

51

mid-air before righting itself and flapping off through the shutters and into the sky.

Mark stumbled a few paces backwards away from the open bonnet of the Picanto holding his right hand aloft. Blood was pouring down his wrist and dripping off his elbow. He turned to look at Fred – who was striding towards him with a look of concern on his face – and promptly keeled over backwards. Fred picked up his pace and was joined by John and their young apprentice, Kaden.

John stood over Mark, who was flat out on the concrete in a state of semi-conciousness. 'Fuck me, mate, the queer's car bites back, eh?!'

Fred pushed him aside. 'Don't mess about,' he snapped. 'Go get the first aid box!' His knees cracked as he squatted down beside Mark. 'You alright, son?' he asked. He was trying to sound calm, despite having spied the blood pooling around Mark's arm and running across the polished concrete floor.

Mark mumbled something incoherent and with a noticeable wobble, tried to prop himself up. He cried out as he put weight on his right hand. Fred pulled a checked handkerchief from his pocket and shuffled round Mark to tend to his injury.

Mark looked at his arm and seethed through gritted teeth. 'Fucking wrench slipped!' He lifted his hand towards Fred.

'Christ, Mark, you've made a right mess of that!' Fred exclaimed as he gently wrapped the hankie around Mark's hand. He looked back over his shoulder. 'Where's John with that sodding first aid box?'

Kaden, who had kept quiet up until now and was looking more than a little queasy said, 'Do you think he needs the hospital?'

Fred looked up at the teenager and nodded. 'Yes, you're probably right, lad. Can you go and call for an ambulance?'

Kaden reached into his overalls and pulled out a mobile phone. Fred rolled his eyes; he'd lost count of the times he had told the boy to leave his mobile phone in the locker, but now wasn't the time to bring it up again.

As Kaden dialled 999, John appeared behind him holding a green plastic box coated with dust. He handed it to Fred. 'Sorry, mate. Couldn't find it,' he said breathlessly.

Fred took the box from him and flipped open the latches to reveal its pitifully meagre contents: a half empty packet of blue plasters, an eye patch and a box of Rennies. 'Brilliant,' he sighed. He looked back at Mark, the handkerchief was now sodden with blood. 'John, get me a tea towel will ya?'

John hurried into the kitchen at the back of the workshop and returned clutching a slightly grubby piece of cloth. He looked down at the puddle of blood and winced. 'Where's he bleedin' from?'

Mark looked up at him and muttered, 'I'm from bleedin' Ilford, ya fuckwit!'

John wasn't sure if the remark was a joke or if his colleague was delirious. Erring on the side of caution, he bridled a sarcastic comeback and handed the tea towel to Fred.

Kaden, who had stepped outside to find a signal, returned looking forlorn. 'They said it's a half hour wait.'

'Half an hour? Fuck me, the man's gonna bleed to death before they get here!' Fred exclaimed, wrapping the tea towel tightly around Mark's injured hand. He rummaged in his pocket and pulled out his car keys. 'Take my car, get him to the hospital or he's gonna end up

53

brown bread!' He threw the keys to John, who caught them and took off at speed.

Mark shot Fred a frightened look. 'Am I gonna die?' His voice was shaky.

'Course you're not, son,' Fred said, feigning reassurance and gently patting Mark's arm to comfort him. 'It was just words. You'll be fine. We'll sort you out.'

Moments later there was a screech of tyres as a light blue Jaguar, with John at the wheel, whizzed across the garage forecourt and, with a shrill squeal of brakes, lurched to a halt outside the open-shuttered entrance to the maintenance bay. John leaned over and threw open the passenger side door.

Fred helped Mark onto his feet and guided him to the car. As Mark eased into the passenger seat with a little groan, Fred looked at John. 'Treat her like she's your own,' he said, an unspoken yet very evident *or else* in his tone. He rested a friendly hand on Mark's shoulder and smiled nervously down at him. 'Try not to bleed on the upholstery, son.'

CHAPTER 4

The pub was filling fast. Katie and Mark were seated at their usual table when a tall man with a bald head and a full beard, dressed casually in a football shirt and shorts, strode purposefully towards them. He grabbed hold of the back of a chair with one of his large hands and without saying a word pulled it out from under the table.

'That seat's taken mate,' Mark said. The bald man didn't acknowledge him. 'Oi! You deaf pal?!' Mark said, getting to his feet.

The large man turned round, his face like thunder. He let go of the chair and it dropped with a clatter. Katie reached up and put her hand on Mark's left arm as the man spoke. 'I didn't see your name on it.' He looked down at Mark's right hand, which was wrapped in bandages. 'Did ya get that fighting over a chair?' he asked sarcastically, smiling to reveal a row of uneven teeth.

The mood lightened a bit as Mark grinned back at the man. 'Yeah, summink like that,' he replied. He gestured to the man with a wave of his hand. 'Take it. It'll teach my mates for rocking up late. Ya snooze, ya lose!'

With a glimmer of triumph in his eyes, the man – who had evidently been willing to start a fight – looked Mark up and down for a moment, then nodded once, grabbed up the chair and returned to his table.

Katie smiled at Mark as he sat back down. 'Well done.'

'Weren't worth the ag,' Mark mumbled resignedly.

'You could have taken that ape easily,' Katie said, knowing full well that Mark would have been on the receiving end of a pounding from the other man. 'But you proved yourself the better guy. Proud of you,' she added, patting his arm affectionately. She took her jacket off the back of her chair and reached over to slip it on to the adjacent chair, then passed her handbag to Mark. 'Here, bung it on that chair and put your jacket on the other one.'

Mark did as he was asked and as he stood up to drape his jacket over the chair opposite him he caught sight of Joshua and Jordan standing at the bar. 'Ah, I see the poofs are here.' He added with a chuckle, 'Seb will just have to sit on the floor.' There was a discernibly cruel hint of menace in his laugh.

'That's enough!' Katie exclaimed. 'Maisie and Josh have split up, so she won't be here.'

Mark guffawed. 'That didn't last long!' He looked over towards the bar where Josh and Jordan were being served their drinks. 'She obviously realised her action man was more into cock than muff.'

As Jordan approached the table carrying two pints of lager in his hands and a loose leaf folder tucked under his arm, Mark whipped his jacket off the back of the vacant chair and sat back down. Jordan set the two glasses down on the table and handed the folder to Mark. Smiling, he bent down to kiss Katie on the cheek. Mark fleetingly bristled and opened the folder, pretending to browse the song titles inside.

'You alright, Jordan? Where's Josh?' Katie asked.

Jordan pulled out the chair beside Katie and sat down. He reached behind to slip her jacket off the backrest. Handing it over to her he replied, 'He's gone for a waz. Where's Seb?'

'He's not here yet,' Katie replied. She pointed across the pub towards a table beside the stage. 'He's gonna be disappointed when he does though, his cute little crush isn't here tonight.'

Jordan followed Katie's finger and spotted the three girls that had been sat with Tilly a fortnight earlier, all huddled around one of their mobile phones and laughing hysterically. 'Aww. Poor Seb. Maybe she'll be along later.'

'Who's going to come along later?' a voice from behind him asked.

Jordan turned around. 'Seb's new love interest.'

Joshua laughed and pulled out the chair next to Jordan. 'I don't think I've ever even seen Seb with a girl.' He set Katie's bag down on the floor near her feet and sat down.

Katie leaned forward. 'Lucy. Remember her?'

Joshua's eyes widened. 'Oh, God, yeah. Loopy Lucy. I forgot about her.'

'I wish *I* could!' Jordan threw his head back and laughed.

With the hubbub around them getting increasingly loud and intrusive, Mark couldn't hear what was being said across the table and it was starting to irk him. He put the folder down on the table. 'What's so funny?' he asked accusingly.

Katie was about to answer when Jordan put his hand on her arm and nodded towards the bar. Katie looked over her shoulder and saw Sebastian coming towards them carrying two drinks. Walking beside him was Tilly. Katie looked momentarily agog, then her mouth formed into a broad smile. 'Here he is!'

'Hiya!' Sebastian said. 'You all remember Tilly?'

Tilly raised her hand. 'Hi everyone.'

Sebastian walked round the table and set the glasses down. He pulled out the chair and gestured for Tilly to sit down. She looked up at him. 'What about you?'

'Oh I'll just stand here and grow good.'

Tilly smiled up at him sweetly. Sebastian caught Mark staring at him out of the corner of his eye. 'You alright Mark?'

Mark was about to reply when the speakers clicked loudly and the karaoke compere took to the mic. 'Good evening, Cauliflower!' He paused for a response and when none came he smiled a little sheepishly and continued. 'Come on up and submit your songs.' He pushed a button on the panel beside him and the throbbing introduction to Robbie Williams' hit *Let me Entertain You* filled the room.

Joshua reached for the folder of songs and flipped it open. Inside a poly pocket there was a bundle of torn-up bits of paper. 'Anyone got a pen?' he asked.

Katie retrieved her handbag from beneath the table and pulled out a biro. 'Here you go, Josh. Put me down for Rita Ora will ya?'

Joshua flicked through the pages until he got to the page headed **O**. 'Which one? There's a few here,' he shouted, hoping she could hear him over the sound of the compere giving the Robbie Williams number his all.

'*Read All About It,*' Katie replied.

'Huh?'

Katie leant closer, almost knocking Jordan's pint over. '*Read All About It*,' she repeated.

Josh withdrew a scrap of paper and wrote Katie's request down. He flicked onward through the pages and stopped on **Q**. 'I think I'll do a bit of Freddie tonight,' he said confidently.

Jordan watched with amusement as Joshua wrote down his song choice. 'Blimey mate, you're brave,' he said with a toothy grin.

Joshua handed the pen to Jordan and pushed the folder along the table.

58

'Nah, I don't fancy it tonight,' Jordan said. 'What about you, er…' He paused, looking at Tilly. 'Er…'

'Ooh, no, I don't think you want to hear me sing,' she said coyly. 'And it's Tilly,' she continued, looking up at Sebastian 'Since *somebody* failed to introduce me.'

Sebastian looked flustered. 'Oh! Didn't I? I'm so sorry, I thought I had.' His face running crimson, he turned to face the table. 'Everyone this is Tilly.' He pointed at Mark. 'Tilly, this is Mark.' He moved his finger across to Katie. 'This is…' He stopped short as Tilly elbowed him in the thigh.

'I was joking you soppy sod! You *did* introduce me. It's not your fault if your mate can't remember my name.' She winked at him.

Joshua laughed. 'She's got your number, bro!' He punched Jordan playfully on his arm. 'Good one, Tilly.'

Sebastian smiled apologetically and bending over he kissed Tilly lightly on the top of her head. Suddenly aware that his friends were all staring at him with silly grins on their faces, he turned towards the stage in an attempt to hide his embarrassment, just as the compere reached the end of his song. Sebastian clapped enthusiastically, but as the music faded his response to what had at best been an average performance drew funny looks from the group sitting at the next table. One of the women openly sniggered at him. Aware he was making even more of a spectacle of himself, Sebastian stopped clapping and quickly buried his hands in his pockets.

Having submitted his and Katie's song choices to the stage, Joshua returned to the table and stepped up beside Sebastian. 'You alright there, Seb?' he asked with an undisguised trace of mockery. Sebastian gave him a wry smile and focused his attention on the stage where the compere was calling out a name.

59

A corpulent woman, probably in her mid-to-late-40s, stood up and slowly made her way onto the stage. Frank handed her the microphone and she immediately launched into Adele's *Hello* with great confidence. The mumbling of chitchat ceased and the pub fell silent as the audience watched transfixed.

Joshua returned to his seat and took a large gulp of his lager.

Tilly looked up at Sebastian. 'She's really good.'

Sebastian nodded. 'Yeah, fantastic!' He tenderly put his hand on her shoulder and she covered it with her own, interweaving her fingers with his.

Jordan nudged Katie and wrinkled his nose, gesturing towards the couple with his eyes. Katie smiled and mouthed 'Awww, sweet' back at him.

The pub erupted in rapturous applause as the woman concluded her rendition of *Hello*. As she returned to her seat, Frank stood at the front of the stage and scooped his hands upwards to encourage the applause. 'Amazing!' he exclaimed, 'fantastic performance there from Belinda.' He reached over to the small table at the side of the stage and picked up a slip of paper 'Josh, you're up!' he called out, grinning broadly. Josh jumped out of his seat and strode towards the stage. He hopped up the steps at the side and Frank handed him the microphone. 'Good luck, son,' he said as he turned to hit the play button on the karaoke machine.

The speakers burst into life and as the lyrics "Can... Anybody... Find me. Somebody to love?" appeared in front of him on the screen, Joshua breathed in deeply and threw himself into the role of Freddie Mercury. Giving it his all, he proceeded to prance up and down the stage, forcing his chest out and bellowing the words for all he was worth. Frank had to move swiftly to the back of the

60

stage to avoid the microphone lead, which was thrashing about like a deranged eel. As Joshua spun on his heels to take another lap of the stage, the lead caught around the handrail to the steps and pulled taut. Joshua gave it a hard yank and it came loose from the microphone and dropped to the floor. His performance cut brutally short, Joshua stood looking at the now divorced microphone in his hand with dismay. The backing music continued to play as the crestfallen lad handed the broken microphone back to the compere. 'Sorry 'bout that,' he said sheepishly.

Frank walked over to the player and stopped the track. Popping open the latches on a silver flight case, he felt the blood in his neck rise as he realised he hadn't packed a spare microphone. The audience started to slow clap and the flustered compere turned to face them. The pub was full to capacity and for a moment he felt a wave of panic pass over him. Struggling to compose himself, he stood up and pressed a button on the mixing desk. The speakers hissed and the sound of *Mr Brightside* filled the air. The audience stopped clapping and Frank breathed a sigh of relief. He slammed the case shut, stood up and felt around in his pocket for his car keys. Walking over to the fire exit and opening the double doors, he went out into the car park where he opened the boot of his car. Rummaging amongst a pile of leads he let out an exasperated sigh as he realised the spare microphone wasn't in the car either. A shadow cast over him and he looked round to see the landlord of The Cauliflower standing beside the car.

'Problem, Frank?' the man asked.

Flustered, Frank tripped over his words. 'Er, yeah. Well, er, no. I, er... well, I er, I haven't got a spare microphone.'

The landlord didn't look happy. 'I've got a full house tonight, Frank,' he replied bluntly.

Frank thought for a moment. 'It's cool, Dave. Don't worry, it's all in hand.' He smiled nervously. 'Have I ever let you down?'

There was a moment's silence as Dave looked him in the eyes, as if he was considering what was clearly intended as a rhetorical question. Then he slapped Frank hard on the back. 'Just get the entertainment back up and running before we have a bloodbath out there, eh?' He turned away and walked back into the pub.

Frank put a hand to his chest. His heart was beating hard. He fumbled around in his trouser pocket and pulled out a small box. Shaking out one of the antacid pills into his hand, he opened his mouth and swallowed the small square tablet whole. Grimacing, he slammed shut the car boot and returned to the pub, where the song he'd left playing was just fading out. Then *Chelsea Dagger* kicked in, another crowd pleaser which kept the audience distracted as they all shouted along to the words.

Frank walked over towards the friends' table. Joshua saw him coming and squirmed in his seat, preparing himself for a telling off. But Frank walked straight past Joshua and stopped in front of Sebastian. Holding out his hand, he smiled warmly. 'Hello, young man. I'm Frank.' Politely getting to his feet, Sebastian took the hand and shook it lightly. 'As you can see,' Frank continued, 'I'm in a bit of a predicament here.' He pointed towards the stage over his shoulder with his thumb. 'I wondered if you could help me out?'

Sebastian frowned. '*Me*?' he said with surprise.

'Yes. I noticed a couple of weeks ago you had some kind of floor show of your own going on during the karaoke.'

Sebastian could feel his neck glowing hot and rising up to his cheeks. 'Er, yeah. I'm sorry about that,' he said contritely.

'No need to apologise, son,' Frank said reassuringly. 'But I was wondering, could you possibly reproduce something like that over there?' He pointed towards the stage.

Sebastian swallowed hard. 'What?' he exclaimed with a note of incredulity. 'When?'

'Now.'

Sebastian's face adopted a worried look as he glanced round to see all his friends watching. They were more than likely unsure of what was being said over volume of the loud rock music and the noise of the audience chanting along, but it was clear to all of them that the conversation had made Sebastian uncomfortable. 'Oh no,' he said shakily. 'It's just a bit of fun between me and my mates, I couldn't do it in front of an audience.'

Frank's expression turned to one of desperation. 'Please, son. I just need half an hour to whiz home and get another mic, that's all.' He looked at Sebastian imploringly. 'You'd really be getting me out of the shit,' he added, turning to face Joshua, 'especially as it's your friend here that dropped me in it in the first place.'

Sebastian looked down at Tilly. Having been able to pick up most of the conversation, she smiled and nodded at him enthusiastically. 'Go on, give it a try,' she said, reaching up and squeezing his hand for support.

Sebastian looked towards the stage, then back towards the packed pub. Coldplay was now playing over the loud speakers; the dreary melody of *Paradise* had completely killed the jovial mood and most of the audience were now absorbed in their mobile phones or chatting amongst themselves.

63

Frank was still looking at Sebastian, his eyes silently pleading with him.

'Okay then,' Sebastian said, only half assured.

Frank beamed. 'Splendid! You're a 24-carat life saver, son.' He snaked his arm around Sebastian's shoulders and gently but firmly ushered him toward the stage. As they climbed the three short steps, Sebastian momentarily hesitated. He glanced back at Tilly, who had a look of reassuring admiration on her face. He smiled at her weakly, then followed Frank onto the stage. Gently dipping the music, Frank adopted his best showbiz stance and with his hands held high and wide he announced, 'Sorry for the small disruption folks, but I have a very special treat lined up for you. Tonight, for one night only, please let me introduce...' He paused. 'What's your name, son?' he whispered.

Sebastian leaned in close. 'Seb,' he whispered back.

Frank, his arms still held theatrically aloft, bellowed 'Myyyyystic... Seeeeeeb!'

Sebastian looked at him. 'Seriously?!' he said with a note of disbelief in his voice.

Frank shrugged his shoulders and grinned, gave Sebastian a hearty slap on the back, then he stepped down from the stage and made a hasty exit through the fire doors.

Save for the hubbub of voices on the far side of the bar, the pub had almost fallen silent.

His heart pounding and his stomach doing little cartwheels, Sebastian looked out across the room. He smiled and spoke. 'Good evening to you all.'

A voice from somewhere over to his left yelled, 'Speak up!' There was a rumble of laughter.

Sebastian stood silently for a moment and then, in the blink of an eye, he transformed himself into a showman.

64

More loudly this time, he announced, 'Good evening ladies and gentlemen. Tonight you will witness something truly mystical. A spectacle unlike anything you've ever seen before.'

'I ain't never seen nothing quite as ugly as you before, that's for sure,' the same heckler shouted out, following the declaration with a combination of a guffaw and a belch.

Sebastian leaned slightly forward and, as if sharing a confidence with the rest of the audience, he raised a cupped hand to his mouth. In a loud stage whisper, he said, 'Clearly the gentleman hasn't looked in a mirror recently.' Though the joke appeared to be lost on the heckler, who just frowned and waved a dismissive hand in the air, the pub erupted with laughter. Sebastian smiled inwardly. He had their attention now. 'As you can see,' he continued, holding out his hands, ' I have nothing up my sleeves. I have no special effects equipment and what you're about to see is completely unrehearsed.'

Another voice rang out across the pub. 'That's blatantly obvious!' There was no accompanying laughter this time though. Most of the people in the pub were now looking expectantly up at him, waiting to see what was going to happen next.

Sebastian carried on. 'I will select two people at random and demonstrate to you just how effective the power of persuasion can be.' He paused for dramatic effect. 'These people will be completely under my spell. Do I have any volunteers?' Sebastian peered out at the sea of blurry faces. Nobody was putting themselves forward. 'Come on, don't be scared,' he said, surveying the room. As he looked over towards the bar, his eyes fell upon a man he inexplicably recognised him from a fortnight ago. He was watching Sebastian with interest. Pointing towards him, Sebastian called out, 'You, sir!' The man shook his head and looked down into his lap.

Sebastian suddenly felt his confidence begin to ebb. He looked towards his friends. 'There's a free beer in it for my volunteers,' he announced. Just as Sebastian knew it would, Mark's hand shot up. 'Excellent. Thank you, sir. Please come on up and join me on the stage.'

As Mark swaggered over to the stage, a man's voice from over at the bar called out, 'Fix!'

Sebastian pointed at him. 'Excellent,' he exclaimed. 'We have our second volunteer, ladies and gentlemen.'

The man's face fell; suddenly he didn't look so cocky. Someone shouted, 'Go on, mate, get yer arse up there!' To save face in front of his friends, who were now mercilessly goading him, the man acquiesced. He stood up and, as a wave of enthusiastic applause – mixed with jeers of derision – resounded through the pub, he crossed to the stage where, alongside Mark, he ascended the steps.

'Please give both our volunteers a hearty round of applause,' Sebastian called out, joining in the clapping as the audience responded with enthusiasm.

Mark extended his hand to the other man. 'Mark,' he said. 'I wouldn't worry about this being a fix, mate, it's all a load of bollocks and I'm gonna prove it!' The other man shook his hand and introduced himself as Kevin.

Before Sebastian could continue, Dave, the landlord, stepped up in front him. 'What's going on here? Where's Frank?'

'He asked me to fill in,' Sebastian replied nervously as the bravado drained from him. 'While he goes back home to get a microphone,' he added nervously.

Dave frowned. The silence only lasted a matter of seconds as the man processed what he'd been told, but to Sebastian it felt like hours. 'Alright, streaky, give the punters a good show and I'll sort you and your mates a free drink afterwards.'

Sebastian smiled and nodded as the landlord started to turn away. 'I'll do my best.'

Dave stopped and looked back at him. 'You'd better!'

Dave stepped down from the stage to return to the bar and Sebastian took a deep breath and looked out at the audience. He felt his confidence come flooding back and turned to address his volunteers. 'What's your name, my friend?' he asked Kevin.

Before Kevin could reply, Mark hissed at him irritably. 'It's Kevin. Can we just get on with this? The sooner this charade is over, the sooner I can enjoy my *two* pints!'

Sebastian raised his hands. 'Ladies and Gentlemen. Tonight I will show you that with just a little persuasion, I have the power to manipulate the minds of these two ordinary men and convince them to do, or become, anything I ask of them.'

A voice rang out. 'Oi, Kev, get him to make ya dick bigger!' Kevin's group of friends, who were flanking the bar, all burst out laughing and the rest of the audience joined in. Kevin stuck up his middle finger and thrust it towards them.

Sebastian spoke again. 'I'm sorry, chaps, I'm not able to fulfil your fantasies for you, but if it's big dicks you're after, The Dreamboys are appearing at the Kenneth More Theatre next week.'

Someone shouted out drunkenly, 'Benders!' and Kevin's friends immediately fell silent, whilst everyone else in the room roared with laughter.

Sitting at the back, the suited man leant forward in his seat, a broad smile on his face. He looked around at the crowd, who were clearly enjoying this impromptu show. This was going to be interesting.

67

Sebastian took a deep breath and swallowed hard. Don't mess this up, he thought. He felt a fleeting urge to look at Tilly – seeing her pretty face would fill him with the confidence he needed – but he resisted. From everything he'd ever read and learned about hypnosis he knew that some people could be easily manipulated, whilst others were completely immune to the power of suggestion. And right now, although he could only hope he'd chosen well with Kevin, he knew for a fact that Mark would be an easy conquest at least; malleable putty in his hands. *I'll start with him first*, he thought. 'I need a couple of chairs please.' He looked over towards his friends and both Jordan and Joshua stood up and brought their chairs up to the stage.

'Break a leg,' Jordan whispered to Sebastian as they returned to their seats.

I hope not, Sebastian thought. 'Please take a seat gentlemen.' Kevin and Mark – who had a look of impatience etched on his face – both sat down. 'Now then, Mark,' Sebastian said. 'I want you to look into my eyes.' Mark did as he was asked. 'There is nobody here except for you and me,' Sebastian continued. 'Look deeply, ever more deeply into my eyes.'

'Just get a room!' a voice called out and, somewhere over to the right of the stage, a woman howled with laughter. Despite the interruption, the audience weren't anywhere near as boisterous now.

I've got them, Sebastian thought. *They might just be waiting to see me make a total pillock of myself, but I've got them.* 'You're beginning to feel tired. *Very* tired. So tired, in fact, that you can't keep your eyes open.' Kevin was watching intently as, almost immediately, Mark's eyelids began to flutter, then drooped and closed. 'I'm going to count backwards from three to one,' Sebastian

68

continued, 'and when I reach one you will be completely under my spell. You will remain that way until you hear me say stop and I snap my fingers. Nod if you understand.' Mark nodded once.

Sebastian executed the countdown, then turned to face the audience. 'Picture the scene,' he said. 'It's a beautiful morning, the sun is shining down on the farmyard. In the distance cows are mooing and the scent of freshly cut hay lingers in the air. Scrabbling in the dust are a clutch of hens.' He raised a hand towards the crowd to hold their attention for a moment and leaned towards Mark, whose face was completely blank now. 'The next time you hear me say the word chicken, you will become one. You will think just like one and you will behave just like one. You will only cease to be one when I shout stop and snap my fingers. Nod if you understand.' Mark nodded again.

Sebastian turned to Kevin, who was beginning to look as if he wanted to be anywhere else but there on the stage. 'Now then, Kevin, I have to confess I'm not on top form tonight. I haven't had anything to eat yet and I could absolutely murder a sandwich. Something really tasty like...' He paused, looked out at the audience and winked, earning himself another small ripple of laughter. 'You're ahead of me, aren't you?' he said, grinning. 'Chicken!'

Behind him, Mark's head shot up and he flung out his elbows. His eyes widened and he made a little clucking sound.

There was a pregnant pause and then someone at the front started laughing. Within moments the audience was roaring with laughter.

Sebastian turned back to Mark. 'Oh, you're awake,' he said, struggling to make himself heard over the din.

'Buk,' Mark responded and jerked his head forward once.

'You're a very *naughty* chicken. What are you doing out of your coop before you've laid your morning egg?'

'Buk-buk.'

The audience was gripped. They were lapping up the evening's bonus entertainment.

'I think you'd better get on and lay that egg for us now,' Sebastian said.

Scraping his feet on the floor of the stage, Mark turned in a small circle and squatted. 'Buk-buk.' A strained expression appeared on his face. 'Buk-buk-buk ba-gawk!'

The audience was howling with laughter as Sebastian stepped forward and took a little bow; this was going even better than he could have hoped. The moment of jubilation was cut short as he heard Kevin say, 'He looks like he's gonna crap himself!'

'No!' Sebastian exclaimed. He spun round to see that Mark, still squatting and straining, now had a protruding vein on the side of his head that looked ready to burst. 'Stop!' he cried. 'You no longer feel compelled to lay an egg!'

Mark immediately stood upright and flapped his elbows once. 'Buk.'

That had been close. Sebastian didn't even want to think about the consequences had he made Mark defecate in front of a pub full of people.

Mark began moving in little circles, scraping his feet and jerking his head about. 'Good chicken,' Sebastian said. 'You've earned your breakfast.' Making little clucking noises of contentment, Mark set off around the stage, making jerky pecking motions towards the floor. The audience burst into a round of applause and Sebastian acknowledged with another little bow. He turned back to Mark and said, 'Time for you to return to your roost for a little rest. But you'd better sit down *very* carefully.' He looked out at the crowd and was rewarded with hoots of laughter. 'Now then,' he said, turning to Kevin.

'You'd better not make *me* crap myself,' Kevin growled at him quietly through gritted teeth. The tacit threat in the words was all too clear.

Sebastian locked eyes with him. 'Look into my eyes. Deeply, ever more deeply. I'm going to count down from three to one...'

Much to Sebastian's surprise – and, no less so, relief – Kevin was quickly engaged and responding to his instructions. Sebastian turned and stepped to the front of the stage. 'And who is the arch nemesis of a chicken?'

'Colonel Sanders!' a portly man yelled out and the audience fell about laughing.

Sebastian licked his fingers. 'Hmmm, finger-lickin' good. We can all see you've had more than your fair share of bargain buckets, sir.' He pointed at the man and the laughter intensified. 'Aside from Colonel Sanders though, a chicken fears a slinky, bushy-tailed animal that slinks around the woodland...' He turned to Kevin. 'The next time you hear the word fox, you will become one. The bane of every farmer and a chicken's worst enemy. A sly, wily and very *hungry* scavenger.'

Turning back to the audience, he cried out, 'What's he going to become?' and threw a hand in the air. In unison the audience responded loudly, 'A *fox*!'

At the sound of the trigger word, Kevin's head snapped up and he leapt out of his chair.

'You're a fox with a beautiful, bushy brush,' Sebastian continued. 'How proud you are of it. Why don't you show the people?'

Kevin turned his back to the crowd, stuck out his bottom and vigorously waggled it about. The audience roared.

71

'Look over there,' Sebastian said to Kevin. 'A nice, plump, juicy chicken just waiting to be eaten.'

Kevin made a little raspy yelping sound. Upon hearing the noise, Mark's head jerked round, his senses on alert. Kevin hunched his shoulders over, stuck out his arms, his hands crooked and fingers extended like claws, and began to advance on his quarry. Seeing him coming, Mark jumped up and scampered to the far end of the stage. 'Buk-buk-buk ba-gawk!' he exclaimed loudly. To the sound of rapturous laughter and applause from the delighted audience, Kevin quickened his pace. Mark took off at speed around the stage, wildly flapping his elbows and squawking loudly as Kevin pursued him. The vigorous movement of his arms caused the bandage on Mark's hand to come unravelled and it flapped wildly behind him as he darted back and forth across the stage.

Sebastian took another bow and cast a glance towards Tilly. He was delighted to see the look of admiration on her face and he felt himself swell with pride. As he was about to turn back, he caught sight of the suited man beside the bar, who was now on his feet, grinning and applauding enthusiastically. He nodded appreciatively at Sebastian. The laughter in the room suddenly intensified and there was a crash behind him. Spinning round, Sebastian saw Mark cowering on the floor clucking for all he was worth and Kevin standing astride him, his teeth bared and snapping.

'Stop!' Sebastian exclaimed and the two men froze. He crossed the stage and said in a commanding voice, 'Kevin, you are no longer a fox.' He snapped his fingers. 'Mark, you are no longer a chicken.' Again, he snapped his fingers.

Shaking his head, Kevin stepped away from Mark, who quickly realised he was splayed out on the floor. Looking a little dazed, he picked himself up. Sebastian stepped between the two men and turned back to face the audience. 'Ladies and gentlemen, let's have a huge round of applause for our two wonderful volunteers!' As the room erupted in the sound of clapping and whistles of approval, Sebastian guided Kevin and Mark to the steps down from the stage. 'Thanks, guys,' he said. 'You can return to your seats now.'

Both looking slightly bemused about what had just happened, the two men descended the steps and returned to their seats.

Sebastian glanced at his watch. The performance hadn't filled as much time as he'd hoped. His mind racing, he wondered how he could keep the audience entertained until Frank returned. He was saved by a sudden shout from the crowd, 'Come on then, mate, do me!'

Before Sebastian could respond, the burly man with a mop of blonde hair and an unkempt beard bounded towards the stage and up the steps. Sebastian noticed that the man's beard bore traces of whatever he'd been eating; something spicy from the smell of his breath. He smiled. 'Well, they say a volunteer is worth ten pressed men.'

'Who?' the man said.

'Excuse me?'

'*Who* says a volunteer is worth ten pressed men?'

The audience laughed. Sebastian looked at the man, trying to gauge if he was being funny. From the quizzical expression on his face, it was apparent he wasn't.

'Never mind. Thank you for offering to participate. May I ask your name?'

'Gareth.'

A lone voice in the audience cheered and Gareth grinned. 'That's my mate, Toby.'

'I see you support the Lilywhites,' Sebastian said, nodding at the Tottenham Hotspur football shirt Gareth was wearing. An idea had already come to him.

Gareth turned to the audience and chanted, 'We love you, Tottenham, we do. Oh, Tottenham, we...' – he punched the air – 'Love...' – another punch – 'You!' – a final air-punch. A few people in the crowd booed and some cheered. 'Oggy, oggy, oggy!' Gareth yelled at the top of his voice.

'Oi, oi, oi!' the audience responded.

Gareth turned back to face Sebastian and chanted loudly, 'Glory, glory Tottenham Hotspur, and the Spurs go marching on!'

'Indeed,' Sebastian said non-committally. His interest in football was minimal. 'I assume it's fair to say you don't care too much for Arsenal then?'

'Arsenal? The scum!'

'Spurs for life then?' Sebastian asked.

'Too bloody right,' Gareth exclaimed proudly. Again, the response from the audience was a mixture of amusement and boos.

Sebastian smiled inwardly. He had the man safely on his side now. It was always easiest to manipulate people if you could lower their resistance to the power of suggestion by striking up a rapport. 'Very well then,' he said. 'Please take a seat and look deep into my eyes.'

It didn't take long to put Gareth under. He was sat upright with his eyes closed as Sebastian circled him, sensing the anticipation of the crowd through the silence in the room. 'So just to recap, there's no way on Earth you'd ever support Arsenal, is that correct?' The corner of Gareth's mouth twitched and he nodded slowly. 'In a moment I'm going to ask you to open your eyes. You will see the colour red and you will become the world's

74

proudest Arsenal supporter, something you'll feel compelled to announce to the world. You will only cease to be an Arsenal supporter when I command it and snap my fingers. Do you understand?' Gareth nodded. 'Then open your eyes now.' As Gareth did so, Sebastian slipped his mobile phone out of his pocket and held up the red leather flip-case in front of the man's face.

Gareth's eyes lit up. 'Guuuunnners!' he exclaimed and began to march up and down the stage singing loudly. 'Arsenal 'til I die. I'm Arsenal 'til I die...' Sebastian could feel the stage vibrating beneath his feet as the march turned into a veritable stomp. 'We won the League at Shite Hart Lane...'

'Shake your rattle!' Sebastian cried out.

Gareth raised his arm and swung it in circles above his head as if whirling a rattle, and he started making clacking sounds.

Through the howls of laughter, there came a loud hammering sound on the fire escape doors. A woman seated nearby got up, pushed the panic exit bar and Frank appeared carrying a microphone.

Sebastian saw him and immediately said 'Stop!' Gareth came to such an immediate halt; it was as if someone had flipped an off switch. 'You are no longer an Arsenal supporter,' Sebastian said, snapping his fingers.

Gareth blinked a couple of times as Sebastian placed a friendly hand on his shoulder. 'Ladies and gentlemen, let's hear it for Gareth!' As the crowd clapped loudly, Sebastian guided the slightly disoriented man to the steps and he returned to his seat beside Toby.

'Guuuunnners!' Toby said, wiping the tears of laughter from his eyes.

Gareth shot him a confused look. 'You *what*?!'

'That was fuckin' hilarious, mate!'

75

Gareth grabbed up his empty pint glass. 'I'm gonna get another drink.' Toby held out his own empty glass and Gareth glanced at it angrily. 'You can get your fuckin' own.'

Toby seemed to find that even funnier. As he watched his friend head over to the bar, Frank hurried up the steps onto the stage. He shook Sebastian's hand vigorously. 'I could hear the laughter from half way down the street, son. Whatever you did, it sounds like it went down a storm.'

'It did go rather well actually,' Sebastian said, beaming.

'Well, thanks again. I owe you one.' Frank slapped Sebastian on the shoulder and resumed his position beside the karaoke machine. He pulled the microphone out of its box and plugged it in. 'Apologies for the intermission, folks. Let's get back to knocking out some more tunes, shall we?'

Feeling pleased with himself, Sebastian made his way back to his friends. Tilly stood up to greet him and planted a soft kiss on his cheek. 'That was absolutely amazing!' she cooed. 'I'm *so* proud of you!'

'Yeah, fantastic job mate,' Joshua said. Katie and Jordan chimed in.

Mark, however, was looking less than impressed. 'Hey, Mystic Meg, I think there was something about a free pint?' he said grouchily. Although he didn't quite understand how, he knew that Sebastian had made him look foolish and the uncomfortable feeling in his bottom made him afraid to ask.

Sebastian rolled his eyes and sighed. 'Okay.' As he stood up to go to the bar, he caught sight of a suited man approaching the table and realised it was the same one he'd made eye contact with during the show.

76

The man stopped in front of Sebastian, adjusted his tie and extended his hand. 'Hi, my name's James Lawrence.' The accent was indefinable but the man spoke with a slightly effeminate tone. 'I represent the Rising Starz Entertainment Agency.'

Sebastian shook the man's hand and smiled. 'Sebastian Matthews,' he said.

'Pleased to meet you, Sebastian. I've got to tell you, my friend, what you did up there this evening was outstanding. Not many people can get up as spontaneously as you did and tame a rowdy crowd like this. But you had them hooked.'

'That's very kind of y...' Sebastian began.

'Pint!'

Sebastian looked around to see Mark glaring at him. He felt his hackles rise. Had Mark got no filter whatsoever? 'I'm just talking to...'

'You owe me a pint,' Mark pressed irritably.

Sebastian wasn't about to get into a spat. Mumbling an apology to the agent, he pulled a £5 note from his wallet and handed it to Mark. 'Here, go get your pint.'

Mark snatched it from him – 'Cheers!' – and sauntered over to the bar.

'Sorry again, Mr Lawrence,' Sebastian said.

'Call me James. No need to apologise. Your mate is evidently thirsty.'

'He's evidently *very* rude,' Katie chipped in, an apologetic expression on her own face. She and the others had heard what James had said when he introduced himself to Sebastian and they were now all sitting waiting to hear what was coming next.

'No worries,' James said. 'You meet all sorts in this place. I'm here for most karaoke nights. I suppose you'd call me a talent scout.' He smiled at Sebastian. 'And let

77

me tell you, my friend, you've got talent by the barrel load. Have you ever thought about a career in show business?'

'Er... yes, I have. But life kinda gets in the way of your dreams, doesn't it?'

'Not for everyone. As I say, I've attended most karaoke nights here the last couple of years and I've seen a lot of talented singers. A heck of a lot of rubbish too, of course.' James chuckled and gestured at the drunk, middle-aged woman on the stage who had just launched into a terrible rendition of *I Will Survive* with the power to make ears bleed. 'But you have to suffer the chaff to discover the wheat.'

'So basically, you identify people who can sing...'

'Precisely that.'

'And then what?' Sebastian asked.

'Attempt to set them on the starry road to fame and fortune. You remember Marty Lucerne?'

Sebastian shook his head.

Despite the background noise his friends were listening intently to what was being said. 'I do,' Tilly said. 'He did that catchy song *Caress My Heart*.'

Everyone looked at Tilly blankly. 'It was a couple of years ago, it played on the radio for weeks,' she added.

'That's him,' James said with manifest pride. 'He was one of mine.'

'You discovered him here?' Sebastian said.

'No, over in Islington. He had a fantastic vocal range.'

'A one hit wonder though,' Tilly said.

James nodded. 'Sadly so.' His face clouded a little. 'He was damned good. Could have gone the distance if he wanted, but he just wasn't committed enough. Threw away a golden opportunity. Such a waste.'

78

'What's all this got to do with me?' Sebastian said. 'I can't sing.'

James laughed. 'You don't have to be able to sing to hold a crowd's attention, my friend. We all witnessed that tonight. I've been in this game for years and I'm telling you straight, you've got talent. I can't always define it, but I sure as hell know it when I see it.' He could see Sebastian wasn't sure. 'Tell you what, Mr Matthews.' He reached inside his jacket, pulled out a business card and thrust it into Sebastian's hand. 'Take my card. I'd really love to get you in to meet my boss and show him what I saw here tonight.'

'I don't know about that,' Sebastian said uncertainly.

James held up a hand. 'All I ask is you think about it over the weekend and give me a bell.'

Sebastian nodded. 'Okay, I will.'

'Sweet. There is one caveat though.'

'Oh?'

'You're going to have to lose the name "Mystic Seb"!'

Sebastian laughed. 'Not a problem. That one was courtesy of Frank.'

'Sounds about right.' James extended his hand. 'Until we meet again...' – he winked – ' and I'm in no doubt we will.'

They shook hands again and, as the caterwauling sound of *I Will Survive* reached its crescendo, James walked away.

'He seemed really nice,' Tilly said, as Sebastian tucked the business card into his shirt pocket and sat down.

'So, what you gonna do, Seb?' Jordan asked. 'You gonna call him?'

'You *so* should,' Katie said. 'If someone had approached me with an offer like that, I wouldn't have needed time to think about it.'

'Me neither,' Joshua chipped in.

'Yeah, go for it, mate,' Jordan said. 'What have you got to lose?'

'I don't know,' Sebastian said doubtfully. His brow was furrowed. 'It's a big commitment to make.'

'Seriously?' Jordan said. 'What commitment? All he did was invite you along to meet his boss. He might take one look at your act and boot you out the door.' He laughed.

'*Or* it might just be the open door to something really exciting,' Tilly said. 'A career in showbiz.'

Before Sebastian could respond, Mark, his face like thunder, appeared clutching a pint of beer. 'Bastard barman wouldn't give me my free pint!'

Katie rolled her eyes. 'That *is* a free one, you greedy sod. Seb paid for it.'

'But Dave promised me one. I'm due two and I *want* two.'

Sebastian needed a moment away from everyone to think. He stood up. 'Okay, okay, I'll get you another one.'

Mark grinned. 'Nice one.'

Sebastian looked at Tilly. 'Would you like another?'

'No, I'm fine.' She gestured towards the toilets. 'If I have any more, I'm going to have to go in there.' She wrinkled her nose.

Thinking back over what James had said to him, Sebastian moved through the crowd towards the bar. As he got nearer, he could see Kevin arguing with the barmaid. 'I'm telling you, Dave *promised* me one.'

'Well Dave ain't 'ere and it's more than my job's worth to give away freebies.'

'Listen up, you stu...'

Sebastian touched Kevin on the shoulder. 'Pint's on me.' He pulled out his wallet and reluctantly withdrew a £10 note. 'A pint of…' He looked at Kevin questioningly.

'Stella.'

Sebastian smiled at the barmaid. 'A pint of Stella for this gentleman, please, and a pint of Waddington's.' When he returned to the table – his wallet now £15 lighter – Mark had already finished his first pint. He eagerly took the fresh one from Sebastian. 'Did I get any change from that fiver?'

Mark winked at him. 'I'll sort it out for you later, mate.' He took a sip of the beer. 'Anyway, from what I just heard, you're gonna be minted soon. It ain't gonna be a hardship to buy your mates a drink.'

'I don't know what you "heard", but I can assure you being wealthy doesn't interest me.'

'Only a halfwit would think like that,' Mark said, taking another draft of beer. 'Everyone wants to be loaded.'

'Not *everyone*.' Sebastian sighed and sat down. 'Here,' he said, pulling out the business card James had given him and handing it to Tilly. 'What do you reckon?'

Tilly inspected the small white card embossed with gold lettering:

JAMES LAWRENCE
TALENT SCOUT

0208 57485748

RISING STARZ
"The Gateway to Stardom"
email: risinstarz@talisa.net

81

'It it legit then?' Jordan asked.

'No idea,' Tilly said. 'I mean, it *looks* professional enough.' She handed it to Katie, who gave it a cursory glance, nodded approvingly and gave it back.

'Let's have a look,' Mark said, reaching over and snatching the card out of Tilly's hand.

He looked at it and then flicked it back across the table to her. 'Looks like a load of old shit to me. Talent scout, my arse. He's probably a raving great queer...' – he glanced at Jordan – '...No offence, mate.'

Jordan shook his head in disbelief. 'None taken. Mate.'

'Well *I'm* offended,' Katie said irritably. 'What the hell's the matter with you?' She rested her hand on Jordan's arm. 'Sorry, he's got absolutely no filter,' she said quietly.

'It's cool,' Jordan said, placing a hand over hers. 'Really.'

Mark, who failed to notice, continued, 'Yeah, I'd be careful if I was you, Seb. He probably just wants to take you up the backstage pass!' Cackling, he formed a small circle with the thumb and forefinger of his left hand and jabbed the forefinger of his right in and out of it. 'Up the old Khyber, mate.'

'Don't be so damned crude,' Katie said. 'And stop being so rude to Seb. That show he put on tonight was seriously awesome. If anyone deserves a shot at success it's him.'

Mark waved a dismissive hand at her and finished his pint.

Tilly reached under the table and gently caressed Sebastian's knee. As she leaned in close and he felt her hot breath on his ear, he felt a little tingle of excitement course through him. 'You do, you know,' she whispered. 'You really do.'

82

CHAPTER 5

The previous evening, when Tilly had dropped Sebastian back to his flat, she'd parked up at the kerb opposite and they remained there for almost half an hour, lost in trifling small talk. They had finally kissed goodnight just as it started to rain and Sebastian had to make a dash across the road to avoid a soaking. When he got in he'd fallen straight into bed, but there followed a restless night; when he wasn't half awake, his mind replaying the encounter with James Lawrence over and over, he had endured a succession of troubling dreams. In the worst of them he had been standing alone on stage, completely naked in a spotlight, surrounded on all sides by hoots of derision from unseen spectators revelling in his predicament. It had been exceptionally vivid and left him feeling inordinately unsettled, and he was only able to shake off its remnants after he'd got up, showered, shaved and sat down to eat his breakfast.

He had just cleared his cereal bowl and was sitting, thoughtfully twirling the Rising Starz business card in his fingers, when his phone buzzed. He picked it up and looked at the screen, smiling as he saw it was a WhatsApp message from Tilly.

> **Morning my little superstar! Still on Cloud nine? X**

Hesitating for a moment, he tapped out a reply, cursing the autocorrect function as he did so and changing the word "wonderful" back to the intended "wondering" twice.

83

Not exactly. I've been awake half
the night wondering what to do.
I feel really nervous!!

Hoping Tilly would respond with the words he needed to help him reach a decision, Sebastian watched the three pulsating dots with anticipation as she keyed her reply. After what seemed like an eternity the message popped up.

Don't be a silly. There's nothing
to be nervous about, you're
absolutely great. You've nothing
to lose by just giving that guy a
call...

In his heart Sebastian knew she was right. What was the worst that could happen? He'd go in and see them and if they didn't like what he had to offer that would be the end of it. And at least he would have tried. But if they *did*...

I guess so. I'll call him now. If I
hang about any longer I reckon
I'll probably chicken out! lol

Don't mention chickens!! ☺
Just let me know what he says.
buk-buk-buk-buk!!! X

hahahaha I will. Thank you. X

With his heart racing 19 to the dozen, Sebastian took a deep breath and called the number on the card. Almost immediately a woman's voice came on the line and said, 'Good morning, Rising Starz Entertainment Agency. How can I help you?' Her tone was typically matter of fact.

'Oh, er, hello,' Sebastian started. 'I wonder if I might be able to speak to James Lawrence please.'

'Who may I say is calling?' the woman said.

'Sebastian. Sebastian Matthews. We met last night at The Cauliflower.' As the words left his mouth, Sebastian realised the woman probably had no idea what The Cauliflower was. 'Oh, er, that's a pub in Ilford. Mr Lawrence saw my act. I'm a hypnotist, you see, and I had to fill in when Frank – that's the man who hosts the karaoke – well, the microphone broke and he had to go and get...' Sebastian trailed off as he realised he was blathering. 'What I mean is, he gave me his business card and asked me to call.'

'Please hold.'

The line went dead for a moment, then there was a soft click. 'Mr Lawrence is on another call at the moment. I can ask him to call you back, or you can hold, but I've no idea how long he'll be.'

Sebastian had suffered enough failed callbacks in his life – banks, doctors, opticians, dentists, even his favorite bookshop – and although a few minutes earlier his nerves would have gladly seen him throw the business card away, suddenly this call had become very important to him. If only to be able to prove to Tilly he'd plucked up the necessary courage. 'I'll hold, thank you,' he said firmly.

'Very well.'

There was another soft click and one of those generic melodies that plays in minute-long loops began playing.

85

Sebastian sighed and sat back, preparing himself for a long wait, but less than a minute passed before the music abruptly ceased and a man's voice spoke. 'Mr Matthews!'

'Hello, is that Mr Lawrence?' Sebastian said, feeling his stomach tighten.

'Indeed it is, sorry for keeping you waiting.'

'It's fine, I'm sure you're a busy man.'

'As a matter of fact,' James said breezily, 'I was just talking to one of my colleagues about you.'

'Oh, really?' Sebastian's stomach twitched again.

'Yes. I'm really glad you called. I can read people pretty well and I had a feeling in my water you'd make the right choice, though I'll be honest, even with all my years in this game, you can never be a hundred percent sure.'

'I wasn't sure myself,' Sebastian said. 'To tell the truth, I'm still not.'

'Listen, Sebastian... Can I call you, Sebastian?'

'Seb is fine.'

'Well, Seb, the one thing everyone will tell you about James Lawrence is he doesn't spout B-S. I meant what I said last night, you're a class act and there's a career in show business awaiting you if you're smart enough to seize it. *Are* you smart enough, Seb?'

'I hope so,' Sebastian said, unable to disguise the note of uncertainty in his voice.

James laughed. 'We're going to have to work on your confidence though. I know it's there, I saw it last night in spades.'

'So, what happens next?' Sebastian asked.

'We get you in here to meet my boss. I only work till noon on a Saturday, so it can't happen today. How does Monday morning at eleven suit?'

'That'd be fine, I think. Where exactly are you?'

'We're in a little office in Brick Lane,' James replied. 'Have you got email?' Sebastian gave him his address. 'I'll ping you over details before I leave for the day. I'll include a little map to help you find us.'

'Thank you. I'll see you on Monday then.'

'Looking forward to being wowed all over again,' James said enthusiastically. 'Bye-bye for now.' A soft click ended the call.

Sebastian immediately opened WhatsApp and sent a message to Tilly, telling her that James had invited him in to meet the boss. He ended the message with a nervous-face emoji. The twin white ticks appeared beneath his message and they immediately turned blue, showing that Tilly was reading it. Sebastian waited excitedly for a moment, expecting the pulsing dots indicating that she was typing a reply to appear. They didn't. In fact, to his dismay Tilly went offline. As he felt his heart sink, the phone rang and he almost dropped it. Tilly's name came up on the screen.

'Hi!' she said breathlessly. 'Too much to text, it was easier to call. I'm *so* pleased for you!'

'It's good to hear your voice again.' Sebastian said. 'I missed you.'

'You only saw me last night!' She laughed. 'And I think we should go out tonight to celebrate.'

'It's a bit early to celebrate, but I'll certainly take you out.'

'It's a date. So, come on, what time are they seeing you Monday?'

'Eleven. I'll get the tube over early to make sure I'm there in time.'

'Don't be daft,' Tilly said. 'I've got Monday off. I'll pick you up about eight-thirty and we can stop for breakfast on the way.'

'Are you sure,' Sebastian said? 'Didn't you have plans?'

'Only seeing my sister. That can wait, I want to come with you. I'm *so* proud of you and you're going to knock them dead.'

Sebastian felt his heart swell. The call ended with the promise he'd meet her at six that evening for a movie date and Sebastian turned his thoughts to what he might wear to impress on Monday. In his head, stage hypnotists wore top hats and capes, but that was a cliché and the more he thought about it, it probably wasn't right anway; wasn't that mostly magicians? He bounded into the bedroom and flung open the wardrobe door. Rifling through his clothing, he pulled out the suit he'd last worn at his cousin's wedding. It wasn't flash, but it was smart and always gave the impression he was making an effort. He tried it on, but to his horror, as he inspected himself in the mirror, he saw that the shoulders had been ravaged by moths. He returned to the wardrobe and pulled everything else from the hangers. Throwing a pile of clothing on the bed, he stood and doubtfully inspected his remaining options. A wave of mild panic descended on him. He picked up his phone and typed a short text to Tilly.

I can't do it!

A few moments later a reply popped up.

Can't do what?

I've got nothing to wear!! ☹

88

As he sat on the end of the bed waiting for a reply, the phone started ringing. It was Tilly. 'What's up? What do you mean you've got nothing to wear?'

'I've got a decent suit, but I tried it on and flippin' moths have made holes in it, I've looked through everything else and there's nothing that doesn't make me look like a tramp, and don't even get me started on shirts, my best one has a stain on the back from some idiot who splashed wine on it at a wedding, besides it's the only white one I've got and...'

'Woah, woah, calm down, you'll have a nervous breakdown in a minute!'

'Sorry, I'm just getting myself in a bit of a state,' Sebastian said forlornly.

'Have you got a pair of black trousers?'

Sebastian looked at the pile of clothes on the bed. 'I have, yes.'

'Good,' Tilly said. 'We can stop off in town after breakfast and pick you up a cheap jacket. That'll take care of your shirt worries.'

'I suppose,' Sebastian conceded.

'There you go then, problem solved.'

Sebastian let out a sigh. 'Thank you. I know I'm being irrational, I'm just nervous. I don't think I could have done this without you.'

'Of course you could. But you don't have to. I'll be behind you all the way to the Palladium.'

On Monday morning Sebastian woke with a start. Another disturbing dream had meant a restless night and, as he sat bolt upright, he reached for his mobile phone to look at the time. Sighing with relief when the digits on the screen revealed it was only 6:30, he plumped up the pillows behind him and started to scroll through his Facebook page. Sleepily losing himself in the virtual world, absorbing the trivial and mundane updates from his network of online friends, before he knew it almost an hour had flittered by. It was the sound of the adjacent flat's front door slamming as his neighbour left for work that startled him out of his daze. He looked at the clock in the top corner of his phone. 'Shit!' Tilly had texted him late the night before to confirm she would pick him up at 8:30. He didn't have to be at the Rising Starz offices until eleven, and the journey shouldn't take them more than an hour, but Tilly had insisted they arrive early – better that than roll up late – so that they could find a coffee shop and have a drink, which would give Sebastian a chance to steady his nerves before attending the audition. He threw the duvet aside and swung his legs round to sit on the edge of the bed. Drawn like a moth to the flame, he looked at his phone again and the red dot beside the email inbox icon caught his eye. The notification stated that he had 11 new emails. He tapped the icon to open his inbox and mentally chastised himself. Why did he *always* do this? He knew what would happen: he would go into his email, then end up spending the next hour farting around on his phone and make himself late. It had happened copious times before and yet here he was dithering about once again. Of course, he knew there was an element of procrastination at play, a way of distracting his thoughts from the morning that lay ahead, but nevertheless that wasn't going to cut it today. No matter that he might let himself down, he sure as heck wasn't going to let Tilly down. Shaking his head, he closed his email and tossed the phone aside onto the mattress. 'Get a grip,' he muttered.

90

Standing up, he stretched and ambled through to the bathroom.

He shaved quickly enough, but showering afforded him yet another opportunity to dither. He was usually in and out in less than five minutes, but today, as he luxuriated for longer than normal beneath the warm spray, he was sorely in need of a good kick up the backside. The kick came abruptly in the form of his intercom buzzing.

The speaker was affixed to the wall just outside the bathroom and the loud noise made him jump. As he spun around in the cubicle, he slipped. His full weight hit the flimsy cubicle door, held in place by only three tiny magnets, and it swung open, depositing Sebastian on the floor.

The buzzer sounded again.

Sebastian rolled onto his side and pulled his knees up to his chest to free his lower half from the cubicle; the bathroom was only small and at just over six foot tall he was almost wedged into the corner. Slipping about on the tiles, he managed to get up onto his knees. He winced as he gingerly poked at the red line running across his shin and down to his ankle, caused by the thin strip of metal along the entrance to the shower cubicle. Cursing under his breath, he suddenly became aware that his mobile phone was ringing. He hoisted himself onto his feet, grabbed his towelling robe from the back of the door and rushed through to the bedroom, snatching up the phone just as it stopped ringing. He saw on the screen that the missed call was from Tilly. Oblivious to the fact he was dripping water on the bedroom carpet, he quickly called her back.

She immediately answered. 'You okay, hun? I've been ringing your doorbell.'

'Yes, sorry, I was... in the shower. Hang on, I'll let you in now.' Ending the call, he went out into the hallway, pressed the outer door release button and opened up his own front door an inch. His ankle was smarting badly now, but before he could inspect the damage further he heard the sound of footsteps on the stairwell. He quickly sidestepped into the bathroom and pushed the door to. Catching sight of his reflection in the mirror, his eyes widened with dismay; his face was red and his hair was hanging flat on his head.

As he quickly ruffled it with his fingers, Tilly's voice called out, 'Seb, are you decent?'

'Yeah, come on in,' he replied with more assurance than he felt. 'I'm just drying my hair, go take a pew in the living room, I won't be long.' He picked up a hand towel and rubbed his hair vigorously, then applied a small blob of wax and ruffled it again. 'That's better,' he said to himself, though louder than he'd intended.

'What was that?' Tilly called.

Sebastian appeared in the doorway to the living room. 'Nothing,' he said, flicking a stray curl away from his eyebrow. He leant casually against the doorframe, endeavouring to exude an air of casualness contrary to how he was actually feeling. 'How are *you* doing?'

'I'm good. All the better for seeing y...' She trailed off and grinned.

Sebastian frowned. 'What?'

Tilly's grin broadened and she nodded downwards towards Sebastian's crotch. He looked down and felt himself go hot and cold as he realised his gown was hanging open and failing dismally in its job to protect his modesty. 'Oh my God,' he exclaimed, hastily pulling it closed. 'I'm *so* sorry!'

92

Tilly stood up and walked towards him. She planted a soft kiss on his forehead and slipped her arms around his neck. 'Don't be silly.'

Almost swooning at the scent of her perfume and the warmth of her soft skin against his neck, Sebastian smiled and pulled her into a closer embrace. 'I'm so glad you're here.'

'I wouldn't want to be anywhere else,' Tilly replied with a warm smile. 'Now go get yourself dressed.' She stepped back out of his embrace. Her eyes sparkled at him. 'You might have impressed *me* with your, er… impromptu presentation. But you're going need some clothes on if you want to wow the guys at Rising Starz!'

Turning away from her to hide his blushes, Sebastian went back through to the bedroom and pushed the door to behind him so that it was half closed. Reaching up to the hook on the back of the door, he lifted down the coat hanger on which his smart black trousers and white shirt were draped. The offensive red wine stain on the shirt caught his eye and he sighed. Throwing his robe on the bed, he bent down and pulled out some socks and a pair of boxers from a drawer in his wardrobe. Balancing on one foot, he was in the process of slipping one leg into the underwear when Tilly drummed her fingers on bedroom door. He jumped, lost his balance and fell backwards onto the bed, grazing his ribs on the bedknob as he did so. 'Ffffff…!'

'You okay?' Tilly said with a note of concern.

'Yeah, yeah, all good,' Sebastian lied. He quickly got up off the bed and massaged his side. Trying to sound as calm and composed as possible, through gritted teeth he added, 'I won't be long.'

93

'Sorry, I didn't mean to interrupt,' Tilly said from behind the door. 'I just wanted to ask if I can use the bathroom?'

'Of course you can.' Sebastian pulled up his boxer shorts. 'It's just to your right.'

Tilly pushed open the bathroom door and frowned at the sight of the wet floor. 'Yep. I've found it.'

Sebastian finished dressing as fast as he could and checked his hair in the mirror. As a child, everyone had made a fuss of his tightly curled locks, cooing at him and fiddling with them, as doting parents and relatives do. *'Awww, he's just like the little boy in the Pears soap adverts!,'* one of his aunts had said when he was about five; it had been an innocent enough observation at the time, but somehow it had stuck, following him through adolescence and well into his teenage years – and it wasn't always remarked upon in a kindly manner. As an adult he still deemed his hair annoying. No matter what he did with it, it just sat in irksome spirals on his head. He had once considered shaving it off completely, but given the choice of becoming a skinhead or resembling a male version of Shirley Temple... well, he'd ultimately decided to live with the curls.

There was another light drumming sound on the bedroom door. 'Come in,' Sebastian called out.

Tilly pushed open the door. 'What's been going on in the bathroom? Does your shower leak?' she asked innocently.

'Oh gosh, no. Sorry. I didn't get a chance to mop up.' Sebastian felt his cheeks burning. 'I, er... I kind of slipped actually. One minute I was in the shower and the next I was flat out on the floor, dripping wet.'

Tilly put her hand to her mouth. 'Oh no! You didn't hurt yourself did you?'

Sebastian bent and rolled up his trouser leg. 'My shin took a bit of a battering.'

Tilly gasped. 'Ouch. You really ought to put something on that, you know. You're going to have a nasty bruise.'

Sebastian let go of the hem and straightened the seam. 'Nah. I'll be fine,' he said, trying to ignore the searing pain in his ribs. He turned to retrieve his mobile and quickly flipped the duvet over the bed, hoping Tilly hadn't noticed the dishevelled state of the sheets.

With his back to her, she could see the faded pink stain across the right shoulder of his shirt. 'Oh dear, I see what you mean about that stain!'

Sebastian turned. 'Yeah. It's not good, is it? But I only have this one. Otherwise it's a Hawaiian shirt with flamingos on, or one of my old blue work shirts.'

Tilly stepped up to him and took his hand. 'Don't you worry, we've got plenty of time. We'll stop off at the retail park on the way to Brick Lane, there are a few cheap clothing shops there. We can easily get you a black jacket.' She laughed. 'Provided you keep it on, no-one will ever know.'

Sebastian smiled. 'Thank you.'

Tilly lifted his hand and gave it a soft kiss. 'Come on then, my little superstar. Let's go make you famous.'

CHAPTER 6

Roadworks punctuated by two sets of traffic lights, along with the ensuing queues passing through Gants Hill and Hackney added another 20 minutes to the journey, and the whistle-stop shopping trip at Leyton Mills to acquire a jacket a further 10 minutes. Nevertheless, Sebastian and Tilly arrived in Spitalfields with plenty of time to spare.

'It helps to know the best spots,' Tilly said. 'Free parking here all day.' She was reversing her car into the one remaining space in the car park when she caught sight of Sebastian biting on his thumbnail. She stopped and frowned at him. 'Hey, you! Relax!' Sebastian turned his head and whipping his thumb away from his mouth he smiled at her nervously. Tilly completed her manoeuvre and applied the handbrake. Killing the engine, she leant over and placed a hand on Sebastian's knee. 'We can just forget about it and go home if you like,' she said with a smile.

'Can we?' Sebastian replied hopefully.

'*No*, of course not!' Tilly squeezed his knee. 'Come on, you've made it this far. Let's go get a cuppa and I'm sure you'll feel much better.'

Sebastian nodded doubtfully and lifted Tilly's hand to his face. He kissed it gently. 'Thank you.'

They climbed out of the car and set off in the direction of Brick Lane. As they walked, Tilly hooked her arm through Sebastian's and when they rounded the corner, she spotted a small café on the opposite side of the road. 'Perfect!' she exclaimed. The traffic was heaving and as they waited for an opportunity to cross the road, she

96

laughed and added, 'Or it will be if we manage to get there before they close.'

A man behind the wheel of a tank-sized 4x4 slowed down and flashed his lights at them. Tilly raised a hand in acknowledgment and they hurried over to the café. As Sebastian held open the door for Tilly and they stepped inside, the woman behind the counter acknowledged them with a cheerful smile.

Aside from an elderly couple drinking coffee and talking quietly, the place was empty. Opting for a table beside the window, Sebastian pulled out a chair and gestured for Tilly to sit. 'Why, how very gentlemanly of you, Mr Matthews. Chivalry is a lovely quality to have.' Tilly sat down.

'Manners maketh the man, or so they say. What are you having?'

'Can you see if they've got a chamomile tea? It's great for nerves.'

Sebastian pulled a face. 'I've already got more than enough of those.'

'No, silly, for *settling* them!' Tilly rolled her eyes, then saw Sebastian grinning at her. 'Oh, very funny.'

Affording Tilly a wink, Sebastian turned and walked over to the counter. 'Good morning.'

The woman looked up and smiled. 'And good morning to you, young man. What can I get for you today?'

'Do you have chamomile tea?'

'I'm really sorry, no'. The woman looked at him apologetically. Turning, she lifted down a jar from the shelf behind her. 'I do have green tea though.'

Sebastian smiled and held up a finger. 'Hold that thought.' He crossed back to the table. 'They haven't got any chamomile, but there's green tea.'

Tilly nodded. 'Yeah, green tea is good too.'

97

Sebastian returned to the counter. 'Can I have two green teas please?'

The woman nodded. 'Coming right up. Sit yourself down and I'll bring to your table.'

Sebastian smiled appreciatively and walked back over to join Tilly. He sat down opposite her and put his hands on the table. She reached across and took both his hands in hers. They stared into each other's eyes for a moment, then Tilly said, 'You know what? I could use something to eat. You ought to as well come to think of it.'

'I don't know if I can stomach anything right now.' He thought for a moment. 'Although it's a known fact that it's remiss to come to Brick Lane and not have bagels.'

'Sounds good to me. How are you feeling now?'

Sebastian squeezed her hands. 'Much better. Thanks to you.'

He was about to say something else when the woman appeared carrying a tray with two tall glass mugs on it. 'There you go my darlings, two green teas.' She set them down. 'Enjoy.'

'Actually, could we have a couple of cream cheese bagels too please?' Sebastian asked.

'Of course, my lovely.' Her eyes fell upon their entwined hands. 'I'll be back in a jiffy.' Smiling to herself, she sashayed back to her station to prepare them.

Sebastian lifted the mug and sniffed at the steaming liquid suspiciously. His nose wrinkled.

Tilly giggled. 'Don't tell me you've never had green tea before?'

Sebastian looked up at her. 'No.'

'It tastes better than it smells, I promise,' Tilly ventured reassuringly.

Sebastian blew on the tea and took a small sip. 'Mmm.' He looked at Tilly and smiled. 'That's alright actually.'

'Told you.'

The woman appeared with their food and the bill, presented on a small saucer. They spent the next half an hour engaged in idle chit-chat. When they had finished their tea, Sebastian glanced at the bill and extracted three £5 notes from his wallet, slipping them onto the saucer alongside the bill.

'Hey, I didn't expect you to pay, you know,' Tilly said.

'I'm pretty sure it's not free here.'

Tilly stuck her tongue out at him playfully. 'It's good to see someone feeling a bit more relaxed. But what I *meant* was you didn't have to pay the whole bill yourself.'

Sebastian smiled. 'I know. But a gentleman always pays. At least that's what my parents taught me.'

'Then they taught you well. Thank you. But next time it's *my* treat, okay?' Tilly stood up. 'Come on then, Seb the Sensational. Let's go knock this talent mogul dead!'

Sebastian pinched his chin thoughtfully. 'Seb the Sensational. I rather like that.'

'It's got a nice ring to it, eh?' Tilly grabbed his arm and they headed for the door. As they left, Sebastian turned and called out to the woman at the counter. 'Thank you.' She waved them off with a big smile.

As they walked hand in hand up Brick Lane it started to cloud over and suddenly, without warning the heavens opened. Picking up the pace, they giggled as they scurried along the pavement, which glistened as the heavy rain danced on the slabs. Tilly pointed up at the sign for Princelet Street and they sprinted around the corner and up the steps to the office block that housed the Rising Starz Entertainment Agency.

Sebastian pushed open the glass door and they stepped inside, wiping their feet on the huge coir mat. Tilly's hair was hanging in strands across her face and her dress was sodden. She was shivering. Sebastian slipped off his jacket and held it out for her. 'Here, this will warm you up.'

Tilly flapped a hand at him. 'Don't be daft. Put it back on quick, you don't want this fella seeing your shirt!'

Sebastian's face fell. 'Oh, lord! I forgot...' He quickly put the jacket back on.

Tilly looked up at him and smiled. 'Your hair has gone into ringlets!'

Sebastian winced. 'Oh no! Really?'

'Yeah.' She reached out and touched a little curl that was hanging down across his forehead.

'You wouldn't happen to have some wax or hair gel in your handbag, would you?'

Tilly chuckled. 'Sorry, no. I don't use that kind of stuff. Anyway, it looks cute. I like it.' She reached up again and twirled a lock of Sebastian's hair in her fingers. He took her face in his hands, gently brushing the damp hair away from her cheeks, and bent to kiss her, but just as their lips met, they were disturbed by the sound of a loud cough.

They spun round to see a stout woman standing behind a mahogany reception desk. She was watching them embrace with undisguised disapproval. 'Can I help you?' she asked curtly.

'Oh, er... I'm sorry we didn't see you there,' Sebastian replied contritely.

'Evidently,' the woman responded. There was sarcasm in the tone.

'I have an appointment with James Lawrence.'

The woman opened a large, leather-bound book that was laid on the desk in front of her. 'Which office?' she asked with an overt note of impatience in her voice.

Before Sebastian could reply, Tilly chimed in. 'Rising Starz Entertainment Agency.'

The woman studied the book. 'Right. That's on the fourth floor.' She pointed to the lift to the left of the desk.

'Thank you,' Sebastian said, and they stepped over to the buttons on the wall beside the elevator doors.

'Er, excuse me,' the woman hissed. 'You need to sign in first.'

'I'll do it,' Tilly said. 'You call the lift.' She walked back to the desk and forced a smile. 'Do you have a pen?' The woman brusquely slid a ballpoint across the desk and spun the book round to face her. 'Thank you,' Tilly said sweetly, with an intentional hint of insincerity. A couple of drips of water fell from the end of her wet hair onto the open page. The woman scowled and made an exasperated tutting sound, but said nothing as she watched the girl print her name in capital letters – TILLY – then scribble her signature as indecipherably as possible in the box alongside it. Glancing up at the digital clock on the wall, she added 10:25 in the end box. She was about to fill in the next line but hesitated and thought for a moment. With a cheeky smile she printed SEB THE SENSATIONAL in capital letters across both boxes and scribbled 10:25 beside it. As she put down the pen, there was a dull buzzing noise from the lift and the doors slid jerkily open. Noticing the wooden name plate on the desk – the slip of card in it said **Harriet Sterne** – Tilly gave the woman another slightly sarcastic smile before joining Sebastian in the lift. Reaching over, she hit the number 4 button. Once the doors had closed, she sniggered. 'Did you see her name? Sterne by name, stern by nature!'

'I know,' Sebastian said. 'Talk about making people feel unwelcome!'

'Never mind.' Tilly slipped her arms around Sebastian's waist and planted a soft kiss on his lips – 'For

101

luck!' – then stepped hastily away from him as a buzzer sounded and the lift ground to a halt.

The doors juddered open to reveal a large open reception area with a small desk in the centre and a handful of chairs arranged at intervals around the walls. Painted eggshell blue, the walls were dotted with prints of theatre billposters. A young woman was sitting at the desk filing her nails. Although the clatter of the lift doors had announced someone's arrival, she didn't even look up.

Sebastian and Tilly walked over to the desk and waited politely for the woman to give them her attention. She ignored them, absorbed by the task of attending to her nails. Tilly gave Sebastian a little nudge of encouragement and he swallowed hard. 'Good morning. My name's Sebastian Matthews,' he said with as much confidence as he could muster. 'I have an appointment with James Lawrence.'

The receptionist managed to look up without actually moving her head, raising her eyes just enough to meet Sebastian's. 'Cool.' The voice was leaden with disinterest. 'Take a seat. I'll let him know you're here.'

'Thank you. I don't suppose you'd have some paper towels or something like that we could use to dry ourselves off with?'

'Paper towels. Hmmm.' The room fell silent while she seemed to ponder the question. Sebastian and Tilly – who had sat down with her wet dress clinging to her legs – exchanged glances of incredulity. 'No,' the woman eventually decided. 'We don't.' As Sebastian turned away to go and join Tilly, the woman added, almost as an afterthought, 'I do have a couple of proper cloff towels if you'd like.'

Sebastian turned back. 'Oh, yes, that would be wonderful. Thank you.'

Giving him a weak smile, the woman spun her chair round. She reached down and pulled open the bottom drawer of a huge filing cabinet, withdrawing two grey hand towels. 'Here you go. I fink they're a fiver each, but you can sort that out with James.'

Sebastian took them gratefully and thanked her again.

She nodded and picked up a telephone receiver and, pressing a button, she nestled the phone between her ear and shoulder and resumed filing her nails. 'Oh. Mr Lawrence, there's a Sebastian Maffhews out here to see you...'

The room fell silent for a moment. Sebastian handed a towel to Tilly and sat down dabbing at his wet neck and shoulders, while the receptionist continued. 'Er, I dunno? Hang on...' She looked at the diary on her desk. 'No, Mr Lawrence, it says 11:00 in the book.' Sebastian listened with interest to the woman's side of the conversation. 'Well, he's here now in the reception, shall I tell him to wait or get him to come back?' Sebastian frowned and looked at Tilly with concern. She was vigorously rubbing at her hair with the towel. She caught the expression on Sebastian's face and shrugged her shoulders.

The receptionist hung up the phone and called across, 'Mr Lawrence will be out in a minute.'

Sebastian let out a small sigh of relief as Tilly pulled the towel from her head and playfully whipped his knee with it. 'Will you please relax!' she implored him.

'I'm trying!'

As she folded the towel, Tilly noticed a five-pointed star emblem and the Rising Starz logo embroidered neatly on the end. 'They must be good, they've got their own towels,' she quipped.

Sebastian ran his finger over the embroidery and nodded his approval. 'Yeah, pretty swish'.

A door opened on the right and James Lawrence stepped out. Sebastian stood up and extended his hand. 'Hello there, James. I apologise for the drowned rat appearance.'

Chuckling, James took Sebastian's hand and shook it warmly. 'It certainly threw it down, didn't it?'

'Yep, and we were right in the middle of it.' Sebastian suddenly realised Tilly had got up and she was standing beside him. 'Oh, sorry. James this is Tilly, my er…'

Tilly held out her hand. 'I'm Seb's girlfriend. Nice to meet you, James.'

James took her hand gently in his. 'Enchanting,' he said. 'Lovely to meet you too.' He looked at Sebastian. 'Listen, Sebastian…'

'Please, call me Seb.'

'Seb. Can I assume you didn't check your email before you left home? I sent you a message around half six this morning.'

'No I didn't,' Sebastian replied nervously. 'Is there something wrong?'

James cupped his hands around Sebastian's shoulders. 'No, dear boy, not at all. It's just that Mr McCleary – that's my boss, the man you've come to see today – had to attend an urgent meeting this morning. I wasn't informed until late last night and I hoped I'd have got to you in time to delay your arrival. But here you are. And looking exceptionally dapper, if I may say so.' He smiled and squeezed Sebastian's shoulders. 'All ready to show Mr McCleary what you can do?'

'I hope so.' Sebastian was starting to feel uncomfortable in the man's embrace. Had he no sense of personal space? He shuffled backwards slightly, hoping it wouldn't be obvious he was trying to put some distance between them. 'May I ask what time Mr McCleary might be back?'

James looked at his watch. 'He told me to reschedule you for midday. So, just under an hour I'd say. You're most welcome to sit here and wait. Gemma will sort you out a tea or coffee. I'd suggest a wander around the market...' – he paused and peered out of the window – '...but it's not looking like great shopping weather out there.'

Sebastian looked at Tilly. She smiled and said, 'We'll wait, eh? Seems daft getting soaked again.'

Sebastian looked back at James. 'We'll wait, thank you.'

James clapped his hands together. 'Excellent! That's great. Gemma could you please get these two good people a nice hot beverage?'

Gemma stood up. 'Sure. What do you want?'

Sebastian looked at Tilly 'Tea?' She nodded. 'Make that two teas please.'

'What about you, Mr L?' Gemma asked.

James thought for a moment. 'I'll have a latte. Could you please bring it through to my office.' He turned back to Sebastian. 'Would you excuse me for a bit? I have a mountain of promo stuff to get through for a pantomime we have coming up in Barking.' He spun on his heels and crossed to his office, where he paused in the doorway. 'As soon as Mr McCleary arrives, I'll get you seen straight away.'

'Sure, of course,' Sebastian replied with a smile as James tuned away. 'Thank you,' he added, but his words were lost as the office door closed with a soft click.

Sebastian looked at Tilly. 'Oh well, looks like we needn't have worried about being late.' Tilly removed the towel from her chair and sat down. 'I'm so annoyed with myself,' Sebastian continued. 'I was going to check my emails, then I thought better of it because I didn't want to get distracted messing about on my phone. Typical, the one time you don't look there's something really important there.'

'It's no big deal, better early than late,' Tilly said reassuringly. 'And now you have a chance to dry off and see this McCleary guy looking your best.'

Sebastian wasn't listening. He was bobbing his head around, trying to see his reflection in one of the framed prints on the wall, but the image wasn't all that clear. 'Is my hair alright?'

Tilly passed him a towel. 'Here, ruffle it up with this and sit down. I have a comb in my handbag, I'll get you looking all showbizzy in no time.'

Sebastian rubbed at his hair and looked down at Tilly. With one eyebrow raised he pursed his lips and struck a pose with his hands on his hips. 'Whaddya reckon?'

Tilly laughed. 'Just sit down, you buffoon!'

He took a seat beside her. His hair was sticking up like little springs. Tilly reached into her handbag and pulled out a small pink comb. She tenderly styled his hair and, with her fingers, pinched at the little curls hanging over his forehead. 'I think you'll pass.'

Sebastian kissed her quickly on the cheek. 'Thank you. When I'm rich and famous, you can be my hair and make up assistant.'

Tilly grinned. 'Make up? It's hypnotism not drag!'

'You know what I mean,' Sebastian replied with a coy smile.

While they waited for their tea, Seb stood up and wandered around the room, inspecting the prints more closely. On one of them he spotted a familiar face. 'Hey,

106

look at this!' he exclaimed. 'Rik Mayall. I used to really like him.'

'Oh me too,' Tilly said, getting up to take a look. 'He was wonderful. *So* funny. It was such a shame he died.'

'Yeah' Sebastian sighed. 'Only the good die young.'

Gemma appeared with two mugs, both emblazoned with the Rising Starz logo. 'There you go,' she said. 'Did you want sugar?'

'No thanks.' Tilly reached out and took a mug from her. 'Thanks.' She sat down.

Sebastian shook his head and Gemma handed the other mug to him. 'I'll just be at my desk if you want anything else. Oh, and those mugs...' – she waved an idle hand in the air – '...I think they're a fiver too. But you can sort that out with James.'

Sebastian looked at Tilly and grinned. 'This gig has cost me a score already, I hope McCleary doesn't send me packing!'

Tilly chuckled. 'Yeah, but you got a nice new mug and a swanky hand towel out of it.'

They noticed Gemma was looking at them. Like schoolchildren caught whispering in class, they both fell silent and lowered their eyes to avoid the girl's penetrating stare. As Gemma turned her attention back to her nails, Tilly playfully slapped Sebastian's knee. 'Oi, you! You almost got us into trouble there!'

Sebastian laughed. He turned the mug in his hand to examine the design. It was a big silver star and **RISING STARZ** was printed around the wrap of the mug in bright pink lettering. He lifted the towel and compared the logos. 'I think I'll give these to my Mum. She'll love them.'

Tilly passed Sebastian her towel. 'She can have this one too.' He smiled, and as he took it from her, she squeezed his hand. 'I reckon your Mum would be dead proud if she could see you here today.'

Sebastian's smile waned. 'I doubt that somehow. My parents were never that happy about my dreams of becoming a stage hypnotist.'

'No?'

'My father told me I lived in a fantasy world and that I should knuckle down and learn a trade. My Mum used to encourage me as a child, she even bought me a little top hat. But she soon changed her mind when one of my stints resulted in Nala, our cat, going to animal A&E with a broken tail.'

Tilly gasped. 'Oh no! What happened?'

'Well I often used to hypnotise her. She was easy. I would just tickle her under the chin and stare into her eyes, and she'd go floppy and nothing would wake her until I snapped my fingers. One day, I was out in the garden and she jumped down off the shed roof and came sauntering along the fence. I stared at her and she went out like a light. Unfortunately she fell off the fence and into a pile of logs in next-door's garden. I climbed up and looked over and she was just lying there limp. Her tail was sticking out in an L shape. It looked broken.'

Tilly was listening intently. 'What did you do?'

'I ran upstairs into my bedroom and hid under the covers. Mum doted on Nala and I knew she'd be furious. Eventually the neighbour saw her and brought her to the front door. When I came downstairs, Mum was sitting at the kitchen table sobbing. She thought Nala was dead. I bent down beside her basket where the neighbour had placed her and snapped my fingers.'

'Was she okay?' Tilly asked hopefully.

'Absolutely. She woke up. At first Mum was elated. Then she hit the roof. *You did this to her!*, she yelled at

108

me. She was apoplectic. I'd never seen her in such a rage before, I was only twelve and it was terrifying. It turned out Nala's tail *was* broken and she ended up having to have it removed. She was a cute little bobcat, but Mum never really forgave me'. He sighed. 'I felt really bad at the time. So after that, I never performed any hypnotism again. Well, at least not until more recently, you know, the odd party trick or…' – he smiled – 'to try and get a girl's attention.'

'Well, you certainly caught *my* attention,' Tilly said, squeezing his arm affectionately.

'How about you?' Sebastian asked. 'You've mentioned your sister, but not your parents.'

'My Mum and Dad split up when I was still in junior school. I've not seen him since. She remarried. He was a lovely guy, Peter, but he sadly died about three years ago from cancer. And now…' she trailed off. Sebastian saw the sadness in her eyes. 'You okay? I'm sorry, I didn't mean to upset you.'

'No, it's fine. Now my Mum has cancer too.' She paused again and ran her index finger along the skin underneath each of her eyes. 'She's been having treatment, but it's not working. She's pretty much given up. It breaks my heart to see it, but in some ways I can understand where she's coming from.'

'Oh, I'm so sorry,' Sebastian said hooking his arms around hers and pulling her close towards him.

At that moment, accompanied by a loud ping, the lift doors opened and a man wearing a white short-sleeve shirt and chinos, with a purple necktie dangling loosely out his back pocket, marched out into the reception area. He was mid-conversation on the phone and his mood plainly wasn't good. 'Max feckin' Reynolds will be the death of me!' The man's accent was broad Scottish and there were

109

flecks of angry spittle in the bristles of his full ginger beard. Sebastian and Tilly watched in silence as he laid the briefcase he was carrying flat on Gemma's desk, removed his Aviator sunglasses and slipped them into the breast pocket of his shirt. 'What's that? Ye listen tae me, Dennis, if ye think the fact he's gonna be Bottom in *A Midsummer Night's Dream* carries any feckin' weight with me, it doesnae. He'll nae be in it at all if he doesnae get a grip!' He flipped the clasps on the briefcase with one hand. 'Why? *Why*?! I'll tell ye why!' He withdrew a folder from the case, all but threw it at Gemma and silently mouthed, 'File these!'

Sebastian leant towards Tilly and whispered nervously, 'I *really* hope that isn't Mr McCleary.'

The man continued in full flow. 'Because Bottom doesnae get to throw a strop at photoshoots because he thinks his rubber ears are the wrong feckin' length, that's why! He's a *donkey*, for feck's sake, what in God's name constitutes the *right* length? I tell ye, Dennis, he'll na be pulling the feckin' luvvie act on Gregor McCleary's watch.'

Sebastian looked at Tilly again and raised his eyebrows. 'Oh, Lord,' he whispered. She rested a comforting hand on his knee.

McCleary closed the case and glanced at his Seiko wristwatch. 'Anyway, I'm back in the office now, and thanks to the Queen dying I've got a shite load of cancelled shows to sort out. We'll discuss this again later. But in the meantime, ye speak tae that annoying little arse-wipe and tell him he's taking the pish!' James appeared in the doorway to his office as McCleary ended the call and strode past him. 'Prissy actors! I cannae be doing with them.' He walked into the adjacent office – 'The bane o' ma *feckin'* life!' – and slammed the door hard behind him.

110

James offered Sebastian and Tilly a weak smile. 'Sorry about that. He can be a bit fiery, but he's an okay guy. I'll give him a minute to cool off, then I'll let him know you're here.' As he turned to go back into his office, he paused and winked at Seb. 'I have to say though, personally I think Max's Bottom is rather splendid.'

Aside from the rustling sound as Gemma rifled through the filing cabinet behind her desk, the room fell silent. A minute, then two passed. Sebastian had his thumbnail in his mouth and his right foot was tapping up and down nervously.

'Sebastian Matthews!' Tilly whispered sternly. 'If I have to tell you one more time. Just chill out. And *stop* biting your nails!'

Sebastian looked at her. 'Ooh, I like it when you're all strict with me,' he said with a cheeky smile. 'You've got to admit that McCleary is a bit scary though.'

'Nah. He'll be fine. Obviously somebody has wound him up, but he's going to *love* you. You'll soon put a smile on his face.'

The door to James's office opened. He smiled at Sebastian. 'You ready?'

Sebastian stood up. 'Yep. Ready as I'll ever be.' He crossed to the door. 'Is it okay if Tilly comes in too?'

'I don't see why not,' James said.

Tilly waved her hand at them. 'You don't need me in there. Go do your thing. I'll be right out here waiting.' Sebastian looked crestfallen. 'Go on with you,' Tilly urged him.

James put his arm across Sebastian's back and gripped his shoulder. 'You'll be fine. A big strapping lad like you. Come on, show Mr McCleary what you can do and the next stop will be footlights and standing ovations.'

Sebastian looked back over his shoulder and smiled at Tilly as he followed James into the office of Mr Gregor McCleary and pushed the door shut behind him.

CHAPTER 7

The office wasn't particularly large, but the blank white walls and sparsity of furnishing gave it the feel of airy spaciousness. The focal point was an ornate oak desk, on which there was an open laptop, a sheaf of paperwork and an intercom. Other than this there were just two large chairs. The one on the far side of the desk was facing the window with its back to Sebastian and James.

'Gregor, this is Sebastian Matthews, the hypnotist I told you about.' James gestured for Sebastian to sit down and stood to his left, just outside his peripheral vision.

Gregor McCleary spun round in his chair to face the two men. Sebastian leaned forward and extended his arm across the desk. 'Pleased to meet you, sir.'

'Aye.' Looking Sebastian up and down, McCleary half-heartedly took his hand and shook it. 'So, what is it ye have that makes ye think I'd wannae put ye up on one o' ma stages?' Sebastian hesitated. 'Well lad, is ye hypnotist act a mime or can ye speak?'

'Yes, Mr McCleary. Sorry, I... Well, Mr Lawrence, he approached me in the pub and...'

McCleary cut him off. 'I know what our Jimmy here thinks. I wannae know what *ye* thinks.'

Sebastian was starting to sweat and he could feel the palms of his hands getting clammy. But as he thought about Tilly sitting outside, and how disappointed she'd be if he fell at the first hurdle, he felt a calmness descend upon him. He looked directly into the Scottish man's hungry blue eyes and said, 'Absolutely, Mr McCleary. But what I have to offer is far too magical to sum up in a mere sentence. I think my act is best seen. If you'll allow me,

113

I'd like to give you a demonstration. Despite the pantheon of hypnotists you've probably seen before, I believe my act will be worth your time.'

McCleary leant back into his leather chair and peered at Sebastian. After a moment's silence, he said, 'Pantheon, eh? Good word. Very well, laddie, you've got ma attention. Show me what ye can do.'

Sebastian looked at James. 'Mr Lawrence, would you mind volunteering?'

'Oh, dear Lord, no.' James laughed nervously. 'I get all squiffy after one glass of wine. There's no way you're taking control of *my* mind!'

'Ah, c'mon with ye, Jimmy,' McCleary said with a thin smile. 'Don't be a diddy.'

'No. Absolutely not. I'm way past waking up not knowing what I've been up to.'

Sebastian smiled. 'It's okay, Mr Lawrence. May I bring Tilly in?' He looked at McCleary. 'She's my girlfriend, she's just outside in reception.'

'Och, no, laddie. I'm nae fallin' for *that* cheap trick. Your lass will be all primed. I wannae see real hypnotism, not some staged performance.'

He banged his forefinger down hard on a red button on the intercom. It buzzed and a voice spoke. 'Yes, Mr Maclearly?'

'Get yerself in here, Gemma. I have a wee job for ye.'

A moment later there was a scuffling noise as the door handle rattled a couple of times. It swung open and Gemma appeared carrying a mug of coffee in one hand and a tin of biscuits wedged under the crook of her arm. She pushed the door wide open with her elbow and came into the room.

'Didnae anyone ever teach ye to knock, lassie?!' McCleary snarled.

114

Gemma stopped in her tracks and looked at her boss apologetically. 'I'm sorry, Mr Maclearly.' She started to back up and tried to hook her elbow around the door to close it.

'What on earth are ye doing now, ye silly wee bampot? You're halfway in for Christ's sake, ye might as well forget about knocking!'

'Of course, Mr Maclearly.'

Gemma hesitated as if she wasn't sure whether she should come or go, but as she came to a decision and shuffled back into the office McCleary slammed his fist down hard on the desk, making both her and Sebastian jump. 'And it's McCleary, girl, clear-*ee* not clear-*lee*. I'm getting pretty tired of having to keep reminding ye!'

'I'm sorry Mr McClea...ry,' she said timidly as she set down the tea and biscuits. McCleary reached greedily for the tin. He struggled with the lid for a moment and it popped off and dropped to the floor, spinning in noisy circles. 'Ah, Jammy Dodgers, ma favourite!' Without offering one to anyone else, he snatched a biscuit from the tin, popped it into his mouth whole, crunched a couple of times and washed it down with a swig of coffee. He let out a satisfied *ahhhh*. 'Sure. I needed that!'

Everyone in the room waited in silence as McCleary took another mouthful of coffee. Then he put the mug down and clapped his hands together.

'Reet. Gemma. Young Sebastian here needs ye to help him with a little performance.'

Gemma looked enquiringly at Sebastian. 'Of course. What do you want me to do?'

Sebastian stood up. 'I'd like to show Mr McCleary my hypnotism act. If you're willing, I would like to put you into a little sleep. Then I'll give you a command and hopefully you'll respond'.

115

Gemma looked unsure. 'It's not going to involve me taking my clothes off is it?'

'Perish the thought!' McCleary chortled. 'I've seen more meat on a butcher's dog.'

'I think it's a butcher's pencil, Gregor,' James said.

McCleary waved a hand at him. 'Aye, well, whatever. I still don' wannae see the lassie in the raw.'

Sebastian smiled at Gemma, whose cheeks had coloured up. 'Don't worry,' he said. 'You won't come to any harm, I promise. And I assure you that you'll remain fully clothed.'

Gemma thought for a moment. 'Okay then, I'm up for that.'

Sebastian pulled out his chair and set it back, a few feet away from the desk. 'Okay then, Gemma, if you wouldn't mind sitting down for me.' He gestured to the chair. She eagerly obliged. McCleary leant forward on the desk and rested his chin on his hands. Sebastian stepped over and stood beside Gemma. 'Mr Lawrence, you may wish to move over beside the desk there and give Gemma some room.' James did as he was asked. Sebastian pulled his mobile phone from his inside pocket and quickly selected his Spotify account. McCleary was peering over his tightly balled knuckles, a curious expression on his face. Resting a hand on Gemma's shoulder, Sebastian spoke quietly. 'Gemma. Please look up and into my eyes.' She did as she was asked. 'You will feel yourself becoming sleepy. Very sleepy. *So* sleepy that you will barely be able to keep your eyes open. I'm going to count backwards from three to one, and when I reach one you will fall immediately under my control. *Three.* Already your eyelids are feeling heavy and there is no other option for you but to give in and close them. *Two.* And now you must sleep. *One.*' It was almost as if Sebastian had flicked a switch; Gemma's eyelids fluttered and closed. Her head lolled slightly onto her shoulder.

McCleary lifted his head. 'Tha silly bint's probably been up all night on the lash.'

Sebastian looked over towards him and placed a finger to his lips. 'Please, sir, we must have complete quiet.' He leaned in towards Gemma's upturned ear. 'Gemma. In a moment you will hear the famous piece of music from the ballet *Swan Lake*.'

'I'd be surprised if she's even heard of *Swan Lake*,' McCleary muttered.

Sebastian was going to repeat his request for silence, but thought better of it. He continued his instruction to Gemma. 'As soon as you hear it, you will leap to your feet and show us your finest, most elegant dance moves. You will pirouette like a pro and we, your audience, will be moved to tears. You will continue in this role until I snap my fingers and you hear my voice telling you to stop. Do you understand?' Gemma grunted something unintelligible. 'Do you *understand* me Gemma? When the music plays, what is it that you will do?'

'I will piri-et like a pro,' Gemma mumbled.

'That's right,' Sebastian concluded. He slid the volume on his phone up to full, tapped the screen and Tchaikovsky's beautiful passage of music filled the room. It took a fleeting moment for the music to reach Gemma's ear, but as soon she registered the tune she stood bolt upright and assumed the pose of a ballet dancer. She moved gracefully around the room, her hands aloft, stumbling only slightly in her kitten heels, which was admirable given they clearly weren't designed with ballet dancing in mind. As she spun around, her chequered kilt flowed outwards. She bumped into the chair briefly, but immediately righted herself. After a minute, Sebastian

117

slowly reduced the volume on his phone until the music had faded to barely audible and spoke softly. 'Well done, Gemma.' He gestured to James and McCleary to clap.

James applauded enthusiastically, but McCleary didn't move a muscle. Sebastian felt his stomach twitch nervously at the agent's mute response. He continued, 'Take a bow, Gemma. Your magnificent performance is done.' Gemma took a deep bow and as she stood upright again Sebastian clicked his fingers and uttered the command. 'Stop.'

Gemma's eyes snapped open and she stood for a moment staring into space. Then she spoke. 'Ooh, I feel a bit dizzy.' She brushed a loose stand of hair from her face and started to fiddle with the scrunchy holding up her hair in a pony tail. She looked around the room and saw the three men staring at her. 'So what we doing then? Was you going to hipmatise me or not?'

McCleary peered at her inquisitively. 'I dunna know if you're *playing* thick or ye just are.'

Gemma's face fell. 'That's a bit rude, Mr... Mr MacClearl... Mc*Cleary*.'

Suddenly McCleary's face lit up and he laughed. A deep hearty laugh. 'Sit yeself down lass before ye hurt yeself.' He looked at Sebastian. 'Aye lad, so ye hypnotised this soft wee lassie alright, but it was nae what you'd call entertaining. In fact I'd go so far as to say it was damned boring.'

Sebastian was bereft of words. He'd blown it.

'If tha's all ye have, then I'm afraid it's a no from me.' McCleary stood up as if to suggest the audition was over.

James stepped over to Sebastian. 'One minute sir.' He rested a hand on Sebastian's shoulder. 'Seb, why don't you show us the chicken?' He turned back to McCleary. 'Honestly, Gregor, this is going to crack you up. *Crack*

118

you up!' James playfully punched Sebastian's arm. 'Get it?' He roared with laughter. 'Cracked. Chickens. You know, eggs...' He suddenly realised that McCleary, Sebastian and even Gemma were staring at him stone-faced and he abruptly ceased guffawing. He cleared his throat. 'Anyway, Seb, over to you. I mean, that is if it's okay with you, Gregor.'

McCleary stood in silence for a moment and then, much to Sebastian's surprise, he nodded – 'Very well. Last chance though.' – and sat down again. James smiled at his boss obsequiously and slunk back into the corner as

Sebastian ushered Gemma to sit and took up position beside her. 'Once again, Gemma, I'm going to ask you to look into my eyes.' Brushing aside the errant strand of hair that now refused to stay bound in the scrunchy, the girl looked up at him. 'You are feeling sleepy,' he continued. 'Your eyelids are heavy.' Before he had a chance to say anything more, Gemma's head abruptly dropped onto her chest.

Sebastian was momentarily thrown. He caught sight of McCleary out of the corner of his eye, the penetrating stare urging him to get on with it. Inhaling deeply, he went on with his commands. 'Gemma. You are a beautiful, golden bantam. A chicken with the most resplendent plumage. What are you?' There was no response. 'What are you?' he repeated softly.

The room remained silent. Sebastian could feel McCleary's impatient eyes burning into him and his neck started to feel hot. He was just about to repeat himself again when Gemma said sleepily, 'I'm a beautiful golden bantam chicken.'

Sebastian breathed an inward sigh of relief. 'It's nice and warm there in your coop, isn't it, Gemma? That cozy hay nest you have built yourself is *so* comfortable.' Again

119

there was no response. Gemma was smiling but appeared to have slipped into a deep slumber. Sebastian leaned in close to her ear. 'When you hear the word cock-a-doodle-doo you will rise. The sun is up and it's be time for you to forage outside for grain.'

McCleary now had a thin smile on his face and his eyes were glistening with anticipation. James was smiling too; he knew exactly what was coming.

Sebastian continued. 'You will scratch and scrape the floor looking for grain until you hear me snap my fingers and tell you to stop.'

Before Sebastian had a chance to say any more, McCleary suddenly yelled out, 'Cock-a-doodle-doo!'

Gemma's head whipped up and she stood bolt upright. Then, with her head bobbing and her hands on her waist, with elbows stuck out like wings, she started strutting around the room making a *buk-buk* sound. McCleary laughed out loud as Gemma scraped her right foot hard on the carpet and her shoe slipped off. She continued to walk jerkily around the room, clucking and scraping at the floor, stopping occasionally to see if she'd unearthed anything.

McCleary snatched up the biscuit tin. He broke up a jammy dodger in one of his big hands and scattered the crumbs on the desk. 'Here chick chick chick,' he cried mockingly. Gemma strutted over towards him and stopped at the desk. Spotting the crumbs, she bent down and started to peck up the tasty morsels. McCleary was laughing uncontrollably and the veins on his temples were standing out. He enthusiastically pulled another biscuit from the tin and crumbled it in front of Gemma. 'Oh my sweet Jesus, I've never seen anything so feckin' funny in all my life,' he managed to splutter through howls of laughter as he bounced up and down on his chair like a hyperactive child.

Suddenly Sebastian felt awful about what was happening to Gemma and the fact that he was the instigator. This wasn't entertainment, it was out and out humiliation. And McCleary was revelling in it. The laughter wasn't born of amusement, it was sadistic, and Sebastian didn't like it. He swiftly stepped up beside Gemma. 'Stop.' She immediately obeyed and stood upright, crumbs tumbling down her cleavage.

Sebastian was about to snap his fingers in front of Gemma's face when McCleary batted his hand away. 'Ah, ye damned spoilsport! I was enjoying myself there.' He glowered at Sebastian. 'Can ye not leave her like that? She'd probably be more useful round here and definitely a damned sight more entertaining.'

Gemma's hair was hanging in large loose strands now and she looked down at her top which was covered in jammy dodger crumbs. She stepped back from the desk looking slightly dazed, and as she did so she realised she only had one shoe on. She looked uncertainly at her boss, who was still sniggering, and then across to James, whose face was etched with amusement.

Sebastian handed her shoe to her. 'Thanks Gemma.' She took it from him. 'I think we're done now. You were *really* great,' he added with a friendly smile.

'Aye. Ye go and get on with yer filing now, lassie,' McCleary said begrudgingly, unable – or perhaps unwilling – to disguise his disappointment that the pantomime was over.

Slightly disoriented, Gemma nodded and silently left the room, closing the door behind her.

McCleary brushed the remaining crumbs off his desk onto the floor. He was still inwardly giggling to himself.

121

He pulled a small, leather-bound folder from the top drawer of his desk and gestured for Sebastian to sit. Retrieving the chair from the back of the room, he pulled it up to the desk and sat down.

'Reet. Based on the hilarious performance ye just put on, I'm willing to give ye a chance.' Sebastian smiled. 'But I'll have ye know this, laddie. When Gregor McCleary puts his name to an act, people know that it means quality. I've been running this company now for three decades and we are a trusted and respected name. The audience has expectations and McCleary delivers. Do ye understand that?'

Sebastian nodded. 'Yes sir, I do.'

'Good. I don' wannae be chasing ye because you've turned up late, or not at all, do ye understand?' Sebastian nodded again. 'Okay then.' McCleary flipped open the folder. He flicked through a couple of the clear plastic inners stuffed with business cards until he found what he was looking for. Pulling out a card, he handed it to Sebastian. 'This is the Ind Coope Social Club in Walthamstow. I've been putting on a show there once a month for the last seven years. Next Saturday there is a magician on and I want ye to be his support act.'

Sebastian studied the card for a moment and looked back up at McCleary. 'Thank you, sir.'

The man continued. 'Ye will need to be there at six o'clock sharp. There's no time for rehearsals or any of that nonsense, so I expect ye to be stage-ready for half past six. Your slot will be 30 minutes and I will pay ye £50. Is all that clear?'

'Yes, Mr McCleary.'

'Do ye have any questions?'

Sebastian thought for a moment. 'No, I don't think so. But thank you for giving me this opportunity, I'm most grate...'

McCleary cut him short. 'Be sure ye don' make me regret it.' He sat back in his chair. 'Liase with Jimmy here, he'll take all yer personal details, etcetera and I'll be back in touch should I deem yer performance next Saturday to have made the grade'.

James crossed to the door and Sebastian stood up. He reached out a hand, but McCleary didn't take it. He slipped the folder back into the desk drawer and slammed it shut. 'Just ye remember, laddie, you're representing Rising Starz noo. Don' ye dare be letting me down!'

Sebastian felt his stomach tighten. 'I won't, sir.' He gave McCleary a weak smile and followed James out of the door and into the reception.

'Take a seat for a minute, Seb. I need you to fill in a couple of forms.' James patted him on the shoulder. 'You did well in there.'

Sebastian looked at Tilly, who had the brightest, most expectant smile on her face. He discreetly gave her two thumbs up and sat down beside her. She shimmied in close and grabbed hold of his hand. Seb squeezed it tight.

James walked over to Gemma, who was staring vacantly at her desk. 'Could you dig out an AE form and a C1 please, sweetheart?' Gemma looked at him blankly. 'The forms please, Gemma,' he pressed. 'For young Sebastian here.'

Her vacant expression changed to one of understanding. 'Oh yes, sorry. I don't know what's up with me this afternoon. My head's all over the place.' She spun the chair round and wheeled it towards the filing cabinet. As she bent down to open the second lowest drawer, a small sprinkling of crumbs tumbled out of her

123

top onto the carpet. 'Oh!' she exclaimed. 'I wonder how they got there?' She pulled out two folders and slid the drawer shut. Spinning back round to her desk she flipped the folders open and extracted two pieces of paper. 'There you go, James.' She glanced down at the front of her sweater. 'I'll have to get the vacuum out. I dunno where all these crumbs came from, I guess it must have been my toast this morning.' She pulled down the neck of her top, exposing the V of her cleavage. 'They're all down my front. How embarrassing!'

Averting his eyes, James asked, 'Have you got a pen I can use please?' Gemma handed him a biro. He went and sat down beside Sebastian, passing him one of the forms and the pen. Resting the paperwork on his knee, Sebastian began to fill in his name at the top of the first page and the point of the biro went straight through. Chuckling, James reached over to the coffee table and picked up a couple of glossy magazines. 'Here, you can lean on these.'

Sebastian placed the contract on top of the magazines and began to fill them in. Half way down the page he paused and frowned. 'It says here that I agree to perform exclusively for Rising Starz for the duration of the contract.'

James nodded. 'Yes, Mr McCleary runs a tight ship here, he doesn't want any of his acts sneaking off and working for other agencies. Is that a problem?'

Sebastian looked at Tilly. She shrugged.

'You can always take the paperwork home and read it,' James said, 'but you really have nothing to be concerned about. We cover more or less the whole of the London circuit and we have many venues across Hertfordshire, Essex and Kent too. Providing you give them a great show next week – which I know you will - you'll have no need to look elsewhere, and you'll never have to worry about

124

finding a day job either. You'll earn a great wage with us, doing what you love best.' Sebastian smiled and without further hesitation he ticked the box and continued to fill out the rest of the form with vigour. He handed it to James, who swapped it for another. 'Now we just need all your credentials and bank details for making your fee payments.'

Sebastian patted his jacket and pulled his wallet from his inside pocket. He withdrew his debit card and copied the account details onto the form. As he got to the bottom of the page he stopped and looked at Tilly. 'Er, this feels a bit weird, but I hope you don't mind me asking?'

Tilly smiled. 'What?'

'Can I put you down as my next of kin? I know we barely know each other, but I'd rather my parents don't find out about all this just yet.'

'Of course you can,' Tilly replied warmly. Sebastian wrote down her name and phone number. 'Hey!' Tilly exclaimed. 'You wrote my number down without even checking your phone.'

'Yeah. I have a good memory for numbers,' Sebastian replied.

'Even I don't know it off by heart. I always have to check my phone if anyone asks for it.'

Sebastian completed the form and handed it back to James. 'Great stuff!' James held out his hand and Sebastian shook it firmly. 'Delighted to have you on board.' He side-stepped to the desk and held the paperwork out to Gemma. 'Will you please put this on the database for me, sweetheart?' Gemma stared blankly at the papers and then up at James. A look of concern flashed across James's face. 'Gemma! Are you listening?'

'Yeah, sorry James. What did you want?'

He sighed. 'Take these papers and enter the details onto the database under new engagements please.'

'Of course. Do you want me to file them when I'm done?'

'That would be great, thank you,' James replied, slightly exasperated. He turned back to Sebastian. 'Is she going to be alright? She's never been the brightest, but she seems to be even more ditsy since her little chicken performance.'

'I'm sure she'll be fine. People often mention that they feel a little muddled after being put under hypnosis, but it doesn't last long.'

James frowned. 'I hope not. Anyway, thanks for coming in today and I'll see you next Saturday in Walthamstow.' With that, he turned on his heels and pushed open the door to his office.

Tilly stood up and handed Sebastian the towels and mugs. 'Oh Mr Lawrence,' he called out. James stopped in the doorway to his office. 'Sorry. We used these and we'd like to pay for them.'

'*Pay* for them?' James chuckled. 'Don't be silly Seb, you're one of us now. Have them on me.'

'Thank you very much, that's very kind.'

James closed the door and Sebastian leant in to give Tilly a kiss. 'Wow! What an afternoon!'

Tilly beamed 'Well done you! I knew you could do it. Let's go for some lunch and you can tell me all about it.'

'I'm actually quite hungry now,' Sebastian said as they walked to the lift. He pressed the call button and after a few seconds the buzzer sounded and the door juddered open. 'Thanks, Gemma,' Sebastian called out as they entered the lift. 'You were an absolute star.' The doors slid slowly shut.

Sebastian and Tilly disembarked the lift and walked hand in hand towards the doors.

'Ahem!' A cough rang out from behind the reception desk, halting them in their tracks. 'Excuse me, you need to sign out.'

Tilly rolled her eyes.

'Sod it, let's just go,' Sebastian said quietly.

'No. Come on, you've gotta create a good impression.'

They returned to the desk where Sterne, who had a pinched expression of impatience on her lips, spun the book around and forcefully slammed a pen down on top of it.

'Thank you *so* much,' Tilly said with a wry smile.

Sebastian scribbled his signature, sniggering as he saw how Tilly had signed him in. 'What's the time?'

Tilly looked up at the clock on the wall. '12:55.'

Completing the entry, Sebastian handed the pen to Tilly. She added her signature to the page and dropped the pen lightly back down on the book. 'Thanks again. You have a lovely day now.'

Sterne forced a smile and whipped the book back to her side of the desk, glowering at the pair of them as they made for the door, unable to stifle their giggles.

CHAPTER 8

Laughing like naughty children, Sebastian and Tilly walked down the steps onto the street. The rain had stopped and the sun was shining in an azure sky dappled with banks of fluffy white cloud, showing its face to congratulate Sebastian on his success. At least that's how it seemed to him at that moment. He inhaled deeply. He'd started the day a bag of nerves and now he felt as if he were walking on air. As they turned left to rejoin the main road, Tilly said, 'Shall we go to Spitalfields market?' She rubbed at her tummy. 'There's bound to be loads of eateries there.'

Sebastian nodded enthusiastically. 'Sounds good to me.' They set off with the sun burning down on them and, beyond a few shallow puddles in the kerb, the ground was already bone dry. It was almost as if it had never rained. The streets were busier now too, with shoppers bustling about on the narrow pavements. 'Crikey, it's heaving!' Sebastian exclaimed.

'Yeah, not my idea of fun,' Tilly sighed.

They could see the entrance to Spitalfields market up ahead and quickened their pace, trying – but failing dismally – to avoid bumping into people pushing through in the opposite direction. As they got closer, the enticing scent of spicy food filled the air. 'Mmm, that's making me feel *really* hungry now.' Sebastian chuckled.

'Yeah, me too,' Tilly agreed as they entered the market.

If making their way through the crowds to get there had been a mission, it was nothing compared to the vast number of people crammed in under the glass enclosure.

'Flippin' 'eck!' Sebastian gasped. They could see a stall selling tapas over to their left and the queue of people waiting to be served was immense. 'Bit busy isn't it? Maybe we should just go back to that little café. That was nice.'

Tilly nodded. 'Yeah, good idea.'

Eventually managing to cross the road, they headed back in the direction of the café.

Tilly suddenly squealed and pointed. 'Oooh, look, a Wagamama's! How on earth did we miss that? I absolutely *love* Wagamama's.'

'Then a Wagamama's you shall have!' Sebastian declared.

Once again crossing the road, which seemed to have doubled in volume of traffic, they eagerly made their way to the restaurant. As they approached the entrance, Sebastian said, 'You know, I don't think I've ever had a Wagamama's. What is it?'

'Japanese.'

'Then I definitely haven't.'

Tilly licked her lips. 'It's lush, you're going to love it.'

They went inside and were immediately intercepted by a young man wearing black trousers and a waistcoat. 'Good afternoon.' He smiled welcomingly. 'Table for two?'

'Yes please,' Sebastian replied.

It was busy, but the waiter found them a table nestled in the corner and they sat down on the wooden bench. 'Can I get you any drinks?' the waiter asked.

'Just a mineral water for me please,' Tilly replied.

'Certainly.' The waiter looked at Sebastian.

'Do you have coke?'

The waiter nodded. 'Full fat or diet?'

'Full fat please.'

The waiter smiled. 'And ice in both of those?'

Sebastian and Tilly nodded in unison.

'Coming right up.' With that the young man hurried off.

Sebastian wiggled his bottom around to get more comfortable. 'Strange seats. They're like blocks of wood.'

'Yeah, a lot of their restaurants are like this now. I guess they can squeeze more seating in without clumsy chairs and people constantly moving them about.'

'Fair point.' Sebastian looked nervously over his shoulder. 'I must remember not to lean back though!'

The waiter returned with their drinks on a tray. He placed them on the table and whipped two menus out from beneath his arm. 'I'll leave you with these and come back shortly to take your order.'

'Thank you,' Sebastian called out as the waiter hurried away, but his words were lost in the hubbub of chatter filling the restaurant. He picked up the menu and inspected the array of choices. Some of the dishes looked exceptionally appetising. He glanced up at Tilly and saw that she was watching him with amusement. 'What?'

'I can see your eyes glazing over.' She laughed. 'I don't blame you, there's so much choice. But whatever you choose it'll be *deeee*-lish.'

'I'm not sure. I can't eat anything too spicy,' Sebastian said. 'What are you having?'

'My favourite is the seitan katsu. It's pretty mild, kinda sweet and quite buttery.' Tilly smiled. 'I don't really do spicy either.'

Sebastian re-examined the menu. 'The chicken katsu might be nice then. I do like my chicken.'

'I'd never have guessed,' Tilly said, laughing.

'How do you mean?'

'Buk-buk-buk!'

130

Sebastian laughed. 'Oh! Yeah, well I don't want to be a one-trick pony. I'm going to have to come up with some fresh ideas if I've got to fill half an hour at the Walthamstow social club.'

Tilly's eyes widened. 'Wow! When?'

'Next Saturday night. I'm gonna be the support for a magic show.'

'Yay!' Tilly squealed. 'I knew you could do it, I knew it! So, come on then, tell me all about it. What was going on in there? I could hear a heck of a lot of laughter, so I sussed it must be going well.'

'Yeah, that was McCleary,' Sebastian said. 'He got a bit carried away. I'm not sure I like him very much.'

The waiter reappeared and took their orders, commended them on their choices, then retreated in the direction of the kitchen.

'You were saying you're not keen on McCleary?'

Sebastian sighed. 'He's very brash. And he was really unkind to his secretary.'

Tilly frowned. 'Gemma? How do you mean?'

'Well, I know James was hankering for me to do the chicken thing, but I thought it might be better to do something that made Gemma look less... I dunno, daft, I suppose. Anyway, I had her do a bit of ballet. *Swan Lake*.'

Tilly smiled. 'I heard the music.'

'Yeah, she was really susceptible actually. I couldn't believe how fast she went under and I had her pirouetting round the room like she'd been dancing for years.'

'Well, that sounds cool.'

'It was. I was really pleased, but McCleary wasn't impressed. He said it wasn't entertaining. In fact, he said it was boring. I really thought I'd messed up my one big opportunity.'

Tilly reached over and took his hand in hers. 'But you didn't.'

'No, but only because James got McCleary to give me another chance and insisted I do the chicken act. It would have been alright, except when Gemma went under McCleary kind of took over. He was taunting her and getting her to eat biscuit crumbs off his desk.'

Tilly frowned. 'I don't understand. Isn't that the how the chicken act works?'

'Sort of, yeah, but it was obvious McCleary was getting off on some sort of power trip. He was really *enjoying* humiliating her. It wasn't fun at all; it was really horrible. I knew if I stopped it I could be jeopardising my chances, but at the same time I couldn't just stand there and watch him doing that to her.'

Tilly squeezed his hand. 'That's because you're a decent guy, Sebastian Matthews.'

'Maybe. But I instigated it, didn't I? Anyway, I had to put a stop to it. At that moment I didn't care what happened to me, so I snapped her out of it. McCleary looked a bit peevish about it, but luckily he was impressed enough that he offered me the Walthamstow gig on the spot.'

'That's absolutely brilliant.' Tilly smiled. 'Course, you'll have to put up with me in the front row cheering you on.'

'If you don't mind.'

'*Mind*? Wild horses couldn't keep me away.' A thought flashed across her mind. 'Hey, why don't you get your mates along? I'll ask mine too. You know, a few fans to support you.'

'I'd really appreciate that.'

'We'll have to have Seb the Sensational badges made up, of course,' Tilly joked.

132

Seb chuckled. 'Of course!'

The waiter reappeared. 'The seitan katsu?'

'That's for me,' Tilly said.

The man set down her dish and placed the other one in front of Sebastian. 'Is there anything else I can get you?' They both shook their heads. The waiter smiled politely. 'Then please enjoy.'

Sebastian sniffed his curry cautiously. 'This smells absolutely heavenly.'

Tilly grinned. 'You'll be a Wagamama's convert before we leave. Guaranteed.'

Sebastian eyed the cutlery and chopsticks standing in a metal container, both of which were wrapped with a napkin. Tilly selected chopsticks and eagerly unravelled the paper. Sebastian's fingers hovered over the remaining pair of chopsticks. His mind raced; would Tilly be impressed if he tried to use them? Or would he just end up making a complete fool of himself? Maybe it would be better to just use the cutlery. But how would *that* look?

Tilly could sense his indecision. 'You can just use the knife and fork, you know. Chopsticks are optional.'

Sebastian smiled. 'I wanted to give it a try, but I'm worried I'll probably just drop most of it into my lap.'

Tilly held out her chopsticks. 'Watch me.' She carefully positioned the implements between her fingers.

'Hang on,' Sebastian said, hurriedly removing the paper napkin from his set. He looked at how Tilly was holding them and tried to mimic her. She lowered the chopsticks to her dish and took a small pinch of rice. 'This is the easiest rice to pick up,' she said as she raised it to her mouth. 'Because it's sticky.' She popped it in and smiled at Sebastian. 'Your turn.' He looked at her nervously. 'Go on,' Tilly urged him. 'What's the worst that can happen?'

Sebastian gingerly scooped up a small ball of rice in the V at the end of his chopsticks. He beamed victoriously and Tilly lovingly smiled back at him. He lifted the food gingerly towards his mouth, but as he turned the chopsticks to eat the rice he pinched them too hard and they separated, sending his rice showering all over the table. Tilly giggled and he felt his cheeks flushing red. 'Oops!' he exclaimed. He set the chopsticks down. 'I knew I'd be useless,' he said, slightly crestfallen.

'You aren't useless.' Tilly stood up and walked round the table. Standing behind him, she reached round, took hold of his chopsticks and put them in his hand. 'Here,' she said encouragingly. Sebastian took them and he felt a little butterfly fluttering in his stomach at the coolness of her skin as she gently placed her hand over his and manoeuvred his fingers into the necessary position. She guided his hand down to his plate and helped him to pick up a piece of the sliced chicken. 'Start with the bigger pieces first, once you master that, then you can tackle the rice'. Sebastian nodded. 'Now, keep the sticks in this position and just slowly turn your wrist inwards. There's no need to release the chopsticks until the chicken is in your mouth.' Sebastian moved his hand and a glob of the katsu sauce dripped off. 'Woah! Slowly.' Tilly gently moved Sebastian's hand and deftly deposited the meat into his mouth. He turned his head over his shoulder and attempted to smile as he chewed the tasty morsel. Tilly returned to her seat and started to tuck in.

Sebastian continued to eat using the chopsticks, slowly at first, then, as his confidence increased, so did his speed; after a few more pieces of chicken and some of the salad had been eagerly devoured he bravely started on the rice. 'Mmm, this is really nice. Is yours okay?'

'Yeah, it's delicious.' She looked up at him and raised her eyebrows. 'Here…' Giggling, she reached across and gently brushed a piece of rice from the corner of Sebastian's mouth. 'Messy!'

Sebastian picked up his napkin and dabbed at his lips. 'Sorry.'

'Don't be a silly, I'm teasing. You're doing great.'

Sebastian looked at Tilly's plate curiously. 'What is that?'

'What *this*?' Tilly stabbed a piece of the seitan up on the end of her chopstick. 'It's seitan, a kind of vegetarian version of what you've got. Wanna try it?' She held out the offering and Sebastian carefully nibbled it from the end of the prong. 'Mmm, that's not bad, what's it made of?'

Tilly looked thoughtful. 'You know, I'm actually not that sure. Some kind of wheat I think.'

They finished their meal in silence, both of them completely clearing their plates. 'Wow! I *really* enjoyed that,' Sebastian declared.

Tilly patted her stomach. 'Yeah! That was lush!'

Seemingly from out of nowhere, the waiter appeared. 'All finished?'

'We are,' Tilly said.

'Did you enjoy your food?'

They both nodded.

The waiter smiled. 'May I take your plates?'

Sebastian leant across the table and lifted Tilly's up onto his own, then moved aside so that the waiter could take them. Spotting the empty glasses, the waiter asked, 'Can I get you both another drink?'

Sebastian looked at Tilly. She shook her head. 'No, we're fine thank you.'

'Can I get you the dessert menu?'

Once again Sebastian looked at Tilly to make the decision. 'No, just the bill please,' she said.

'Of course,' the waiter replied and hurried away to deposit their plates and get the bill.

'I'm paying for this one,' Tilly said. 'No arguments.'

'But…' Sebastian ventured, then he saw the look of determination on Tilly's face.

'No *buts*. Let's call it my congratulatory gift to you.'

Sebastian reached over and took Tilly's soft hands in his. 'Thank you.' They stared into each other's eyes for a few moments, both of them smiling from ear to ear, words unnecessary. Their little moment of happiness was disturbed by the waiter, who reappeared with the bill on a small black plastic tray. With a polite smile, he slid it across the table towards Seb and hurried away again.

'So, what do you fancy doing now?' Sebastian asked. 'Assuming you haven't got anything else planned.'

'I haven't. I left the whole day open just for you, so I'm in no rush to get home,' Tilly replied, looking past him in the direction their waiter had retreated.

'It would be nice to get out of the Smoke for a bit.'

Tilly's face lit up. 'I know just the place.' She frowned as she spotted the waiter attending to someone else on the other side of the restaurant. 'Have you noticed how waiters always lose interest in you at the end of the meal? The minute you say no to dessert or coffee and they realise there's no more money to be had out of you, that's it. You become invisible. He was quick enough to take our plates away. He was serving someone over there just now, but he's disappeared again.'

'Let's stand up as if we're going to leave,' Sebastian suggested mischievously. 'That'll get his attention.'

Tilly giggled and picked up the plastic tray with the bill on. 'Come on, let's just go and pay at the bar.'

A young girl who was wiping down the pumps looked up and smiled as they approached. 'Hello there, how can I help you?'

'We'd just like to settle the bill, please.' Tilly handed the plastic tray to her.

'No problem. One minute please.' The girl took the tray over to the till. 'Are you paying cash or card?'

Tilly waved her debit card in the air. 'Card.'

Sebastian hastily pulled out his wallet. 'Please, let me pay.'

Tilly smiled at him sweetly. 'Put that away immediately! I said I wanted to treat you.'

'You really don't have to, I...'

Tilly placed her hand on his arm. 'Really, I *want* to. If you're that concerned, you're buying the ice creams when we get to where we're going. Deal?'

'Deal.' Sebastian affirmed with a nod.

The girl appeared with the card machine. 'That's £32.60, please.'

Tilly examined the screen and frowned. She pressed the red button, waited for a moment and then swiped her card.

The girl handed her the receipt. 'Thank you. Have a pleasant day.'

Sebastian gave the girl a little wave as they made for the exit. 'Which way is it to the car?' he asked as they stepped out into the street.

Tilly looked left and right. 'Do you know what? I've lost my bearings.'

Sebastian chuckled and pointed up the street. 'Look. There's that little café.'

Tilly laughed. 'Well done, eagle-eyes.' They hooked arms and strolled along the road. 'I don't suppose you

137

noticed, but when I paid the bill just now the card machine asked if I wanted to give a £4 tip.'

'Really?' Sebastian said incredulously.

'Yeah! Bloomin' cheek! I mean, sometimes I'll tip if the service has been particularly good, but I'll be damned if I'll let them dictate how much I should give. Especially as our attentive waiter disappeared and left us sitting there.'

'Absolutely. Eating out is expensive enough as it is these days, they can't expect everyone to tip. It's all well and good if you can afford to, but it should always be optional. And while we're setting the world to rights…' – he chuckled – '…another thing that irks me is people saying *no problem*. It's not just in restaurants, it's everywhere. It's spread like the plague. The girl at the bar said it. I mean, I know it's just an expression and they're acknowledging your order or whatever, but it's their *job* to serve you, dealing with customer requests is what they've been employed to do!'

Tilly laughed. 'It would be all the same if it *was* a problem, wouldn't it? They'd never serve anyone.'

'Exactly.'

As they rounded the corner and walked across the car park, Tilly let out an exasperated cry. 'Oh, great!'

A large, olive-green SUV had parked right up close to the driver's side door. Tilly pipped the door release on her car and walked round to the passenger side. 'Looks like I'm climbing in.' She hitched up her dress. 'Avert your eyes, please.'

Ever the gentleman, Sebastian did as she asked. He waited until he heard the engine turn over before he turned back around and climbed in. 'Well done. I'm not sure I could've managed that.'

Tilly grinned. 'Not the most ladylike of manoeuvres, I'll grant you. But needs must.'

CHAPTER 9

If Sebastian had been pleased with the way the audition had gone, McCleary was absolutely delighted. He couldn't remember the last thing that had made him laugh as much as the sight of his secretary pecking biscuit crumbs off his desk. It had filled him with renewed optimism about a career that he'd frankly found himself tiring of in recent months. After Sebastian had left, McCleary had spent some time on the phone, killing himself laughing as he recounted the morning's entertainment to Harry Nelson, an old colleague in the profession. 'Aye, well, ye probably had to be here,' he said with a note of disappointment when his hilarious story was met with bemusement. Arranging to meet Nelson for lunch later in the week, and assuring him that Sebastian's was an act well worth seeing, McCleary hung up and – still chuckling to himself – went out through reception on his way to the toilet.

As he passed Gemma, who was bent over at the filing cabinet, he paused. 'Reet ma little chicken,' he began. For an instant he thought he'd made the girl jump. She stood bolt upright and jerked her head round to face him. 'Can ye pull the file on the *Midsummer Night's Dream* show at the New Wimbledon Theatre? And Johnnie Crawford's contract while you're at it.'

'Buk!'

McCleary eyed her uncertainly. 'Aye, very funny. And when ye go for lunch pick up another packet of Jammy Dodgers, will ye? Take the money out of petty cash.'

Gemma cocked her head to one side. 'Buk-buk.'

McCleary frowned. 'I'm going for a whiz, just be sure to have the damned paperwork on ma desk when I come back.'

'*Bukee*!' Gemma scraped her foot once on the carpet. 'Buk-buk.'

McCleary could feel his hackles rising. 'It was funny before, but the show's over, ye can give it a rest now.'

Gemma stared at him quizzically for a moment, then began to circle her desk, making little clucking noises, her head jerking around.

'I said *stop*!' McCleary exclaimed angrily.

Gemma immediately came to a halt beside the filing cabinet, shaking her head and blinking.

Muttering under his breath – 'This feckin' girl is gannae have te go!' – McCleary made his way to the toilet, leaving Gemma rocking unsteadily on her feet, confused as to what on earth had just happened.

*

The drive out of East London was laborious. The traffic was heaving and an accident on the A12 near Newbury Park had resulted in one lane being closed, meaning cars were all crawling at a mind-numbing pace. 'I really wish I'd taken the back roads now,' Tilly said with a sigh.

Sebastian craned his head to try and see the road in front of them. 'I can see blue lights flashing. It doesn't look like it's too far ahead, so hopefully the road will be clear after that.' As they passed the accident, they could see a car upside down on the verge and another with the left side of its bonnet staved in. 'Jeez!' Sebastian exclaimed. 'That looks nasty.'

Tilly kept looking straight ahead as they passed. 'I hate seeing car accidents. I've seen some near misses on the road and it makes me go cold.'

Sebastian placed his hand on her knee and squeezed it gently. 'Yeah. I had a little 50cc motorbike when I left school, but I had a few close scrapes and it scared me off. I rode a pushbike for a long time too, but it's got way too dangerous for that. It's actually been in the shed downstairs for the last couple of years. I just don't feel confident riding it any more.'

'Did you never think about learning to drive?'

'Not really. I grew up just outside Romford so there were always plenty of trains and buses. And as you know I'm right on a bus route now, so I didn't really see the point. Plus, it's so expensive to run a car.'

Tilly sighed 'Yeah, tell me about it. It's ridiculous. Almost two quid a litre for fuel and my insurance seems to shoot up every year. I would miss having my little car though. I can walk to work, but I love just being able to jump in and go wherever I like whenever I like.'

Sebastian smiled. 'That's something. Public transport is convenient, but you can't always rely on it. Especially the trains.'

With the traffic moving faster, they soon reached their destination. Tilly indicated left at the entrance of Hainault Forest Country Park.

'This looks nice,' Sebastian said as Tilly pulled in on the far side of the car park beside a huge lake.

'Yeah, I used to come here all the time as a kid. I love it.' Tilly applied the hand brake. She slid the ashtray out from under the stereo and fished around in the small plastic container for some coins.

'Oh, let me get this one,' Sebastian said. Before Tilly had a chance to argue, he got out and walked over to the

142

parking meter. 'What's your registration?' he called back over his shoulder.

Tilly climbed out of the car and shouted it to him. She slipped on a cardigan. As she shut the door, Sebastian stepped up behind her and put his arms around her waist. 'I didn't really know how long we were likely to be staying so I bought four hours. It says on the machine that they lock the gates at dusk. Whenever *that* is.'

'Yeah, what is with that? Somewhere else I went recently had that. I mean when exactly *is* dusk? Who decides?' Tilly said.

'When it gets dark, I guess. But then again, on a stormy day dusk could be at 4 o'clock.' He chuckled. 'Maybe they have hi-tech dusk-reading equipment.'

Tilly laughed. 'Nothing would surprise me. And it would be some annoying jobsworth using it and locking you in for the night!' She shut the car door and pipped the remote to lock it. 'Anyway, I reckon four hours will be about right.' She pointed across the car park towards a small building. 'That's the café. Shall we have an ice cream now in case they're closed when we get back?'

'Ooh, yes, let's have one now.'

They walked towards the café, holding hands and laughing like excited children. As they entered, a burly man stepped out from behind the counter. 'I'm not doing hot food today,' he said bluntly.

'That's okay, we'd just like an ice cream, please,' Sebastian replied.

'Whippy machine is off,' the man muttered. 'But you can have something from the freezer if you like.'

Tilly looked disappointed. Sebastian peered through the misted-up sliding glass lid. 'Ooh, Feast! I haven't had one of those for years,' he exclaimed, pulling out the lolly.

143

Tilly's face lit up. 'Neither have I. Have they got a mint one?'

'Yup!' Sebastian said. He took the ice creams to the counter. There was a plastic tub beside the till, filled with clear polythene bags containing seed and grain. 'I'll have a couple of bags of the duck food as well, please.'

The shopkeeper dropped two bags of feed onto the counter and held out his hand. 'Six pounds.' He watched Sebastian withdraw a £10 note from his wallet and sighed. 'Haven't you got the right money?' he asked tetchily.

'No, sorry mate.' Sebastian held out the £10 note, waiting for the man to take it. He snatched it from him and made a show of holding it up to the light to check it wasn't a forgery. Grunting, he pushed a button on the till and the drawer sprang open. His fat fingers scrabbled to pull out four £1 coins, which he banged down heavily on the counter. Then, without a word of thanks, he slammed the till drawer shut, turned his back on them and wandered off through the door into the back room.

'That was a bit rude,' Tilly said under her breath.

'Thank you,' Sebastian called out with a deliberate note of sarcasm.

They eagerly ripped the wrapping off their Feast lollies and dropped the shreds into the bin outside the café door. Sebastian slipped one of the bags of duck food into each of his jacket pockets and they skipped down the steps and crossed the car park back in the direction of the lake.

'He was a real ray of sunshine, wasn't he?' Tilly said, rolling her eyes.

'Yeah, he sure knows how to make customers feel welcome. Not!'

'Mr Whippy's not on,' Tilly mockingly bellowed in a deep voice.

Sebastian laughed.

144

They found a bench beside the lake and sat down to eat their ice creams. Within minutes an audience started to gather. At first half a dozen ducks stepped up out of the water and waddled over towards the bench, stopping and loitering just far enough away from Sebastian and Tilly that they could scurry back to the lake if they felt threatened. Sebastian finished his ice cream, reached into his pocket and pulled out the bag of duck food. As if sensing something tasty was in the offing, the ducks started to quack excitedly. Sebastian noticed Tilly had finished her ice cream. 'Let me deal with that,' he said, taking the stick from her and dropping it along with his own into his pocket. 'Here,' he said, and handed her the bag of food.

Tilly took it from him and smiled. 'You big softy.'

'Well, you can't come to a duck pond and not feed the ducks.'

Tilly opened the bag and carefully poured a little of the mixed seed and grain into the palm of her hand. Sebastian pulled the second bag out of his pocket, but in an attempt to open it he managed to split it clean in two, showering the ground around the bench with seed. There was an immediate frenzy as the ducks rushed over and, amidst a flurry of wings and a cacophony of delighted quacking, they hoovered up the spilt offerings. Tilly burst out laughing as Sebastian hitched up his knees to get his feet out of the way of the marauding mallards. 'Crikey!' Sebastian cried above the din. 'It's like a scene out of an Alfred Hitchcock film!'

'And it's about to get worse,' Tilly spluttered through tears of laughter. She pointed to the lake where a froth was forming as a huge flock of Canadian geese made their way across the water towards them. '*The Birds* had nothing on this!'

'Oh, crap!' Sebastian cried. He stood up and as the geese launched themselves out of the water he froze on the spot.

Startled by his reaction, Tilly got up. 'Are you okay?'

'Yeah, I'm fine,' Sebastian replied unconvincingly.

There were angry squawks as the geese muscled in on the ducks. All the feed they had scattered had been gobbled up and the geese honked at Tilly and Sebastian expectantly, while the ducks retreated to the water. The couple were left surrounded by the gaggle of hungry geese. As Tilly opened the bag up fully, one of them advanced and started pulling at her skirt. She held the bag aloft and scattered the remainder of the feed all over the ground.

'C'mon, let's leave these greedy buggers to it,' she said, taking Sebastian's hand. 'There's another bench up on the hill, you can see all across London on a clear day.' Sebastian glanced back at the squabbling geese and shuddered as he followed Tilly away from the carnage.

'Those geese really freaked you out didn't they?'

'Yeah, they did a bit. It stems from childhood. My parents took me to Raphael's Park once to feed the ducks and the same thing happened there. I was only four or five and I got mobbed by geese. They pecked the bread out of my hand and were tearing at my clothes and hair. My Dad just laughed. Looking back now, I guess I wasn't in any real danger, but that kind of thing can scar you. I've never forgotten it.'

Tilly squeezed his hand. 'They can be spiteful birds.' She let go of his hand and spun round. 'Isn't this beautiful though? You can't beat the great outdoors!'

They trekked up the hill. It was quite a steep incline and although Sebastian could feel his knees aching, Tilly marched on seemingly unaffected, so he did his level best

146

to keep up. When they reached the peak, just as Tilly had said, there was a bench. Unfortunately, it had been vandalised. 'Oh look at that!' Tilly exclaimed forlornly. 'Why would someone do that?'

Sebastian sighed. 'You can't have anything nice these days without little scrotes wrecking it. It's like it everywhere.' All three seat struts had been snapped across the middle and one of the backrests was completely missing. Scattered around the area there were a load of beer cans, crisp packets and little silver canisters. 'Looks like they've been at the laughing gas too,' Sebastian said pointing to the debris.

'Yeah. And I bet they found smashing up the bench absolutely hilarious.' She shook her head in disbelief.

Sebastian turned around and caught sight of the view. 'Wow!' he gasped. 'You really *can* see London.'

Tilly stepped over to join him. 'Told you.' She pointed. 'Look over there, you can just see the Millennium Dome.'

Sebastian followed her finger. 'Oh yeah! Or the O2 Arena as it's now known.'

Tilly stuck out her tongue. 'Smarty-pants.'

Sebastian grinned and took off his jacket and laid it down on the grass. 'Let's just sit on the ground, eh? The view is splendid.'

'You'll get it all dirty!' she exclaimed. 'You only bought it a few hours ago.'

'It's fine,' Sebastian said. 'It served its purpose.'

Tilly looked at him aghast. '*Seriously*?'

Sebastian laughed. 'I'm kidding. The ground's bone dry.' He sat down and patted the jacket, inviting Tilly to join him.

Tilly looked disdainfully at the broken bench and litter, then carefully sat down on the ground beside him. 'It's sad, isn't it,' she said with a sigh. 'We came here almost every weekend as kids. My Mum would pack a picnic, and my sister and I would bring a bat and ball or a frisbee. We had crisps and cartons of drinks and Mum would always make sure we picked up all our litter and took it home with us. What has gone so wrong these days that people think it's okay to leave the countryside in such a mess?'

'They just don't care,' Sebastian replied resignedly. 'They think it's perfectly okay to leave it there for someone else to pick up. If they think at all.'

They sat quietly for a minute and stared out across the London skyline. 'This is really lovely,' Sebastian said quietly, breaking the silence.

'Yeah, it is.' Tilly shifted closer to Sebastian and he put his arm around her.

'So is this the exact spot you used to come for your picnics,' he asked.

'Sometimes. We didn't have a lot of money and Mum wouldn't have dreamt of paying to eat in the café. We'd usually walk around the animal enclosures, feed the ducks and that sort of thing. She'd sit on the bench and read a book whilst Grace and I entertained ourselves.'

Sebastian's eyes lit up. 'They've got animals here? What type?'

'Oh, mostly farm animals. Sheep, goats, pigs and donkeys. I did hear they got some meerkats recently, but I've not actually been here for a while.'

'Meerkats? Cool!' Sebastian replied excitedly.

'Sorry, I didn't think you'd be interested in the animals. We should have gone there first.'

Sebastian pulled Tilly in tight. 'Next time.' She smiled and leant in to give him a soft kiss on the cheek. Sebastian felt a warm glow pulse through his body. 'It sounds like you had a lovely childhood.'

148

'We did. Mum struggled for a while when my Dad left, but she always made sure we were okay, you know? When Ken came along we weren't sure at first, in fact Grace gave him sheer hell for a while. But he was a good man and he worked hard. He loved the bones of Mum and she loved him too. It hit her really hard when he was diagnosed with cancer.' She breathed in deeply. 'He was...' She faltered. 'He was on chemo for over a year... Mum quit her job and became his carer.' She made a little sobbing noise.

Sebastian hugged her. 'I'm sorry. You don't have to carry on. I didn't want to upset you.'

Tilly reached into her cardigan pocket and pulled out a tissue. 'No, it's okay.' She dabbed at her nose. 'He was slowly wasting away in front of our eyes. He lost so much weight and in the end he was barely recognisable. He spent the last couple of weeks of his life in a hospice. Mum would visit every day and come home crying. She tried to hide it from me and Grace, but we knew.' She blew her nose, taking a moment to compose herself. Sebastian waited in silence. 'And now... well, it's got her too.'

'I'm so sorry,' Sebastian said, gently rubbing his hand up and down her arm.

'Witnessing how Ken suffered through the chemo and with the outcome as it was, Mum has decided that she doesn't want the treatment.' Tilly sighed shakily.

She looked out across the fields, where a small dog was running at incredible speed to catch his ball as it rolled away down the hill. The dog's owner stopped and raised his hand to wave. 'Evening.'

Tilly and Sebastian waved back. 'Aww, so cute,' Tilly said as the dog retrieved his ball, bounded back up the hill and dropped it at his owner's feet. 'Anyway, what was I saying?'

'You said your Mum wasn't going to have treatment.'

'Yeah. I remember the day she told us. Grace had just come back from Turkey with her husband and Mum asked us both to come over. I didn't live with her then, I shared a flat with Keira, one of my friends – you met her at the Cauli a while ago.' Sebastian nodded. 'I picked Grace up and on the car journey we were both trying to guess what the summons would be about. Neither of us expected what Mum had to say. She'd been diagnosed with Stage 4 breast cancer. The oncologist had recommended a full mastectomy, then a course of chemotherapy, followed by radiotherapy. We were both shocked and couldn't stop crying. Grace is a lot tougher than me, but she was really upset too. Mum, being strong as ever, told us to pull ourselves together as it wasn't a time for crying.'

Sebastian frowned. 'That's a bit harsh'.

'I thought that too at the time. But she went on to tell us that she'd made a decision and needed us to support her. She was booked in for the mastectomy the following week. She said she would have her breasts removed but she wasn't going to have any treatment. We both pleaded with her, but she shut us down. Her mind was made up.' Tilly pulled out another tissue and cleared her nose. 'After the operation, she really struggled lifting things. Both her arms were in pain because they'd removed nodes from under her armpit whilst doing the mastectomy. I offered to move in temporarily to help her around the house and that's where I've been since.'

'How is she doing now?' Sebastian asked.

'She has good days and bad days. She spent a long time looking at holistic remedies and ways to boost her immunity through various foods and supplements.

150

I know she's in pain, though she rarely lets you see it. And she has really aged suddenly. Grace is always full of anger and says Mum has just given up, but I disagree. I fully respect her decision. She potters in the garden, she loves her plants and flowers. She reads a lot and on the good days she always manages to get out and meets with friends. She's making the most of her life while she can. I think it's admirable.'

Sebastian nodded. 'It is.'

'I admit I'm scared though,' Tilly said. 'The doctors say that without treatment the cancer will advance but…' She started to sob again. 'We just take each day as it comes.'

Sebastian hugged her tight and she lay down, resting her head in his lap. He bent down and kissed her tenderly on her head. They sat in silence for a while, words unnecessary as they savoured the simplicity of each other's company and the beauty of the vista before them. Sebastian tenderly stroked Tilly's hair as he gazed out across the sky. The birds were beginning to gather in the trees around them and the chirrupy evening song was almost deafening.

Tilly sat up and groaned. 'Ooh I'm getting a crick in my neck,' she said, wincing.

Sebastian helped her to straighten up and gently massaged her neck.

'That feels good.'

'The sun's beginning to set over there,' Sebastian said, pointing to the now almost silhouetted sight of the Canada Square Tower in Canary Wharf, which had a surreal shard of light shimmering across its glass facade.

Tilly sighed. 'London looks so beautiful from afar.'

'It's a beautiful city,' Sebastian concurred. 'It's just a shame it's been ruined by all the traffic and over-

151

development. It's changed dramatically in just the last ten years.'

Tilly yawned and shivered slightly. 'It's got a bit chilly.'

Sebastian put his arm around her and the pair huddled close, sitting in silence again as the sun set slowly over the capital.

Tilly suddenly gasped as she realised the light was going fast. 'We'd better get back to the car before we get locked in for the night!'

They got up and as fast as they could descended the hill. Approaching the car park, they could see that the lights were out in the café. 'Oh, Lordy, I hope Mr No Whippy isn't responsible for locking the main gate,' Tilly said breathlessly. 'If he is we're doomed!'

Other than Tilly's car there was one small yellow van in the car park. 'Well, at least we won't be the only ones locked in,' Sebastian said, panting hard as they reached the car. They both climbed in, Tilly pulled away and the car spun in a full circle, sending up a cloud of dust before swiftly negotiating the narrow private road towards the main gate. 'Fingers crossed!' she exclaimed as they approached the exit. They both breathed a sigh of relief to see the gate was still open.

As they passed through, Sebastian chuckled. 'Whoever owns that yellow van back there might not be so lucky.'

Tilly pulled out and joined the traffic on the dual carriageway, picking up speed as they headed towards Chadwell Heath to drop Sebastian off home.

CHAPTER 10

The next few days passed slowly for Sebastian. Jobless and with only meagre savings to his name, going out wasn't an option. Tilly was at work during the days and attending appointments with her mother during the evenings. But they had made plans to see each other on Thursday evening to go shopping at Lakeside for a whole new ensemble, and Sebastian had been counting down the days.

He had only ever had one girlfriend before Tilly. He was 17 and had just started work in a shop selling video games. The girl's name was Sheryl. She had been a regular customer and they had got talking over the popular life simulation series of games, *The Sims*. Sebastian asked her on a date and they went to a pizza restaurant. Over dinner he discovered that she was six years older than him – she actually looked younger – and was extremely forward. She invited him back to her flat and he lost his virginity with her that very first evening. It wasn't a pleasant experience for Sebastian and he did his best to distance himself from her after that, which was difficult when she knew where he worked. She called his mobile phone relentlessly and kept coming into the shop. He would often duck out the back when he saw her coming, but one day Sheryl caught him unawares while he was stacking the shelves. She made a scene in the shop, shouting at him for ghosting her, and later that day his boss summoned him to the office where he was promptly sacked. From that day on he had never made much of an effort to find love. There had been a girl in his office at Mapp Apps who he quite fancied, but she always referred to him as "sweet" and "a great mate". He had been well and truly friend-zoned there and had neither the courage nor the ability to try and move it up to next base.

The day Tilly referred to herself as his girlfriend had made Sebastian's heart skip a beat. They'd been on a couple of dates, but even though he really liked her he didn't dare go so far as to assume they were in a relationship. Nevertheless, it had happened – naturally and unexpectedly, everything had just fallen perfectly into place. And on that same day, he also got a step closer to becoming the stage hypnotist he always dreamt he would be.

Thinking about this meteoric turn around in his fortune, on the Thursday morning Sebastian felt the sudden urge to tidy his flat. Living on his own, he had become a little tardy with the housekeeping. He made a conscious decision that now was the time to grow up and that would mean giving the man-cave he called home a complete overhaul. Starting in the kitchen, Sebastian emptied all the cupboards and spray-cleaned each and every inch. He disposed of food, which was long since out of date – a lot of it from the Co-Op – and restocked the cupboards with almost obsessive organisation. The room sparkled when he had finished and he stood back and admired his handiwork. 'Now *that's* clean!' he said aloud. He continued throughout the flat until every room was cleaned and reorganised. He had taken the curtains down and stripped the covers off the cushions. He'd whipped off his bedding and changed the bath towels and it was all spinning lazily in the washing machine. He'd even found a screwdriver and started to fix the shower door. It had been slightly hanging off the wall since his unfortunate accident earlier in the week, some of the screws had pulled the rawl-plugs out and the plaster was split. Sebastian studied it for a moment and then remembered he had bought some decorator's caulk a while back; that should do the trick he thought. He rummaged in the airing cupboard where he kept his tools and other bits and bobs. Locating the tube, he checked the nozzle, only to discover it was bunged up. With the help of a nail, a bit of scraping managed to clear it, and he was just about to set to work when his phone rang. He set down the tube on the toilet seat and answered.

It was Tilly. 'Hiya. What you doing?'

'Hi! I've been doing a bit of tidying up round the flat. You'd be proud of me.' Sebastian caught sight of himself in the bathroom mirror. There was a blob of white caulk on the end of his nose. 'I was just...' He trailed off as he glanced down and saw that the tube was leaking, dripping a long string of caulk onto the floor tiles. 'Oh no!'

'What's up? You okay?'

'Yeah, hang on a sec.' With his free hand, Sebastian awkwardly tried to tear off a sheet of toilet paper, but the roll spun once and began to unspool. He tried to grab hold of it to stop it spinning, but it fell off the holder and rolled across the tiles. 'Flip! Can I call you back in a minute?'

'Of course.'

Hastily rewinding the long stretch of tissue back onto the roll, Sebastian pulled a couple of sheets off the end and bent down to wipe away the spillage from the floor. He cleaned the end of the nozzle, firmly replaced the cap on the tube, then perched himself on the edge of the toilet seat and called Tilly back. 'Sorry about that. Had a small caulk crisis.'

Tilly burst out laughing. 'I beg your pardon?'

'Caulk. You know, that sealant stuff.'

Tilly sniggered.

Sebastian looked a little puzzled. 'What did you think I said?'

'Never mind,' Tilly said, stifling another giggle. 'So, you're decorating too?'

'No, just filling some holes where I managed to pull the shower door off the wall on Monday. Anyway, sorry, you called me.'

'Yeah, I couldn't wait till tonight to tell you the good news. I spoke to my friend Keira about the show on Saturday and she just phoned me to confirm she's going to come. She thought you getting Mark to act like a chicken a couple of weeks ago was hilarious! And better still – wait for it – she's bringing Helen, her sister *and* Helen's boyfriend. She's going to book tonight.'

'Wow, that's brilliant!' Sebastian said.

'Isn't it though?' Tilly said excitedly. 'I'm still waiting to hear back from a couple of my other girlfriends. At this rate the whole audience will be made up of the Seb the Sensational fan club, all cheering you on.' She laughed. 'Have you asked your friends?'

'Er, no, I don't think I mentioned it yet.'

Tilly frowned. 'You don't *think* you mentioned it? You mean you don't *know*?'

'Well, no, I haven't.'

'What's the matter?' Tilly could detect the note of doubt in his voice. 'You don't sound very enthusiastic.'

'The thing is, I'm not sure they'd be interested.' Sebastian sighed. 'They kind of put up with my hypnosis act, but I don't think they're that impressed really. Especially Mark.'

'I'm sure they'd come along to support their mate if you asked them to,' Tilly said encouragingly. 'They'll be fighting for free seats to see you when you're a superstar!'

Sebastian laughed. 'Yeah, I guess. Okay, I'll call them later. Anyway, enough about me. How was *your* day?'

'Okay, I guess.' Tilly sighed. 'A bit sad. We had to take down all the memorial stuff for the Queen. It felt really... well, final, if that makes sense?'

'Of course. But you'll soon be replacing it all with coronation stuff when Charles gets his crown.'

'That's true enough.'

Sebastian stood up. 'Are we still on for tonight then?'

'You bet. Pick you up at six?'

'I'll be ready.'

'By the way,' Tilly said. 'Did the props arrive?'

'Oh, yes!' Sebastian exclaimed enthusiastically. 'I've still got my Prime, they all arrived yesterday. Sorry, I should have called to let you know.'

'Are they good?'

'The Freddie jacket's a bit plasticky to be honest, but I guess it was cheap. The other stuff is great though. Especially the spider!'

Tilly laughed. 'I can't wait to see it. I'll look forward to seeing what you've done with the flat too.'

'Oh, crikey,' Sebastian said. 'Don't expect it to be up to showroom standards.'

'I'm sure it looks fantastic. And I promise I won't criticise the odd speck of dust.' She gasped. 'Oh! I didn't mean to invite myself round. Sorry.'

It was Sebastian's turn to laugh. 'Don't be silly, you're welcome here any time. You know that. Tell you what, I'll even mop the bathroom floor this time. I wouldn't do that for just anybody y'know.'

'See you at six then.'

Sebastian heard her blow a little kiss down the line and then she was gone.

CHAPTER 11

Sebastian spent most of Friday rehearsing his act. He practiced in front of his door-length mirror over and over, ensuring his stance was charismatic and his hand movements were engaging. He had written out a script for the whole show and repeatedly read it out loud, tweaking his jokes to ensure he got the timing right.

On Saturday afternoon, sitting on the bed waiting for Tilly to arrive and looking sharp in the brand new suit he'd bought from Lakeside, he knew in his heart that he was as ready as he would ever be.

The intercom buzzer sounded and he got up and pressed the button to open the outside door. He quickly checked his hair in the hallway mirror; it was gelled tight to his head and for once he actually felt good about it. He opened the flat door just as Tilly was about to knock.

'Ooh, you startled me!' Her eyes sparkling, she smiled up at him. She was wearing a bright orange knee-length dress with a crocheted white cardigan over the top.

Sebastian bent and kissed her on the lips. 'You look sensational.'

'Aww, thank you. You look pretty spiffy yourself. Are you ready?'

'Yep. Ready and raring to go!' He unhooked his keys from behind the door and stepped into the communal hallway, closing the door and locking it behind him. They descended the stairs and as Sebastian opened the main door he stopped short. 'Oh rats!'

'What's up?' Tilly asked.

'I forgot my props!'

Tilly laughed. '*Really*?! Go back and get them. I'll wait in the car.'

Sebastian dashed back up the stairs as Tilly stepped out into the street. A few minutes later he returned carrying a shopping bag bulging with props. Tilly lowered the window and called out, 'Put them on the back seat.' Sebastian opened the rear door and dropped the bag on the seat behind her. He waited for a gap in the traffic, then nipped smartly round to the passenger side and hopped in.

'How are your nerves?' Tilly asked.

'Nerves? What nerves?'

Tilly poked out her tongue. 'No, really.'

'I'm as cool as cucumber,' Sebastian replied, brushing a mark off his sleeve. 'At least I look the part, eh?'

'One hundred percent.' Tilly leant and kissed him lightly on the cheek. 'Are you sure you've got everything?'

Sebastian thought for a moment. 'Yes. Definitely. All good.'

'Right then,' Tilly said as she turned the ignition. 'Let's get this show on the road.'

The drive to Walthamstow was surprisingly smooth and hassle free. The traffic on the A406 was moving quickly and as the satnav instructed them to turn off at the next junction Tilly noted that they were less than two miles from their destination, the Ind Coope Social Club. They turned into Billet Lane and the car shuddered as they drove over a cattle grid spanning the road. 'Ooh! I wasn't expecting that,' Tilly exclaimed.

'Yeah, it's a bit odd in the middle of a big place like this.'

'We're really close. How are you feeling?'

'I'm grand,' Sebastian replied. 'In fact I can't wait!'

Tilly smiled. She could detect a hint of bravado in Sebastian's voice, which she suspected was for her benefit, but she didn't say anything. Inside she was bursting with pride and, although she wouldn't have admitted it, a little nervous on his behalf; she would never give him any reason to lose confidence. 'I can't wait to see you perform,' she said. 'I'm really proud of you, you know.'

Sebastian moved his hand across and wrapped it around Tilly's just as she was about to change gear. She selected the gear, but left her hand resting on the stick with Sebastian's cupped over it. 'I know you're doing the Freddie act and the thing with the spider, but will you be having Mark up there again doing his chicken parade?'

'I've been thinking about that.' Sebastian removed his hand from Tilly's. 'I want to play this completely straight tonight.'

'How do you mean?'

'I'm going to pick three completely random people. James is going be there and I want to leave him in no doubt that my abilities are genuine. I want to prove that hypnosis really works. If I use friends all the time, people will start to think it's all set up. It has to be authentic. I know it is and *you* know it is, but most people are sceptical. I get that, it's normal. But they look for any little chink to latch on to that proves it's phoney. And finding out I'm using friends would seal it. So it *has* to be strangers.'

'That makes sense. How will you pick them?'

'Well, I've worked it all into my act. I don't want to spoil it for you, but trust me, it will all be perfect.'

Tilly indicated left. As the satnav announced that they had reached their destination, she spotted the club on the corner, turned right into the car park and pulled into a

160

space just inside the entrance. Leaning over to kiss Sebastian on the cheek she said, 'I have absolutely no doubt.' She reached behind her seat and grabbed her handbag. 'Oh. I forgot to show you this.' She pulled out a piece of card from the inside pocket and handed it to Sebastian. It was a ticket.

'You paid?' Sebastian said with surprise. 'You didn't have to buy a ticket, you're with me.'

Tilly smiled. 'I wanted to. You've got to show this Rising Starz lot you can sell tickets.'

Sebastian studied it. 'So, this magic man is called Zayn Bauer. Is that a German name?'

'Yeah, I think so,' Tilly replied.

'And who's this?' Sebastian said, tapping a finger on the card. 'Support Act.'

'Yeah, I was a bit gutted it didn't have your name on,' Tilly replied.

Sebastian grinned broadly. 'Maybe next time.' He handed the ticket back to Tilly. 'Shall we go in then?'

Tilly pulled him over to her. 'In a minute.' She kissed him softly on the lips. 'For luck.' He moved closer and the kiss became more passionate. The moment was shattered by the loud crunching of gravel as another car pulled in beside them. It was a large Audi with blacked-out windows. A man wearing black trousers and a black shirt stepped out. He reached into the back of the car and pulled out the suit protector that was hanging behind the passenger seat.

'Do you reckon that's Zayn?' Tilly asked.

'I reckon it could be,' Sebastian replied.

'Go and say hello,' Tilly urged.

'Nah. I'll wait till we're inside.' He pecked her again on the cheek and, waiting until the man had crossed the car park and disappeared inside, he opened his door and stepped out. Tilly climbed out and smoothed down her dress. Sebastian looked at his jacket. 'I probably should've hung mine up too,' he mused. 'Oh well, you live and learn.' He reached into the car for his bag of props and together they walked into the club.

A man was sat inside the doorway beside a small table. 'Tickets please.' Tilly handed him her ticket. He tore it down the perforated line and handed the stub back to her. He looked up at Sebastian.

'Er, hello. My name is Sebastian Matthews. I'm the support act tonight.'

The man scanned a sheet of paper on his table. 'Yes, of course. Go on through.'

As they walked through the double swing doors into the club Sebastian's eyes widened. It was only just six o'clock and the place was packed to capacity. He spotted a poster on the wall beside the bar advertising the evening's show. 'Cool poster.'

Tilly turned to look. 'Yeah, that's great. I see that strange bloke Support Act is on there too.'

'Yeah, I hope he's good,' Sebastian said with a grin. 'We're early. Shall we get a drink?'

'Definitely. We must put money behind the bar, it all gets measured to gauge the success of tonight.'

'Sure, but I'm only the support act.'

'Oh, *you're* Support Act!' Tilly winked at him. 'Seriously, doesn't matter. Chances are they've had this German bloke here before. If the ticket sales and takings are up on last time, they might attribute some of that to you.'

Sebastian smiled. 'There might be some truth in that.' He stepped up to the bar. 'What are you having?'

'Just a Diet Coke for me, please. No ice.'

As Sebastian was about to give the barman his order, Tilly's mobile phone rang. She pulled it out of her bag. Frowning, she cancelled the call. 'Everything okay?' Sebastian asked curiously.

'Yeah, it's just Mum. She knows I'm out tonight. I'll call her back a bit later.'

'You sure? I don't mind if you want to do it now.'

'Nah, honestly, she's probably just forgotten I was going out straight from work'.

The barman approached Sebastian. 'What can I get you mate?'

'Two Diet Cokes please.'

'Pint or half pint?'

Sebastian looked to Tilly. 'Might as well have a pint,' she said, switching her phone to silent and slipping it back into her bag.

Sebastian paid for their drinks and they looked around for a table. Realising they were all taken, they moved over to the window and rested their glasses on the sill. 'It's great to see a full house,' Sebastian said.

'Yeah. And there's more to come. Your mates aren't here and neither is Kiera or the Bradleys.'

Sebastian looked at all the people. 'Well, I hope they bought tickets because I'd wager this is a sell-out show.'

Tilly scanned the room. 'It's a nice place. It has a friendly atmosphere.'

'It does,' Sebastian concurred.

Out of the corner of her eye Tilly saw a group of people coming through the doors. She jabbed Sebastian in the arm. 'There's Jordan and Joshua. Looks like they've brought someone else with them too.'

Sebastian looked over towards the door. 'That's Pete, Jordan's Dad.' Sebastian put up a hand and waved them over.

'Well, well. Don't you scrub up well,' Joshua said, pulling Sebastian into a shoulder bump.

Jordan held out his fist and Sebastian reciprocated with a bump of knuckles. 'You've met my dad?' Jordan asked.

'Indeed I have.' He smiled and held out his hand. 'Hi, Pete. Thanks for coming.'

Pete gripped Sebastian's hand tightly. 'It's a great pleasure. My boy has told me all about you and your clever tricks. I wasn't gonna pass up the chance to see it wit' my own eyes.' He turned to Tilly. 'And who's this lovely lady?'

'This is Tilly,' Sebastian said. 'My girlfriend.'

Tilly stepped forward and held out her hand. 'Nice to meet you.'

Pete took her hand in his and kissed it. 'The pleasure is all mine. I have to tell you I'm besotted by your beauty.' Tilly felt herself blush. Pete pointed at Sebastian. 'You dis boy's manager?'

Tilly laughed. 'Yeah, I suppose you could say that. I'm also a chauffeur, roadie and the costume department!'

Pete roared with laughter. 'Good for you.' He elbowed Sebastian. 'You got yourself a keeper here.'

Joshua leant in and kissed Tilly on the cheek. 'Glad you're looking after our Sebby.'

Sebastian spotted Katie in the doorway and she wasn't looking very happy. Mark appeared behind her. Over the noise in the room, Sebastian couldn't quite make out what, but he heard Mark shout something over his shoulder, presumably to the man on the door, and it didn't look pleasant. Catching Katie's eye, Sebastian waved. She pushed her way through the people towards them, but Mark went straight to the bar.

'You alright Katie?' Sebastian asked.

'Yeah, all good. Mark's just behaving like a twat again!' She hugged Tilly and then worked her way round the others, hugging each of them in turn. Jordan introduced his father, who gave Katie exactly the same line he'd used on Tilly.

Katie laughed and Jordan rolled his eyes. 'Really, Dad, haven't you got any new material?'

'Hush your mouth, boy. What do you know about wooing a lady?'

'Well seeing as I'm gay, not a lot.'

'Exactly, batty boy!'

Jordan shot his father a dirty look. '*Really*?!'

Pete kissed his teeth and headed for the bar.

'Besotted by my beauty?!' Katie said, laughing. He's a bit of a character, isn't he?'

'That's one word for him,' Jordan replied with a rueful sigh.

Mark appeared carrying two drinks. He handed one to Katie and then took a big slug of his own. 'Whatcha, Seb. You all ready to fall on your arse then, lad?'

Katie back slapped him across the chest.

'Hopefully not, Mark. I'm going to raise the roof on this place.'

Mark guffawed. 'I'll believe it when I see it.'

Sebastian looked at his watch. He took hold of Tilly's arm. 'I'm going to have to go and get ready. Do you wanna come?'

'Do you need me to?'

Sebastian looked down at his shoes. 'I'm starting to feel a bit nervous,' he confessed.

'Not because of what Mark said I hope?' Sebastian didn't reply. 'Look. You've rehearsed, you'll be fine. Go show that Wally what you're made of!' She stood on tiptoe and gave him a kiss on the forehead.'

165

Sebastian beamed and bent to pick up his bag of props. He collected his drink from the window sill and walked towards the door leading backstage. Tilly smiled as she watched Sebastian disappear. She hung on her gaze for a while, her head doing cartwheels.

'He'll be fine,' a voice beside her said quietly.

Tilly turned to face Katie, who was standing at her shoulder. She was looking at Tilly reassuringly, almost as if she had read her mind. 'Oh yeah, I know he will,' Tilly said. 'It's just it means so much to him. I really hope it goes well and everyone here likes him.'

Katie smiled warmly and squeezed her arm. 'They're going to love h…' She stopped as her eye was drawn to something going on behind Tilly. 'Oh, for Christ's sake! What's he doing now?!'

Tilly looked round to see Mark over near the stage, standing at a table with his palms flat on top of it, seemingly in the midst of an animated argument with an elderly man.

'Excuse me a moment,' Katie said. 'I can't flippin' take him anywhere!' She pushed her way through the tables. 'Mark!'

He spun round, his eyes blazing.

'What's going on?' Katie hissed angrily.

'Doddery old Fritz here is taking up a whole table to himself,' Mark replied irritably. 'All I'm doing is politely suggesting that he goes and sits with someone else so that we can have this table.'

'It didn't look to me like you were being very polite,' Katie said. The old man was looking at her with a confused expression on his face. She smiled apologetically. 'I'm so sorry, mate. Ignore my boyfriend, he can be a bit of a d… a so and so.'

166

The man afforded her a gummy smile. 'I really don't know what your friend wants. I'm a bit deaf you see. Does he need to clean the table?'

Katie smiled inwardly and raised her voice a little. 'No, it's fine, really. You enjoy your beer. I'm sorry we troubled you.' She grabbed Mark's arm and firmly pulled him back to join the others. 'Just get back over here and stop causing a scene.'

'Fucking Kraut!' Mark protested loudly. 'I'm surprised he didn't have his towel laid out on the table.'

'Seriously, Mark, I wonder sometimes what I ever saw in you!' Katie exclaimed.

Mark snorted. 'I think you'll find it was my massive cock.'

Almost lost for words, Katie stared at him angrily for a moment, then turned her back on him. 'Yeah, right,' she muttered under her breath.

'When's this poxy show supposed to start anyway?' Mark bellowed.

'Any time now,' Tilly said.

'I'm gonna get another pint then,' Mark declared and sauntered off towards the bar.

Tilly looked over to the stage. The thick red drapes were pulled shut, but she could see them swaying occasionally; someone was moving about behind them. Lost in her thoughts, she was startled by a hand touching her shoulder. She looked round to see Keira, Helen and her boyfriend, Glen. 'Oh, hiya!' Tilly said cheerfully. 'Thanks so much for coming.' The friends hugged.

'Can I get you a drink?' Kiera said.

'Thanks, but I have one,' Tilly replied. She looked round to see what she'd done with her glass. 'Somewhere, anyway.' She laughed.

Kiera went up to the bar with Glen.

'This seems like a nice place,' Helen said.

'Yeah, it is.'

'So, it's your boyfriend performing tonight?' Tilly nodded. 'Keira has told me all about his act, it sounds hilarious. I can't wait to see the chicken hypnosis.'

'Oh he's...' Tilly began, but she was cut short by a burst of loud music from the speakers. It was *Mirrors* by Justin Timberlake and the bass was overpowering.

'Here we go!' Josh exclaimed.

'Yeah, man,' Pete said with a grin.

The curtains opened slowly and Sebastian strode confidently out from the wings and into the middle of the stage. There was a small ripple of applause around the room as Sebastian gestured to someone out of view at the side of the stage and the music faded out.

CHAPTER 12

Tilly's eyes were transfixed on the stage. Arranged neatly were three chairs to Sebastian's right and a small square table with a box on it to the left. He had a microphone in his hand. There was a low hubbub of chatter in the crowd, but it ceased as soon as he lifted the microphone to speak.

'Ladies and gentlemen. Thank you for having me here tonight. My name is Sebastian Matthews and I would like to introduce you to the mystical world of hypnotism.' He looked out across the vast, brightly lit room where a sea of expectant faces was staring back at him. 'Barman. Could we please have the house lights off?' A moment later the lights went out and the performance area was awash with subtle blue lights from a rig above the stage. Sebastian continued with his address. 'What I am about to show you tonight will defy reason. I will be asking for volunteers, who before your very eyes will succumb to my hypnotic spell and will assist me in demonstrating to you just how powerful the art of persuasion under hypnosis can be.' He moved to stand behind the chairs, placing his hand on the first in the row of three. 'I am looking for somebody who likes music. Who amongst you would like to be my first volunteer?'

After a moment's silence a voice called out, 'I'll do it!'

Sebastian looked in the direction of the voice and traced it to a tall man stood by the bar. 'Then please come on up, sir. Thank you very much. Come on everyone, let's give my first volunteer a round of applause.'

The room erupted with the sound of enthusiastic clapping. As the man strode towards the stage, Sebastian looked out across the room and saw James stood leaning

169

on a fruit machine at the far end of the bar. His stomach tightened a little as the sight of him standing there suddenly reminded him of the importance of this show.

The man who'd volunteered came up the steps at the side of the stage. As he crossed to the chairs, it became apparent he was quite tall, standing a good couple of inches over Sebastian.

'What's your name, sir?' Sebastian asked.

'Nigel,' the man replied. He had a big grin on his face.

'Great. Thank you for volunteering, please take a seat.' Nigel did as he was asked. Sebastian moved along and stood behind the second chair. 'I'm now looking for someone who likes to travel, someone with a full book of air miles to their name.'

He looked out across the room and saw a man walking towards the stage waving an arm in the air. 'Yep, I'll have some o' that,' the man shouted out, scrambling up onto the stage from the front.

'Thank you. And what's your name, sir?'

'I'm Steve.'

'A round of applause for Steve please, ladies and gentlemen.' He waited for the short burst of clapping to cease. 'Fantastic. Thank you for coming up, Steve. If you'd like to take a seat please.' As the man sat down, Sebastian moved along and stood behind the final chair. 'My third volunteer needs to have a specific fear,' he announced. 'I'm looking for an arachnophobe. Someone with a genuine fear of spiders.' He stepped around the chair and scanned the room. All eyes were fixed on him, but nobody was coming forward. His heart began to beat faster, but the rising panic was quickly quelled by a kerfuffle going on at a table to his right. A group of friends were egging on one of their party to volunteer. The woman timidly stood up and stared at Sebastian. He

170

walked over and stood on the edge of the stage in front of her. 'Do you hate spiders, madam?'

'She's shit scared of them, mate!' one of the men at her table called out. The audience laughed and the poor girl looked as if she wanted the ground to open up.

Sebastian smiled at her warmly. 'Please, come up and join me up on the stage. He walked to the steps and held out his hand towards her. Hesitatingly, the woman came over and took Sebastian's hand and he guided her up the steps. 'What's your name?' he asked softly.

'Karen,' the woman replied shakily. 'You've not got spiders on stage have you?' she added warily.

Sebastian smiled. 'Honestly, you can relax. I assure you that you won't come to any harm.' Asking the audience to show Karen their appreciation, he led her across to the third chair and waited for her to sit down. 'Ladies and gentlemen, as you have seen, these three people have freely volunteered to participate in the show tonight. I do not know them. Can you all please confirm we have never met before?' The three of them nodded and Sebastian continued. 'Through the power of persuasion, I will infiltrate the subconscious minds of our volunteers, and for your entertainment I will take them to a different realm, way beyond the here and now.' He stepped swiftly across to the first chair and bent down close to Nigel. Speaking softly into the microphone, he said. 'Nigel. Listen to my voice. Very soon you will begin to feel sleepy. Your eyelids will become heavy and you will be unable to resist falling into a deep sleep.' He took a pace back as Nigel's head lolled.

A series of raucous claps rang out from a single member of the audience. Sebastian raised his finger to his lips. The culprit looked down into his lap with embarrassment. Sebastian returned his attention to Nigel.

171

'Nigel. You are a powerful rock god. You're on stage at Wembley Stadium with your band behind you. You are the ultimate frontman, the one and only Freddie Mercury! Who are you?'

Nigel mumbled 'I'm Freddie Mercury.'

'That's right. You will hear me count down from three to one, after which you will hear the drumming begin for the song *We Will Rock You* and you will give us the performance of your life. You will *own* this stage, Freddie Mercury. You will only cease your performance when you hear me shout stop and click my fingers. Nod if you understand.' Nigel nodded slowly. Sebastian stepped over to the box of props and pulled out a yellow jacket. He gently slipped it over Nigel's arms as he remained slumped in the chair; it was a tight fit, but Sebastian managed to get it on him quite swiftly.

He glanced up to see Tilly illuminated in the darkness by a thin shard of streetlight beaming in through the window. He smiled at her and she smiled back.

Confidence oozing out of his every pore, he stepped back and moved onto the second chair. 'Steve. I want you to listen to my voice. Very soon you will feel sleepy. Your eyelids will become heavy and you won't be able to resist falling into a deep sleep.' He stepped back a pace as Steve's head fell forward, his chin resting onto his chest. 'Steve. You are an airline pilot. You're at the helm of a Boeing 737 on a flight to Barbados. Who are you?' Steve didn't reply. 'Steve. Can you hear me?' There was still no reply. Sebastian leaned in and he could hear faint snoring. Perplexed, he tapped Steve on the shoulder and whispered. 'Steve. Are you awake?' Still nothing. He could feel himself starting to sweat. He looked over towards James, who was staring directly at him. Sebastian stood up straight. 'Oh well. Must be past this one's bedtime,' he

172

said throwing up his hands and shrugging. 'You snooze, you lose.'

The audience burst out laughing.

Sebastian quickly moved across to the third chair. 'Karen. You have a fear of spiders, is that correct?'

'It is,' she replied nervously.

'Okay. Listen to me very carefully. Listen to my voice. Very soon you will begin to feel sleepy. Your eyelids will become heavy and you won't be able to resist falling into a deep sleep.' Karen blinked a few times and her eyelids slowly closed. 'Spiders cannot harm you. They are small and fuzzy and actually very sweet. You will no longer find spiders frightening and if by chance you happen to see one...' – he paused, looked out at the audience and winked, raising a ripple of laughter – '...if you happen to see one,' he continued, 'you will not run away screaming. Repeat after me, Karen. Spiders will not hurt me. I am not afraid of them.'

Karen sleepily repeated, 'Spiders will not hurt me. I am not afraid of them.'

Sebastian leaned in close again, the microphone pressed between his mouth and Karen's head. 'You will hear me count down from three to one and when I get to one your fears will be completely forgotten until you hear me say stop and I click my fingers. Do you understand?' Karen nodded. Sebastian stepped over to the prop box and pulled something out, deftly popping it into his jacket pocket.

He moved in close behind Nigel, bent and counted down from three to one, then stepped swiftly over to the front of the stage. 'Ladies and gentlemen, I want you all to follow my lead.' He glanced over at the sound engineer in the wings and nodded. As the introduction to *We Will*

173

Rock You started, Sebastian stamped his feet twice and clapped once. The audience immediately joined in.

With a start, Nigel jumped to his feet. He threw his fist high up in the air and began strutting round the stage. With his chest pushed out, he half shouted, half sang, 'Buddy, you're a boy, make a big noise, playing in the street, gonna be a big man someday, you got mud on your face, you big disgrace, somebody better put you back into your place.' He turned to face the crowd. 'Singing we will, we will rock you!' The audience enthusiastically sang it back at him.

Sebastian watched the show play out and smiled inwardly. *This is going really well*, he thought. He looked across to James and was thrilled to see that he appeared to be enjoying it.

When the track came to an end, Nigel came to a stop, his face red and sweat dripping from his brow. He stood stock still in the middle of the stage as if in a state of suspended animation. Sebastian walked over and said softly, 'You may stop now.' He guided Nigel to his chair and gently eased him down onto the seat. 'A round of applause for Nigel, please.' The room responded enthusiastically.

Sebastian walked past Steve – 'Still in The Land of Nod,' he quipped, and the audience laughed – and stopped behind Karen. Standing at the back of her chair, he pulled out a large, very realistic-looking rubber tarantula from his jacket pocket and held it aloft above Karen's head, drawing gasps from the audience. Returning the spider to his pocket, he stepped around to the side of Karen's chair and spoke softly, keeping the microphone close to his mouth. 'Karen. I am going to count backwards from three to one. When you awaken you will notice that there is a big spider on your knee.' Sebastian retrieved the rubber

174

spider from his pocket and placed it on her left knee. 'Remember, this spider cannot harm you. You do not fear spiders at all. Three. Two. One.'

Karen's eyes sprung open. She blinked for a moment and then caught sight of the tarantula sitting on her knee. There was no reaction. The room was completely silent and almost everyone in the audience was leaning forward in their seats waiting to see what would happen next.

Sebastian put his hand on Karen's shoulder. 'Karen.' She slowly turned her head to look at him. 'There is a massive spider on your knee. How do you feel about that?'

Karen looked away and stared at the tarantula for a few moments. 'I feel absolutely fine. Spiders cannot harm you. Spiders are cute and fuzzy.'

A man in the audience sniggered; it was one of Karen's friends.

Sebastian spoke again. 'Can you pick the spider up, Karen?'

She turned her head again and looked up at Sebastian. 'Sure,' she said with complete calm and assurance.

'Go ahead,' Sebastian prompted.

Karen reached out and paused, her hand hovering an inch or two above the spider. Her eyelids fluttered for a second, then she smiled and very gently lifted the spider from her knee and held it up for Sebastian to see.

'Well done, Karen. You can put it back down now.' She responded by placing the spider into her lap, then looked up at Sebastian as if awaiting further instruction. 'You can stop now.' As the words left his lips, Karen's head fell to one side and rested on her right shoulder.

Sebastian turned to the audience and held up his hands. 'Ladies and gentlemen, a round of applause for Karen, please.' The room went wild. Clapping, cheering and whistling rang out throughout the room. Sebastian looked out at Tilly, who had a smile a mile wide on her face and was clapping furiously. Through the din he heard a man shout out, 'Fuck me, he's cured the woman's fear of spiders in five minutes. He's way better than that McKenna tosspot!'

Lapping up the applause, Sebastian moved to the front of the stage and took a bow. The whooping and whistling was almost deafening. 'Thank you!' He took another deep bow. When he straightened up he caught sight of the sound engineer out of the corner of his eye gesturing for him to wrap up the show. He stepped back around behind the chairs and individually clicked his fingers beside the ears of his three guests. 'Thank you very much for being a part of my show. You've all been great. You may now go back and join your friends.'

The volunteers rose and shuffled forward to leave the stage. 'Oh, Steve,' Sebastian said, placing a friendly hand on the man's shoulder. Steve stopped. 'You can come and collect your underpants from me later!' Sebastian said, which earned him another deafening round of applause accompanied by raucous laughter. Steve looked a bit sheepish as he felt around his bottom and realised he was being ribbed. He gave Sebastian a sarcastic smile.

The sound engineer hit play on his desk and, giving the audience an appreciative wave, Sebastian left the stage to the sound of the Timberlake track.

Tilly pushed through the crowd to make her way to the door beside the stage. She opened it and saw Sebastian standing over by the far wall drying off his neck with a towel. 'You were amazing!' she exclaimed, running over and throwing her arms around him. Sebastian hugged her close and they kissed.

'Ja. Your lady friend is correct.'

176

Sebastian and Tilly broke their embrace and turned to see who had spoken.

'Hallo. I am Zayn Bauer.' The man held out his hand and Sebastian shook it warmly. He spoke perfect English, but with a very slight hint of an accent. 'May I?' he asked as he moved towards Tilly. Sebastian was momentarily thrown, unsure what Bauer was asking permission for. Before he could say anything, without waiting for an answer, Bauer took hold of Tilly's hand and kissed her once on each cheek. 'Charmed.' Tilly stepped back and forced a smile, unable to conceal her surprise. 'I was watching you from the wings,' Bauer said. 'You gave a very impressive show.'

Sebastian smiled. 'Thank you.'

'I have rarely seen such a positive reaction for my support acts. You are a very hard act to follow,' Bauer added with a throaty chuckle. Sebastian felt himself blush. He wasn't sure how to respond so he simply smiled and thanked the man again. 'You will remove your things from the stage now, please, so my assistant can get it ready for me.' Again, without waiting for a reply, he nodded politely at Tilly, turned on his heels and walked off along the corridor and into his dressing room.

Tilly looked at Sebastian and shrugged.

'Well, he was a bit, er… strange,' Sebastian said.

'Who cares?' Tilly replied. Her eyes were sparkling. 'This is *your* night!' She grabbed Sebastian's face in her hands and gave him a big kiss. 'C'mon superstar, let's go get your props. Then I think you deserve a well-earned drinky!'

They walked out onto the stage behind the closed curtains and retrieved the box of props. The sound engineer had moved the chairs and was rearranging the stage ready for Bauer. Sebastian stepped back offstage and emptied the contents of the box into his shopping bag. He slid the box under the sound man's table and called over to him. 'Cheers, Paul.' The man looked up and gave Sebastian a quick thumbs-up.

As they stepped through the door to return to their friends, they were mobbed by a small group of people from the audience, who rudely pushed past Tilly to get at Sebastian. She managed to relieve him of his bag and, laughing, she said, 'I'll leave you to speak to your fans. Would you like me to get you something a bit stronger to drink this time?'

Sebastian looked distinctly out of his depth as the people surrounded him. 'Yes please,' he replied, as Tilly was swept aside in the melee. 'Could I have a vodka and Diet Coke?' he shouted. 'I won't be long!'

Tilly nodded and headed for the bar, leaving Sebastian to contend with his first taste of fame. He smiled awkwardly at the man who had grabbed hold of his hand and was shaking it vigorously. 'Alright mate?' Sebastian said, releasing himself from the man's grip.

'That was absolutely blindin', son! I never really believed all that hypnosis bollocks before, but now I've seen it wiv me own eyes… well, I'm just gobsmacked!'

Sebastian smiled appreciatively. He could see an eager queue of people forming behind the man, all seemingly wanting to speak to *him*. It was almost as if he were dreaming.

'Seriously, son,' the man continued, 'it's the best fing I've ever seen in this club, and I don't mind tellin' ya I've bin comin' here 20 years or more.'

'Thank you very much. I'm so glad you enjoyed the show.'

The man grabbed his hand again and shook it hard, before being pushed aside as another man forced his way

178

between them, breaking the handshake. ''Ere, can you cure any phobia?' he asked.

'Well, it's not really a cure,' Sebastian said. 'You see, while...'

The man cut him off. 'It's just I've got this fear, see, and I don't wanna go down the docs with it cos it's a bit like... kind of sensitive, if you know what I mean.'

Sebastian placed his hands on the man's shoulders and leant in so he could speak discreetly. 'I'm sorry. My act is purely for entertainment. If you have a serious concern, I really think you should speak to your GP.'

The look of hope on the man's face faded as Sebastian patted him on the back and started to move forward. He was promptly intercepted by a young woman wearing a tight-fitting tee-shirt. 'Hi, luv. D'ya think I could get your autograph?'

'Yes, sure,' Sebastian said hesitatingly. He could hardly believe what was happening. It felt surreal. 'Do you have a pen?'

The woman pulled a sharpie from her handbag. 'I think you're really sexy,' she said, giggling as Sebastian blushed and fumbled with the lid of the pen.

As he pulled it off, it shot out of his fingers into the air and dropped down amongst the feet of the crowd. 'Er. Do you have some paper or a beer mat or something?' he asked.

Grinning, the woman shook her head.

'Well, what do you want me to sign?' he asked.

'These!' she exclaimed, lifting her top up over her head. For a moment Sebastian froze. Then, while the woman struggled to get the neck of her tee-shirt up over her head, he seized the opportunity to get away, apologetically pushing his way through the other people to go and join his friends.

'Here comes Harry Houdini,' Mark said scornfully as Sebastian approached them.

Katie rolled her eyes. 'Houdini was an escapologist, you plank!'

'That was really great!' Joshua said. 'And I think it's safe to say everyone else here thought so too.'

Sebastian smiled. 'Thanks. Glad you enjoyed it. I have to say, I froze for a moment there when that Steve guy didn't react!'

'You covered it well, Seb,' Katie said. She laughed. 'When you said he could have his pants back later his face was a picture.'

Sebastian was just about to reply when loud music filled the room and the lights went out.

As the curtains opened and Zayn Bauer stepped out onto the stage, a single cheer rang out from the table at the front; it was the old man Mark had been haranguing. He got to his feet, clapping for all he was worth and looking back over his shoulder at the audience behind him, proudly exclaiming, 'Das ist mein sohn!'

The music ceased and the small ripple of applause in the room died away. Bauer moved forward and took a bow.

Sebastian stopped talking and turned to face the stage. The introductory music ceased abruptly and something more dramatic started. The magician began his act with three illuminated rings, which he was moving rhythmically to the soundtrack. He held them aloft, swiftly rotating them in his hands to show that they were solid, then with a flick of his wrist they linked up. Sebastian noticed that a lot of people were talking amongst themselves and paying very little attention to what was happening on the stage. As Sebastian watched Bauer spinning around on the spot and flipping the rings high up into the air, a woman appeared and stopped right in front of him, blocking his view of the stage.

'S'cuse me,' she said loudly, staring at him intently. 'Can I ask you a question?'

'Sure,' Sebastian replied, only half focussing on her whilst trying the watch the performance over her shoulder. Bauer had just introduced three more rings and was seamlessly linking and separating them again in time to the music.

Oblivious to the fact she didn't have Sebastian's full attention, the woman continued. 'It's my fella, he snores, like *really* loud.' She proceeded to demonstrate the sound.

Up on the stage, Bauer was momentarily distracted and looked directly at Sebastian. Embarrassed, he hissed at the woman, 'Not now, please!'

She ignored him. 'Fing is, I was wondering, could you hypnotise him so he don't do it no more?'

Sebastian put his hand on the woman's elbow – 'Come with me,' he whispered loudly and guided her across the room towards the doors. Gesturing for her to follow him, he stepped outside into the car park. 'Hi,' he said, smiling politely at the woman. 'I'm really sorry. My act is purely for entertainment, I am not a medical hypnotist.'

'But I saw what you did on that stage. You made that woman hold a spider after she'd told everybody she was frightened of them. You cured her of her fear! Why can't you do something simple like stop my husband from snoring? We'll pay you, of course.'

Sebastian held up a hand. 'It's not about money. It's just not what I do. That woman's phobia was only temporarily allayed. If she finds a spider in the bath tonight, I guarantee you she'll be screaming the house down. It's not a cure, it's just a momentary lapse of consciousness during which people become pliable and I do the moulding.

The woman looked confused. 'So you won't help me?'

'Not won't. *Can't*. The long and short of it is I'm not able to cure phobias or snoring or anything else like that. I'm sorry.' He turned away and walked back towards the club leaving the dumfounded woman standing in the car park.

As he walked through the main entrance, James appeared and stopped him. 'Sebastian! That was sensational! A really great show. And I've just been speaking to the club owner, he's really pleased too.'

Sebastian smiled. 'Thanks, James. I'm over the moon everyone enjoyed it.'

'Just one thing though,' James continued. 'What happened with the second man?'

Sebastian's smile faded. 'Oh. Well, sometimes people don't react. Not everyone is susceptible to hypnosis. Also, when he got up on stage, he reeked of alcohol. He was definitely three sheets to the wind and I guess when I put him into a sleep, he just stayed there.'

James laughed and patted him on the shoulder. 'Well, you handled it like a true professional. Honestly, Sebastian, that was one of the best shows I've seen in a long time. Mr McCleary is going to be very pleased when I tell him.' Sebastian's smile returned. 'You go on back to your friends now. I'll be in touch real soon.' He patted Sebastian on the shoulder again – 'Really, first class stuff.' – and strolled out into the night.

Sebastian walked back inside and joined Tilly, who slipped her arm around his waist, and together they watched the remainder of the show.

Bauer was ploughing through his tricks and Sebastian observed that the confidence he'd shown them backstage was waning as he fought to keep the audience engaged.

The first half of the show drew to a close and Bauer took a bow. Sebastian gently nudged Tilly and began to clap enthusiastically. She joined in too and soon the rest of the room followed suit. Bauer acknowledged the applause with a curt bow and walked off the stage as the curtains closed for the interval. The house lights went on and music started playing. The hubbub in the room increased even more as people tried to talk over the sound of David Bowie's *Let's Dance*.

'I'm getting myself another beer,' Mark declared.

'Don't you think you've had enough already?' Katie asked scornfully.

'Who are you, my friggin' mother?!' he snapped back at her.

'Well one of us has to be mature. Have you forgotten we're taking the bus home?'

'And?!'

'*And* the last time you got rat-arsed the driver wouldn't let us on and I ended up having to prop you up whilst we walked three miles in the rain.'

Mark waved a dismissive hand at her. 'Whatever,' he said, and sauntered off towards the bar.

Katie sighed. 'Seriously, I've had it up to here with him!'

Pete stepped up behind her and snaked his arm tightly around her waist. 'Don't you go gettin' upset, little lady. You're way too good for that raasclaat!'

'Yeah, damned right I am!'

Clutching a pint of beer, Mark returned from the bar and spotted Pete with his arm around Katie. 'What the fuck?' He spat the words out.

183

Pete grinned. 'Well, if you can't take care of your lady, pussy 'ole, someone else gonna step up, ain't it!'

Katie wormed free of Pete's arm and stepped away from him. 'Er, *what*?!' She glared at him. 'I can take care of myself, thank you very much!'

His face like thunder, Mark stepped forward. 'What did you call me?!'

'Pussy 'ole,' Pete repeated with a broad grin.

Mark raised his fist and was about to throw a punch when Jordan stepped between them. 'Enough!'

Pete kissed his teeth. 'Let the big man roll, see what he's got.'

Jordan looked angrily at his father. 'I won't have you brawling and ruin the night for everyone. Calm the fuck down or piss off home!'

Pete was clearly taken aback by his son's outburst. 'All right, boy. Cool your jets, innit.'

Mark was still stood poised ready to fight. Jordan turned to face him. 'Enough, yeah?'

With evident reluctance, Mark dropped his fist and swallowed a large mouthful of beer. 'Whatever.'

Sebastian leant over and spoke in Tilly's ear. 'Wanna get out of here?'

'I'm ready if you are.'

'Yeah, it's been a long day.'

They quickly said their goodnights and Sebastian picked up his shopping bag. He took hold of Tilly's hand and they made their way to the exit.

CHAPTER 13

As Tilly backed her car out of the parking space and turned the car around, the headlights briefly illuminated someone standing over near a row of dustbins. His shoulders were hunched and he was smoking a cigarette. He squinted and raised a hand to shield his eyes from the light.

'There's that Zayn fella,' Tilly said.

'He looks a bit hacked off,' Sebastian replied.

'Probably because a certain someone upstaged him tonight,' Tilly said with a grin.

'Oh, God, really? I hope not. That wasn't my intention.'

'Don't be daft. You rocked that stage tonight and that's nothing to be ashamed of.' Tilly pulled out of the car park and turned onto the main road. The radio in the car was playing quietly. Sebastian looked out of the window into the darkness, replaying the evening's events over in his mind.

Tilly pulled up at a set of traffic lights and glanced at him. 'Penny for them.'

Sebastian looked over. 'Huh?'

'I said penny for them.'

'Oh, I was just thinking about tonight. It did go okay, didn't it?'

Tilly selected gear and they continued on. 'It was better than okay, silly. You were fantastic. I felt so proud watching you up there. I saw you talking to that James guy. I hadn't noticed him arrive. I assume he saw the whole act?'

'Yeah.'

'Was he impressed?'

'He was. *Very*. He said he'd be in touch soon. I must admit, I got a real buzz out of being up there tonight. I just hope he finds me a few more gigs like that.'

'I've no doubt he will. I think you'll be in very high demand.'

Sebastian smiled and rested his head on the glass, idly watching the cars pass by until his eyes slowly closed and he nodded off.

The gentle bump of the car as Tilly pulled up onto the kerb to park woke him with a start. 'Oh, sorry,' he said, sitting up sharply. 'I must have dozed off.'

Tilly smiled. 'Don't apologise. You must've needed it.' She leant over to give him a kiss. 'Anyway. Home sweet home.'

The pavement outside Sebastian's flat was still heaving with people. A few doors down, there was a late night mini-mart, with customers bustling around the colourful display of fruit and vegetables laid out on pavement stalls, and they could hear faint music coming from the pub across the road.

'Is it always this busy here so late at night?' Tilly asked.

'Yeah, pretty much. The pub closes at midnight, but I don't know about the mini-mart. It seems to be permanently open to me.'

Tilly yawned. 'Ooh, sorry. Looks like you're not the only one who's tired.'

'Did you want to come up for a coffee?' Sebastian asked.

Tilly nodded. 'That might not be a bad idea actually. Hopefully it'll wake me up a bit for the drive home.'

They climbed out and Sebastian politely held the outside door to the building open for Tilly. As they

186

ascended the stairs, loud music and the acrid stench of cannabis greeted them. 'I'm sorry about that,' Sebastian said apologetically as they reached the front door of his flat. 'It's my neighbour. I'd love to know how he affords that stuff.' There was a note of annoyance in his voice. 'He hasn't done a day's work in the three years I've been here, and all he does all day is listen to that racket and smoke dope!' He opened the front door and stepped aside to let Tilly in. 'Brr, it's a bit chilly in here. Get comfy on the sofa. I'll whack the heating up and get the kettle on.'

'Can I do anything?' Tilly asked.

'No, no, it's all in hand. Put your feet up. You can stick the telly on if you want.'

Tilly crossed the hallway into the lounge and settled down on the sofa. She reached across to a table lamp and switched it on.

Sebastian called out from the kitchen. 'Do you take sugar in your coffee?'

'Two please.' Tilly called back. She surveyed the room. It was spotlessly tidy and she smiled as she recalled the conversation she'd had with Sebastian earlier in the week. She noticed a spider plant on a stand in the corner, its leaves hanging limp and pale. 'I think your plant needs some water,' she called out.

'Huh?' Sebastian responded.

Tilly raised her voice a little. 'I said your plant...' She trailed off as Sebastian appeared in the doorway.

'My plant?'

'Your plant needs some water.' Tilly pointed to the spider plant.

Sebastian chuckled. 'Oh, that old thing. It's tough as old boots. I've been trying to kill it off for years, but it just keeps going.' He put the mugs of coffee down on the table and slumped into his armchair.

187

Tilly raised her eyebrows. 'Kill it off?' She got up and inspected the sad looking plant more closely. 'Why would you want to do that?' She picked it up, went out to the kitchen and ran the tap over it. Returning to the living room she held it up. 'Poor little thing. Is daddy Seb being mean to you?'

Sebastian laughed. 'You can have it if you want it. My Nan brought it round as a housewarming present. When I remember to water it I do, but to be honest I don't really want it.'

'You do know they purify the air?' Tilly said.

'Do they?'

'Oh yeah. They're great plants to have around the house.' She placed the pot back on the stand and stepped across to the table. Picking up her mug, she took a sip. 'Mmm that's nice'. She perched on the arm of Sebastian's chair. Resting her mug on her left knee, she reached over and started to fiddle with his hair. She smiled at him. 'You really have got lovely hair.' He shivered a little as her fingers touched his scalp. 'I know I said it earlier, but I'm so proud of you.'

Sebastian looked up at her, his blue eyes sparkling in the half light from the lamp. 'Thank you. But you know I couldn't have done it without you.'

Tilly continued to twirl his curly locks around her fingers. 'It's funny, you know. I watched all those people cheering and clapping for you and I was just bursting with pride. I don't think I've ever felt like that before.'

Sebastian hooked his arm around her waist. Tilly leant over, set her cup down on the table, and allowed him to pull her gently onto his lap. 'When I was up on the stage, I looked over towards you,' he said. 'And seeing you standing there with your pretty smile made me want to

188

give the best performance I could. It didn't matter who else was there, all I could think of was you.'

Tilly slipped her arms around his shoulders and they kissed. She moved her fingers up and down his neck and around his earlobe as the kiss intensified. Suddenly Sebastian pulled away. 'What's the matter?' Tilly asked, slightly concerned.

Sebastian eased himself out from beneath her and stood up. Tilly watched him curiously as he began to pace the room. 'The thing is...' He paused beside the spider plant, his back to her, and reached out and nervously twiddled the end of one of the wiry stems. 'The thing is, I haven't had a girlfriend for quite a long time.' Tilly sat back in the armchair and listened. 'I really like you,' he continued, 'and I'm frightened if we go on it will... well, stir certain things, and then I'm going to want you to stay, and...' He was startled as he felt Tilly step up behind him.

She reached round and took his hand in hers, leading him to turn and face her. '*Do* you want me to stay?'

'Of course I do, but...'

Tilly put her index finger to Sebastian's lips. 'No buts. I'd love to stay over.'

Sebastian took hold of Tilly's hands. 'Are you sure?'

She smiled and kissed Sebastian on the lips. 'Come on,' she whispered, and turning away, she led him towards the bedroom.

As she took hold of the handle on the bedroom door Sebastian snaked around past her. 'Er, just one minute.' He pushed the door open just enough to squeeze through and pushed it shut behind him, leaving Tilly standing in the hallway. She smiled to herself and stifled a little giggle with the back of her hand.

Sebastian switched on the light and hurriedly bent down to retrieve something from under the bed. He stuffed a pair of underpants and a lone sock into one of the drawers and let out a small sigh as he hunted round for the other one; it was nowhere to be seen and he gave up. Quickly checking his reflection in the mirror, he nervously called out, 'Okay, you can come in now.'

Tilly pushed open the door and stepped into the room. Sebastian was standing on the opposite side of the bed with his hands thrust deep into his trouser pockets. She stepped over to the bedside lamp and switched it on, then flicked the main celling light off. 'So?' she said to Sebastian. He looked back at her blankly. 'Are you just going to stand there all night like some kind of sentry guard?'

Sebastian had the look of a lost child on his face. Tilly sat down on the side of the bed and kicked off her shoes. She removed her cardigan and plumped up the pillow behind her. Swinging her legs around and up onto the bed, she straightened her dress and shuffled herself upright. 'Are you going to sit down?' She patted the bed beside her.

'Yeah, yeah, of course,' Sebastian said as casually as he could, hoping against hope that his face wasn't betraying his inner turmoil. He stepped up to the bed and launched himself onto it backside first, bouncing Tilly as the mattress springs moved under the weight. Leaning forward, he moved the pillow up behind his back and the pair of them sat for a few moments in silence.

Tilly reached across and took hold of Sebastian's hand. He rolled on to his side to look at her. 'This has been one of the best few weeks of my whole life,' he said softly.

Tilly smiled and squeezed his hand. 'Mine too.' She craned her head upwards to give him a kiss. As the embrace became more passionate, she unbuttoned Sebastian's shirt. She moved her hand slowly inside,

190

stroking his chest with her fingers and then, moving her hand around to his back, she gently ran her nails up and down the nape of his neck. Sebastian shifted and with his right hand he caressed Tilly's face and neck. She sat up and took hold of Sebastian's shirt, easing it up and over his arms, then turning her back to him she pulled her hair away from her neck. 'Could you undo me?'

Sebastian fumbled with the tiny zip pull; his hands were shaking and it was difficult to see in the dim light. He finally managed to grip it between his finger and thumb and slowly pulled it down. Tilly stood up and removed her dress. As Sebastian gazed at her stood there in only her underwear, he could feel his heart beating out of his chest. She lay back down on the bed and rolled towards Sebastian, and they resumed their embrace, holding each other tightly and kissing passionately.

Sebastian lifted his head . 'Do you think you should call your Mum to let her know you won't be home tonight?'

Tilly was undoing the belt around Sebastian's waist. 'She'll be sound asleep by now,' she replied, slightly breathlessly. She flipped open the buckle and undid Sebastian's trousers. She could feel him trembling, but so as not to embarrass him she decided it was best not to say anything.

Sebastian got up, hooked his foot around his shoes and flicked them off one at a time, then slipped out of his trousers, while Tilly rolled onto her side and removed her underwear. She turned off the bedside lamp and pushed the duvet to the end of the bed. As she rolled back towards Sebastian, she cried out, 'Ow, what's *that*?!'

Sebastian tried to see, but there was barely any light now. Tilly moved and pulled out a balled-up sock from

191

under her ribs. She threw it onto the floor. 'What was it?' Sebastian asked.

'I think it was a sock,' she exclaimed, giggling.

Sebastian was suddenly grateful for the darkness; at least it was hiding his crimson cheeks. 'Sorry!'

Tilly propped herself up on her elbows and, running her fingers through Sebastian's hair, she found his lips again. They kissed fervently, each of them surrendering to the moment, their bodies and souls entwining as they lost themselves in the blissful feeling of togetherness.

After they had made love, Sebastian lay on his back with his arms wrapped around Tilly, who slowly fell asleep in his warm embrace. He stared at the ceiling through the darkness for ages, unable to sleep as he basked in the afterglow of what had undoubtably been the best day of his life.

CHAPTER 14

A number 86 bus pulled up at the stop just outside Sebastian's flat and sat with its engine running for over five minutes. The low rumble of the diesel vehicle permeated through the thin walls of the flat and as it noisily revved and pulled away Sebastian awoke. He hadn't pulled the curtains the night before and light streamed in through the window. He squinted and shielded his eyes as his mind came into focus and returned to the night before. He turned his head to see Tilly on her side with her back to him, her hair laying in neat strands over her shoulders and down her back. *It wasn't a dream*, he thought. As carefully as he could, he rolled over and curled his arm around her waist beneath the duvet. She didn't stir at all and before long the soft rhythmic sound of her breathing lulled Sebastian back to sleep.

An hour later they woke simultaneously to the sound of a phone ringing. 'Ah sorry, that's mine,' Sebastian said groggily. 'I should have switched it to silent.' Tilly rolled over onto her back and he leant over to kiss her. The phone continued ringing. 'Morning.' Sebastian said with a smile. 'You look absolutely gorgeous,' he added.

Tilly raised her eyebrows. 'Aren't you going to get that?'

'Nah. If it's important, they'll ring back.' Sebastian pulled her closer, feeling the warmth of her skin against his chest. As he kissed her again the ringing stopped. 'Did you sleep alright?'

Tilly yawned. 'Yeah, I did actually. You have a very comfortable bed.'

Sebastian looked into her eyes. 'You are *so* beautiful.' Their lips met again, but as the passion intensified Sebastian's phone started to ring again.

'You'd better answer it,' Tilly said. 'It might be important.'

Sebastian swung his legs out and bent over to retrieve his trousers from the floor. He coyly slipped them on before standing up and reaching for his phone. As he picked it up, it stopped ringing. He tapped the screen and the name of the missed call notification read KATIE. Sebastian's brow furrowed. 'It's Katie. I wonder what she wants this early on Sunday?'

'Call her back and find out,' Tilly said.

Just as Sebastian was about to do exactly that, it rang again. He pressed the answer icon. 'Hi Katie.'

'Oh, thank God,' Katie said. She sounded worried.

'Is everything alright?' Sebastian asked.

'Not really, no. Is Tilly with you?'

Sebastian suddenly felt embarrassed. He glanced at Tilly. She was sitting up against the pillow with the duvet covering her chest. 'Er... Yeah, she is,' Sebastian said. 'Why?'

Katie sighed loudly on the other end. 'Could I speak to her?'

To Sebastian she sounded on the brink of tears. He frowned. 'Of course.' He held out the phone to Tilly. 'Katie wants to speak to you.'

'Me?' Looking suitably confused, Tilly reached up and took the phone from him. 'Hello?'

Sebastian watched her face while she listened and felt his stomach tighten as her expression changed from one of confusion to shock, and the warm glow on her cheeks seemed to drain before his eyes. He quickly moved round the bed and sat down beside her.

194

'Okay. Thanks for letting me know.' Those were the only words Tilly uttered before ending the call and slowly placing the phone down on the bed.

Sebastian placed his hand over hers. 'Is everything okay?' Even as the words left his lips, he knew it was a stupid question; everything was patently far from okay. Tilly remained silent. 'Please tell me what's happened.' He squeezed her hand. His eyes were filled with concern.

Tilly stared at him for a moment. 'It's my Mum,' she said quietly. 'She was admitted to hospital late last night and...' Her voice became choked. 'She... she died.'

Sebastian's eyes widened in shock. 'What?!'

'Katie said Keira called her this morning at the animal sanctuary. They've all been trying to get hold of me.' She put her hand to her mouth. 'Oh my God! Mum called me last night and I ignored it!' She started to sob.

Sebastian shuffled up close and put his arm around her. She buried her head in his chest and he could feel the cold wetness of her tears trickling down his bare torso. He hugged her tight. 'I'm so, *so* sorry,' he whispered, barely able to contain his own tears. Tilly was shivering between deep sobs. Sebastian reached behind him and pulled the duvet over. Wrapping it around her, he held her to him tightly, gently stroking her hair. He was completely lost for words. He knew anything he said would sound empty and pointless so he just held her close and said nothing. They stayed that way for almost half an hour until Tilly sat up, her face strewn with tears and mascara running down her cheeks.

'Would you like a cup of tea?' Sebastian asked.

She nodded. 'Please. Is it okay if I have a shower?' she added solemnly.

'Of course.' Sebastian went to the airing cupboard and pulled out a towel. 'Here, use this. It's clean. There's shampoo and shower gel on the shelf.'

Tilly pushed aside the duvet and stood up, taking the towel from Sebastian and wrapping it around herself. She walked slowly past him and into the bathroom, closing the door behind her.

Sebastian looked up to the ceiling and ran his hands through his hair. He let out a big sigh. 'Oh God,' he said under his breath. His heart was breaking for Tilly, but he simply didn't know what to do or say. He quickly made up the bed and picked up his shirt and underwear from the floor. Unplugging his phone charger, he stepped out of the bedroom and paused momentarily outside the bathroom door. He could hear the shower running. He went through to the lounge and plugged the phone in beside the television, then he went out to the kitchen. Filling the kettle, he made two teas and heaped a spoonful of sugar into both; he had heard that sweet tea was good for shock, and as pathetic as it seemed it was all he could think to do right now to try and help. He took the drinks through to the lounge and set them down on the table, then he sat down on the sofa, biting at his lip as he drummed his fingers on the arm. He got up again, crossed to the window and looked down at the street below. The sun was shining brightly and a throng of Sunday morning shoppers were merrily going about their business, all of them oblivious to the awful news that had just rolled in like a dark, violent storm in the flat overhead. He rested his palms on the window sill and stared up at the cloudless blue sky, and a single tear trickled down his cheek. He quickly wiped it away and returned to the sofa where he sat and stared at the swirling steam rising from the two mugs of tea, his eyes following it as it snaked up and

196

evaporated in the air. Soon there was no more steam and he looked over through the lounge door towards the bathroom. He suddenly wasn't sure how long he'd been sitting there. It felt as if Tilly had been in the bathroom a long time. Nervously fiddling with his fingers, he got up and walked out to the bathroom door. He couldn't hear the water running any more. He pressed his ear right up against the door; there was nothing but silence. He thought for a moment, biting his bottom lip, then he tapped lightly on the door. 'Tilly. Are you okay?' There was no reply. He tapped again. 'Tilly. I'm coming in okay?' He pushed the handle down and with trepidation opened the door.

Tilly was sat naked on the floor, her knees pulled up to her chest and her back against the shower door. She looked utterly bereft. Her wet hair was dangling down over her face and Sebastian saw that the towel he had given her was unused, folded neatly on the lid of the toilet. He quickly grabbed it and knelt down beside her, lovingly wrapping it around her and pulling her close. She started to cry. 'Oh, please don't cry,' Sebastian said and he hugged her tightly.

'What am I going to do?' Tilly said between breathless sobs. 'I should have taken her call. She needed me and I just ignored her.'

Sebastian closed his eyes, desperately searching for the right words. 'You weren't to know. Don't blame yourself.'

Tilly was sobbing uncontrollably now. 'But I do. I *do* blame myself.' She looked up at Sebastian, her blue eyes wet with tears. 'She tried to reach me and I just ignored her.'

Sebastian gently carefully pushed the strands of damp hair out of her face. 'You didn't know.'

Tilly sighed and her expression turned to anger. 'I was out having fun and all the while she was in hospital

197

dying.' She banged her fist down on the hard tiles and screamed, 'I should have taken her call!'

Sebastian was momentarily taken aback by the rage in her voice, but he responded in the only way he knew how; he wrapped his arms around her and hugged her tight. Tilly submitted to his embrace and she lay helplessly in his arms like a broken doll. 'Come on. It's cold in here,' Sebastian said. He gently helped her up onto her feet and took his dressing gown down from the back of the bathroom door. He slipped it over her shoulders and led her through to the lounge. Guiding her onto the sofa, he handed her one of the mugs of tea, but she pushed it away. 'Just try and have a little, it should be just warm now.' Sebastian smiled encouragingly and handed the mug back to her.

Tilly wrapped her hands around it and held it for a moment before placing her lips on the rim and taking a small sip. She put the mug down on the table. 'What do I do now?'

Sebastian took hold of her hand. 'Whatever you want to do. I'm right here beside you.'

Tilly squeezed his fingers tight. 'Thank you. I guess I should call my sister. Or should I go to the hospital?' She looked at him for an answer.

Sebastian felt so useless. He really didn't know what was the right thing to suggest. After a moment he said, 'It might be best to call your sister.' He looked at Tilly hoping that she would agree.

She took another sip of tea. 'Yeah. She's probably at the hospital with Mum.' She cradled the mug in her hands.

A few minutes passed in silence.

'Shall I get your phone?' Sebastian asked gingerly.

Tilly stared across the room, leaving him waiting for an answer. After what felt like an eternity she sighed. 'Yeah.

I'd better call Grace.' She put the mug down and went out to the hall where she retrieved her handbag and rooted about inside for her phone. She tapped it and the screen lit up. She returned to the sofa. 'Blimey!' she exclaimed as she sat down. '16 missed calls!' She looked at the notifications; most of the missed calls were from Grace. There were a number of text messages too, also from Grace. Sebastian watched her as she silently scrolled through them. As she let out a big sigh and shook her head, her phone made a small bleeping noise. 'Have you got an iPhone charger? My battery is almost flat.'

'Yes. Hang on,' Sebastian said, walking over to a charger that was plugged into the wall. He unplugged his own phone and held out his hand. 'If you give me your phone, I'll plug it in. You can use mine to call Grace.' Tilly handed him her phone and he inserted the charger. He sat back down, unlocked his own phone and handed it to her. She took it and stared at it for a while.

'There's no hurry if you're not ready,' Sebastian said reassuringly.

'No, I'd best call her.' Tilly went to dial the number but the screen was black. 'Oh, it's locked itself. Here.' Sebastian took it from her, unlocked it and handed it back. She tapped in the number and waited as the phone rang.

'Hello?' a voice on the other end said. It was Grace's husband. 'Hi Jason, it's Tilly. Can I speak to Grace please?'

'Oh, hi. She's in with your Mum at the moment. I'm sat outside. She left her bag and phone with me. I can get her to call you back.'

Tilly thought for a moment. 'No, don't worry. I'm going to make my way to the hospital. Is she in King Georges or Queens?'

199

'She's in the chapel of rest. They moved her there this morning.'

'Oh… so where's that?'

'Ilford. Chapel Road.'

Sebastian could hear what Jason was saying and he scribbled down Chapel Rd Ilford on a piece of paper.

'Okay,' Tilly said. 'I'll make my way there now. Thanks, Jason.'

'No worries. See you in a bit.'

Tilly ended the call and handed the phone back to Sebastian. 'I'm going to get dressed, then I'm going to join Grace. They moved Mum to the chapel of rest at…'

'I heard,' Sebastian said. 'I wrote it down.' He handed her the scrap of paper. 'I'll go and get dressed too and I'll come with you.'

'Oh, no, you really don't have to. I'll be fine.'

'Nonsense.' He got up and kissed her lightly on the cheek. 'Just give me five minutes and I'll be ready. I need to use the bathroom quickly, so you can get dressed first.'

*

As they stepped out of the car at the chapel of rest, Tilly faltered. 'I really don't think I can do this,' she said.

Sebastian closed the passenger side door and walked round. He took Tilly in his arms and hugged her, kissing her softly on the top of her head. 'There's no rush. We don't have to go straight in if you don't want to. There's a bench over there by the door. Let's sit for a bit until you're ready.'

Tilly closed the car door and remote locked it. A huge grey oppressive tower block loomed over the chapel, casting a shadow across the car park. The sky was a bright blue and there wasn't a cloud in sight, yet everything surrounding the chapel felt cold and dark. Tilly eyed the bench 'No. I'll be fine. You can wait outside for me if you'd rather not come in. It's not like you knew my Mum or anything.'

Sebastian put his arm around her shoulder. 'Would you prefer me to stay outside? I'm happy to come in, but I don't want to be in the way.'

Tilly smiled up at him. 'You could never be in the way.'

They walked across to the chapel, but as they approached the arched doorway the wooden doors opened outwards and Tilly stopped short as Grace and Jason appeared.

Grace's face was red and wet with tears. 'Oh, so you finally decided to show up then!' she snapped. Tilly looked at her sister in disbelief. 'Bit fucking late now though, isn't it?' she continued.

Jason looked awkward. 'Grace!'

Tilly walked up to Grace, tears welling in her eyes. 'I'm sorry,' she said weakly, reaching out to hug her sister.

Grace stepped smartly aside, shunning the embrace 'Sorry? Sorry?! Where the *hell* were you last night? It's way too fucking late now to be sorry!'

'My phone was on silent and, I... I was...'

Grace glared at her. 'I really don't give a shit what you were doing or where you were. All I know is our mother was dying and she *really* needed you, and you were nowhere to be found!'

'I don't know what to say. I'm sorry,' Tilly said quietly.

'Yeah? Well sorry doesn't fucking cut it!' With that, Grace pushed past her sister and stormed off across the car park.

201

Jason looked at Tilly apologetically and followed quickly after Grace.

Tilly broke down in tears and Sebastian, who had been watching dumbfounded by the venom in Grace's voice, rushed over and caught her in his arms as her knees started to buckle. He walked her over to the bench near the doors and they sat down. Tilly was crying uncontrollably and shaking, her shoulders rising and falling as she gasped for air between sobs. Sebastian wrapped his arms around her and watched as the black BMW, with Grace at the wheel, sped out of the car park, sending up a cloud of dust.

Sebastian looked up at the sky. Until this day, his life had been carefree and easy. He wasn't a selfish man by any means, but since he had no dependents and only himself to worry about he had casually taken life in his stride. His default emotion was usually apathy and he'd never really had to handle anything particularly serious or important. And so now, as Tilly lay broken in his arms with her whole world falling apart around her, he felt completely redundant. A weaker man might have wanted to turn his back and run away, but Sebastian wasn't weak. And the fact was he loved Tilly dearly. His heart was aching for her and he reached into his brain for the right words; words that might help in some small way. They didn't come. He just sat there, defeated, stroking Tilly's hair until her crying ebbed away and finally ceased. She sat up. Her face was red and blotchy and she looked exhausted.

'What have I done?' she asked quietly.

Then, from nowhere, the words came. 'Listen. Your sister was upset,' Sebastian said. 'She didn't mean what she said. Please, Tilly. This is an awful time for you both. A *truly* awful time. But nobody is to blame.' He put his hand gently on her face and lifted her chin to face him. '*You* are not to blame.'

Tilly nodded slowly, but Sebastian wasn't sure she had truly accepted what he'd said. 'I want to go inside now.' She pulled out a small packet of tissues from her handbag and blew her nose. 'I want to see my Mum.'

They stood up and Sebastian put his arm around her shoulders as they stepped through the archway and into the chapel.

CHAPTER 15

The following morning, James Lawrence, Gregor McCleary and another associate of Rising Starz, Harry Bean, were sitting huddled around James's mobile phone. He had propped it up on McCleary's desk and it was playing the footage he had filmed of Sebastian's performance at the social club on Saturday night.

'This was the first guy!' James exclaimed eagerly. The small screen showed Sebastian's volunteer, Nigel parading up and down the stage and posturing like Freddie Mercury.

'Tha' jacket's a bit shite,' McCleary declared, his beady eyes squinting at the screen.

'Look at how the audience are all joining in though,' Harry remarked. 'They're loving it.'

'Aye, I'll nae dispute that,' McCleary said.

The footage came to an end and James picked up his phone. 'Now watch this bit,' he said, selecting the next video file and placing the phone back on the desk. Sebastian was hypnotising Karen now and McCleary leaned in closer to see the screen better. 'Wha's that the laddie has in his hand?'

James looked over McCleary's shoulder. 'It's a plastic spider. The girl has an irrational fear of spiders.'

McCleary shuddered. 'So do I, tha nasty wee bastards!' He watched in silence as Sebastian's act played out.

When the video finished, James picked up his phone and looked hopefully at his boss for a reaction.

McCleary turned to his associate. 'Wha do ye think then, Harry?'

Harry smiled. 'I loved it. Variety acts are really making a comeback. I reckon this guy's got potential.'

McCleary grinned. 'Aye I make ye right. With a bit of work to boost the production and some decent props I think we could have a household name in our stable.'

James was feeling distinctly pleased with himself. 'The video really doesn't do him justice, Gregor. Honestly, the punters loved him, they were going wild when it ended. Even Ted was impressed and he asked me if he could book Seb's act as a headliner around Christmas time.'

'Aye, well, we'll see about that,' McCleary said. 'Tight-fisted Ted might have to rethink his budget. I won't be letting this one out cheap.'

'So, shall I get onto the marketing girl? Get her to draw up some artwork?' James asked.

'Aye.' McCleary popped a jammy dodger into his mouth, crunched twice and swallowed it down. 'We'll have to get the laddie in fer a photo shoot too. Check with the studio and see when they're free.'

James nodded and left McCleary's office.

'I think you've got yourself a great bit of talent there, Gregor,' Harry said.

'Aye,' McCleary conceded with a sly smile. '*Really* great.'

Next door, James sat down at his desk and scrolled through the contacts on his phone. He found the number he wanted and pressed it to call. A voice on the other end answered. 'Good morning, Golden Shots, how can I help?'

'Morning, Debs. It's James from Rising Starz.'

'Alright, James? How ya doin'?'

'Pretty good, thank you. Listen, we've just taken on a new performer. He's a hypnotist. We need some promo stuff sorted pronto, is there any chance you can you fit him in sometime this week?'

'Oh, I'm sorry, James. I'm off to Cancun tomorrow for a fortnight. I can organise something for when I'm back.'

James thought for a moment. He knew McCleary would probably kick off; the man wasn't exactly renowned for his patience. But Golden Shots had been their go to outfit for years and they always provided superb results. So, although he might grind his teeth a bit, he'd ultimately accept the delay.

'Okay, that'll be great, Debs,' James said. 'Could you book our guy in for a photo shoot, makeover, all the usual stuff and ping the details over to Gemma for me?'

'Yes, of course.'

'Thanks, sweetheart. You have a lovely holiday.'

'Cheers, James. Catch ya soon.'

James sat back in his chair and smiled as he looked around at the collection of framed photos filling the walls. Most of the acts he had discovered were nothing more than pub, club and holiday camp performers, but he had a feeling in his water about Sebastian Matthews. He bent down, opened the bottom drawer of his desk and pulled out a black 10x8 inch frame. It was still wrapped in cellophane. He smiled and left it out on the side in readiness for a photograph of his most recent acquisition.

*

Tilly was awake early. In truth she had hardly slept. She had been sitting on the sofa in darkness in Sebastian's lounge since before 5.00 am, replaying her sister's words over and over in her head. She was wrapped in a tartan

206

throw-over with her knees up, staring at her phone. Grace had sent 16 text messages and there were several other texts from her friends and Kathy, their next-door neighbour. She read them over and over again, as if doing so repeatedly might change the words within and alleviate her overwhelming feelings of guilt. It didn't. Her head in a whirl, she eventually threw the phone onto the floor. It skittered across the carpet and hit the skirting board. Letting out a big sigh, she pulled the throw up under her chin.

Tilly wasn't sure how long she had been sitting there when she heard movement in the bedroom. A light went on and Sebastian, dressed only in his underpants, appeared in the lounge doorway. 'Hey. I'm sorry, I didn't mean to sleep that long. I was out for the count.' He stifled a yawn. 'How long have you been up?'

'I'm not sure. Not that long. I didn't want to wake you, so I came in here.'

Sebastian padded over to the sofa and bent to kiss her. 'Did you sleep ok?'

Tilly gave him a small smile 'Not too bad I guess. Thank you for letting me stay. I don't think I could have faced going back home on my own last night.'

Sebastian placed his hand on her shoulder and squeezed it lightly. 'You don't have to thank me. Would you like some tea? Or coffee?'

'Tea would be lovely please.'

Sebastian crossed to the window and opened the blinds. 'It's a lovely morning.' As he stepped away from the window he almost trod on Tilly's phone. He picked it up and handed it to her. 'Here, you must have dropped this.' She placed it on the coffee table and followed Sebastian out to the kitchen.

'What do you suppose I have to do? You know, about my Mum?'

Sebastian turned to face her. 'I'm not too sure. I've not been in this position myself. I would imagine the funeral directors would be the first port of call.'

'I'm going to have to speak to Grace too I guess.'

Sebastian nodded. 'Definitely.'

'Hopefully she'll have calmed down a bit,' Tilly said with a sigh. 'I'll have to go back to the house at some point today too. Would it be okay if I stay here with you for a few days?'

Sebastian stirred the tea and removed the teabags. 'Of course. You can stay for as long as you want.'

Tilly smiled appreciatively. 'Thank you. I'll call work in a minute. I hope I'll be able to get some time off.'

'You'll definitely be entitled to leave,' Sebastian said, handing her a mug.

Tilly nodded. 'Yeah. I just have to get a few bits of clothing and stuff from the house and then I need to arrange to meet up with Grace.'

'Okay.' Sebastian took a sip of his tea. 'We can have a bite of breakfast and then make our way over to the house if you want. Maybe call Grace from there and see if she'll meet you. If you want some moral support I'll gladly come along.'

Tilly nodded. 'Yeah, let's do that. Thank you.'

*

A little over an hour later Tilly stood on the doorstep of her mother's house with the key in her hand. Several attempts to insert it had failed, so Sebastian offered to help and took it from her.

'I'm sorry,' Tilly said. 'It's ridiculous.'

Sebastian unlocked the door and held it open for her to go in first. He followed her and they walked through to the kitchen.

'I don't know what I was expecting,' Tilly said. 'But it all looks the same as when I left on Saturday.' She shook her head. 'God, that feels like a lifetime ago now.'

Sebastian brushed his hand across her back. 'A heck of a lot has happened over the last two days.'

'I'll just get some bits together. Do you want a drink or something?'

'No, I'm fine. Can I help?' Sebastian asked.

'It's okay. I won't be long. I'll just throw some clothes and toiletries in a bag and be back down. Go and wait in the living room if you want.'

Tilly went upstairs and Sebastian walked through to the living room. The curtains were pulled and the room was dim. He stepped over to the window and took hold of the curtain, then thought better of it. Turning back, he walked over to the sofa and sat down. The soft cushions sank beneath him. In the half-light he could see a small table beside the sofa. On it was half a cup of cold tea and a paperback book laid open upside down. Propped up against the mug was a white envelope with *TILLY* written neatly across middle. Sebastian stared at the envelope for a moment, then picked it up. It was sealed. Behind it was another envelope with *GRACE* written on it. He was about to pick it up when he heard footsteps on the stairs and quickly returned Tilly's envelope to the table.

A moment later Tilly reappeared carrying a bulging holdall. 'Okay, I've got what I need. Let's get out of here.'

'Erm.' Sebastian pointed at the table. 'There's an envelope here with your name on it.'

Tilly put her bag down and walked over to the table. She picked up both envelopes and stared at them. 'There's one for Grace too. They're from my Mum,' she said, recognising the handwriting. 'I'll look later.' She slipped them both into her jacket pocket and reached down for her bag.

'Let me take that,' Sebastian offered.

Tilly gratefully passed him the holdall and they left the house.

*

Tilly sat with the envelope in her hand studying the neatly written name on the front of it. Sebastian was in the kitchen cooking a pizza for their dinner. She put the envelope down on the table and then promptly picked it up again. Carefully splitting the top with her fingernail, she tore across the seam and withdrew a folded piece of notepaper. Taking a deep breath and exhaling, she slowly opened it and felt her heart beating heavy as she stared at her mother's handwriting.

My dearest Tilly,

This will be one of the most difficult letters I'll ever have to write. If you're reading this then you will now know that I have left this world.

Tilly stopped for a moment. The tears streamed down her cheeks. She reached for a tissue, dabbed them away and continued reading.

You and Grace are the most wonderful gift and it breaks my heart to know I will be leaving you. You have always been the strongest and I am asking you to please look after your sister. She may be older than you and she may act tough and seem like she's got it all figured out but I know a lot of the time it's a front. Jason is a good man but sisters will always need each other - please be there for her.

I'm sorry that for the last couple of years or so you've had to care for me, often putting your own life on hold. But I want you to know that I appreciate everything you've done and I wouldn't have come this far without you. You have been the best daughter any mother could wish for.

Please don't grieve for me. I've had a wonderful life and I have accepted that my time has come. Let me go and please enjoy your life. I won't be far away.

There is a red plastic folder in the sideboard beneath the TV. Inside you will find all the documents needed for my funeral. I have arranged and paid for it all so you and Grace won't need to worry. Everything else you'll need is also in the folder. Just hand it all to the solicitors.

With all my love. Mum xxx

Tilly folded the piece of paper and held the letter to her heart. 'Oh, Mum,' she said quietly to herself. 'I love you *so* much.'

Sebastian appeared carrying two dinner plates. As he placed them on the table he saw that Tilly had the letter in her hand. 'Everything okay?'

Tilly smiled up at him. 'Yes. Everything is fine.'

'Are you ready for pizza then? I think I just about managed to salvage it from burning.'

Tilly nodded. 'I'm sure it'll be lovely. Thank you.'

They ate their meal in silence. When they'd finished Sebastian took the plates to the kitchen. Tilly followed him out. 'Let me wash up,' she said.

'No, no, it's fine. I'll do that later,' Sebastian replied.

'Please, I like washing up.'

'Nobody likes washing up!' Sebastian smiled. 'But if you insist.' He stepped aside so Tilly could get to the sink. While she rinsed off the plates and cutlery, he set out two glasses on the counter and reached for a bottle from the top shelf of the cupboard. 'I fancy a cheeky vodka. Would you like one?'

Tilly saw the bottle of Grey Goose in his hand. 'Yeah, go on then!'

Sebastian poured a generous measure of vodka into each glass, then took a bottle of lemonade from the fridge and topped them up. Leaving the dishes to drip dry on the drainer, Tilly hung the cloth over the tap. Sebastian handed her a glass and they returned to the lounge. She put the glass onto the table and rummaged in her handbag for

212

her mobile. 'I'm just going to give Grace a quick call and see if she'll meet me tomorrow.'

Sebastian nodded and turned to leave the room. 'I'll leave you to it.'

'Don't be daft. You sit down, I won't be a minute.'

Tilly was surprised when Grace answered the call almost immediately. 'Oh. Hi. It's Tilly.'

'Obviously,' Grace replied coldly.

'Look. I realise you're feeling pretty angry with me right now, but we have things to sort out.' Tilly heard Grace huff. 'Mum left us each a note,' she continued. 'She's also left a folder full of stuff for us to go through for the funeral and whatnot.'

'You said there's a note for me? What does it say?'

'It's sealed in an envelope,' Tilly said. 'Are you free tomorrow?'

'I start work at two tomorrow, but I'll have an hour in the morning... if you can make it.'

Were those last words inflected with sarcasm? Tilly let it go. 'Sure, we can meet up then. Say 10 o'clock?'

'I'll see you at the house. Ten-thirty.'

There was a moment's silence.

'Could we meet somewhere else?' Tilly asked. 'The café by the station maybe?'

'*Which* station?'

Tilly knew Grace was being facetious but wasn't about to start an argument. 'Sorry. Seven Kings, just up from the house. The café is called Ali's.

'Yeah, okay. I'll see you there.' Grace hung up the phone without even saying goodbye.

Tilly sighed. 'Oh, well. At least she agreed to meet me.'

213

Sebastian gestured for her to join him on the sofa. She sat down and picked up her glass. He put his arm around behind her and she rested her head on his chest.

'Would you like me to come with you tomorrow?' he ventured.

'I'm sure you must have better things to do,' Tilly replied.

'Nah, not really. I mean, it's crossed my mind I'd better start looking for a job, but that can wait a day or two. It doesn't look like the Rising Starz thing is going anywhere, so I need to start thinking about earning some money. My savings sure won't last long.'

Tilly sat up. 'Oh crikey. I'm so sorry. All this going on, it's really taken the shine off your big moment.'

'Of course it hasn't!' Sebastian exclaimed. 'I'm just being realistic.'

'What makes you think the Rising Starz contract isn't happening?'

'Well, James said he'd be in touch, but I haven't heard a dicky bird.'

'But it's only been two days. I doubt they work Sundays. These things take time.'

Sebastian sighed. 'Yeah, I know, but even so, I can't rest *all* my hopes on them. I'm going to have to try and get a job for now, if only to keep up with the bills.'

'When I'm back at work, I'll see if they've got anything going. It's not the best pay in the world but it might tide you over.'

'That would be really great.' Sebastian planted a big kiss on her cheek. 'Shall we watch a movie?'

'Yeah, sure,' Tilly replied. 'Something light hearted though.'

'Definitely.' Sebastian reached for the TV remote. 'Let's see what Netflix has to offer.'

CHAPTER 16

The following day, Tilly sat nursing a cup of green tea in Ali's café as she nervously waited for her sister. Earlier that morning she had stopped by the house to retrieve the folder her mum had left for them and it was laid on the table in front of her. She had decided she wouldn't open it until Grace arrived so that they could discuss the contents together. As she took a sip from her cup, the bell over the door tinkled and she looked up to see Grace coming in. She put down the tea, feeling a knot in her stomach tighten as Grace strode over towards her with a distinctly tense expression on her face. Tilly smiled up at her sister, but her welcoming disposition was met with a grimace.

'What a ridiculous place to meet!' Grace exclaimed angrily. 'There was nowhere to park and I've had to walk bloody miles to get here!'

'Where did you park?' Tilly asked.

'Tesco's!' Grace snapped back.

'You could have parked outside Mum's. That would have been nearer.'

Grace glared at her sister. 'It's a bit late to be making suggestions now, isn't it?'

'Would you like a tea or coffee,' Tilly said, taking out her purse.

'I'll get my own thank you!' Grace hissed. She ordered a coffee at the counter and sat down opposite Tilly. 'Where's your shadow today then?'

'My shadow? If you mean Sebastian, he's at the job centre.'

Grace scoffed. 'A real keeper that one!'

Tilly frowned. 'Don't be so unkind, you don't even know him.'

Grace took a sip of her coffee. 'Is this going to take long?' she asked testily.

Tilly looked a little bemused 'Probably not.' She drew a breath. 'Look, I understand how you feel. I'm upset too. But we need to go through Mum's wishes together and...'

Grace cut her off. 'So you're upset are you?' Her eyes burned with rage.

'Yes, I...'

'Just shut up and let me speak. I'll tell you now, you forfeited your right to be upset when you went out gallivanting around while our mother lay dying.' Tilly was mortified. Her eyes were brimming with tears. She opened her mouth to speak but Grace held up a hand. 'I haven't finished. Mum tried to call you and you ignored her. Thankfully she gave up on you and called me. We tried and tried to reach you and if you'd had a thought for someone other than yourself for a change you'd have checked your messages. But no. Too wrapped up in yourself. Leave someone else to deal with it. You're so selfish! And you sit there and tell me you're upset? Don't make me laugh.' Grace practically spat out the last few words.

Tilly had sat there in silence listening, the sick feeling in her stomach intensifying as her sister laid into her, but suddenly she felt herself flare. 'Enough!'

Taken aback, Grace stopped speaking. There was only one other person in the café and he swivelled in his seat, frowned at the two women, then turned his back on them and resumed reading his newspaper.

Tilly lowered her voice. 'That's not fair and you know it,' she said. 'I did *everything* for Mum. Everything.' Now it was Grace's turn to listen in silence. 'I did her

216

shopping,' Tilly continued. 'I cooked for her. I helped her administer her meds when she was having a bad day and was too weak to do it herself. I was there to put her to bed every night and there to get her up and washed and dressed every morning. But I have a life of my own too, you know. Mum used to encourage me to go out, but more often than not I didn't. I stayed in and watched TV with her just so she wasn't on her own. Yes, I feel guilty as hell that I wasn't there for her Saturday night, and that's a cross I'll have to bear. But what did you do? Nothing. Ever. You were so busy getting on with your life, you barely gave Mum a thought. You lived just down the road and if you visited her more than once a fortnight it was a miracle – and then usually only because you wanted something. So don't you *dare* tell me I'm selfish. If there's a selfish one here it's *you*!'

Grace had been staring at Tilly, her face getting paler and paler. Suddenly she stood up. 'I didn't come here for this shit!' she exclaimed. She snatched up her handbag and turned to leave.

'Grace, wait. I'm sorry.' Grace stopped but remained facing the door. Tilly opened the folder and pulled Grace's envelope out. 'At least read Mum's note.'

Grace turned around and stepped back towards the table. She snatched the envelope from Tilly's hand and stormed off out of the café.

Tilly sighed and leant back in her chair. 'I'm sorry,' she whispered under her breath.

While Grace stood at the lights, waiting for the traffic to stop so she could cross, she studied her mother's handwriting on the envelope. She could feel a tear trickling down her cheek and she quickly wiped it away. The pedestrian crossing bleeped and she walked across. Beside the station entrance there was a wooden bench.

217

Grace sat down on it and opened the envelope.

My dearest Grace,

This will be one of the most difficult letters I'll ever have to write. If you're reading this then you will now know that I have left this world. You and Tilly are my entire world and it breaks my heart to know I will be leaving you.

I know you didn't agree with my decision not to have treatment and I understand your reasons. But the last couple of years watching you and Jason fall in love and being present at your wedding was so much better being relatively well and lucid.

You have a great life now and I know Jason will look after you. I know you and Tilly don't always see eye to eye but I am asking you to please to look after her, she's not as confident and grounded as you and I hope someday she will find a good man like you have and settle down. Sisters will always need each other - please be there for her as I know she will be for you.

Please don't grieve for me. I've had a wonderful life and I have accepted that my time has come.

218

Let me go and please enjoy your life. I will always be there by your side.

Tilly has my folder. Inside you will find all the documents needed for my funeral. I have arranged and paid for it all so you and Tilly won't need to worry. Everything else you'll need is also in the folder, please help Tilly to sort through it and give whatever is needed to the solicitors.

With all my love. Mum xxx

Grace quickly folded the letter and slipped it back into the envelope. She hurried back to the crossing, hammering on the button until the beep sounded and the icon of the green man appeared. She dashed across and pushed open the door to Ali's café and stared around the room. The old man was still sitting reading his paper, but a young girl was wiping the table where she and Tilly had been sat – and Tilly was gone.

Grace rushed back out the door and looked to her right. In the distance she caught a fleeting glimpse of her sister's familiar denim jacket as Tilly disappeared around the corner. Grace hurried after her at speed.

'Tilly! Wait!' she called breathlessly as she caught up with her sister right outside their mother's house. Tilly stopped and turned around. She had her keys in her hand and was just about to unlock the car. Grace panted for a moment and finally managed to catch her breath. 'I'm sorry.' Tilly looked at her sister uncertainly. She saw that Grace had tears welling in her eyes. Putting down her bag, she ran forward and threw her arms around her sister, hugging her close. 'I'm *so* sorry,' Grace repeated between sobs.

Tilly rubbed her sister's back comfortingly. She was fighting back tears herself. 'It's okay. Let it all out.'

After a few moments passed Grace managed to find a tissue in her handbag and blew her nose. She handed a clean tissue to Tilly, who took it and did the same. 'Shall we start again?' Grace ventured.

Tilly smiled. 'I'd like that.'

'Seeing as we're here now, shall we go inside and look over this paperwork?'

Tilly took a deep breath. 'Yeah, sure.'

They walked up the steps and Tilly unlocked the door. She stood back and let Grace go in first. They walked through into the living room and Grace opened the curtains. Bright sunlight burst in and a pretty trail of dust particles shimmered in the shards of light.

'I'm not sure what's in the fridge, but if we have milk, do you want a coffee?' Tilly asked.

Grace thought for a moment. 'I'm really thirsty actually. I bet ya there's a can of Lilt in the fridge. Mum never let that run out.'

Tilly laughed. 'That's true!' She went out to the kitchen and opened the fridge; sure enough the top shelf was loaded with cans of Lilt. Tilly picked up a couple of the ice-cold drinks and reached into the cupboard for two glasses. Then she pulled the folder out of her bag and sat down next to Grace. She poured their drinks and smiled to herself as she remembered her mum heaping lumps of pineapple, mango and melon into a jug and filling it up with Lilt. 'Remember when Mum made us Lilt cocktails and put umbrellas in our glasses? She used to say "Looks more posh dun' it"?'

220

Grace nodded. 'Of course, once we'd gone to bed, you could bet your bottom dollar she'd top it up with gin!'

Tilly laughed. 'Yeah, definitely.' She opened the folder and laid the contents out across the coffee table. 'Shall we tackle this then?'

Grace leant forward and put down her glass. 'Blimey! This is unlike Mum. She was *never* this organised!'

'Oh, you'd be surprised. I'd say in the last few months she'd definitely started to get things in order.' Tilly separated the papers and handed Grace a small wodge held together by a staple.

'Pure Cremation?!' Grace exclaimed incredulously. 'Isn't that where no-one turns up? You just get cremated with no service or anything?'

'Yeah, I think so,' Tilly replied sadly.

'Well, that's a bit callous. What if people want to come to the funeral?' Grace said, clearly perturbed by her mother's choice of arrangements.

'Nobody *wants* to go to a funeral. You just kinda do it because you feel you should,' Tilly replied. 'But I reckon she's made a good choice.'

'I suppose,' Grace replied, but she didn't sound convinced. 'But what about all her friends though? And Uncle John and Aunt Wendy? They're going to want to pay their respects.'

Tilly lifted up another sheet of paper. 'Ah, look!' She handed it to Grace.

She glanced at it. 'Oh, okay. That's different then.' Stapled to the sheet of paper was a receipt for a pub in Loughton and a note from their mother.

> I know you're all going to want to get
> together and I would be much happier

221

*knowing it's somewhere nice without
gravestones, hearses and solemn music.
I've paid for a buffet and booze at The White
Lion in Loughton and I want you all to
enjoy yourselves. No weeping and wailing,
just remember the good times we shared
and say your goodbyes with a drink
in your hand. XXX*

'She's thought of everything,' Grace said with a smile. She handed Tilly back the note. 'What's all that other stuff?'

Tilly moved the pages around looking at the headers. 'Life insurance, bank statements, names and addresses of everyone she wants us to contact. She really has sewn everything up.'

Grace stood up and wandered around the room. She picked up a framed picture from the mantelpiece. 'I remember that day out like it was yesterday.' She stared at the photo and laughed. 'You got chased by a sheep and slipped on that cow pat!'

Tilly frowned. 'Yes, hilarious. Not.'

'Oh, come on, it was *so* funny. You were crying because you'd got your new dress covered in it and Mum had to carry you at arm's length to the toilets and clean it off.' Grace put the frame down. 'We had to have the windows down in the car on the way home because you smelt so bad.'

'I'm glad you found it funny! That scarred me for life that did. I'm still a bit wary of sheep.'

Grace sat down in the armchair opposite Tilly.

'I was at Hainault Park a few days ago.'

'Yeah?'

'I took Seb over there. We sat up on the hill where Mum used to take us.' As the words left her mouth Tilly felt an all-consuming wave of sadness. She let out a gasp and started to cry. Grace rushed around the table and sat beside her on the sofa. She put her arm around her and hugged her. Tilly sobbed. 'I'm going to miss her so much, Grace.'

'I know. I will too.'

CHAPTER 17

Just over a week into his new job, Sebastian was struggling. In a relatively short space of time he had fallen out of the routine of getting up to go to work and the job he'd taken meant an unfeasibly early start. Loading flowers into crates at the Columbia Road market wasn't a career he'd ever have hoped for, but when the woman at the job centre had mentioned it, he thought it sounded a doddle and the pay was reasonable too, so he'd seized it with both hands. The job itself wasn't too taxing; all he had to do was make sure the correct crates had the correct labels on and went into the correct van. But it was the early starts that were beginning to take their toll, especially as his inconsiderate neighbour was keeping him awake all night with his infernal drum and bass music.

Sitting on the bus after his shift, he was staring out of the window, his eyelids drooping, when his phone pinged. It was a text from Tilly.

How was today?

He tapped a short reply.

It was okay.

Just okay?

Well, nothing to write home about. Gotta say, I'm bloody knackered though.

Are the flowers heavy then? ;-)

LOL. No, I'm just not sleeping too well. That selfish pothead Craig has been blasting out muisc late every night and it's keeping me awake.

Hang on, I'll call.

A few seconds later Sebastian's mobile rang. 'Hey gorgeous!'

Sebastian blushed and looked quickly around the bus in case the other passengers had heard; of course they hadn't. Nevertheless, the old lady sat across the aisle nodded and smiled at him, so he kept his voice low. 'Hiya,' he replied. 'How's your day going?'

'Better than yours by the sound of it.'

'I don't think I'm ever going to get rid of the scent of hyacinths!' Sebastian sniffed the sleeve of his jacket. 'It's stuck in my nose.'

Tilly giggled. 'At least it's a nice smell.'

225

'Yeah, it could be worse. But I could do without these 4am starts. It's pitch-dark and it's so depressing riding the night bus with all the drunks and weirdos.' Sebastian yawned. 'Oh, excuse me! I think it was gone one o'clock this morning when Craig finally turned his music off.'

'Yeah, about that,' Tilly said. 'I've been thinking. I'm rattling about in this big house on my own. You can say no if you want to, but what do you reckon to you moving in with me?' The line fell silent as Sebastian considered the idea. 'You can say no,' Tilly ventured to break the silence. 'I won't be offended.' She laughed. 'Much.'

'No, I'd love to. Maybe just for a little while though, see how it works out?'

'Yeah, of course. You don't have to give your flat up or anything. It'll just give you a chance to catch up on some sleep for a while. You probably won't be at that flower market for long anyway, but at least while you are you won't have to contend with the ministry of sound next door keeping you awake all night.'

Sebastian chuckled. 'Thank you. I really appreciate it. I hope you're right about the job being temporary too. It's not really what I want to do with my life, but it definitely looks like I blew the Rising Starz gig. I know James said he'd call, but I'm starting to think it was a brush off. I'm sure he'd have been in touch by now if they wanted me.'

'Maybe, maybe not. But if that's true, it's their loss, eh?'

'I guess so.' Sebastian sighed. 'I'm off tomorrow so I might pop back down the job centre, see if there are any new ads up.'

'That sounds like a plan. Anyway, if you want to get some essentials together, I'll pick you up later when I finish work.'

'Will do,' Sebastian said, trying hard not to yawn. 'I love you.'

'Love you too. Bye for now.'

Sebastian took a quick look round the bus and put the phone close to his mouth. 'Mwah!' He ended the call, sat back in the seat and stared out of the window, watching the world flash past as the bus made its way through the mid-morning traffic. A warm glow of happiness coursed through him as he thought about Tilly and how lucky he was. The job might suck, but everything else in his life was pretty damned good.

When the bus reached Chadwell Heath High Street, Sebastian got off. He'd decided to pick up a bottle of wine and something tasty to cook for dinner as a thank you to Tilly for her offer of sanctuary away from Craig. He walked into the supermarket and picked up a basket. As he started to peruse the shelves of home takeaways and fresh meat his phone started ringing. Awkwardly hooking the shopping basket over his arm, he reached into his pocket. The display showed that the number was withheld. Probably a cold caller, he thought. Tutting, he cancelled it. He was just about to slip the phone back into his pocket when it started to ring again. He looked at the screen, which displayed the same withheld number message. He didn't like answering unknown numbers, but this time he instinctively accepted the call. 'Hello?' he said abruptly.

'Sebastian?'

'Yes.'

'It's James. James Lawrence from Rising Starz.'

Sebastian put the shopping basket down on the floor. 'Oh, hello James! How are you?'

'I'm dandy, Seb, absolutely tickety-boo. Listen, are you free tomorrow to attend a photoshoot in Limehouse?'

'Er, yes, I am. What's it for?'

227

'Well, we need to get you on the website and whatnot, so you'll need some promotional materials. Obviously, you'll be paid tomorrow too. Gregor has a few gigs lined up for you, but I don't have the details right now. I'll get back in touch with those. But the priority is to get your portfolio drawn up.'

Sebastian grinned to himself. 'Yes, of course. What time do I need to be there?'

'10:30 on the nose. I'll ping the address over to you. When you arrive ask for a lady called Debbie. She's an amazing make-up artist and photographer, we use her all the time, and she'll take care of you.'

'What do I need to wear?' Sebastian asked.

'Oh, what you had on the other night will be fine. Simple but stylish.'

'Great! Thank you, James.' Sebastian's heart was beating double time. 'I'll see Debbie at 10:30 tomorrow then.'

'Splendid. I'll be in touch later with those gigs. Toodle-pip.'

'Bye.' Just as Sebastian hung up an elderly woman pushed rudely past him. He stepped back and looked at her in disbelief.

'I can't get to the chicken with you standing there lollygagging about on your mobile phone!' the woman muttered irritably.

'An excuse me wouldn't have gone amiss,' Sebastian replied, shaking his head.

'I *did* say excuse me,' the woman spat back. 'You just weren't listening! That's the trouble with you youngsters these days, no respect for your elders. We're invisible to you!'

Sebastian suddenly felt very ashamed. It wasn't in his nature to be rude to anyone, let alone a little old woman.

228

'I'm *really* sorry.' He hastily picked up his basket and made a quick exit out of the fresh foods aisle with the old woman's voice echoing in his ears: 'I should think so too!'

He thought about calling Tilly to tell her the good news, but decided it would be better to spring it as a surprise over a nice meal that evening. He loitered at the end of the aisle for a minute, pretending to inspect the range of regional cheeses, then peered cautiously around the corner to see if the old lady had moved; he was relieved to see there was no sign of her. He gingerly returned to the selection of oriental dishes on the home takeaway shelf. Selecting a rather tasty-looking Chinese meal for two, he made his way round to the alcohol aisle. Unsure what Tilly might like, he settled for a bottle of white Lambrusco – anything medium sweet with bubbles was usually a safe choice – and proceeded to the till to pay for his goods.

When he left the supermarket, an idea popped into his mind. Smiling to himself, he walked along the street to the B&M store. Finding what he wanted, he was making his way home when he caught sight of something in a shop window. He checked his wallet, made a quick mental calculation and went inside.

*

'Wow!' Tilly gasped as Sebastian set down the two plates of steaming hot food on the table. 'This looks deeeeelish.'

'It might have been more impressive if I'd prepared it from scratch,' Sebastian said, sitting down opposite her. 'But it wouldn't have been anywhere near as appetising.'

Tilly laughed. 'Don't be silly. This is lovely. You really didn't have to buy dinner though, I've got plenty here we could have had.'

Sebastian unscrewed the cap from the bottle of Lambrusco and filled two wine flutes. 'It's just my little way of saying thank you for letting me stay for a bit. It means a lot.'

They chinked glasses. 'Here's to us,' Sebastian said, and they each took a sip.

Tilly's eyes lit up. 'Mmm, that's good. I haven't had Lambrusco for years. It was the first wine I ever tasted. Grace and me were only kids, but Dad let us have half a glass each as a treat one Christmas. We felt so grown up.' Her eyes misted over.

'Well, we'd better eat while the food is still hot,' Sebastian said, changing the subject. 'Rice gets cold really fast.'

Tilly looked down at the table and smiled. 'It would help if someone hadn't forgotten the cutlery.' She started to get up, but Sebastian reached into his back pocket and produced two pairs of chopsticks.

'Ta-dahhh!'

Tilly laughed. 'Where on earth did you get those?'

'I picked them up in the B&M store on the way home.' Sebastian handed a pair to Tilly. 'I know I fumbled about a bit at Wagamama, but practice makes perfect.'

'Absolutely.'

They tucked into their food – sweet and sour chicken, chicken chow mein, egg fried rice and vegetable spring rolls, with a side of prawn crackers. It wasn't the best Chinese food either of them had ever eaten, but it was pleasant enough for what it was. The conversation while they ate was convivial and they soon cleared their plates. Better yet, Sebastian thought as he took them out to the kitchen, aside from one small spillage of rice into his lap he'd managed to get through the meal without making too much of a fool of himself with the chopsticks.

230

Tilly fetched some chocolate ice cream from the freezer and as they sat down again to have their dessert, Sebastian said, 'There's something I've been aching to tell you.'

Tilly was about to eat a scoop of ice cream. The spoon paused at her lips and she raised her eyebrows. 'Aching, eh?' She slipped the ice cream into her mouth.

'Yeah. I had a phone call while I was in the supermarket this afternoon. It was James Lawrence.'

Tilly's eyes widened. 'Oh! What did he say?'

'He said they want me to do a photoshoot so they can make up a portfolio.'

'So does that mean...?'

'It means they want me.' Sebastian grinned. '*And* they're lining up some more gigs.'

Tilly squealed. Dropping her spoon, she jumped up, ran round the table and threw her arms around Sebastian. 'I told you, I told you!' she cried, planting a big kiss on his mouth. 'You just needed to be patient. So, when's the photoshoot?'

'Tomorrow. In Limehouse.'

Tilly suddenly stood upright and stepped back. She playfully punched his shoulder. 'Why didn't you tell me straight away?!'

Sebastian smiled. 'I wanted to surprise you.'

'You certainly did that.' Tilly returned to her seat. 'How did you manage to hold it in all day?' She laughed. 'If it was me, I'd have been shouting it from the rooftops.'

'I nearly phoned you immediately, but I thought I'd save it and tell you over dinner,' Sebastian said. 'But then I nearly caved and told you in the car on the way home.'

'So why didn't you?'

'Because there's something else too. One moment.' Sebastian got up, went out to the hallway and collected a

231

small package from his jacket. He returned to his seat and put the package on the table beside him. Tilly was looking at him inquisitively. 'I wanted to get you a little something to say thank you.'

'You got the Chinese food to thank me. That was more than enough.'

'No, not for letting me stay here. Well, that too. But for everything. If it weren't for your encouragement and support, I'd not have had it in me to follow my dream. You made me realise it could actually happen. And now... well, it has.' Sebastian slid the package across the table. About eight inches long, shallow in depth and wrapped in gold foil gift-wrap, it was neatly tied with a red ribbon.

Tilly shook her head. 'Oh, Seb. You shouldn't have. Really.'

'I wanted to. I love you.'

Tilly smiled. 'I love you too.'

'Go on,' Sebastian urged her. 'Open it.'

Tilly pulled the bow and removed the foil wrapping to reveal a slender, black velvet-covered box. She opened it and inside there was a pendant; a fine silver chain with a tiny, heart-shaped sapphire attached to it. Tilly gasped and put a hand to her heart. 'Seb!' Her eyes teared up.

'Do you like it?' Sebastian asked hopefully.

'*Like* it?' Tilly carefully removed the pendant from the box. 'I *love* it.'

'I'm sorry it's so small.'

'It's perfect!'

Sebastian stood up and walked round behind her. 'Here, let me do the clasp for you.'

Tilly handed him the pendant and held her hair away from her neck so that Sebastian could put it on for her. 'They say that sapphires are supposed to symbolise undying loyalty and devotion,' he said, bending to kiss her cheek.

Tilly gazed down at the gemstone nestled in the top of the V between her breasts. 'Thank you so much. I don't know what to say. It's absolutely beautiful.'

'So are you.' Sebastian's eyes widened as he noticed her dessert dish. 'Crikey, we'd better eat our ice cream,' he said. 'It's gone all melty!'

CHAPTER 18

Tilly awoke to the sound of an electric razor buzzing in the en-suite bathroom adjacent to her bedroom. She got up quietly and stood in the bathroom doorway silently watching Sebastian as he shaved. He was wearing a pair of black trousers but his top half was unclothed.

He caught sight of her reflection in the mirror and switched off the razor. 'Good morning. I hope I didn't wake you.'

Tilly crossed the bathroom and threw her arms around his neck. 'No, I was half awake already.' She reached up and wiped a little blob of gel off his chin before kissing him. She brushed his cheeks with the back of her hands. 'You look lovely and fresh.' She ran her fingers down his neck and across his bare chest, making him shiver.

'I wasn't sure what they'd be looking for today at this photoshoot but I've never been able to carry off the stubble look very well,' Sebastian said. 'So I thought I'd better go clean shaven.' He looked into the mirror and fiddled with his hair, trying to comb it straight. He sighed as the curls stubbornly refused to behave and sprung back into place.

Tilly slapped him playfully on the bottom. 'I'll leave you to carry on. Would you like a hot drink?' Sebastian thought for a moment. 'No I don't think I will, thank you.'

'Fresh orange juice?' Tilly offered.

'Yeah, go on then. Just a small glass though please.'

Tilly walked downstairs and flicked on the kettle. She poured a glass of juice for Sebastian and switched on the television, groaning as the screen came alive showing a parliamentary debate in Westminster. She reached for the remote and turned it off again.

Doing up the buttons on his shirt, Sebastian came into the kitchen. 'Was that our new PM?' Sebastian asked.

'Yeah. Dopey mare. I give her till Christmas.'

'That long?'

Tilly laughed and looked up at Sebastian. 'Wow, you look fantastic!' Sebastian looked down at his shoes, which shone back up at him. 'Don't be embarrassed,' Tilly said, stepping up to him. She took hold of his shirt collars and pulled them straight, then stepped back and looked him up and down. 'Where's your jacket?'

'It's in the hall.'

'Well go get it. I want to see you in your full outfit.'

Sebastian collected his jacket, slipped it on and stood with his arms out wide. 'Ta-dahhh!'

'Hold that pose,' Tilly said, grabbing her mobile phone from the worktop. She snapped a couple of photos and turned the phone around to show Sebastian. 'You look sensational.'

'Well that's me, isn't it?' He smiled. 'Seb the Sensational!'

Tilly laughed. 'Absolutely.'

'Apart from my hair,' Sebastian added forlornly.

'How many times do I have to tell you? Your hair is lovely. Stop fretting about it.'

Tilly handed Sebastian his glass of juice. 'I wish I could come with you, but we have two off on annual leave and another two off with Covid this week, so I couldn't get the time off and they wouldn't let me change my shift either.'

'Don't worry. I would have loved for you to come, but to be honest I doubt it'll be very exciting. Just silly old me trying to look cool in front of a camera.'

'You'll be great.'

'I'll try my best.' Sebastian glanced at his watch. 'Anyway, I'd better get going, don't want to rock up late.' He hugged Tilly and gave her a kiss. 'So, I'll see you later tonight?'

'Oh crikey, yes, I'd better give you a key.' Tilly rummaged in one of the kitchen drawers and pulled out a set of keys on a lanyard. 'Here. This is for the porch door and the gold one is for the inside door.'

Sebastian took them from her. 'Thanks. Hope you have a good day at work. And I'll see you tonight. Walking to the front door, he stepped out into the porch, turned and blew Tilly a kiss.

A quick change at Mile End station and Sebastian was on the train to Limehouse. By the time it arrived his confidence was starting to waver. Leaving the station, he paused and opened his email to double check the address James had sent him. He spotted a newsagents a few doors down from the station and went inside to ask directions.

The elderly man behind the counter peered at him with disinterested eyes over the rim of his spectacles. 'Do I look like tourist information?' he said sarcastically.

'I'm sorry?'

The man scowled. 'Did you see a big sign on the door saying tourist information?'

'Er, no, I...'

'No, you didn't.' The man was glaring at him with what could almost have been contempt. 'I sell papers, fags and sweets. So, what *can* I help you with?'

Sebastian frowned. 'Nothing. Thanks a lot, pal.' He went back out into the street where he opened up Google maps on his phone and entered the address. The location

236

icon showed that his destination was nearby. He started to walk in a straight line until the flashing blue dot on his phone moved along the road map. Realising it was taking him away from his destination, he turned around and set off back in the opposite direction. Finally, the blinking dot started moving again, indicating he was going the right way. He followed it until he saw an illuminated sign above a glass fronted shop: **GOLDEN SHOTS Promotions**.

Sebastian turned away for a few seconds in a vain attempt to compose himself and looked off along the street, bustling with people going about their daily business. Lost in his thoughts for a moment, he didn't notice the doors behind him opening wide.

A husky voice said, 'Sebastian?'

Startled, he turned around. 'Yes. That's me, I'm Sebastian.'

'Well, please come on in. I'm Debbie.'

Sebastian studied the face briefly then extended his hand. 'Thank you for seeing me today.'

'My pleasure entirely. James appears to be very proud of his new protégé, so it's an honour to be able to help launch your career.' Debbie ushered him to follow. 'Come on through to my studio.'

As Sebastian walked through the immaculately clean waiting area he smiled at a young girl who was sat crossed legged posing into her mobile phone. She cast him a slightly dismissive glance and resumed her pouting. Debbie pushed open a heavy swing door and gestured for Sebastian to enter. 'Take a seat on the sofa whilst I set up.'

Sebastian looked around the room. There were various tripods, large white umbrellas on stands and lighting rigs scattered about. He noticed several different backdrops hung on frames and wondered which one of them he would be posing in front of. Debbie had disappeared into a side room and he started tapping his foot nervously. He stood up and walked slowly around the room. He could feel his brow dampening under the heat of the lights.

Suddenly a voice spoke, giving him a start. 'Sebastian, sweetheart. I'm ready for you.' He spun round and saw Debbie standing in the doorway to the side room. 'We're just going to do a little hair and make-up before your shoot.'

Sebastian entered the room to find a young girl waiting. 'This is my assistant, Ava,' Debbie said.

The girl gave him a welcoming smile. 'Good morning, Mr Matthews, would you like to take a seat?' She gestured to a leather swivel chair in front of a vast mirror, which spanned the whole wall.

Sebastian sat down as instructed and eyed the array of products on the trolley beside the chair. 'Er, I don't really wear make-up,' he said nervously.

Debbie bellowed a throaty laugh. 'Don't worry, we won't be turning you into Liberace. It's just a little eyeliner to accentuate your eyes and some powder to take the sheen off your forehead.' Sebastian glanced at his sweaty brow in the mirror and suddenly felt embarrassed.

Ava draped a gown across him and Debbie stepped up behind him. 'So how do you usually wear your hair, sweetheart?'

Looking at himself in the mirror, Sebastian tilted his head to one side. 'I do try to style it, but it kind of has a life of its own.' He laughed. 'As you can probably tell.'

Debbie took hold of a few strands of his hair. 'It looks to me like you try to straighten it, am I right?' Sebastian nodded. 'Why?' Debbie asked.

'Because it looks silly curly. It makes me look... I dunno, boyish I guess.'

Debbie caressed it. 'I think curls are wonderful. You just need to learn how to manage them. May I show you?'

'Sure.'

'This is curl-defining cream.' Debbie selected a tube from the trolley. 'It contains argan oil. It's very good for the hair, it'll separate your curls and make them look as if you intend them to be that way. By attempting to straighten them you end up with it sticking out in all directions, yes?' Sebastian nodded. Debbie finished styling his hair and stepped back. 'You see?'

Admiring himself in the mirror, Sebastian smiled. 'That looks way better. Thank you.'

Debbie winked. 'No worries, sweetheart. We want the very best photos, right?'

'Absolutely,' Sebastian replied enthusiastically. He was finally beginning to relax.

''Right then. I'll leave you with lovely Ava here to get made up and then if you come back through to the studio, we can get your photos done.' Debbie strolled out of the room and closed the door behind her.

Ava came over and asked Sebastian to close his eyes whilst she applied his make-up. When she was done, Sebastian looked into the mirror. The man peering back at him looked distinctly different. *Suave maybe,* Sebastian thought. *Or glamorous perhaps. Showbizzy? Yes, that's it,* he decided.

'Okay, Mr Matthews, all done.' Ava removed the gown.

Sebastian stood up and, with a last glance in the mirror, he thanked her and walked back out to the studio. A camera on a tripod and a reflective shade were set up in front of a bright white backdrop. There were also two large white umbrellas and a pair of lights on either side.

Debbie looked up from the viewfinder of her camera. 'Oh, great, you're all done. You look sensational!'

Sebastian felt himself blush slightly. He was really warm and began to wonder if whatever it was Ava had put on his face might start to run.

'If you could just stand in the middle of the screen there, I can get my camera adjusted,' Debbie said gesturing to the backdrop. Feeling his nerves kick in again, Sebastian walked onto the white canvass and stood with his hands in his pockets. Debbie looked at him through the lens. 'Okay, if you could just turn slightly to your left.' She adjusted the settings on the camera. 'Take your hands out of your pockets, sweetheart.' Sebastian did as he was asked. 'Lovely. Now drop your head slightly and look towards me.' It took Sebastian a few seconds to compute the instructions. He looked down and turned to face the camera. 'No, sweetie, stay where you are. I just wanted you to turn your head slightly.'

'I'm sorry.' Sebastian was beginning to feel slightly flustered. He tried to resume the position he was in before, but as his nerves shifted up a gear, he suddenly felt really awkward. 'I'm sorry,' he apologised again.

Debbie stepped away from the camera. 'Hey, Sebastian. Relax.'

He smiled weakly. 'I'm not really used to all this. I feel such a fraud. I mean, you and Ava have done a really great job but...'

Debbie stepped up beside him. 'But *what*, sweetie?'

'But... Well I'm hardly a model. I'm stood here in a cheap suit, posing for photos, and I just feel a bit ridiculous.'

Debbie placed a hand on his shoulder. 'Can I tell you something?'

Sebastian felt really deflated. He nodded and stared at the floor. 'Sure.'

'Look at me,' Debbie said softly. Sebastian raised his head. 'How do you think I look?'

Momentarily thrown by the question, Sebastian muttered, 'I'm sorry, what do you mean?'

'My face, what do you see when you look at me?'

Sebastian didn't quite know what to say. 'I, er... well, you look... erm...'

Realising that the question had made Sebastian feel uncomfortable, Debbie changed tack. 'I used to really struggle with my appearance. Throughout the whole of my teenage years, I hated myself. I felt as if I was living a lie. I felt that whatever I did, however I wore my hair I just didn't feel like me. The outside didn't match the inside is the best way I can put it. Do you understand what I'm saying?'

Sebastian nodded.

Debbie continued. 'When I turned 18, I decided that I would start living *my* life the way *I* wanted to. I'd been a slave to conformity, too afraid to be myself. And now? Well, I'm the person I was always meant to be. I'm entirely comfortable in my skin and that gives me the confidence and conviction to do anything I want.'

Sebastian half smiled. 'I don't have any confidence. I'm scared that people will suss me out and I'll make a fool of myself.'

'Exactly the point I was trying to make, sweetie.' Debbie took hold of his shoulders. 'Are you a good hypnotist?'

'Yes. Yes, I am.'

'And when you're on stage do you feel as if you're in control of your performance?'

Sebastian nodded. 'Yes. Well, at least I think I do.'

241

'And *that*, my friend, is all you need. You're a good-looking young man and however much you've spent on your suit you wear it well. Having faith in your performance is all you need. I know Gregor McCleary very well, we go back a long way. And, trust me, that man is *sharp*. His business and reputation mean everything to him. If he's willing to add you to his roster, then he believes you have something special.'

Sebastian beamed and stood up straight. 'Thank you.'

Debbie smiled. '*Now* you're shining! Come on, let's get these photos done.'

Sebastian was buzzing when he left Golden Shots. Debbie had really struck a chord with him and he departed the building feeling more confident than he ever had before. For the best part of his life, he'd felt self-conscious and lacked any real esteem; he hadn't been popular at school or at work and would always shy away from social events. The only thing he ever felt self-assured about was his ability to hypnotise people. With just a few words Debbie had made him realise that, if he was true to himself, he would always walk tall. He was absolutely bursting to tell Tilly about his morning, but it wasn't quite lunchtime and she was at work; he didn't want to risk getting her into trouble. He decided instead to go to Hornchurch and pay his parents an impromptu visit.

He hopped off the train at Emerson Park station and strolled along the road to the florists. It had been almost a year since he'd seen his mum and dad and he thought it might mitigate the lecture slightly if he were to present his mother with a nice bunch of flowers. Purchasing a fulsome bouquet, he carried on across the street to his childhood home. He rang the bell and after a few moments he heard the internal door open and the click of the latch.

'Hello, Mum,' he said cheerfully as his mother peered round the door.

'Sebastian!' Her face lit up. 'Aren't you a sight for sore eyes.' Sebastian kissed her on the cheek and handed her the flowers. 'Well, aren't these beautiful! But what's the occasion? It's not my birthday.'

'Do I need an excuse to buy my Mum flowers?'

'No, of course not.' She beckoned to him. 'Come on in and I'll put the kettle on.'

Sebastian followed his mother inside. 'Where's Dad?' He peered round the door into the living room. It was empty.

'Oh, he's in the garden. Sit yourself down, I'll let him know you're here.' Putting the bouquet down on the worktop, his mother went out into the back garden.

Sebastian peered out of the window over the kitchen sink and watched his mother hobble down the garden. She suddenly looked older and he felt a twinge of regret at having left it so long to visit. He could see his father on his hands and knees beside one of the flowerbeds, seemingly pulling up weeds. He stopped what he was doing and stood up and a few words passed between them, but although the top window was open Sebastian couldn't make out what was said. Yet as his mother came back up the cobblestone path to the kitchen door she looked a little sad, which told Sebastian all he needed to know about what must have been said. His father got back down on his knees tending to the flowerbeds.

'He'll be in in a minute,' she said as she closed the kitchen door. 'Tea or coffee?'

Sebastian took a seat at the kitchen table. 'Could I have a tea please, Mum?'

His mother started making the tea and then rummaged under the sink for a vase. 'These are really beautiful flowers, Seb. Thank you so much.'

'I remembered you always liked peonies.'

'I do, they're my favourites.' She set about arranging them in the vase. 'So. What brings you here? It must be a good six months since we saw you?'

Sebastian knew it was longer than that and he felt another twinge of guilt, but he didn't correct her. 'Oh, I have been meaning to visit for a while, but you know what it's like, time just runs away with you. I had a few hours to spare today so thought I'd pop over. I also wanted to tell you…'

The back door opened and his father walked in, scraping his boots on the mat. He looked at Sebastian. 'Well, well. Your mother wasn't hallucinating after all.'

Sebastian stood up. 'Hi, Dad.' He held out his hand, but his father ignored it and turned to the sink.

'Where have you come from, a funeral?'

'No.'

'What's with the fancy whistle then?'

'Sebastian works in an office, Adam,' his mother interjected. 'He would have to wear a suit.'

It's now or never, Sebastian thought. 'Well, actually Mum, I don't work there anymore. I was… er… I finished there a couple of months ago.'

'Oh?' His mother looked surprised. 'I thought you loved working there. Making all those space invader games and whatnot. What was it now? Maps?'

'Apps, Mum. We developed Apps.'

Sebastian's father turned around, drying his hands on a tea towel. 'I suppose they sacked you. What you doing now then? Is this your interview suit?' There was an evident note of sarcasm in the question.

244

'Actually, no. As I was just about to tell Mum, I have a new job and I've just been for a photoshoot.'

His mother put her hands together and smiled. 'A *photoshoot*? Gosh. What for?'

'I've been signed to an entertainments agency. I'm a stage hypnotist.'

'Ha!' his father guffawed. 'That's not a job, boy. What are you doing to actually earn a living?'

'This *is* my job. It *is* how I earn a living. Or at least it will be.'

His father shook his head resignedly. 'Still away with the fairies,' he scoffed as he left the kitchen and disappeared into the living room, pushing the door to behind him.

Sebastian sighed and sat back down. His mother handed him a mug of tea and sat down opposite him. 'Never you mind your father, Seb. Come on, tell me all about this new job.'

After spending a couple of hours at his parents' house Sebastian decided he would stop off in Romford and see a film. It had been ages since he'd been to the cinema and he quite fancied seeing the new *Halloween*. He refused point blank to pay the extortionate prices cinemas charge for refreshments, preferring to get himself a drink and some sweets at half the price and smuggle them in, so he popped into The Range.

As he stepped up to the till he was greeted by a cheerful lady. 'Are you going up to the pictures?' she asked as she scanned his bottle of Pepsi, a bag of popcorn and some Jelly Babies.

Sebastian chuckled. 'How did you guess?'

'Just call it intuition,' the woman said with a wink, waggling the bag of popcorn at him. 'One of our best sellers. What are you going to see?'

'The new *Halloween* movie,' Sebastian replied.

'Another one?!' the woman exclaimed, shaking her head. 'You'd think they'd have run out of ideas by now. I remember the original from 1978. Really good.' She laughed. 'I do love my horrors though. That'll be £3.24 please.'

Sebastian swiped his debit card. As he picked up his supplies, he caught sight of the woman's name badge. 'Thank you, Sandra. Have a great day.'

'You too. Enjoy the film,' she called after him.

Two and a half hours later Sebastian stepped out of the cinema and as he travelled down the escalator, he recalled Sandra's words. *The makers have indeed run out of ideas*, he thought to himself; *Halloween Ends* was one of the most disappointing films he'd seen in many years. He looked at his watch. It was approaching six o'clock. He thought for a moment. If he caught the 86 to Ilford, he should make it just in time to meet Tilly from work. He walked to the bus stop and just as he reached the shelter it started to rain. A few minutes later the bus arrived and Sebastian hopped aboard.

The journey from Romford to Ilford was slow. It was a busy route at the best of times, but tonight half the world seemed to be on the road. Nevertheless, Sebastian sat thinking about the film and what a shame it was that the series had gone out with a whimper, and before he knew it the bus had reached his stop.

Tilly smiled with surprise when she saw him stood waiting beside her car. 'What you doing here?' She stepped up and kissed him.

'I thought I'd come and meet you.'

Tilly eyed his wet jacket. 'You should have come inside. You're soaked!'

'Yeah, it was just starting to rain when I got on the bus, but the skies really opened when I arrived just now.'

Tilly unlocked the car. 'Quick, get inside.' They climbed in and Tilly leant over to kiss Sebastian again. 'It's lovely of you to meet me from work, but I thought you'd have gone home and changed first.'

Sebastian smiled as the word "home" made him feel all warm inside. 'I've been out all day actually. After the shoot I went to see my parents, then I decided to take myself off to the cinema.'

'Your parents? That's lovely.' Tilly started the car and they set off.

Sebastian sighed 'Yeah, it was okay. Well...' he paused. 'A bit disheartening truth be told.'

Tilly glanced at him as she slowed down at the lights. 'Disheartening? Why's that?'

'My Dad hardly spoke to me. I don't think he even cared that I was there. And my Mum... I dunno, she seemed really pleased to see me, but it all just felt a bit strange. I'm glad I went though, I hadn't seen her for a while.'

'What about the photoshoot? How did that go?'

'It was amazing. The person taking the photos was great, really inspirational. And, yeah, for the first time in my life I actually felt confident in myself.'

Tilly reached over and squeezed his knee. 'I'm so happy for you. When will you get to see the photos?'

'I'm not sure. I expect McCleary will want to vet them first.' Sebastian shifted uncomfortably in his seat. He hadn't realised that his trousers had also got a little wet on the dash from the bus stop to Tilly's car and his legs were starting to feel damp. 'Anyway, enough about me. How was *your* day?'

'Oh, nothing exciting, same old same old really. Except guess what came in on today's delivery?'

'Er...' Sebastian shrugged his shoulders.

'Advent calendars. And chocolate Santas! I mean, we've not even had Halloween yet and we had to put those on the shelf!'

Sebastian laughed. 'It'll be Easter Eggs before you know it! Speaking of Halloween, the film I went to see this afternoon was the new *Halloween* one – *Halloween Ends.*'

'Oh! I wanted to see that. The trailer looks great.'

'Don't bother, it was rubbish,' Sebastian said.

'Oh no, really? That's a shame.'

'Yeah. Trust me, it's not worth the effort. Two hours I'll never get back. Well, two and a half what with all the adverts.'

'It's meant to be the last one though, isn't it?'

'Supposedly.' Sebastian laughed and rolled his eyes. 'Until the reboot.'

Tilly slowed the car and indicated, then turned right into her road and pulled up outside the house. 'Come on then, my gorgeous little superstar. Let's get inside and you can dry off while I get dinner on.'

CHAPTER 19

Sebastian could hardly contain his excitement when he picked up the card-backed envelope that the postman deposited on Tilly's doormat. James had called on Tuesday and told him to expect a package and the wait had been torture, but it was finally here. James had requested he open it immediately upon receipt as he needed approval on the photos, but Sebastian wanted Tilly to be there so he waited patiently until she got home from work.

'You mean to tell me you've sat here all day with this and you weren't even tempted to have a sneaky look?' Tilly said.

Sebastian was standing in front of her clutching the envelope. 'Nope. I wanted to open it with you here,' he replied, anxiously turning it his hands.

'Well, come on then!' Tilly said, almost as excited as he was. 'What are we waiting for?'

Sebastian hooked his thumbnail under the flap and ripped open the top of the envelope. Carefully slipping two fingers inside, he pulled out an 8x10-inch glossy photograph. He studied it for a moment and a small smile appeared in the corner of his mouth.

'Let's have a look then,' Tilly said eagerly. Sebastian turned the photograph round and she beamed, clapping her hands together. 'Oh, wow! That's fantastic! *You* look fantastic!' Sebastian looked at it again. 'Do you like it?' Tilly asked.

'Yeah. It's alright, eh?'

Tilly took the photo from him and gently laid it on the kitchen table. She cupped his face in her hands and stood on tiptoe to give him a big kiss. 'It's more than alright. It's

249

absolutely wonderful. I'm *so* proud of you. Everything is falling perfectly into place.'

Sebastian hooked his arms around her waist and held her tight. 'Yeah. It is.'

'Is that all that was in the envelope?' Tilly asked.

'Ooh, I don't know.' Sebastian picked it up and peered inside. 'No, there's something else.' He pulled out a smaller photograph and an A4-sized sheet of paper.

'Look at that!' Tilly exclaimed, taking the smaller photo from him. It was a reproduction of the large one. 'It's got a space for your autograph.'

Sebastian looked a little embarrassed. 'Who's going to want *my* autograph?'

'I'd say a lot of people will once your show starts to become popular.' She giggled. 'I'll want one.' She saw Sebastian looking at the sheet of paper. 'What's that?'

'I'm not sure.'

Tilly waited expectantly, watching his eyes darting back and forth.

'It's a biography type thing.' Sebastian chuckled. 'It's not bad actually. Makes me sound like a proper entertainer.'

'You *are* a proper entertainer!'

Sebastian handed her the sheet of paper and she read it. 'I'd better call James,' he said. 'He wanted to know if I approve of the photos and stuff.' He opened his phone and found the number. It rang a couple of times before a voice came into the line.

'James Lawrence.'

'Hi James, it's Seb Matthews.'

'Seb! I was just about to call you, I was getting concerned. Did the package arrive?'

'Yes, it did.'

'And? Are you happy with the portfolio and promo shots?'

'They're great, James. Thank you.'

'Super. Have you got a pen handy?'

Sebastian looked around the kitchen, silently mouthing 'Pen?' to Tilly. 'One minute, James,' he said, as Tilly rummaged in a drawer. She handed him a pen and a small notepad. 'Okay, I've got one.'

'Right. I have some dates for you. Jot these down and check your availability for me, can you? The last one is very special, Seb, so I hope you'll clear your diary for us.'

James reeled off a list of dates and Sebastian scribbled them down. 'I'll let you know as soon as possible,' Sebastian said excitedly.

'Great! I look forward to hearing from you soon. And Seb, I can't stress enough how big the New Year's Eve one is. It would definitely be in your interest to keep that date free.'

Sebastian's mind was racing. 'Okay.'

'Speak soon, Seb. Bye for now.'

'Bye, James. And thanks again.' Sebastian ended the call and looked at Tilly, who was staring at him with excitement in her eyes. 'Wow! I wasn't expecting *that*!'

'Have they got a gig for you?'

'Quite a few actually,' Sebastian said, handing Tilly the notepad.

Her eyes scanned the list of dates. 'Seven. And one of them is on New Year's Eve too. That should pay well.'

Sebastian grinned. 'Yeah, I guess it will.'

'Are you going to do them all?' Tilly said, handing back the notepad.

'James asked me to check my diary, but to be honest, there's nothing in it.' Sebastian chuckled. 'In fact, I don't even own a diary.'

'Well I'd say you'd better get one.' Tilly smiled. 'It looks like you're going to be in high demand.'

'Yeah, I guess I should.' Sebastian wrapped his arms around her. 'I wouldn't even be doing this if it wasn't for you. I love you so much.'

Tilly kissed him and picked up the photo from the kitchen table. 'Can I have this?'

'Of course. You can have them both if you want.'

'Nah, just this one. Signed of course! You should give the larger one to your Mum.'

'You know, I think I'll do that,' Sebastian said tucking it back into the envelope.

'I think we should go out to celebrate.' Tilly declared. 'What do you say?'

'Sounds good. What do you have in mind?'

'There's a nice bar up the road called McCaffety's. They do a great selection of food.'

'Then McCaffety's it is. But do you think I should ring James back first?'

'Hmm.' Tilly thought for a moment. 'I reckon you should leave it until the morning. You don't want to appear too desperate'.

'Maybe. But what if he gives the gigs to someone else?'

'I'm just going to pop upstairs and get changed so if you really want to call him, go for it. But I don't think you'll lose those gigs. You're their new star boy!'

Tilly trotted off upstairs and Sebastian slumped down on the sofa. He looked at his phone. Accessing the recent calls he stared at James's number at the top of the list. Deciding that Tilly was most probably right, he made up his mind to leave it until the following morning.

*

The pipping sound of Sebastian's phone alarm woke him from a deep and dreamless sleep and he stirred, groaning at the ridiculously early hour. Tilly turned over, blinking in the half-light and he apologised for waking her. 'I'm sorry, bubs. Go back to sleep.' He kissed her lightly on the forehead and then, scooping up a neatly folded pile of clothes from the stool beside the dressing table, he crept out of the bedroom and silently pulled the door to behind him. He washed and dressed in the bathroom and set off for his shift at the flower market.

Twenty minutes later, sitting on the empty bus and staring idly out of the window, he thought about the engagement with Rising Starz. His first gig was two weeks away, after which he had one every weekend up to January. If things picked up for him in 2023 as well as he hoped they would, he could actually think seriously about ditching the job at Columbia Road.

The day dragged and Sebastian couldn't wait to leave. He found a quiet spot on a bench in the Jesus Green park around the corner and called James.

The phone rang for what seemed like an eternity until finally someone answered. It was a woman's voice. 'Good morning, Rising Starz, how can I help?' Sebastian recognised Gemma's voice.

'Hi Gemma. It's Sebastian. Sebastian Matthews. Is James Lawrence there please?'

'No, I'm afraid he's just stepped out, Mr Maffews. Would you like to leave a…' the line suddenly went quiet.

Sebastian frowned. 'Hello?'

'Sebastian!' The familiar voice of Gregor McCleary boomed down the line. 'How ye doing son?'

'I'm good, thank you. I was just calling to…'

'Yes, yes, very good. Listen, have ye had a chance to look at those dates our Jimmy gave you? Tha' big German jessie windbag Zach Bauer has let me down and I need to get those slots filled pronto. Do ye get me?'

'Yes, Mr McCleary. I'm available and I'd love to do it.'

'Aye. Tha's great. Did Jimmy tell ye about the Hogmanay do?'

'Hogmanay?'

'New Year's Eve, son.'

'Er... well he told me to keep that particular date free. He said it was an important gig.'

'Important? This could be your big break, laddie. You're going to need to speak to our stage people. It'll be a big production and it has to be spectacular. There will be a film crew there and I've staked ma whole reputation on you, so ye need to be thinking about what you're going to do.'

'Oh, wow. Thank you, Mr McCleary.' Sebastian's heart was beating hard. He felt incredibly excited and very nervous in equal measure. 'May I ask where the show is being held?'

'Aye. It's Bloomsbury lad, tha' big theatre there. But I'll get Jimmy t' call ye with all the details, okay?'

'Okay. Thank you.'

'Oh and Sebastian. Just one thing.'

'Yes sir?'

'When ye do tha' theatre I insist you do the chicken routine, okay?'

'Yes, sir, Mr McCleary, of course. Anything you say.'

Without even saying goodbye, McCleary hung up. Sebastian clenched his fists. 'Yes!' he cried out. A woman walking her dog gave him a sideways glance and he felt his cheeks flush with embarrassment.

Against the distant hum of traffic, Sebastian sat for a while, musing upon what McCleary had said. He thought about how quickly his life had changed in just a few short weeks and the excitement that lay ahead. Feeling the warm sun on his face, he looked up at the trees, swaying gently in the breeze and occupied by countless small birds flitting from branch to branch. And then his thoughts turned to Tilly. He smiled. *Life can't really get much better than this*, he thought.

CHAPTER 20

Sebastian stepped through the doorway of yet another charity shop – the umpteenth he'd visited that morning – and headed straight for the Bric-a-Brac shelves. He was already carrying a large shopping bag bulging with his purchases and he struggled to squeeze past the clothing rails with it. Catching it on a coat hanger he yanked it and a dozen or more knitted jumpers dropped onto the floor.

'Are you alright there?' a voice called out.

Sebastian quickly bent down to pick up the jumpers. He tried to return them to the rail but the coat hangers had become tangled and he started to get flustered.

'Here, let me sort those out,' the elderly volunteer said. There was a note of annoyance in her tone.

'I'm sorry,' Sebastian said. 'The gap was very narrow and my bag got caught.'

'Yes, everything has become very tight in here since we've had to put the Christmas cards out on display,' the woman grumbled.

Sebastian could see he had touched a nerve and decided to make a hasty retreat. He was crossing to the door when he caught sight of something poking out of a pile of knitting magazines and craft materials. His eyes lit up; he couldn't believe what he was seeing and he quickly grabbed up the piece of treasure. He turned it around in his hands and beamed from ear to ear. A small tag was dangling from it and Sebastian examined it. Satisfied with his find and the more than reasonable price attached to it, he negotiated his way back through the clothing racks to get to the till.

The same volunteer came over. She looked up at Sebastian and down at the wooden-rimmed steering wheel he had placed on the counter top. 'Well, I have to say I never thought I'd see *that* go,' she said as she punched the details into the till. 'Would you like a raffle ticket to win a luxury Christmas hamper?' she asked robotically. Sebastian politely declined. 'That'll be £7.50 then please.'

'Is a debit card okay?'

The woman slid the card machine across the counter. Sebastian paid for the steering wheel and apologised again for his mishap with the coat hangers. The woman afforded him a smile, then returned to the rack to finish arranging the jumpers. Sebastian paused at the door and, managing to wedge his new purchase into his bag, he strolled out of the shop feeling inordinately pleased with himself.

With the bag full to bursting and now weighing heavy, he really wanted to get on the bus and head for home. But there was one more prop he needed to acquire, and having trawled all the charity shops in Romford – and there were a few – he decided to try one last place. He'd walked past the fancy dress emporium in the shopping hall many times but had never had a need to go inside; it was a big shop and always looked pretty full, so he was certain he'd find *something* in there along the lines of what he needed.

As he stepped through the door, he was startled by a life-size animatronic Grim Reaper display just inside the entrance, where it had been set up for Halloween. With a whirring sound, it turned to face him and its eyes blazed red. Cackling maniacally, it spoke in a raspy mechanical voice: '*Beware! Everything is doomed!*' It laughed again and repeated '*Doooomed!*' Sebastian shuddered and was slightly alarmed that, as he moved quickly past it, the figure swivelled on its base to track him; it was of course only resetting itself in preparation for the next unsuspecting customer to walk through the door, but Sebastian still felt a chill run through him. Taking one last look back at the monstrosity, he glanced around at the vast display of costumes and novelties.

A voice suddenly spoke in his ear. 'Is there something specific you're looking for?'

Sebastian jumped. He hadn't heard the man approach. 'Oh, hi. Yes. I want something a musician would wear.'

'Would that be male or female?' the shopkeeper asked.

Sebastian pondered the question for a moment. 'It doesn't really matter.'

The man led him to the back of the shop where there was a mannequin dressed up as Freddie Mercury. He pointed to the outfit. 'Freddie?'

Sebastian shook his head. 'No, I've got a Freddie jacket already.'

The man waved a hand at a huge wall rack filled with multiple costumes in packets. 'Well then, we have Cher, Alice Cooper, a generic boyband look, Rod Stewart, Madonna…'

'Oh, can I see the Madonna one please?' Sebastian said enthusiastically.

The man pursed his lips and eyed Sebastian up and down. The trace of a smile appeared at the corner of his mouth. 'Of course, sir.' He reached up and unhooked the plastic package. Sebastian studied the image on the front. It showed a young girl wearing a shiny body suit with a pointed bra built into it. The shopkeeper was watching Sebastian with mild suspicion. After a few moments he said, 'Any good?'

'It's great,' Sebastian said thoughtfully. 'But I think that's going to be a bit of a faff to put on quickly.' He caught sight of the expression on the man's face. 'Oh, it's not for me,' he added hastily.

The man smiled broadly and turned to a shelf laden with a variety of accessories. 'We have the cone bra separately if that's any better?' He handed it to Sebastian and took the packaged outfit from him.

'Yes, that's perfect.'

The man grinned. 'Great. Is there anything else you need? A nice wig perhaps? Or a pair of tights?' There was notable sarcasm in his voice.

'No, this will do fine. How much do I owe you?'

The man glanced at the sticker on the bra. '£9.99.'

Sebastian handed him a £10 note. 'Keep the change,' he said with deliberate sarcasm. The man handed over the bra and Sebastian managed to squeeze it into his bag. 'Thank you,' he said confidently, and being sure to keep as clear as possible of the Halloween display, he swaggered out of the shop, trying desperately not to burst out laughing as the man stood staring at the £10 note.

*

Sebastian laid out his purchases on the kitchen table. Spotting the conical bra, Tilly grabbed it up and slipped it on. 'Like a virgin – ow! – touched for the very first time!' Sebastian raised one eyebrow as he watched her dancing around the kitchen. She caught sight of the look on his face and grinned. 'I do love a bit of 80s Madonna. She went rubbish after *Vogue* though.'

'Do you know what I love?' Sebastian bent forward to whisper in her ear. 'You.' He put his arms around her and suddenly cried out. 'Ouch!' He stepped back. 'Those things are lethal,' he declared rubbing his ribs.

Tilly laughed. 'Perhaps that's why Madonna created them, to keep lecherous men at bay!'

'Are you calling me lecherous?' Sebastian said, sticking out his bottom lip.

Tilly unhooked the bra and put it back on the table. She went to give Sebastian a hug, but he turned sideways and crossed him arms. 'Nope! I'm not going to stand here and be called a letch!'

Tilly frowned and mimicked him. 'Fine,' she said, turning her back on him and crossing her arms. Sebastian grinned and grabbed her from behind, spinning her round into a strong embrace. They both giggled impishly. 'Madonna has nothing on you,' he said kissing her on the top of her head.

'I've got something for you.' Tilly reached for her handbag, pulled out a brown paper bag and handed it to him.

Sliding out the contents, he smiled. 'A diary! Oh brilliant. Thank you.' He opened it and saw there was a handwritten message on the inside cover:

> I feel lucky every day that I'm with you.
> All my love always. Tilly. X

Sebastian felt a lump forming in his throat and he swallowed hard. 'Thank you,' he croaked.

Tilly smiled at him. Her eyes twinkled in the light. She leant over and picked up the old MG steering wheel from the table. 'This is pretty cool. What are you going to do with it?'

'I had an idea I'd make one of the volunteers into a racing driver. I thought it might be funny if they zoom around the stage with that in their hands. I might try that one out next week.'

'And this?' Tilly said, picking up a red tablecloth.

260

'I'm not sure yet, but I have a few ideas. I just thought something bright and vivid would be a good visual, you know for one of the bigger venues.'

Tilly wrapped it around her shoulders and up over her head. 'You could always do Little Red Riding Hood,'

'As long as I can be the Big Bad Wolf!' Sebastian let out a loud howl before nuzzling his face in Tilly's neck and growling.

'Get off, you big dope,' she said playfully, whipping him with the red cloth.

'Well, I think I've got enough new props here to change the shows up a bit each time.'

'You certainly have. Where did you get all this stuff anyway?' Tilly asked, picking up a brass bugle and curling her lip as she looked down into the mouthpiece.

'Charity shops mostly. I was bloody knackered by the time I finished. Do you know there's nine charity shops in Romford and I went into every single one of them.' He picked up the steering wheel. 'I got this little gem in the last one. I couldn't believe my luck when I saw it.'

Tilly rolled her eyes. 'Have you never heard of eBay? You could have saved yourself a lot of time and shoe leather.'

'Yeah, but the hunt is all part of the fun.' Sebastian picked up the bugle and blew into it. A plume of dust shot out the end and the sound was nothing more than a strangled whimper. He licked his lips and winced.

'Ew!' Tilly exclaimed. 'You don't know where that thing has been!'

'In someone's attic, I'd wager. And judging by the amount of dust in it, for a very long time.' Sebastian wiped his mouth with the back of his hand and smacked his lips. 'Hmm. 18th century dust if I'm not very much mistaken.' Tilly laughed. Suddenly he felt his mobile

261

phone pulsing in his pocket. He pulled it out. 'Ooh, it's the agency.' Tapping **Accept**, he answered. 'Hello?'

'Sebastian, dear boy. How are you?'

'I'm good thanks, James. Yourself?'

'I'm tip-top. Thank you for asking. Now listen. Gregor tells me that you've given us the thumbs up on all those dates I gave you.'

'Yes, I'll put them all in my diary. Thank you, James, I'm really grateful for the opportunity.'

'My pleasure, dear boy. I knew from the first time I saw your act in that grotty old pub that you'd be a star and I'm glad we're the ones to help you get there.' James chuckled. 'Now then, New Year's Eve. Gregor explained it's in a big theatre and it will be filmed?'

'Yes, he did. I wanted to ask you more about that.'

'Okay. So, the show is a fundraiser for a charity event. It's invite only and I believe tickets are something like £200 each.'

'Wow!' Sebastian exclaimed.

'There will be four acts on throughout the evening and you are top billing. We have a full sound and light crew at your disposal, but we need to start thinking now about the production. Time is not on our side.'

'I do have a few ideas already. Mr McCleary said I have to do the chicken stunt and I've devised three others that I think will be suitable for a large stage.'

'That's great. But I'm afraid I'm going to have to insist on something, Seb. And you may not like it.'

Sebastian frowned. 'Oh?'

'What happened at the social club with that uncouth bald fellow, is it possible it could happen again?'

Sebastian could detect the concern in James's voice. 'Well, in a word, yes. Not everyone is susceptible to hypnotism. That guy was pretty drunk, so I think he was

262

already half asleep when he came up on stage. But the fact is there's always going to be the possibility that somebody won't go under or follow my instructions.'

The line went quiet for a moment. Sebastian felt a wave of nervousness.

'Right. Thing is, with this show being filmed, and given the calibre of guests we will be entertaining, I'm afraid we can't afford for that to happen.' Sebastian suddenly felt sick inside. Where was this leading? 'When you first performed your act in the Cauliflower,' James continued, 'when that dreadful karaoke fellow's microphone broke, you called up your friend and did the chicken routine.'

'That's right.'

'And before then, I saw you do something to your friend's drink.'

'Well, kind of, yeah.'

'What I'm trying to say, Seb, is that you must tailor your show so that there is no room for error. You need to be certain that your participants will perform.'

Sebastian's face fell as the penny dropped. 'Are you saying I have to fake it? I don't think I c…'

'No, no, no, dear boy, not fake it. Just handpick your volunteers using people you *know* will respond well to hypnosis.'

Sebastian thought for a moment. He wasn't happy about deceiving the audience, yet he could see how it could become very embarrassing – for him *and* Rising Starz – should he end up with a volunteer that he couldn't hypnotise. It also occurred to him that if he didn't agree he could possibly lose the best and maybe only chance of stardom he would ever be offered.

'Well, Seb? Are you on board?'

263

'Okay, sure. I can ask my friends if they'll do it. But we're going to have to work it so that there isn't a sliver of doubt with the audience that I've picked random strangers.'

'I'm sure you can figure all that out,' James said reassuringly. 'Gregor has arranged several rehearsal sessions for you at a theatre in Ilford. The sound and light crew will be there and we'll also be sending a set designer down so that you can discuss any ideas you have. The first one is this coming Monday. Can you be there?' Without even thinking Sebastian said that he could. 'Great! You'll need to be at The Kenneth Moore at 9am sharp. A man called Douglas will meet you there. I'll be back in touch mid-week.'

'Okay, James. Thank you.'

'Once again, dear boy, it's my absolute pleasure.'

'Oh, one other thing, James. Would I be able to bring my girlfriend to the show?'

'Of course. I'll make sure you have a few complimentary tickets to hand out to your friends or family. Toodle-pip.'

Sebastian hung up the phone and sighed. 'Bugger.'

'What's up?' Tilly asked.

'I just said I can go to a rehearsal on Monday when I'm supposed to be at work.'

'Can't you pull a sickie, just this once?'

'Yeah, I *could*, but there are going to be a few of these sessions and I can't *keep* calling in sick.'

'Then hand in your notice' Tilly said firmly. 'You'll be earning from these shows soon enough.'

'But until then, how will I pay for stuff?'

'You won't have to. You know you can stay here for as long as you want and there's always plenty of food in.'

264

'That's really kind, but I can't expect you to pay for everything. And how will I cover my rent on the flat?'

'Give it up.' Tilly smiled at him. 'Move in with me permanently.'

'Hmmm.' Sebastian started to pace the room.

'You're pacing!'

'Yeah, I know, sorry. I always do that when I'm trying to figure stuff out.'

'What is there to figure out? I've loved having you here and as long as you're not bored with me... well, it makes sense right?'

'Of course I'm not bored with you. It's just...'

'Just what?'

'Well, it's a big step and... I'm going to have to give notice on the flat.'

'Ring the landlady and explain the situation. I'm sure she'll understand. Come on, live a little. You hate that job anyway.'

Sebastian sighed again. Then he smiled. 'You're right. Let's do this.'

Tilly threw her arms around him. 'Yay!'

CHAPTER 21

'Oh, my God, I'm so nervous I think I'm going to be sick!'

Sebastian was leaning against Tilly's car in the staff car park adjacent to the Bloomsbury Theatre.

Tilly was standing in front of him vigorously rubbing her hands up and down his arms. 'You're going to be fine. Just relax.'

'But what if it all goes wrong?' Sebastian started to pace the length of the car and back again. He was breathing hard and the icy cold, early evening air was turning every rapid exhalation into a billow of steam. 'I should never have agreed to do this. What if I cock up and let James down? And Mr McCleary! Oh, my God, he'll be livid and...'

'Seb. Darling. It will be fine. Every show you've done the last few weekends has been fantastic. Standing ovations at every one. You've rehearsed this over and over, you have a crew in there who will ensure everything goes to plan. It's going to be great!' Sebastian looked at her, his face etched with worry. 'Honestly,' she continued, 'I'm behind you all the way. I'll be there in the wings, so if you feel nerves creeping over you just look for me. I'll be there.'

Sebastian took a deep breath and exhaled slowly. He nodded. 'Okay.'

'Now come on, it's freezing out here. Let's get your things together and check this place out.'

Sebastian collected his suit bag from the hook inside the rear car door. Tilly opened the boot and pulled out a large bag with string handles.

'What you got there?' Sebastian asked.

'Oh nothing, it's just my jacket in case it gets cold later.'

'It's cold *now*. Don't you want to put it on?'

Tilly rolled her eyes. 'Stop stalling, you.' She playfully slapped him on the bottom. 'Come on. Inside. Now!'

They walked up the steps to the front entrance of the theatre. As soon as they entered the foyer a member of the security staff stepped up to them. 'I'm sorry, folks, the box office isn't open today.'

'I'm Sebastian Matthews. I'm the... er... well, the headline act tonight.'

'One second sir.' The man pressed a button on a walkie-talkie attached to his jacket. 'Control. I have a Sebastian Matthews down here in the foyer. Over.' He waited for a response and smiled politely at Sebastian.

The walkie-talkie crackled. 'Roger that, Paul. I'll send someone down to collect him. Over and out.'

'Someone will be down to meet you in a few minutes.'

Sebastian nodded. 'Thank you.'

Tilly stepped up next to him and took hold of his hand. She squeezed it tight. Sebastian looked down at her and smiled. A minute passed, then a set of swing doors opened and a man appeared. Giving Sebastian's hand another quick squeeze, Tilly gently released it.

'Mr Matthews?' the man enquired.

'Yes, that's me.'

'Splendid. My name is André, I'm the house manager tonight. If you'd like to follow me, I'll show you to your dressing room.'

'This is my girlfriend, Tilly,' Sebastian said.

'Lovely to meet you, Miss.' With that, the man took off at a pace, and they hurried to keep up as he led them through the auditorium and down the sloped walkway

267

towards the stage. As they rushed along, the large bag Tilly was carrying kept banging against the wall. She jabbed Sebastian in the arm and whispered, 'Mr Matthews, eh?'

Sebastian grinned. 'I know,' he whispered back. 'Do you want me to take that bag for you?'

'No, it's fine.'

Sebastian's brow furrowed. 'You sure?'

'Yes. Honest, I'm fine.'

As they reached the stage André paused at a gap in the barrier leading to the orchestra pit. 'Through here, please.' He gestured for them to follow him into the pit and through a door beneath the stage.

Sebastian stopped and stood in the pit for a moment, looking back out into the house. Rows upon rows of red velvet seats climbed way up to the roof. It was an astounding site.

'This way please,' André called.

They went through the doorway, passed through a dimly lit space and out into a corridor. André veered swiftly off to the right and Sebastian and Tilly followed. The sound of laughter and voices echoed from somewhere off along a side corridor as they passed by. André carried on down the passageway and came to a stop outside a door on the left. 'This is your dressing room, Mr Matthews. I hope everything will be to your satisfaction. I'll leave you to settle in. The corridor we just passed takes you to the green room. There are snacks and refreshments there if you'd like them. Do you have any questions?'

Sebastian's head was in a bit of a spin. 'No, I don't think so. Thank you.'

André nodded at Sebastian and turned to face Tilly. 'Miss Tilly,' he said with a small nod, and she smiled and waved at him as he hurried out the door and they heard the sound of his heels receding along the corridor.

Waiting until they were sure he was gone, Sebastian looked at Tilly and the pair of them burst out laughing. She closed the door and put her bag down on the floor. Stepping over to Sebastian, she took hold of his hands. 'Well, Mr Matthews, this is all rather special, isn't it?' she said, looking around the room.

'Yeah. I'm a little bit dumbstruck as it goes. I mean it's all a bit of a whirlwind. André, that huge theatre and now this,' he said, sweeping his hands open wide.

Tilly kissed him. 'It's no more than you deserve.'

Sebastian hung his suit bag on a hook on the back of the door. There was a small cube-shaped fridge against the wall. He opened it to reveal it was brimming with various drinks. 'Do you want something to drink?'

'Don't you want to go through to the green room, get something there?' Tilly asked.

'To be honest, I'm a bit nervous. Do you mind if we just stay in here for a bit?'

'Of course. Whatever you want. What you got in there then?'

Sebastian bent down. 'All sorts of miniatures, spring water, Coke, Diet Coke, Tango.'

'I'll have a spring water please.'

Sebastian took out two bottles of water and handed one to Tilly. They both sat down on the red leather sofa in the corner and gazed around the room. 'I wonder who else has sat on this sofa?' Tilly mused.

'Hmm. Loads of stars, I guess.' He stretched back.

'Don't you think we should show our faces out there?' Tilly said. 'After all, we don't want them to think you're unsociable or rude.'

269

'Sebastian sighed. 'You're probably right. But I dunno. I feel *really* nervous tonight. It's strange, I was fine at all the other shows, even that really weird little club in High Beech. But tonight I just have a horrible feeling in my stomach.'

'That's perfectly understandable,' Tilly said, resting a hand on his knee. 'I'm sure the other acts feel the same. This is a big deal.' She could see Sebastian wasn't convinced. 'You already know some of the crew, right? That Dougie guy you introduced me to? He was nice.' She took his hand. 'Come one, let's just go say hi and we can come back again. Tell them you need to get changed and we can bail.'

Sebastian leant over and kissed her. 'Okay. A quick hello, but then I'll make my excuses.'

They stood up and put the bottles down on the dressing table.

'Ooh, what's this?' Tilly said, picking up a sheet of paper from the table.

Sebastian peered over her shoulder. 'It looks like the running order for tonight.'

'Colin the cunning linguist?' Tilly exclaimed. 'What sort of gala *is* this?!'

Unsure he'd heard her correctly, Sebastian said, 'Huh? Show me.' Tilly handed him the paper. 'Crikey! With a name like that I'm guessing he's some sort of comedian. You wouldn't want to say his name after a few vodkas though.' He studied the list. 'So, there's a ventriloquist on at 7:00, a singer at 8:00, Colin at 9:00 and then me at 10:00. That's a fast turnaround – it says here they all get 45 minutes and I've got an hour.'

'I guess it'll be pretty slick. Places like this know what they're doing.'

270

Sebastian dropped the paper back on the dressing table. 'Come on then, let's go find the green room.'

They walked along the corridor to the T-junction. The laughter and chat was still in full flow and Sebastian stopped just short of the doorway. 'You okay?' Tilly said. Just as he was about to answer a voice sounded behind them.

'Sebastian!' They turned to see James. 'Delightful to see you, dear boy. I was just going to pop by your dressing room, but you saved me the trip.' He looked at Tilly. 'Hello there, erm... sorry...'

'Tilly.'

'Of course, yes, Tilly.' He tapped his head. 'Brain like a sieve. Are we going in then?'

Sebastian nodded and stepped into the brightly lit room with Tilly and James following closely in his wake. The room was filled with people, some sitting at tables eating and others stood chatting. In the far corner, sat on a sofa, Sebastian recognised Dougie, the technician he'd met at rehearsals a few weeks earlier. He raised a hand to wave and, as he caught his eye, Dougie stood up and came over.

'Hey! Good to see ya, man.' He held up his hand and Sebastian high-fived him. He looked at Tilly and James 'Hey, Tilly. James.'

James and Dougie shook hands. 'All set for this evening, young Douglas?' James said.

'Aye, all good. I had a wee run in with the comedian, but I think we're all sorted now.'

James frowned. 'Problem?'

'Nothing major. He was just throwing his weight around a bit, complaining about the backdrops being...' – Dougie raised his hands and made a little inverted commas gesture in the air – '..."in his way". It's all sorted now though.'

271

'Good-oh.'

Dougie looked at the clock on the wall and turned to Sebastian. 'Would you like to see the setup quickly before they start letting the punters in?'

'Yes please,' Sebastian said eagerly. 'Can Tilly come?'

'Of course,' Dougie said with a grin. 'More than welcome.'

'Sorry, James, I won't be a minute,' Sebastian said.

'That's absolutely fine, dear boy. I'll wait here for you. There's a plate of vol-au-vents over there with my name written all over them.'

Sebastian and Tilly followed Dougie out of the green room and off towards the stage. Behind the thick red curtain, the stage was bare, all but for a stool and a small, colourful wooden dog kennel sitting on a table. The lighting engineer was testing the spotlights and Sebastian squinted as a bright shard of light swept across the stage.

'Basically, each set will be moved forward as the curtain closes,' Dougie said as he pulled aside thick black curtains at the rear of the stage. Sebastian and Tilly followed him behind the drapes. 'You see, everything is set up here ready to be moved as soon as each act finishes.'

'Wow! Is that for you?' Tilly exclaimed, pointing at a wooden construction of the front elevation of a barn with a stack of hay bales next to it.

'Yeah, that's for the chicken stint. Where's the car, Dougie? I'd like to show Tilly.'

'It's parked up behind the farmyard set.' They walked around and behind the ply-board scenery was a shiny red racing car.

Tilly's eyes widened. 'Is that real?' she exclaimed.

'Yeah,' Sebastian said excitedly. 'Dougie found it. Isn't it great?'

272

'It's *fantastic*,' Tilly agreed. She pointed to a podium beside the car. There were a couple of props laid out on it. 'So you're doing Madonna I see,' she said, spotting the gold conical bra. 'What's that funny hat on the red cloth for?'

'Oh, that's for the...'

Sebastian was cut off by an angry voice. 'I say, you, technical guy!' A man approached them from the side of the stage. He was wearing tight black drainpipe trousers, a burgundy velvet jacket and a ruffled, open neck shirt. His straight auburn hair hung like curtains across his face. He flicked his head to one side and the hair parted to reveal circular, rimless spectacles. '*What* has occurred here with my display stands?' the man snarled. 'I specifically asked that they not be moved. Is this really so difficult for you people to comprehend?'

Dougie sighed. 'I already told you earlier, Colin, the stands need to be kept *behind* this curtain until it's time for your act.'

'But I placed them in the optimum position and I have no doubt whatsoever that when your grubby little stage-hands move them, they'll be in the wrong place. I can't be expected to move them once I have made my appearance.'

Dougie's brow knotted. 'I beg your pardon? Grubby little stage-hands? Who the hell do you think you are?!' Sebastian looked awkwardly at Tilly. 'Look here, Colin,' Dougie continued. 'I'm the stage manager and technician. This show is way more important than just you, so either you go back to your dressing room and leave the stage logistics to us or you'll find yourself removed from tonight's program.'

'You can't speak to me like that, you odiferous prole!' Colin hissed.

'I think you'll find I just did.' Dougie raised his eyebrows awaiting a response. But after glaring at Dougie for a moment, Colin harrumphed loudly, turned away and strode off. Dougie looked at Sebastian and Tilly. 'Sorry about that.'

Sebastian smiled. 'He's a little, er... fiery.'

'He's a jumped up, toffee-nosed prat is what he is. I don't know what people find so amusing about him. Anyway, look, it's almost time for the doors to open so we'd better get back to the green room.'

Dougie led them off the stage and back down into the corridor.

'If you don't mind, Dougie,' Sebastian said, 'I'm going to go back to my dressing room and start to get ready.'

'Sure, man, no problems. If you need anything just give me a shout. You'll hear an announcement from the speaker in your room when you're needed at the stage. Will you remember your way back?'

'Yeah, I'll be fine.'

Dougie nodded politely at Tilly, turned on his heels and hurried off along the corridor.

CHAPTER 22

Sebastian and Tilly returned to the dressing room. 'Wow, that Colin guy is really up himself,' Tilly said quietly as Sebastian closed the door behind them. She removed her cardigan and slung it onto the sofa.

They had left the house earlier in a bit of a rush and Sebastian hadn't noticed what Tilly had chosen to wear. Now his eyes widened and his heart skipped a beat. 'You look gorgeous!'

Tilly smiled. 'Thanks. Just a little something I found in the back of my wardrobe. But back to the cocky linguist. I can't believe the way he spoke to Dougie.'

'Yeah, I know. I wouldn't have blamed Dougie if he'd chinned him.'

Delighted to see the pendant he'd bought for her hanging around Tilly's neck, Sebastian picked up her cardigan from the sofa and slipped it onto the hook on the back of the door. He removed his own hooded jacket and hung it next to Tilly's. In the far corner of the room there was a closed door. 'I wonder what's in here?' he said, opening it to reveal a small bathroom with a shower cubicle. 'Oh, this is nice.'

Tilly came over to take a look. 'Oh, wow, this really is a swanky dressing room.'

'A marked improvement on some of the ones I've had the last few weeks.'

'That one at the serviceman's club was the best!'

Sebastian laughed. 'Oh, you mean the broom cupboard? Yeah, that was *really* great.' He looked at his watch. 'You know, as it's here I might just have a quick shower.' He winked at Tilly. 'Wanna join me?'

'Ooh, the offer is *very* tempting, but it took me an age to get into this dress.'

Sebastian grinned. 'I bet I could get it off quicker!'

'I bet you could too, but it'll take me ages to look this gorgeous again and I didn't bring my make-up bag. You go ahead and jump in.'

Sebastian pouted at her. 'Okay, spoilsport. I won't be long.'

'Good. And when you come out, I'll do your hair for you. Did you bring that styling cream?'

'Yeah, I did.'

Sebastian stepped into the bathroom and undressed. Tilly took a quick peek around the door and smiled to herself, then went and sat down on the sofa. She pulled out her mobile phone. Seeing that she'd had a missed call from Grace, she tried to return it, but her signal was weak. She held the phone aloft and waved it about hoping that might help, but it wasn't finding anything. She suddenly remembered having spotted a code for the venue's WIFI at the bottom of the run order they'd looked at earlier. Tapping in the password, she connected and called Grace back via WhatsApp. 'Hiya, Sis. Sorry I missed your call. The signal here is naff, so I'm on the theatre's WIFI.'

'No worries,' Grace said. 'I was only calling to say Jason and I have arrived in London. We're going for something to eat and just wanted to check how we get our tickets.'

'Seb has arranged comps for you and his mates. When you get here just speak to the man on the door and tell him you have tickets reserved. He'll get them from the box office for you. If there's any problems tell him to contact André.'

'André?'

'Yeah. He's the one in charge here.'

'Okey dokey. I'll see you a bit later then.'

'Yeah, WhatsApp me when you arrive and I'll come and find you.'

'See you soon.'

As Tilly ended the call Sebastian was coming out of the shower. He was clad in a white towelling dressing gown with The Bloomsbury Theatre embroidered on the breast. 'Who was that you were you speaking to?'

'Grace. She's having something to eat before the show and she wanted to know how to get her tickets. I told her they're at the box office.'

Sebastian frowned. 'That's a point actually, that security fella said the box office was closed. How *will* they get the tickets?'

'I just told her to ask him. I'm sure he can get them. He probably just meant they're closed for sales. Someone will be there to deal with enquiries and stuff.'

'I guess so,' Sebastian said. 'But I invited my Mum and Dad along and they're not that savvy. Do you think I should text Mum and tell them to speak to the security guard?'

'I'm sure Jordan, Josh, Mark and Katie will figure it out, but if you think your Mum and Dad might get a bit confused it wouldn't hurt.'

'Yeah. I'm a bit doubtful they'll even come, especially Dad. But maybe I will, just in case.'

'You'll need the WIFI password.' Tilly read it out to him and Sebastian quickly fired off a text. Then he pulled a tube and a comb from his jacket pocket and handed it to Tilly. 'I'll do that once you're dressed,' she said. 'It'll get all messed up otherwise.'

Sebastian nodded. 'Duh! Yeah, makes sense.' He took down the suit bag and disappeared back into the bathroom to get dressed.

Just to prevent any problems impacting on the smooth running of Sebastian's performance, Tilly decided to text Katie to let her know where to get the tickets from. Not wishing to add to Sebastian's nerves, she decided not to mention it to him. When he re-emerged from the bathroom, he was wearing a crisp white shirt, jet black waistcoat and dress trousers. His jacket was hung on the bathroom door. 'Can you help me with this?' he said, fiddling with the clasp on his bow tie.

'Come here,' Tilly said, taking the bow tie from him. She lifted the collars on his shirt and stepped round behind him to fasten the bow tie. 'Imagine if you had a traditional one you had to actually tie!' She stepped back around the front and adjusted it slightly. 'They have a habit of going crooked.' She looked him up and down and smiled. 'Very handsome. Put the jacket on.' Sebastian did so and Tilly buttoned it up for him and took a few paces backwards. 'Wow! There *is* one thing missing though.'

Sebastian's face fell. 'Oh no, what?' he said, a note of panic in his voice. Tilly picked up the bag she'd brought with her, pulled out a circular box and handed it to Sebastian. 'What's this?' he said.

Tilly beamed at him. 'Open it.'

Sebastian took off the lid and removed some scrunched-up tissue paper. 'Wow!' he exclaimed as he pulled out the contents. 'A proper top hat!' He placed it carefully on his head. 'And it fits perfectly!' Bending down to look at his reflection in the mirror, he tilted it to a slightly jaunty angle. 'Oh my goodness, thank you!'

'Let's have a look then,' Tilly urged him. Sebastian turned to face her. 'That's the cherry on top. You look sensational.'

Sebastian leant forward to kiss her and the brim of the hat bashed her forehead. 'Sorry!' he said, removing the hat. They kissed passionately and Sebastian felt his stomach doing little back-flips.

'Did your Mum answer your text?'

Sebastian picked up his phone and a worried expression crossed his face. 'No, she hasn't.'

'Maybe it would be a good idea to call them. I mean, I'm sure they'll sort out how to get their tickets okay, but just for peace of mind?'

Sebastian nodded. 'I think I will.'

'I'll leave you to it,' Tilly said. 'I need a wee.' She went into the bathroom and shut the door.

Sebastian scrolled to the number on his phone and made the call. After just two rings his mother answered. 'Hi, Mum. Where are you?'

In the bathroom, Tilly stood in front of the mirror and finished brushing her hair. As she straightened her dress, she caught sight of the pendant Sebastian had given her and she placed a hand on it lovingly. Smiling to herself, she stepped out of the bathroom. Sebastian was sitting on the sofa. 'Did you get through?'

'Yeah. They're not coming.'

Tilly's smile faded. 'Oh, no. Why?'

Sebastian looked up at her. 'Apparently Dad refused point blank to come in to London on New Year's Eve, said it's full of drunks and nutters. But Mum said it wasn't just that, she said she hasn't been feeling too good since Christmas either and didn't want to venture out. To be honest, I think she was just saying that to divert a bit of the blame from Dad. I know he's not interested. But I don't

279

know why she stands up for him. So, anyway, that's it. My big night and they won't be here to see it.'

Tilly sat down beside him. 'I'm so sorry.' She rested a hand on his knee. 'But, hey, listen, there will be lots of other big nights. They can come to the next one.'

Sebastian sighed. 'I guess.'

'I *know*.' Tilly squeezed his knee. 'Come on then, come and sit down over here and I'll do your hair.' She smiled. 'Although no-one's going to notice now you have a hat!'

'I'd still like you to,' Sebastian said, moving over to the swivel chair in front of the mirror.

Tilly kissed him on the top of his head and picked up the tube of cream. She gently massaged it into his hair and styled it with her fingers. Then, reaching for the comb, she neatly straightened out the back. 'There you go. Very dapper indeed.'

Sebastian smiled at her reflection in the mirror. 'Sensational Seb, eh?'

Tilly laughed. 'The *very* Sensational Seb!'

There was a rapping on the door and Sebastian stood up to open it. 'Oh, hi James.'

James gasped. 'Wow! Seb, my boy, you look sensational!'

Sebastian exchanged glances with Tilly and they smiled at each other. He picked up his top hat. 'I have this too,' he said proudly, putting it on.

James nodded approvingly. 'Very fetching indeed.'

Sebastian smiled. 'Tilly got it for me.'

'Very well chosen, young Tilly. Seb, have you got a few minutes? Gregor has just arrived and he'd like to see you before you go on.'

'Sure.' Sebastian looked at Tilly. 'Coming?'

280

She shook her head. 'No, I'm going to go out the front and see if I can find Grace.'

James handed her a lanyard with a pass attached to it. 'Here, wear this then you won't have any trouble getting in or out. The access code is 1920.'

'Thank you,' Tilly said, slipping the lanyard around her neck. She retrieved her cardigan from the back of the door and kissed Sebastian on his nose. He had the expression of the last puppy in the pet shop on his face. 'Don't worry, you'll be absolutely fine,' Tilly said reassuringly. 'I'll be in the wings. You go knock 'em dead!'

'I'll do my best.'

Slipping the cardigan over her shoulders, Tilly went out. Sebastian smiled and watched as she walked off along the corridor and disappeared round the corner.

'Lovely girl,' James said, breaking Sebastian's concentration. 'You're a lucky fellow.' Sebastian felt himself glowing with pride. 'Come on then,' James continued. 'Let's go and see Gregor.'

As they turned into the passageway leading down to the green room they were met by the sound of raised voices, one of which was patently McCleary's. They entered the room where there was an argument in full swing between the Scotsman and Colin.

'I dinnae bring ye here to show me up ye frilly-clad, aggravating streak of pish!'

Colin looked indignant. 'Mr McCleary. I was merely pointing out in the most cogent way that the current presentation bares no semblance to the projected and indeed vaunted bestowment of my performance which our revered audience is expecting.'

McCleary squinted at him angrily. 'Talk feckin' English, ye dandy weirdo!'

'The backdrops are *not* as discussed. They are in the wrong place upon the stage!' Colin ranted through gritted teeth. 'That ridiculously ineffectual stage manager, Douglas hasn't got a clue what he's doing.'

'They're feckin' pull-up banners, fer Christ's sake!' Gregor leaned forward, his eyes blazing. 'And tha stage manager you're referring to is my nephew, so I'd watch ye tongue if I were ye!'

'Yes,' Colin argued, 'but if one is to properly present oneself...'

McCleary moved forward so that his face was merely inches from Colin's. 'Now ye listen to me, sonny,' he seethed. 'I've had just about as much crap as I can take. Ye have five minutes to get your lanky arse up on that stage or I'll be shoving those roll up banners where the sun don't shine. Are ye getting me?'

Colin stood blinking at McCleary resentfully through his rimless spectacles.

'*Four* minutes,' McCleary snarled.

With a flick of his hair Colin turned away, brushing past the dumbfounded Sebastian and James as he thundered out into the corridor.

Sebastian looked at James in dismay as McCleary pulled a handkerchief from his jacket and mopped his brow.

The two men hesitantly approached him. 'Gregor,' James began. 'Are you okay?'

'Aye, Jimmy. Sometimes I wish I'd just become a car salesman like me Pa though. I've taken more than enough shite from arseholes today and that feckin' pound shop Russell Brand was just about my limit! Jesus *Christ*!'

'The public seem to like him,' James said. 'But ever since we signed him he's been trouble. I think I'll have him in next week for a stiff talking to.'

'Aye. And I suggest ye sack the snivelling shargar, I've no more time for him!'

'Anyway, Gregor, you wanted to speak to Sebastian.'

McCleary finished mopping his brow and returned the handkerchief to his pocket. The anger in his eyes subsided and his expression softened as he looked at Sebastian. 'I'm sorry about that, laddie. Ye get some real bawbags in this business. Anyway. I just wanted to check ye were alreet for tonight's show?'

Sebastian tried his best to muster a winning smile. 'I am, thank you, Mr McCleary. Everything is set up and I'm feeling great.'

'Aye, ye certainly scrub up well, laddie.'

Sebastian had been holding his top hat behind his back. He whipped it out and put it on. McCleary grinned. 'Aye, now tha's what I'm talking about. Ye look beltin', laddie.'

'Thank you, sir,' Sebastian said, feeling a wave of confidence at having received the man's approval.

'Well. I'm going t' find my seat up in the box,' McCleary said, adjusting his tie. 'Ye coming, Jimmy?'

'Yes, I'll catch you up.'

McCleary strolled out and Sebastian let out a big sigh of relief. James patted him heartily on the back. 'You're all cool, dear boy. Gregor likes you.' He looked Sebastian straight in the eyes. 'But whatever happens tonight, it must be perfect. No slip-ups, okay?'

'Of course not, James. The show has been well rehearsed, my friends have been allocated specific seats around the theatre, it's all completely in hand.'

James slapped him hard on the back. 'Excellent! I'll go and join Gregor now. Break a leg!'

Sebastian waited until James was out of earshot. 'I hope not,' he murmured. He went and stood in the wings and watched the last ten minutes of Colin's set, craning his

283

neck to look out into the audience. The theatre was full and as Sebastian scanned the endless sea of faces the reality of it all suddenly hit him like a ton of bricks. He felt his knees buckle slightly.

Colin concluded his act and left the stage to rapturous applause. He smirked at Sebastian as he passed him. 'I'll just give the rabble a few minutes before I return for my encore.'

Sebastian smiled back at him politely and returned his attention to the stage. The red velvet drapes were slowly closing and he grinned.

Realising what was happening, Colin stormed over to the man operating the console. 'Hey, you, sound guy! What's going on? I haven't had my encore yet!'

The sound technician shrugged. 'You're out of time, man.'

Colin pouted and thrust his hands onto his hips 'Open those curtains *immediately*!' he hissed.

Unfazed, the technician waved at a man standing by the steps leading down to the backstage area. He strode over. 'Is there a problem?' he asked in a deep voice.

The technician gestured towards Colin. 'I think this gentleman needs help getting back to his dressing room.'

The security officer stepped over to Colin, casting a shadow over him. 'Follow me sir,' he said gruffly.

Colin, who himself stood over six feet tall, looked up at the man and nodded. 'Okay,' he replied weakly.

Sebastian watched as several men scurried onto the stage and started to assemble his backdrops. His mind was racing and his stomach was doing back-flips. Feeling his brow dampening with sweat, he reached up to mop it with a tissue and suddenly realised he wasn't wearing his top hat. In a mild panic he ran back to the dressing room to retrieve it. As he hurried down the walkway he passed

Colin, stood in the corridor arguing with André. He smiled awkwardly as he slipped past them.

Out in the main bar another argument was in full flow. 'This is ridiculous!' Mark was holding his ticket in one hand and a plastic tumbler half-filled with lager in the other. 'Why are we all seated separately?'

As Jordan and Joshua looked on in dismay, Katie pulled him to one side. 'Are you really *that* thick?' she seethed. 'Have you forgotten what we're here to do tonight?'

Mark took a large swig from his plastic tumbler of lager. 'Of course I haven't,' he huffed. 'But I don't understand why we aren't sitting together. I bet we've got the crappiest seats too.'

'*Seriously*?!' Katie was trying to keep her voice low, but with Mark proving as blatantly clueless as usual she felt as though she needed to hammer home her message once more. 'It needs to look random when Sebastian selects us. People will be suspicious if he chooses his four volunteers from the same row of seats, all sitting together. *Surely* you can see that?'

Mark thought for a moment. 'Yeah, well, I suppose. But I'd better not be sat next to some fat stinking old girl taking up two seats, or behind a tall guy blocking my view. I didn't pay to watch the back of some bastard's head all night!'

'*Really*?!' Katie rolled her eyes. 'You didn't pay at all, the tickets were free for crying out loud!'

'Oh yeah!' Mark replied oafishly. He started to turn away and bumped into a man standing behind them, slopping some of his drink on the carpet in the process. 'Balls!' The man gave him a filthy look and moved away.

285

Mark drained the last of the beaker. 'Is there time for another?'

'I doubt it. And you've had two at almost nine quid a pint anyway!'

'Bloody tell me about it. That was a good three quid's worth I just watered the carpet with.'

Katie scowled at him. 'Just don't you go and mess this up for Seb tonight.'

'Yeah, yeah, alright!' Mark replied petulantly as they returned to join their friends.

Jordan looked at Katie and smiled, mouthing 'Are you okay?'

She nodded discreetly.

'Hiya!' a voice called out.

'Oh, it's Tilly!' Joshua exclaimed as she came over and hugged Katie.

'How's Seb?' Jordan asked.

'Yeah, he's alright. A little nervous, I think, but looking forward to it.'

'This place is massive!' Joshua said. 'I'm pretty nervous myself!'

Katie patted him on the arm. 'You'll be fine. That Grenadier routine he had you doing at The Red Lion last week was hilarious. You're a natural.'

Joshua licked his lips. 'Yeah, I can still taste that horrible horn!'

Jordan raised an eyebrow. 'Oh yeah?' he said playfully.

Joshua back-slapped him across the chest. 'Not funny!'

'What did you think of the other acts?' Tilly asked.

'We didn't see them, we only just got here,' Katie replied. 'There was a bloody train strike. We had to come on the bus and the traffic was murder. Talk about stressful.'

286

'Oh, really? I didn't know about that.' Tilly pointed across the room to where her sister and brother-in-law were stood having a drink. 'Grace and Jason drove here, but they arrived early and they said it was okay.'

The loud speaker behind the bar suddenly burst into life. 'Will all patrons please return to your seats, as the final act of this evening's show is about to commence.'

'Ooh, I'd better go,' Tilly said. 'I'm going to watch from the side of the stage. See you all after the show.'

The friends waved her off and joined the throng of people filtering through the doors and back into the auditorium.

As Joshua got to his row, he saw that it was already full. He looked at his ticket and then back at the seats. Counting along the row he gestured to a man three seats in. 'You're in my seat, mate,' he called out. The man glanced at him, frowned and then looked away. 'Oi, mate! That's my seat,' Joshua repeated. As the words left his mouth, the house lights dipped and went out and music started to play.

Joshua stood deliberating over what he should do. The woman seated on the end of the row beside him started to get agitated. 'There's an empty seat down there!' she whispered irritably, pointing to a gap four rows in front.

Joshua stood for a moment staring at the man occupying his seat; he was doing everything he could to ignore him. As a man appeared on stage and started to speak, the woman nudged his hip angrily and pointed emphatically towards the empty seat. Joshua sighed and walked down to the end of the row. Tutting and giving him dirty looks, three people stood up to let him in. Joshua squeezed past and sat down. His mind was racing. He twisted round and looked back up at the row where he should have been sitting. He wasn't *too* far away, he mused. If he waved his hand fervently enough Sebastian would surely be able to see him. He turned back to face the stage, where the evening's compère had started to speak.

CHAPTER 23

Sebastian was standing in the wings while the compère addressed the audience. His heart was pounding in his chest and he jumped as he felt a hand touch his arm. He spun round to see it was Tilly.

'How you feeling?' she whispered with a smile.

'Nervous. But better now you're here.'

The introductory music started to play and as the compère stepped off stage and into the wings, the sound technician gave Sebastian a thumbs up sign. He bent down and quickly kissed Tilly, then turned and stepped confidently out onto the stage, appearing from amongst a fog of dry ice to the sound of deafening applause.

Tilly was glowing with pride as she watched him introduce himself to the crowd. She looked towards the sound technician and he smiled at her. 'He's good,' the man mouthed. He pointed to a couple of plastic pint glasses on his desk. 'Do you want a drink?' he whispered loudly.

Tilly shook her head and held up a hand, mouthing 'No, thank you.'

The man smiled and took a small sip from one. Placing it back down on the console desk, he slid a series of switches, which swathed the stage in a mix of blue and pink light.

Sebastian walked the length of the stage and back with the microphone in his hand, explaining to the audience about the mystic art of hypnotism. His well-rehearsed routine was flowing perfectly and Tilly looked on with excitement.

289

'What I would like to do now, ladies and gentlemen, is select four volunteers at random from the audience to help me with tonight's show.'

A series of dazzling spotlights swung round into the auditorium and slowly swept across the vast assembly of seats. Subtle music was playing as Sebastian stepped to the edge of the stage, theatrically placing his flattened hand on his forehead to look out into the audience. He spoke into the microphone. 'Who among you would like to join me on stage and surrender your mind to me this evening? Please raise your hands.'

On cue, Jordan thrust up his hand. The spotlight swung across to illuminate him. 'Please make your way to the stage, sir,' Sebastian said. 'Give our first volunteer a round of applause.' As the audience clapped, several other hands around him were bouncing up and down. But as Jordan stood up, the spotlight swept away, scanning the stalls again.

The lighting technician checked the piece of paper taped to his desk and swung the spotlight upwards to pick out Katie. She was on her feet and waving her hands enthusiastically.

'Our second volunteer,' Sebastian announced. 'Please show the lady your appreciation.'

The clapping commenced again as the spotlight continued its search of the auditorium. Jordan arrived at the steps leading to the stage and was escorted up by two women wearing sparkling bodysuits. They led him to one of the four chairs that had been set out and returned to the steps to collect Katie.

As the spotlights danced up and around the stalls, there was a shout from a man leaning over the front row of the balcony, waving his arms frantically. One of the beams fixed on the balcony, and Mark, wearing his white football shirt, was lit up like a beacon. Sebastian pointed to the balcony. 'Our third volunteer. Come on down!'

A member of the theatre staff appeared, ready to help Mark out of his row, but he rudely pushed her aside and rushed down the steps.

'Right, just one more volunteer, please,' Sebastian said. The lights swooped left and right, up and down, and a drum roll sounded. Hands were thrust into the air and people shouted and whistled as the theatre erupted with excited anticipation.

The lighting engineer checked his sheet of paper again and toggled a switch to cast a light on seat 3 in row J.

Sebastian squinted against the glare from the footlights to where the spotlight had fallen. He could see a hand waving wildly. 'We have our fourth volunteer,' he announced.

With a cry – 'Woo!' – the man jumped up excitedly, pushed his way out of the row and made his way down the aisle.

As he got closer, Sebastian realised to his horror that it wasn't Joshua. A surge of panic coursed through him. At the same moment, Mark appeared at the rear of the stalls and came hurtling down the aisle, almost tripping over himself in his haste. He pushed rudely past the unknown volunteer and reached the bottom of the steps.

Katie was watching him from the stage. 'Jesus Christ,' she muttered under her breath.

As the two women escorted Mark and the other man up to the stage, Mark reached down behind his escort, cupped her bottom in his hand and gently squeezed. She shot him a filthy look. He grinned at her and winked.

Sebastian's mind was racing – what on earth had happened to Joshua? – but he quickly composed himself and while his assistants directed Mark and the other man over to their chairs, he turned to address the audience. 'Ladies and gentlemen, please give it up for our last two volunteers.' There was an audible moan of disappointment, but it was quickly drowned out by the roar of cheering and applause.

With all the candidates seated, Sebastian set about his act.

The lights dipped, casting four subtle circles around the chairs, and Sebastian bent down beside the first and spoke into the microphone. 'Good evening, sir. Thank you for joining me here on the stage. May I ask your name?' He moved the microphone closer to his volunteer.

'Jordan.'

'Ladies and gentlemen, please show your appreciation for Jordan.' The audience responded with applause. 'Now, Jordan, in a few moments you are going to feel very sleepy. Your eyelids will feel heavy and you'll be unable to fight the urge to sleep. I will count backwards from three, and when I reach one you will fall into a deep, deep sleep.' Sebastian stood up straight and glanced out at the audience. He smiled as he saw their eyes all fixed on him. He slowly counted, 'Three. Two. One,' and as Jordan's head slumped onto his chest the crowd applauded loudly. The spotlight over Jordan winked out, plunging him into a smoky darkness. Sebastian moved along to the second seat. He knelt down beside the chair. 'Good evening. Would you mind introducing yourself to the audience, madam?' Sebastian flipped the microphone to his right.

'Katie,' the woman said nervously.

'Thank you, Katie. In a few moments you are going to feel very sleepy, your eyelids will feel heavy and you will not be able to fight the urge to sleep. I will count backwards from three to one and you will fall into a deep, deep sleep.' Sebastian stood up straight and placed a hand

292

on Katie's shoulder, gently squeezing it. 'Three. Two. One,' he said and Katie's head slowly dropped onto her shoulder. Sebastian stepped back and the crowd once again applauded loudly. As the light over Katie dimmed, he moved on to the third chair. He bent down to speak. 'Hello, sir. And what's your name?'

'Sir?' Mark said, grinning. Sebastian glared at him, his eyes imploring him to play along. 'Mark, *sir*. My name is Mark.'

Sensing that Mark's childish tendencies could land him in trouble, Sebastian wasted no time in putting him under. 'Mark, I will count down from three to one and you will fall into a deep sleep.'

Mark sniggered. 'Yeah, right!'

'Three. Two. One.' As the last word left Sebastian's lips, Mark slumped to his right, almost falling off the seat. Sebastian stepped around and straightened him up. 'There's always one!' he said into the microphone, soliciting a rumble of laughter from the audience. Moving on to the final volunteer, Sebastian felt the knot in his stomach tighten. Taking a deep breath, he stepped up beside the man and leaning towards him he asked, 'And last, but by no means least, what is your name, good sir?'

The man tilted his head to speak into the microphone. 'Jeff.'

'Okay, Jeff, in a few moments you are going to feel very sleepy. Your eyelids will feel heavy and you will be unable to fight the urge to sleep. I will count backwards from three to one and you will fall into a deep, deep sleep.' Sebastian counted down and let out a small sigh of relief as the man succumbed to his words and his head dropped forward.

Sebastian walked to the edge of the stage. A single spotlight followed him and the rest of the stage was

293

plunged into darkness. Behind him, stagehands were stealthily manoeuvring the farmyard scenery into place. 'Ladies and gentlemen, tonight you will bear witness to the incredible phenomenon known as hypnosis. I will temporarily take control of my four volunteers and, using the power of subconscious suggestion, I will commandeer their minds and will them into performing for you tonight.'

The lights behind him slowly faded in, illuminating the farmyard backdrop. Music started to play and the audience laughed as they realised it was a jaunty version of *Old MacDonald Had a Farm* played on a banjo.

Sebastian stepped up to the first chair and, with the microphone held between his mouth and Jordan's ear, he spoke. 'Jordan. Listen very carefully.' Jordan's head slowly lifted off his chest. 'When you awake you will be a prize-winning bull. You are a kind and gentle bull. Until, that is, you see the colour red, which sends you into a rage.' Sebastian reached behind him and grabbed the red cloth from the podium, holding it high for the audience to see. There were gasps from around the auditorium before Sebastian tucked it away out of sight in his jacket pocket. He leaned in. 'Jordan. What are you?'

'I am a kind and gentle bull,' Jordan said sleepily.

'And what colour enrages you?' Sebastian asked.

'Red.'

'Very well. In a moment I will pat you on your shoulder and you will awake. You will be that strong and powerful bull. You will remain this way until you hear me say stop and I click my fingers. Do you understand?'

'Yes,' Jordan replied.

Sebastian reached over to the podium again and took hold of a looped rope. 'Lift up your arms, Jordan.' He slipped it gently over Jordan's arms until it rested on his

294

middle, then he picked up a pair of plastic horns from the podium and slipped them onto Jordan's head. Sebastian clicked his fingers and Jordan awoke with a start and let out a large grunt. The audience started to clap and laugh. Sebastian gently pulled the rope. 'C'mon, boy.' Jordan stood up and slowly followed Sebastian over to a stack of hay bales beside the farmyard set. Jordan let out another grunt. The auditorium fell silent as Sebastian carefully lifted the rope up over Jordan's head and slung it over his own shoulder. He took a few paces backwards and the lights faded until there were only two spotlights, one on Jordan and the other following Sebastian as he backed away to the far side of the stage. As he passed the podium, he put the microphone down and took off his top hat, replacing it with a black felt matador's montera. Taking a deep breath, he pulled the red cloth from inside his pocket, held it out to his left with both hands and whistled.

Jordan's head shot up and he started to scrape his right foot on the floor.

The audience were transfixed and suddenly, like lightening, Jordan thundered across the stage, letting out a horrifying bellow. With his head held downwards and the plastic horns pointing at Sebastian, he charged into the red cloth. Sebastian whipped it away and called out, 'Olé!'

Jordan stopped just short of the sound engineer's console, and turned around. Sebastian had backed up a few more paces and, as Jordan scraped his foot again, he positioned himself to take another charge. Jordan flew at him and under the cloth as Sebastian held it high. Before Jordan had a chance to turn back around again, Sebastian swiftly tucked the cloth back into his jacket out of sight.

Jordan stood looking at him for a moment, his chest heaving. Sebastian took the rope from his shoulder and slowly walked towards Jordan. Patting him on the back, he looped the rope over his head and led Jordan to the front of the stage. He took a bow and the audience went wild with excitement.

Sebastian pulled on the rope. 'C'mon,' he said, and led Jordan over to the farm set where he tethered him to a hook on the wooden backdrop. As the applause died away, he returned to the podium and retrieved his microphone. Switching the montera for his top hat, he walked back to the front of the stage to address the audience. 'Now then, ladies and gentlemen, the farmyard is looking a bit empty.' He gestured to the back of the stage where Jordan was peacefully standing tethered to the scenery. 'Who wants to suggest an animal that's missing from our very own Bloomsbury city farm?'

The audience started to call out the names of various animals. 'How about a nice big cock?', a man's voice from the back yelled out loudly, eliciting a swathe of laughter.

'Really, sir, what you like to do in your spare time is no business of ours,' Sebastian retorted, generating an even louder roar of laughter.

'Chickens!' a woman from somewhere down in the front row screeched.

'Yes, madam! Chickens are certainly very useful to have around a farm.' From the side of the stage, Tilly was beaming as she watched Sebastian step up behind Mark's chair. He bent down and spoke into the microphone. 'Mark. When you hear the word chicken you will awake, and you will be a beautiful bantam with feathers so soft and a resplendent, bright red comb. You will remain this way until you hear me say stop and I click my fingers. Do you understand?'

'Yes,' Mark replied.

Sebastian reached over to the podium and picked up an elasticated rubber beak. He slipped it over Mark's head and carefully aligned it. Then he stood upright and looked out at the audience. 'You know what to say!'

In unison the crowd bellowed out, 'Chicken!'

At the sound of the word, Mark let out a loud *ba-gawk* and got up from the chair. The audience clapped and whistled. Mark jerked his head to one side and looked out at them curiously for a moment, then he started to wander around the stage, occasionally stopping to scrape his foot on the floor.

Sebastian picked up a bag of popcorn from the podium and followed Mark around the stage. He briskly shook the bag and Mark stopped and turned around. As he began to strut back towards Sebastian the lights on stage dimmed and a single spotlight cast a glow over the unfolding charade. Sebastian opened the bag and poured some of the popcorn into his hand. He held out his cupped palm and Mark cautiously crept over, letting out small, inquisitive *buk* sounds. 'There you go. Who's a pretty little clucker?' Sebastian said, tilting his head towards the audience and giving them a cheeky grin. Mark's head suddenly darted forward and he eagerly started to eat the popcorn. The rubber beak had become dislodged and was hanging to one side of his nose as he greedily pecked at Sebastian's hand. Scoffing down the last piece of popcorn, he squawked loudly for more. 'Now, now, don't be a greedy hen,' Sebastian said, wagging his finger at him. 'That's enough for now.' He scrunched up the top of the bag and slipped it into his pocket.

Mark looked miffed and squawked again. 'Ba-gawk!'

Sebastian walked towards the barn backdrop and the spotlight followed him; Mark scuttled along behind him, excitedly flapping his bended arms as he went. Sebastian stopped by the stack of bound hay bales. 'It's getting dark now,' he said, and on cue the spotlight dimmed slightly. 'I think it's time for you to roost down for the night.' He patted the hay bales and Mark hopped up on top and settled down cross-legged. 'There's a good hen,' Sebastian said. Reaching up and readjusting the rubber beak on Mark's nose, he glanced over at Jordan, who was still standing calmly on his tether, a serene expression on his face.

With the two farm animals settled, Sebastian returned to his remaining volunteers. 'I'm going to ask you to help me choose who should go next,' he said, addressing the audience. Standing between the two chairs, he held his hands out wide. 'If you'd like Katie to go next, I want you to cheer for her. If you would rather it be Jeff, cheer for him. Whomever gets the loudest cheer will be our next performer.' Sebastian stepped a few paces to the left where just he and Katie were illuminated by the spotlight. 'Cheer if you want Katie next,' he said, and the auditorium filled with loud cheers, whoops and whistles. Sebastian waggled his outstretched hand from side to side, indicating *not bad*. The spotlight followed him as he walked over and stood behind Jeff. 'Okay, let's hear you cheer if you'd like Jeff to be up next.' Again, the auditorium went wild. It was a close contest and difficult to honestly discern who had received the loudest cheers. However, deciding that Jeff might have elicited the most raucous response by a sliver, Sebastian motioned for the audience to quieten down.

'Very well,' he said, 'the majority have spoken. Jeff is to be our next performer.' He dropped his hand and winked at the audience. 'Now, unfortunately I had planned a little musical interlude for this half of the set.' He strolled over to the podium and lifted up the gold-coloured conical bra. He waved it above Jeff's head and stretched it out in front of his dozing volunteer. 'Hmm. I don't think these are going to fit, do you?' he said with a grin. The audience laughed. He stepped over to Katie and gently tilted her forward to slip on the bra over her clothes. 'I guess that's spoiled the surprise a bit. But don't worry, we'll give Katie a chance to get into the groove in a moment. Right now you're going to witness something truly epic!'

He reached beneath the podium and whipped out a dazzlingly luminous yellow crash helmet. Stepping up behind Jeff, he gently placed it over his head, then he leant in and spoke. 'Now, Jeff...' He trailed off. 'Doh!' Theatrically smacking his forehead with his hand, he said, 'He's not going to hear me through *that* now, is he?' He was rewarded with a roar of laughter from his now adoring crowd, and he carefully removed the helmet. Bending again he spoke into Jeff's ear. 'Now, Jeff. When you hear the famous *Formula 1* theme music you will wake to the sound of screeching cars at Silverstone ringing in your ears, and you will be seven times world champion driver Lewis Hamilton.'

As he was speaking two men clad in black were shuffling the racing car out from behind the farmyard scenery. With an open top, it was set on a slight angle, and there were gasps of awe from the crowd as the stage lights fell upon the bright red Ferrari. Sebastian looked over his shoulder as the car was positioned and silently mouthed 'Wow!'. He had only seen the car in daylight and even then, it was an impressive mock-up, but under the magical glow of the stage lights and swathed in dry ice it looked absolutely fantastic.

Sebastian turned back to Jeff and for a split second a wave of fear engulfed him again. Jeff had gone under

299

okay, but what if he didn't respond to commands? He felt cold sweat running down the back of his neck. Shaking his head, he bent and spoke into Jeff's ears. 'Jeff, now is your moment to shine. Remember, when you awake you will be Lewis Hamilton. Do you understand?'

Jeff nodded slowly. 'Yes, I understand.'

Sebastian took a deep breath and stood upright, and the *Formula 1* theme music burst out over the speakers. The spotlight glowed over Jeff as he stood up. Sebastian handed him the helmet and, as he took it from him, Jeff looked over his shoulder and spotted the Ferrari. He pulled the helmet over his head and strode confidently towards the car. The audience clapped furiously. With its top removed it was easy to see the interior from all angles of the stage, and as Jeff climbed in, two large screens – one on either side of the stage – lit up, showing a driver's view of a racetrack; the same image was projected onto a screen inside the windshield of the car.

Sebastian walked up to the podium and picked up a chequered flag. He walked over to the car and stood in front of it. The *Formula 1* theme slowly faded out and Sebastian held the flag high. He looked out across the auditorium and dropped the flag.

Jeff clutched the steering wheel and slammed his foot down on the accelerator. Sounds of racing cars were screaming out across the PA. Jeff furiously spun the wheel of the immobile car, his eyes fixed on the screen in front of him as it played out a virtual race.

The booming sound – the deafening roar of the engine and the screech of tyres – began to agitate Jordan and he let out a loud snorting noise. But over the cacophony Sebastian didn't hear him. Jordan pulled on the tether, causing the backdrop to rattle slightly, which in turn disturbed Mark. He clucked a couple of times in protest at

300

being woken up and turned around to resettle himself. As he did so, Jordan caught a flash of the number seven and the name *Beckham*, which were printed in vibrant red on the back of Mark's football shirt. He started to scrape and tap his foot on the floor and his nostrils flared. Reacting to the perceived threat, Mark let out a frightened squawk and quickly hopped down from the hay bales.

From the corner of his eye Sebastian caught a movement as Mark flew into full panic mode, flapping his arms and circling the stage. With the red logos out of his line of vision, Jordan fell calm again, but it was too late; Mark had worked himself into a frenzy. Sebastian quickly walked towards him, but Mark saw him coming and took off speedily in the other direction, heading for the wings. He dashed off stage left, flapping his arms up and down and squawking for all he was worth, and promptly collided with the sound desk. The engineer looked on in horror as a pint and a half of best British lager was sent flying, splashing liquid all over his console. There was a spark followed by a crackling sound and the sounds of the racing car immediately ceased as the lights all died at once and the entire theatre was plunged into darkness. All that remained was the dim glow from the emergency sidelights and one in the wings.

There was a moment of deafening silence, then a small ripple of laughter, which turned into mumbles of confusion as the audience quickly became unsure whether this was all part of the hypnotism act or something had gone wrong.

Backstage, a solitary ba-gawk rang out from Mark, who was standing dumbfounded in the darkness. A pool of light filled the area as André appeared holding a flashlight. 'What 'appened 'ere?' he asked as he spotted a thin trail of smoke spiralling up from the console towards the ceiling.

'Er…' the sound engineer began.

'Oh, never mind!' André snapped impatiently. He was about to demand that the man get things up and running again immediately when another spark snapped on the desk. The engineer jumped up and Tilly, watching from a few feet away, gasped as she saw a small flame spread out across the controls. It triggered the detector on the ceiling and there was sudden uproar in the auditorium as the sprinklers were activated and water cascaded down upon the audience. Screams were soon drowned out by the ear-splitting clanging noise of an alarm. Grabbing an extinguisher from the wall, the engineer quickly doused the fire, but the damage was done.

André rushed out onto the stage where Sebastian was standing in a state of confusion. 'Ladies and gentlemen,' André shouted, trying to make himself heard over the alarm bell. 'Please make your way to the nearest exits and our staff will escort you safely out of the building.'

Theatre employees appeared around the perimeter of the auditorium,. Flinging the fire doors open wide, they began ushering people out into the cold.

CHAPTER 24

Sebastian made his way across the stage into the wings, where he took off his top hat and held it with both hands close to his chest, staring in disbelief at the foam-covered console. He could feel his eyes welling up.

André appeared behind him. 'Come on, get yourselves out of the building now!'

Tilly rushed over to Sebastian, who was now looking utterly bereft. 'Come on, Seb, we need to get Katie and Jordan out,' she cried urgently. 'And the other man!' They rushed out onto the stage.

Mark was cowering in the corner and the sound engineer hurried over to him. 'Come on, mate, we've gotta get out of here.'

Mark squawked.

'Yeah, very funny,' the man said angrily, grabbing hold of Mark's shirt and pulling him up onto his feet. 'Come on, this way.' He led Mark down the steps and out into the corridor.

Sebastian untied Jordan and quickly stepped over to Jeff, who was still sitting in the car. Sebastian removed the helmet and was just about to speak to him when he felt a hand grab his shoulder and he was pulled roughly aside by the security officer. 'Come on, it's a full evacuation.'

'Yes I know, but...'

'No *buts*. Out!' The security guard pushed Sebastian aside and wrenched Jeff out of the car. Dragging Jeff by his jacket, he pulled him over to Jordan and grabbed hold of him with his other hand. 'I don't know why the hell you're just standing here, but in case you haven't heard there's a fire alarm ringing, which means everyone *out*!'

He dragged the pair of them off stage. 'You lot too, no messing around!' he shouted back over his shoulder at Sebastian and Tilly, who were attending to Katie.

'I can't wake her up!' Tilly exclaimed. There was fear in her voice.

Sebastian dropped the racing helmet and stepped up to Katie. He clicked his fingers. 'Katie, awake!' he cried out.

She stirred and Tilly grabbed her arm. 'Quick, Katie, we have to get outside!' Katie blinked and as she started to come round she looked up at Tilly, who was pulling frantically at her arm. 'Come *on*, Katie!' Tilly urged. Katie stood up and with a puzzled expression she stared down at the conical bra hanging from her chest. 'I'll explain in an minute,' Tilly said. 'Come on, we've gotta go!'

Sebastian led the way down into the backstage corridors and Katie stumbled along behind, with Tilly's arm locked around hers.

The corridor was heaving with people but they managed to find Mark. As they all pressed on through, a burly security guard loomed up in front of them and in the melee they were separated.

'We've lost Katie and Mark!' Tilly shouted to Sebastian.

'We can't go back, this is hell on earth. We'll find them again when we get outside!'

They made it to the fire escape doors at the rear of the green room, where they joined theatre staff and the evening's other performers outside in the loading bay. It had been snowing hard for a couple of hours and the unspoilt carpet of white on the ground glistened. The snow was still tumbling down and it wasn't far short of blizzard conditions.

The pavements outside the front of the theatre were full with the jostling patrons who had been swiftly ejected.

Faced with the awful weather conditions, most of the audience had decided to give up and go home, but a considerable number were still lingering on the offchance they'd be let back in.

Joshua saw Jordan stood amongst the throng of people and rushed over to him. 'Oh, jeez man, there you are. Are you okay?' Jordan turned his head slowly and looked at him, a glassy-eyed expression on his face. Joshua stepped up close and snapped his fingers a couple of times in front of his friend's face. 'Jordan, mate. Are you okay?'

Jordan's eyes appeared to focus and he smiled. 'Hey man.'

Joshua let out a huge sigh. 'Thank God! I thought something had happened to you for a minute.'

Heartily slapping Joshua across the arm, Jordan laughed. 'Nah, man. I'm all cool.' He looked around as if only just noticing they were outside. 'What's going on? Why's everyone out here in the cold?'

'There was an evacuation, don't you remember?' Joshua said. Jordan looked at him vacantly. 'Oh never mind. I doubt they're going to carry on with the show now. Shall we just make a move?'

Jordan shrugged his shoulders. 'Yeah, sure man. Whatever.'

'Right, we'd better see if we can find Mark and Katie amongst this lot!'

They pushed through the crowd and spotted Katie stood on the steps with Mark, who was slumped up against the railings.

'Hey, Katie!'

Katie looked up and saw Joshua and Jordan approaching. It was clear she wasn't very happy.

'I was worried I wasn't going to find you guys,' Joshua said. 'How did you get out front?'

'We got off the stage, but nobody seemed to know what the hell was going on. Then this big security guy manhandled us back through the doors into the auditorium and we kind of got carried by the crowd and came out the front entrance. It was bloody chaos.'

'Thank God you're safe,' Joshua said. 'We're gonna go home.'

Katie nodded. 'Us too. Can you help me get this idiot up?' She pointed at Mark. 'He's pissed out of his brain – *again*!'

Jordan bent over and spoke softly to Mark. 'Hey, Mark. We're heading home, mate. You coming?' Mark looked up at him groggily and his head lolled in a half nod. 'Okay then. Up you get,' Joshua said, hooking his arms under Mark's armpits and helping him to his feet.

'Hang on,' Katie said. Unzipping her coat, she took it off and, with Joshua's help, managed to get it onto Mark.

'You'll freeze!' Joshua exclaimed.

'It's okay, I'm wearing a thick sweater and I'll be warm once we get moving.'

Almost dragging him along, the friends set off in the direction of the train station. Visibility was minimal and they walked quickly with their heads down against the gusting snow, trying to protect their faces from the biting cold. When they reached the station Jordan and Joshua helped Mark down the steps and they sat him down on a bench to wait for the train. Jordan sat down beside him.

Katie came over to Joshua, who was leaning against the wall, and hooked her arm around his. 'I'm absolutely frozen,' she said, shivering.

Joshua's teeth were chattering. 'Me too.' He shot Mark a disdainful glance. 'You shouldn't have given that idiot your coat, he doesn't deserve it.'

306

'It's okay, train's due in a couple of minutes.' Katie huddled in close to him. 'What the hell happened back there? And why didn't you come up on stage?'

Joshua looked down at her arm linked through his and then over at Mark, who was sat staring into space and paying no attention to either of them. 'Well, some stupid bloke – that Jeff to be precise – was sat in my seat. I tried to get him to move, but he wasn't having it. The show started, so I had no choice but to sit a few rows down, I'm assuming where *he* should have been sitting. Then he went and got bloody picked!'

Katie rolled her eyes. 'Typical! What about the fire alarm? What caused that?'

Joshua gestured his eyes to Mark. '*He* did!'

'What?!' Katie exclaimed. 'You're kidding me!'

'Nope. He started running around the stage like a loony and ran off out the back. Next thing all the lights went out and the sprinklers came on.'

'What the hell did he do?' Katie said with a mix of anger and disbelief.

'I dunno. I mean, I can only assume it was him, cos everything was fine until he ran off the stage.'

'I tell you, I've had it with him,' Katie seethed. 'Once I get him home that's it. We're *done*!'

The screech of metal echoed down the empty platform as the train arrived. Jordan got on first, while Joshua and Katie helped Mark aboard, then the doors hissed shut and the train moved off.

In the loading bay, André had made a head count whilst the fire brigade were inside checking the theatre. A fire officer approached him and said it was safe to return to the building. As the engine reversed and manoeuvred its

307

way out of the service area, André turned to the staff. 'Okay, ladies and gentlemen, we can all now go back inside. Would all staff personnel please assemble in the green room. Performers and their guests must retrieve their belongings and please go home. Bob, our security officer will stay by the door to see you out. Thank you all for your cooperation.'

He stood back and watched as the people hurried back into the theatre. Sebastian hung back until everyone else had gone in, then he approached André.

'André, I'm so sorry,' he said. 'I don't know what to say.'

André looked at him with a puzzled expression on his face. 'Young man, I don't know what happened here tonight, but we will investigate further and you will be contacted via your agent. Now if you could please just retrieve your belongings and leave that would be very much appreciated.'

Sebastian nodded solemnly and he and Tilly went inside and along the corridor to the dressing room. He could hear arguing coming from the direction of the green room; it was the unmistakable voice of Colin doing most of the shouting. Sebastian shook his head and opened the door to the dressing room.

'Seb, are you okay?' Tilly asked. 'That wasn't your fault you know.'

Sebastian smiled at her weakly. 'Let's grab our stuff and get out of here. I just want to go home.'

As the train reached Ilford station, Joshua and Jordan stood up.

'You sure you'll be alright, Katie?' Joshua asked.

She sighed. 'Yeah, I'll be fine. I'll just make sure this dopey twat doesn't end up dead in a gutter, then it's just a short drive home from his.'

'Well, go careful, the roads are going to be dodgy.'

'I will.' She stood up and, as the doors opened, she kissed both her friends on the cheek.

'Happy New Year,' Joshua said.

Katie smiled. 'It's not midnight yet.'

'I know, but I won't see you at midnight.' As the doors opened, he kissed her again, then he and Jordan got off.

'Night, babe,' Jordan called back over his shoulder.

The train moved slowly away and Katie sat back down next to Mark. She sighed again. He was snoring loudly and a long strand of dribble was hanging out of his mouth and across his cheek. Katie rolled her eyes and pulled out her phone. She texted Tilly to say they were almost home and she'd catch up with her the following morning. As she finished, she noticed they'd just left Chadwell Heath station and the next stop was Romford where they had to alight. She punched Mark the arm. 'Oi, Hooch! Wake up!'

Mark muttered something incoherent.

'Come on,' Katie said angrily. 'We're getting off!' She stood up and Mark unsteadily got to his feet.

'What did you call me?' he mumbled.

'Hooch! Look at that drool coming out your mouth. Jesus Christ, you're an embarrassment!'

They got off and Katie strode ahead at speed while Mark stumbled along behind her trying to keep up. They walked out of the side entrance and down the slope. Mark's feet were slipping about in the snow and he almost went over. 'Slow down, will ya?' he shouted. Katie stopped and allowed him catch up, and they made their way back to his flat in Victoria Road in silence.

When they reached his front door, Mark fumbled in his pockets for his key. Suddenly there was a loud bang. 'What the fuck was that?!' As he said it, there was a series a crackling sounds and the sky lit up with a shower of gold.

'It's just fireworks,' Katie said. 'Happy New Year,' she added dolefully.

Mark frowned. 'It's bloody snowing, why would people be out in this letting off fireworks? Morons.'

Katie gave him a pitiful look. 'Because it's New Year's Eve! It's what people do.'

Mark finally found his key. 'You coming in?'

'No, but I'll have my jacket back,' Katie said bluntly. She held out her hand and rolled her eyes as Mark somehow managed to get tangled up trying to remove it. 'Don't bloody rip it!' Katie cried angrily. 'Here, let me.' She pulled at the sleeves and whipped it off, and Mark stumbled and fell against the door. She put the jacket on, gave him a last look of contempt and pipped the door lock on her car. Without even saying goodnight, she climbed in and drove off into the night.

CHAPTER 25

Sebastian sat on the sofa in the dark nursing a cup of tepid tea. He was staring at the TV screen, on which there was a weather map showing most of the UK had been stricken with heavy snowfall. The volume was so low it was all but inaudible. Lost in thought, he took a sip of his tea and was startled as the ceiling light came on.

Tilly was standing in the doorway tying her dressing gown cord. 'Why are you sitting in the dark?' she asked concerned.

'I didn't want to wake you,' Sebastian replied sullenly.

Tilly came over and sat down beside him. 'Are you okay? You're not still worrying about last night are you?'

Sebastian's eyes fell. 'A bit yeah,' he said with a sigh. He put his mug down on the coffee table. 'I just keep playing it over and over in my head.'

'It wasn't your fault, darling. I told you last night, that sound man should never have had those drinks so close to his equipment.'

Sebastian looked at her. 'I know, but if Mark hadn't run into it… well, it would never have happened.'

Tilly put her arm around him. 'We could go over this a hundred times, but that man had a responsibility to keep his equipment safe. I'm sorry, but it was negligence pure and simple. I know your night was ruined and it makes me really sad, but none of it was your fault. Okay?'

Sebastian pulled her close and hugged her tightly. 'Thank you.'

She kissed him lightly on his cheek. 'You don't have to thank me, silly.' She hitched her legs up onto the sofa and snuggled into Sebastian's arms, resting her head on his chest. 'I haven't got to work today. How about we have a duvet day? There's still loads of food and stuff left over from Christmas, let's bring the duvet in, watch trashy movies and eat crap all day. What do you say?'

Sebastian chuckled. 'Now *that* sounds like a plan.'

Tilly picked up the remote control for the television and switched it on. 'Let's see what Netflix has to offer shall we? What do you fancy? Action, thriller, horror…'

'Oh, God, no!' Sebastian exclaimed. 'Not horror.'

They sat for a moment waiting for the menus to load, then Tilly began scrolling through. 'There are loads of kids' films on here if you want something light. Or a comedy?'

'That sounds the ticket.'

Tilly selected the comedies menu and the screen filled with poster images. 'There's loads on here,' she said. 'Okay, let's see.' She started to scroll. '*American Pie. Beverly Hills Cop. Bilko. California Man. Daddy Day Care. Drop Dead Fred…*'

She stopped and looked at Sebastian and they simultaneously exclaimed, '*Drop Dead Fred*!'

'Got to be!' Sebastian said.

Tilly giggled. 'Okay, wait here, I'll go get the duvet and the goodies.'

*

The sound of banging from above woke Mark. He turned over and picked up his phone from the bedside cabinet. The clock on the screen showed 14:25. He sighed and swung his legs out of the bed. Still wearing his clothes from the night before, he padded heavily to the bathroom. After a minute he re-emerged and went through to the kitchen. He switched on the kettle and heaped two

312

spoonfuls of instant coffee into a mug. The banging from the upstairs flat intensified and Mark yelled up at the ceiling, 'Turn it in, for fuck's sake!' The banging stopped momentarily and Mark returned to his coffee. As he scooped out a spoonful of sugar the banging resumed, causing him to jump and shower the worktop with granules. 'Fuck!' he seethed. 'Right!' Throwing the teaspoon into the sink he went out into the hall. Without bothering to undo the laces, he stepped into his trainers and scuffed them hard on the floor to force his feet in. Angrily flinging open the front door, he marched out and around the side to the overhead flat's front door. Pressing the bell several times he stood and waited. After a few seconds with no answer, he started pressing it repeatedly until he eventually saw the shadow of a man coming downstairs through the patterned glass.

The door opened and a bulky man wearing jeans and a T-shirt appeared. Standing a good 6'4" tall, his unshaven face was red and running with sweat. 'Can I help you?'

Mark stepped back a few paces. 'Er... yeah. Your banging woke me up. I was just going to ask if you could ease off a bit for today?'

The man raised one eyebrow. 'You *just* woke up? It's the middle of the afternoon.'

'Who is it, babe?' a woman's voice called down the stairs.

'Who are you?' the man asked.

'Mark. I live underneath.'

The man called back up the stairs. 'It's Mark. Says he lives underneath.'

'Tell 'im to sod off!'

The man moved forward and leant on the frame. 'The thing is, mate, I'm back at work tomorrow and my bird...' – he gestured a thumb up the stairwell behind him –

'…she wants laminate flooring down.' He sniffed. 'If I don't do it today it'll never get done. I'll only be a couple more hours. *Tops.* Okay?'

The big man took a pace forward and Mark noticed his biceps were rippling.

Mark gave him a feeble smile and turned away. 'Yeah, sure.'

'Cheers mate!' the man called out after him and shut the door.

'Fuck you,' Mark mumbled under his breath.

He walked back into his flat and slammed the door loudly behind him. He returned to the kitchen and retrieved the spoon from the sink, adding a heaped serving of sugar to the mug. He went to the fridge and stood for a moment staring at the sparse selection inside, then pulled out a two-pint bottle of milk. It was half full. He opened it and took a sniff, instantly recoiling and gagging. Emptying the rancid liquid into the sink, he opted for a can of lager, slammed the fridge shut and opened the cupboard. Choosing a family size bag of crisps, he lazily padded into the sitting room where he slumped down on the sofa.

The sound of banging was still ringing out from overhead. Sighing loudly, he reached for the remote and switched on the TV, flicking through endless animated movies before switching it off again and tossing the remote onto the cushion beside him. He shouted 'Alexa!' and waited for a response.

'Yes Mark?' the smart-device replied in a sultry voice.

Mark loved hearing the voice say his name. 'Play Oasis,' he said.

'OK.' The device acknowledged his request and the sound of *Force of Nature* by the Mancunian band filled the room.

314

'Alexa. Louder!' Mark commanded and the volume increased. He opened the crisps and took a huge handful, spraying crumbs everywhere as he forced them into his mouth. He coughed as the dry morsels hit his throat. Grabbing the can of lager, he took a large gulp and cleared his throat. Then he lay back with his legs up on the arm of the sofa, listening to the music and doing his level best to ignore the banging above. 'Alexa. Louder!' he called out and the volume went up to an ear-splitting level.

Time passed and the light outside started fade. Mark looked up at the ceiling. 'Couple of hours my arse!' he seethed. He got up and walked into the bathroom, returning with a handful of toilet paper. Twisting it around he wedged a piece in each ear and shouted, 'Alexa. Off!' The music stopped and the room fell silent – except for the banging upstairs, which seemed to have intensified.

Mark stomped through to the bedroom and fell face first down on the bed. He pulled the duvet up over his head and turned over, then suddenly flung the cover off and reached for his mobile. He had work in the morning and if he didn't set his alarm it was pretty much a guarantee he'd oversleep. *If I get any sleep at all*, he thought bitterly. With the alarm dealt with, he pulled the duvet back over himself and lay there staring at the ceiling until, eventually, he drifted off.

CHAPTER 26

Through the darkness a high-pitched beeping filled the bedroom. A groan sounded from under the duvet and a hand reached out to silence the alarm. With a yawn, Tilly gently pushed off the duvet and reluctantly climbed out of bed. She looked over her shoulder to where Sebastian was sleeping soundly, his back to her. Picking up her clothes from the chair, she collected her mobile phone and crept out. Silently pulling the bedroom door to behind her, she stepped into the bathroom and turned on the shower.

A little over an hour later Sebastian stirred. He rolled over and reached out his arm. Opening his eyes, he realised the bed beside him was empty. Stretching, he got up and opened the curtains to reveal a blanket of white. He could see tyre tracks from the driveway disappearing off along the road and he felt a little sad. *A day home alone it is then*, he thought, unhooking his dressing gown from the back of the door. He used the bathroom and made his way downstairs. Beside the kettle he could see a neatly folded piece of paper with his name on it. He picked it up and opened it.

> Dear Sebastian. I didn't want to wake you.
> I should be home around three.
> Hope you have a lovely day.
> See you soon. T XXX

Sebastian smiled and pressed the note against his heart. He flicked the kettle on, made himself a cup of tea and took it back up to the bedroom. Slipping out of his dressing gown, he climbed back into bed and picked up

316

his mobile phone. The screen showed a missed call notification; it was the office number for Rising Starz. Feeling his stomach tighten, he set the phone back down on the bedside cabinet and read Tilly's note again. He smiled, took a sip of his tea and rested back on the pillows. The memory of his show at The Bloomsbury was still plaguing him and he was still gutted at the untimely end of his act. Up until that point everything was going so well, and now... well, now he felt an overwheming sense of disappointment and sadness that his career as a stage hypnotist was over before it had even really begun.

His phone started vibrating and he looked at the screen. It was the Rising Starz number again. His hand hovered over the phone, then he quickly withdrew it; he wasn't quite ready to talk to them yet. Finishing his tea, he got up to take a shower.

*

'I don't see the point in us opening today,' Mark moaned as John removed the padlock from the roller shutters.

'I'm flippin' *glad* we are!' John retorted. 'I've had just about enough of the mother-in-law and her stinking little mutt. I would've worked Christmas Day if I could.'

As the shutters went up and the light streamed in, Mark squinted. 'But look at it out there. Who in their right mind is gonna come out in that?'

No sooner had the words left his mouth than a woman appeared in the doorway.

'Mornin', love,' John said as she stepped into the reception area.

'Hi. I'm so glad you're open. I wasn't sure whether anyone would be today. Do you replace tyres?'

'Depends what vehicle you've got,' John said.

'It's a Vauxhall Corsa,' she replied.

John walked over to the computer. 'Registration?'

The woman gave him her registration number and John typed it in. 'Yes, you're in luck, we have tyres in stock. Do you want Budget or Premium?'

She smiled. 'Budget will be fine.'

'Okay, drive her in and we'll get you sorted.'

As the woman went back outside, a young man bundled up against the cold was on his way in. He bid her a good morning as she passed.

'Wow, she was hot!' Kaden exclaimed, unwrapping his scarf and removing his coat.

'Bit young for me, son. But yeah, cracking pair of boobs, I'll give you that.' John winked at Mark. 'Told you it was worth opening today, didn't I, Mark?'

'Where's Fred?' Kaden asked

'Probably in bed if he's got any sense,' Mark grumbled.

There was a sound of crunching gears and they all turned to see a silver Corsa slowly pulling into the workshop. The near-side front tyre was completely flat and torn in several places. As the woman climbed out, John said 'Oh crikey, what happened here then?'

'I slid on the ice and hit the kerb,' the woman said. 'Is it bad?'

Kaden knelt down beside the wheel. 'How far did you drive it like this?'

'Not far. It happened near the White Swan.'

Mark came over to the car. 'The White Swan? That's Leyton!' The woman nodded. He bent to look at the shreds of rubber. 'You're gonna need a new wheel too.'

'Oh no, really?!' the woman exclaimed.

'Yep,' Mark said. 'Sorry, love.'

318

'We'll have to book it in for one day next week,' John said.

'Oh no! Can't you do it now?' She looked at John then back at Mark, her eyes pleading with them. 'Please?'

Mark looked at John and raised his eyebrows. John shook his head and the woman's face fell.

'Ah, come on, John,' Mark said. 'We can help her out, surely?'

'I don't think we have any of these wheels in stock,' John replied.

'I'll go check!' Kaden chimed in eagerly.

'It's okay, squirt, I'll do it,' Mark said. He hurried off through swing doors to the stockroom.

The woman stood awkwardly as both Kaden and John stared at her. 'Horrible weather,' she said.

'Yeah, really sucks,' Kaden said.

John just nodded.

The doors burst open and Mark appeared carrying a wheel and a tyre. 'Sorted,' he announced, clearly pleased with himself. 'Would you like a cup of tea whilst I change this?' he added.

'Ooh, yes please,' the woman replied. 'I'm freezing!' She shivered.

'John,' Mark said. 'Get the kettle on would you mate?'

'Thank you *so* much,' the woman said. 'I really appreciate this.'

'No problem at all,' Mark said with a big grin.

She walked over to him and, as she bent over to see what he was doing, her breasts almost fell out of her top.

Mark's eyes widened. He dropped his wrench and it skittered away under the car. 'Shit!' he said under his breath.

319

'I'd better wait outside,' the woman said. She stepped away from the car and went out on to the forecourt. Pulling out her mobile phone, she made a call.

John elbowed Kaden. 'Looks like you've missed out there, son!'

'Yeah, what's with Mark? He's not usually this helpful,' Kaden replied.

'He's caught a sniff of ginger, son!' Kaden looked at him confused. 'Skirt. *Pussy*, son! All this is his pathetic attempt at flirting.'

'Oh, I get you.'

John took a cup of tea out to the woman. She was pacing up and down the forecourt, talking on her phone, and sounded as if she was in the middle of an argument. Nevertheless, she paused long enough to accept the tea and mouthed 'Thank you.'

John returned to the reception and picked up his own mug, and he and Kaden stood watching as Mark changed the wheel and dealt with the tyre. When the job was done, he came over to create the invoice.

John winked at Kaden. 'I reckon you're in there, Mark.'

'You what?' Mark replied as he typed the details into the computer.

'That bird. Why don't you ask her out?' John pressed.

'Oh, fuck off, she's young enough to be my daughter!'

'Yeah, bruv,' Kaden chipped in. 'She's my age innit. Reckon I've got more chance.'

'Oh, you do, do ya?' Mark retorted. 'I reckon she's the sort who'd prefer a real man.'

'So arks her out then bruv. Prove it!'

John chuckled. 'Yeah, go on, Marky! Look, she's coming over, now's your chance.'

Mark glared at him as he retrieved the invoice from the printer. 'How old are you?' Mark said sarcastically.

John continued to twist the knife. 'He's scared, Kaden. Whaddya reckon?'

Kaden laughed. 'Yeah. Chicken shit!'

Mark looked directly at Kaden and let out a loud *ba-gawk*, which echoed around the room. John and Kaden stared at him, unsure what had just happened.

The woman stepped up to the counter with her debit card in her hand. 'Can I pay now?'

Mark's head twitched twice and made several soft *buk-buk* sounds.

Bemused, the woman looked at John. He shrugged his shoulders. 'Come on, Mark, the lady wants to pay.'

Mark dropped the paperwork and started to walk around the room, bobbing his head up and down and flapping his bended arms. He squawked and strutted out into the workshop.

'Sorry, love,' John said. 'Think he must have had one too many last night.' He looked at the invoice 'That's £179.65 please.'

The woman paid and then, giving Mark one last puzzled look, she walked to her car, got in and reversed out of the workshop.

'What's going on, John?' Kaden asked, as Mark continued walking round the garage, stopping occasionally to look into the tool boxes and cabinets. 'He's freaking me out.'

'Mark!' John shouted. Mark stopped and turned to face them. As John and Kaden approached him, he flapped his arms, squawking loudly. 'What the fuck, mate?'

Mark turned and ran waving his arms frantically.

'He's heading outside!' Kaden screeched.

321

The pair took off after him and managed to catch him just as he was about to run out in front of a bus. John grabbed him firmly by the arm. 'Jesus, Mark!' he exclaimed breathlessly. Although Mark was struggling and making a racket, squawking loudly, between the two of them John and Kaden managed to drag him back inside the garage. 'Get the shutters down!' John demanded, as he struggled to keep hold of Mark. Kaden ran over to the button and pressed it. The steel rollers slowly descended and when they were fully closed John let go of Mark. He immediately scuttled away and hid in the corner behind a stack of tyres.

'I dunno what the fuck is going on, but I think we'd better call his missus!' John said with a mixture of concern and anger.

'Yeah, bruv. I fink he's had a nervous breakdown or summink innit.'

John walked into the staff room and reached into Mark's coat pocket. He pulled out his phone and pressed the button to awaken it. 'Bollocks!' He walked back into the workshop.

'What's up?' Kaden asked.

'It's locked. Needs a password.'

'Give it to me bruv. It might be face recognition innit.' John handed Kaden the phone and he took it over to Mark, who was still cowering in the corner and looking very sorry for himself. Kaden held the phone up in front of his face and the phone screen lit up. Kaden handed it back to John. 'Here, bruv, it's unlocked now.'

John opened the contacts list and scrolled down to find Katie. He pressed call and the phone rang a few times before Katie came on the line.

'Yes?' she said abruptly.

'Katie, it's John. From the garage.'

'Oh, hi John,' she said, slightly taken aback. 'Everything okay?'

'Erm. I don't really know how to explain this, but there's something wrong with Mark. I wondered if you'd come and get him?'

'Wrong? Is he okay?'

'Well, yeah, he's fine I think, but he's acting a bit weird. I think he might have had too much to drink or something.'

Katie rolled her eyes. *Why aren't I surprised*, she thought. 'Look, I'm not being funny, but I'm at work. And to be honest I finished with Mark a few days ago, so I'm not really interested.'

John was a bit lost for words. 'Oh. Er. Okay. Sorry, I didn't know.'

The phone went silent and then beeped a couple of times as Katie hung up.

Kaden was looking at John expectantly. 'What's up?'

'Well apparently they've split up. What the hell do we do now?'

'See if his mum or dad are in there?' Kaden ventured.

John scrolled through the contacts list again. 'Nope. There aren't many numbers in here at all.'

'Ring the last number dialled, bruv. Hopefully it's not Uber or Just Eat!'

'Good idea.' John found the recent calls list and selected the last dialled number. He hit call and a man's voice answered.

'Alright, Mark?'

'It's not Mark. My name's John. I work with Mark at the garage. Are you a member of his family?'

'No. I'm a friend. My name's Josh. What's up?'

'Are you local? Only he's, er… not very well and I was hoping someone could come and get him.'

323

'Have you rung his girlfriend, Katie?' Joshua asked.

'Yeah. She didn't want to know.'

'Oh. Er... okay.' Joshua was mystified. 'Alright, look, give me half hour I'll be there. It's Stratford, right?'

'Yeah, Manor Road.'

'Okay. I'm on my way.'

John ended the call and looked over at Mark. He was still sitting on the floor behind the tyres shaking. He looked back at Kaden and the pair of them burst out laughing.

*

A broad smile appeared on Sebastian's face as he heard the key turn in the lock. He switched off the TV and got up to greet Tilly as she walked through the door. She paused on the outside step, her hands full with shopping bags, and stamped the snow from her boots.

'Hey, gorgeous!' Sebastian called out.

Tilly stepped inside and quickly shut the door. 'It's taters out there!' she exclaimed. Removing her boots, she put her bags down and hung up her coat. Then she came over to Sebastian and mischievously put her palms on his cheeks.

He shuddered. 'Oooh, you're *freezing*!'

Tilly giggled. 'I told you, it's cold out there.'

'Come here, I'll warm you up.' Sebastian grabbed her and held her tight, vigorously rubbing his hands up and down her back. 'I was going to crank the heating up, but with the cost of it these days I thought I'd better not.'

'You shouldn't have sat here in the cold. Honestly! Put it on.'

'It's fine, really. I wasn't cold.' He pointed to the sofa. 'I've been snuggled up under blanky.'

Tilly smiled. 'You liked my Christmas present then?'

'I *love* it!! And I love you too!' They cuddled again and Sebastian kissed her lovingly. 'How was work?'

'Fine. All the Christmas sweets and stuff were reduced so I spent most of my day with a roll of orange labels!'

Sebastian's eyes lit up. 'Reduced sweets?' Tilly reached over for one of the carrier bags and opened it to show Sebastian the contents. It was almost full to the brim with a variety of chocolates and nibbles. 'Oh my God, it's like Christmas all over again!' he exclaimed.

Tilly grinned. 'Isn't it though? You can help me put it away later.' She set down the bag. 'So how was your day? Did you hear from James?'

Sebastian shuffled awkwardly. 'Er... well, they did ring, but...' He looked down at his feet.

'But what?' Tilly asked.

'I couldn't bring myself to answer it. I'm sorry, I know that sounds weak, but I just couldn't. They've been ringing on and off all day though.'

'Oh, darling. You're going to have to speak to them some time.'

'Yeah. I know. And I will.' Sebastian sighed resignedly. 'Tomorrow.'

'Promise?'

'Promise. Would you like a cuppa?'

Tilly smiled. 'Ooh, yes please.'

'Okay, put your feet up and I'll get the kettle on.'

Tilly went and sat down on the sofa, pulling Sebastian's blanket up over her legs. There was a faint humming sound and she looked to see Sebastian's phone gliding across the coffee table. 'Seb, darling, your phone's ringing.'

Sebastian's head appeared round the door. 'Huh?'

325

'Your phone,' Tilly said, pointing at the table. 'It's ringing.' Sebastian stood staring at it. 'Come on, hun, bite the bullet.' She picked up the phone and handed it to him, but as he took it, the ringing stopped.

'Oh well…' Sebastian said.

'Call them back,' Tilly urged. Sebastian looked at her, his bottom lip protruding. 'Come on, be strong!'

'Okay,' Sebastian said reluctantly. He pressed the recent calls icon and the missed call showed. 'Oh! It wasn't the agency,' he said with undisguised relief. 'It's Joshua.' He tapped call-back option and it started to ring. While he waited for the call to connect, he returned to the kitchen to finish making the tea. When Joshua answered he said that he was with Mark and explained what had happened at the garage. Sebastian told him that he'd make his way over as soon as he could. Bringing the tea through, he repeated to Tilly what Joshua had told him.

Her face fell. 'I'll run you over there.'

'Let's just quickly have our tea first. It'll warm us up before we go back out into the cold.'

Ten minutes later they were in the car on their way to Joshua's.

*

The January sales had brought crowds of people to the market town of Romford. The streets were heaving and the shops packed with eager consumers, all seeking a bargain.

Jordan's television had been playing up for months, but he'd purposely held off replacing it; he knew he could make a considerable saving if he was patient and waited for the sales. Now, however, he was beginning to wish he'd just ordered one online. It was approaching 4 o'clock, freezing cold and the light was fading, yet unbelievably

326

the town centre was still bustling with shoppers. Nevertheless, he'd made the effort to come out, so he decided rather than shop around he'd just head for the Sony dealership, buy a TV and get the hell out of there.

Meanwhile, in a nearby Primark, Laura Baxter was having a similarly hellish experience. The place was in chaos; clothes were strewn all over the floor and the queues to pay were immense. Her five-year-old daughter, Daisy, needed a new coat for school. Having chosen one, the little girl had gone into meltdown in the middle of the store because she wanted to put it on straight away.

'We need to pay for it first,' Laura tried to explain.

'But Mummy,' the child whined petulantly. 'I want it *now*!'

They joined the queue and Laura stood trying to hide her embarrassment as Daisy continued to whinge. Other people in the queue were staring at her, some of them shaking their heads and tutting. Laura couldn't recall the last time she had felt so self-conscious. Finally, they reached the checkout and she paid for the coat, took Daisy's hand and guided her towards the exit.

'Mummy. Can I put it on now?' the little girl asked.

Laura sighed. It was just easier to give in. 'Yes, okay.' She pulled the new coat out of the paper carrier bag and ripped off the price labels. Her daughter had already removed her old coat and thrown it to the floor. Laura handed her the new one and Daisy gleefully put it on.

'Thank you, Mummy!' the girl exclaimed.

Her mother smiled. 'Come on then. Let's get you home and you can show Daddy.'

As Laura retrieved the old coat from the floor and stuffed it into the bag, Daisy skipped out of the store ahead of her, pleased as punch with her new, bright red coat. Laura caught up with her daughter on the pavement

327

outside. 'Just one moment, sweetheart, Mummy has to send Daddy a text.'

At the same moment that Laura was rummaging in her bag for her phone, Jordan was moving swiftly along South Street. Suddenly something on the pavement up ahead caught his attention, stopping him in his tracks. His nostrils flared.

Illuminated by the bright lights streaming out from the windows of the clothing store, Daisy was standing admiring the reflection of her lovely new coat in the glass. In a flash, she was knocked off her feet by a man hurling himself at her. A piercing scream rang out and all the noise and hubbub of the high street seemed to cease as people stopped and turned to see what had happened.

Laura had dropped her shopping bag and was standing with her hands to her face, screaming. 'Help! Please, somebody *help* me!'

Two men came rushing over and pulled Jordan off the little girl, dragging him away across the pavement as a group of others moved in and pinned him down. Aside from some muffled cries of distress, he made no attempt to resist; he simply lay face down on the pavement with the weight of a dozen people on top of him.

'Somebody call the police!' a man's voice cried out.

Laura fell to her knees beside her seemingly lifeless daughter. Between heavy sobs, she was screaming. 'Daisy! Please, not my little Daisy!' Her face was red, her cheeks streaked with tears. Shoppers in the immediate vicinity gathered around them, stunned into silence by what they had witnessed.

Within a few minutes a siren sounded and the pavement and walls were swathed in an electric blue flashing light. Two car doors slammed and the crowd surrounding Jordan dispersed. He made no attempt to get

328

up. One of the police officers knelt down, manoeuvred Jordan's arms behind his back and handcuffed his wrists; still he made no attempt to resist.

The second officer ran over to Laura. He stopped short as he caught sight of the little body laying crumpled on the pavement. Her face ashen, Laura looked up at him, unable to speak. Then all at once people around them started to talk and a cacophony of voices rattled out about what they'd just witnessed.

The officer appealed for calm. 'Please, I'd ask anyone who didn't see what happened to move along now. Anyone who *did* see, if you'd be kind enough to wait a few minutes an officer will speak with you.'

Still barely able to comprehend what appeared to have occurred, most people began to shuffle away; only a handful remained.

Another siren sounded and an ambulance pulled up beside the police car. As Jordan, looking dazed, was bundled roughly into the back of the police car, a paramedic jumped out of the ambulance and rushed over to the stricken child and her inconsolable mother. Several other police cars arrived and the officers moved the remaining morbid sightseers along. They waited for the ambulance with Daisy and Laura inside to leave before applying a blue tape barrier, using nearby trees and benches to form a ring around the spot where the incident had occurred. The main doors of Primark were closed and locked as the police completely cordoned off the area.

As quickly as it had all happened, it was over. Several of the police officers took statements from people who had been asked to stay, while the car carrying Jordan and the two arresting officers set off and crawled away along South Street.

CHAPTER 27

Vaughan drained his fifth coffee of the day and rested the empty mug on his desk. He looked at the legend emblazoned in blue on the side – **WORLD'S BEST POLICEMAN!** – and smiled to himself as he recalled the excitement on the faces of his grandchildren on Christmas morning, urging him to open their gift before anyone else's.

It was his first day back in the office since Christmas Eve and even though incidents had been surprisingly light over the period, there had still been a significant amount of paperwork to attend to. He'd be headed home for dinner in an hour, but he pulled out a custard cream from the open packet in his desk drawer and was just about to bite into it when there was a knock on the door. He frowned and dropped the biscuit back into the drawer.

'Come.'

The door opened and Sue Dorrington, the station's desk sergeant appeared. 'Sorry to bother you, sir, but Foster and Price have just brought in a guy and they're asking if you can come out.'

'What did they pull him on?' Vaughan said wearily. He could see his plans for home and dinner disappearing.

Dorrington's expression was grave. 'He attacked a little girl, sir.'

Vaughan stiffened. He'd dealt with all manner of crime during his 35 years on the Force, some of it showing humankind at its worst, but anything involving children had never ceased to make him feel sick to his stomach. 'Some sort of domestic?'

'No, sir,' Dorrington replied. 'The girl's mother was in a pretty awful state, but as far as Foster and Price could ascertain it was totally unprovoked. The guy was a complete stranger to her. And he's keeping schtum.'

'Is the girl okay?'

'I'm not sure. She's been taken to hospital.'

Vaughan scowled and stood up. 'Okay, where is he?'

'They put him the interview room. Bringsley is in with him keeping an eye.'

Vaughan's face clouded over. 'Sounds to me as if the bastard should be in a cell.'

Dorrington shook her head. 'Cells are still full, sir. That fight that broke out at the New Year party last night. But the guy didn't resist arrest and he's not behaving violently. Completely the opposite in fact, he's been meek as the proverbial lamb since they pulled him.'

Vaughan followed her out to the reception desk where Price and Foster were stood talking. 'What's the story then, Alex?' he said.

Price looked up. 'Guy attacked a little girl in the street, sir. Set about her pretty savagely. Came out of nowhere, apparently, and her mum couldn't do anything to stop it. Fortunately, a couple of guys passing by managed to drag him off and pin him down. Weird thing is, they said once they'd taken him down, he didn't put up any resistance. Just lay there kind of dazed.'

Vaughan thought for a moment. 'What's the guy's name?'

'He said Jordan King, sir,' Foster replied. 'In fact, that's *all* he said.'

'Right, let's see what we can find out about Mr King, then we'll go have a word with him. Sue, can you accompany me, please?' He nodded appreciatively at the two officers. 'Thanks, guys. Good job.'

Half an hour later, armed with all he'd managed to find out about Jordan, Vaughan accompanied Dorrington to the interview room. She knocked and the door opened. 'Everything okay?' she asked.

Bringsley nodded. 'Not a peep out of him.'

Vaughan looked over Bringsley's shoulder to where Jordan was seated quietly at the table, his head bowed. 'Okay, thanks, Peter. Would you mind bringing in a couple of teas? And a coffee for me.'

Bringsley nodded. 'Right away, sir.' He went out and closed the door softly behind him.

Vaughan and Dorrington went over and sat down opposite Jordan, who raised his head and looked at them apprehensively.

Vaughan sized him up. The lad's coat looked dishevelled and grubby. His eyes were slightly bleary and he looked exhausted. There was a cut on his cheek.

Vaughan nodded at Dorrington. She set the digital recorder going and cautioned Jordan, who sat passively listening to her. Then Vaughan took over. 'Good afternoon, Mr King,' he began amicably. Jordan said nothing. 'My name is Vaughan. Do you understand why you're here?'

After a moment Jordan shook his head. 'No.'

'May I ask what your relationship to Daisy Baxter is?'

Jordan frowned. 'I don't know anyone by that name.'

'Daisy Baxter is the name of the little girl you assaulted in South Street in Romford this afternoon.' Jordan looked at him blankly. 'Outside Primark?' Vaughan added helpfully. 'Can you tell us why you did that?'

Jordan rubbed his eyes. 'I don't remember.'

Vaughan looked at him curiously. 'You don't remember why you assaulted a little girl – allegedly unprovoked?'

332

'I don't remember *doing* it.'

Vaughan glanced at Dorrington. She raised an eyebrow.

'I see,' Vaughan said. He consulted the sheet of paper in front of him. 'It says here you're a carer at Wisteria Heights. Shooters Hill, that's a nice area.'

'Yeah.'

'You like it? Caring for people, I mean?'

'I do. Very much.'

'From what I can piece together about you, that doesn't surprise me at all, Mr King.' Vaughan said. 'It's a very admirable career choice. But, you see, that presents me with a problem.' Jordan looked at him blankly. 'What prompts a man who chooses caring for the elderly as his vocation to suddenly turn on an innocent little girl and ruthlessly attack her?'

They were interrupted by a light rap on the door and Dorrington paused the recording. Bringsley appeared in the doorway carrying a tray bearing three mugs. He came over and set it down on the table. Vaughan nodded a thank you and Bringsley retreated.

'Here.' Vaughan slid a mug across the table towards Jordan. 'You look like you could use this, son.'

Jordan wrapped his hands around the mug as Dorrington started the recording again. 'Interview with Jordan King resumed 18:27. Inspector Vaughan and Sergeant Dorrington present.'

Vaughan took a sip of his coffee. 'So, what *do* you remember, Jordan? You don't mind if I called you Jordan?'

Jordan nodded. 'It's cool. May I ask you something, Mr...? Sorry, I've forgotten what you said your name is.'

'Vaughan.' Jordan seemed to falter. 'Go on, what did you want to ask?'

333

'The little girl. Daisy.' Jordan swallowed hard. Did I...?' The words stuck in his throat. 'Is she...? What I mean is, is she...?'

Vaughan looked Jordan in the eyes. 'She's in hospital,' he said bluntly. He could sense there was genuine remorse and he certainly appeared to be a good lad. But whether or not it was true he was oblivious to what had happened was another matter. Anything was possible, of course, but given the ferociousness of the attack, it didn't seem likely. 'We don't know any more than that at the moment.' He moved on. 'Take me through your afternoon.'

Jordan took a mouthful of tea. 'I was going into town to get a new TV in the sales. It was heaving with bargain-hunters and I immediately regretted it. I thought about giving up and going home. But I'd made the effort to turn out and I was there, so I abandoned my original plan to browse around for the best price and headed straight for the Sony store. I was walking along the pavement and...' He faltered and fell silent.

'What then?' Vaughan prompted.

'I... I don't know. I can't remember.'

Vaughan leant forward and looked at Jordan hard. 'Do you have a medical history that might have been responsible for this? Schizophrenic episodes? Anything at all like that?' Jordan shook his head. 'Have you been taking *any* sort of medication at all?' Jordan shook his head again. Vaughan sat back in his chair. 'Tell me, do you like a drink, Jordan?'

'A drink?'

'Yes. Alcohol.'

Jordan nodded. 'Some, yeah.'

'Were you drinking before you left the house?'

334

'No. I mean, I had a couple of lagers yesterday, sure. Who doesn't like a drink on New Year's Day? But I haven't had a drop since about nine o'clock last night.'

'What about drugs?'

'Never!'

Vaughan finished his coffee and looked at him for a moment. 'You know what, Jordan? I believe you. But I have to ask you if you'd be prepared to submit to a drugs test to verify that?'

'A drugs test?'

'Yes. I'm sure you understand I need to get to the bottom of what happened this afternoon. And we have to rule out the obvious possible causes. You understand that?'

Jordan nodded. 'Sure.'

'Good man. We use a system called Drugwipe. It's mostly used at roadside and it gives an instant result. It only requires you to give a saliva sample.'

'Okay,' Jordan said.

'If you'd like to go with Sergeant Dorrington, she'll explain exactly what's required and administer the test.' Vaughan nodded at Dorrington and she stopped the recording.

A few minutes later, Jordan's test had revealed a negative result and he'd been escorted to one of the now vacated cells, where he was left looking like a broken man.

'What do you think, Sue?' Vaughan asked. He was back in his office and Dorrington was seated opposite.

''He seems so nice,' she replied. 'I mean, I genuinely believe he doesn't know why he did it. He seemed mortified to hear what he'd done. And if he hadn't actually been detained at the scene, I'd have said we had the wrong man.'

Vaughan scratched his head. 'My thoughts exactly. And *if* he genuinely has no recollection, there's nowhere left to go with this. We need to speak to someone else. His next of kin, parents or a girlfriend or someone. *Anyone* who might be able to shed some light on this. Go ask him for a number we can call.'

Ten minutes passed, during which Vaughan tried to focus on some of the outstanding mound of paperwork needing his attention, but he found he couldn't concentrate. *It can wait till tomorrow anyway*, he thought. He had just given in to the lure of a custard cream when Dorrington returned.

'Well?'

'No mother or siblings, just a father. But he didn't want us to call him. Sounds like they don't have the best relationship.'

'So where does that leave us? A friend? Work colleague?'

Dorrington held up a scrap of paper. He gave me the number for his best friend, a Joshua Hunter.'

'Excellent. Give him a call.'

'Already did, sir. I didn't tell him what happened, but he was genuinely shocked to hear his mate had been arrested. He asked if a couple of King's other friends could come along...' – she consulted the piece of paper – '...Sebastian Matthews and Tilly Shaw. He said they were with him and I thought it made sense to say yes. If Hunter can't help, I figured maybe Matthews or Shaw might be able to. Anyway, they're on their way in now. Should be here in about half an hour.'

Vaughan nodded approvingly. 'Damned good work. Has King had anything to eat since we brought him in?'

'He said he was hungry so I had a word with Bringsley. He's sorting a sandwich for him.'

336

Vaughan smiled. 'We're going to miss you round here when you retire, Sue. Here.' He pulled out the packet of biscuits from his drawer and offered it to Dorrington. 'I think you've earned yourself a custard cream. Let's just hope these youngsters can help make sense of this bloody mess.'

A little over twenty minutes later, Bringsley knocked the door to inform Vaughan that Jordan's three friends had arrived and they were waiting in reception. Vaughan went out to greet them. 'Vaughan,' he said. 'Thank you for coming in so quickly.'

'What's going on?' Joshua asked. 'Why has Jordan been arrested?'

Vaughan looked at him. 'You are?'

'Joshua. Joshua Hunter.'

Vaughan gestured at Sebastian and Tilly. 'And your friends?'

'This is Seb – Sebastian I mean – and his girlfriend Tilly.'

Vaughan smiled at them politely. 'So just to clarify, Joshua, Mr King doesn't have a wife? A girlfriend?'

'No,' Joshua said. 'He's gay.'

'I see, so you're his…?'

Joshua shook his head. 'No. I'm his best friend.'

Vaughan nodded. 'I see. Well, normal procedure is to speak with next of kin in the first instance, but Mr King very specifically didn't want us to call his father. So I'm hoping you might be able to help us make sense of what happened today.'

'But what *has* happened?' Sebastian said.

Vaughan noted that both he and the girl appeared rather shaken. 'If you'd like to accompany me, I'll explain.' He nodded at Dorrington and she escorted Joshua, Sebastian and Tilly into the interview room where they sat in

337

stunned silence while he appraised them as to what Jordan had been arrested for.

'So, as you can see,' Vaughan concluded, 'we're at as much of a loss to explain Mr King's actions as he appears to be himself. As far as we can ascertain he wasn't on drugs, he hadn't been drinking, he has no medical hist…'

'I think I might know.' It was Sebastian who had spoken. 'I think it's my fault,' he added quakily, dropping his eyes sorrowfully to the floor.

'Go on, Sebastian,' Vaughan said quietly. 'Anything you can give me to explain this will help. *Is* it drugs?'

'No.' Sebastian said. 'I think he did it under hypnosis.'

Vaughan peered at him curiously. If he'd had to make a wild guess as to why Jordan King had attacked a little girl he didn't even know, in public and with no apparent motive, hypnosis wouldn't have even made the list. 'So, you're telling me that someone hypnotised him and made him do it?'

'No, he *was* hypnotised, but there's no way I could have known it would result in this.'

Vaughan sat forward and rested his elbows on the desk. 'So, *you* hypnotised him?'

'Yes.'

'What was it, some kind of party prank?'

'No.'

Vaughan frowned. Somehow, as crazy as it sounded, what Sebastian was saying made sense. It was certainly one explanation as to why he had a man sitting in a cell, seemingly oblivious to an act of extreme and inexplicable brutality. 'Okay, Sebastian,' he said. 'Let's say for the sake of argument I believe you. You're still going to have to give me more than that.'

'I'm a stage hypnotist,' Sebastian said. 'It's my profession. It's all done for entertainment.' He looked at

338

Tilly. She smiled at him encouragingly. 'On New Year's Eve I was performing my act at a charity event at The Bloomsbury Theatre,' Sebastian continued. 'Jordan was one of my volunteers and I got him to behave like a bull. I did a silly matador act and made him react to my red muleta.'

'Your *what*?' Vaughan said.

'Muleta,' Sebastian repeated. 'It's a matador's cape. Jordan was charging around the stage like... well, like an angry bull.'

Vaughan sat back in his chair. 'Okay, let's go with this for a minute. Explain to me why he was still hypnotised two days later. Isn't it normal to bring people out of their trance – or whatever you want to call it – when the act is finished?'

Sebastian swallowed hard. 'Yes, it is. But there was a fire backstage, you see, and the lights went out and the sprinklers started, and...' Sebastian swallowed again. 'Well, it was chaos and the theatre had to be evacuated. I hadn't had a chance to bring them back out and usually the effect wears off naturally. It never even occurred to me it wouldn't. Can I ask a question?'

Vaughan raised an open hand and nodded. 'Sure.'

'Was the little girl that Jordan attacked wearing red?'

Vaughan squinted at him. 'She was, yes.'

Sebastian exhaled deeply. 'That's it then.'

'That's what?'

'Her red clothes triggered him. That's why he behaved the way he did. He wouldn't have even been aware.'

The gravity of what Sebastian was saying hit home. 'You said *them*,' Vaughan mused.

'Them?'

339

'Just now you said you didn't have time to snap *them* out of it. How many people exactly were involved in this show?'

'Four.'

Vaughan raised an eyebrow. 'So, tell me about the others.'

'Well, there was my friend Katie and her boyfriend, Mark, and...'

The corner of Vaughan's mouth twitched. 'Are you telling me you *knew* all these so-called volunteers?'

'Yes, well...'

'That doesn't sound very professional to me. If you can really hypnotise people, why is it you were using your friends instead of random volunteers? Are you saying this show was a sham?'

'I had to use my friends because I was asked to by the agency I work for. I *can* hypnotise people, but occasionally there'll be someone who isn't susceptible. It was a very prestigious event and they didn't want to take the chance anything would go wrong. I knew I could guarantee putting my friends under, I've done it before.'

Vaughan was trying to process what he was hearing. 'What did you get your friends to do?'

'Katie, nothing,' Sebastian said. 'The blackout occurred before I could get to her. I got Mark to behave like a chicken every time he heard the word. And...' He trailed off.

'What is it, Sebastian? What about the fourth person?'

Joshua interjected. 'The other guy wasn't one of our friends.'

'Oh?' Vaughan looked at him quizzically. 'I thought the volunteers were all your friends.'

'It was meant to be like that,' Joshua said. 'It was set up that Sebastian knew where we were all sitting so he

340

could pick us out. I was meant to be one of the volunteers, but there was some other idiot sitting in my seat and he wouldn't move. So, I wasn't where I was meant to be. I ended up in what I guess must have been his seat instead.'

Vaughan nodded thoughtfully. 'I'm not entirely sure I'm buying all this. I mean, it's a little bit out there. But I have to concede it *is* feasible, and right now I don't have anything better.'

Tilly had remained silent while Sebastian explained, but now she spoke. 'Everything Seb is saying is true,' she said. 'We had a call from Josh earlier because he'd had to go pick up Mark from work. He was behaving like a chicken. When we got there Seb was able to snap him out of it.'

'Which is what he *would* have done on the night of the show, but couldn't,' Joshua added.

Vaughan looked at Sebastian. 'I assume you've no idea who this other man was?'

'No,' Sebastian replied. 'He was the one genuine volunteer. Albeit inadvertently.'

'And what did you make him do?'

'I had him believe he was Lewis Hamilton. The trigger was the *Formula 1* theme tune.'

'Well, I don't see him being too great a concern then,' Vaughan said. 'All the same, we're going to need to find out who he was.' He looked at Joshua. 'I don't suppose for one moment you remember the seat number you occupied, son?'

'I can, actually. J3 in the stalls.'

'Good. For now we're going to work on the assumption J3 was the seat our mystery man paid for.' Vaughan looked at Dorrington. 'Can you give the theatre a call in a minute and find out who booked that seat?'

'Yes, sir.'

341

There was a knock on the door.

'Come,' Vaughan called out.

The door opened and Bringsley appeared. 'Some good news, sir. We just had a call from the hospital to say that the little girl is fine and her mother is taking her home. She'll almost certainly want to press charges, but right now she's just relieved her kid is safe.'

'Thanks for letting me know,' Vaughan said. Bringsley acknowledged with a nod and closed the door. 'Right then,' Vaughan said decisively, clapping his hands together. 'This brings us back to Mr King.'

'Are you going to let him go?' Joshua asked.

Vaughan held up a hand. 'Not so fast.' He looked at Sebastian. 'If I believe everything you'd told me, son – and I stress *if* – and I were to ask you to snap him out of this supposed state of hypnosis, I'd need to be one hundred percent certain he's not going to be a danger to anyone before I can release him. Otherwise, I'm afraid he spends the night here under lock and key.'

'I think I can prove it to you,' Sebastian said. 'If you're willing to let me.'

CHAPTER 28

As his friends appeared in the doorway of his cell, Jordan couldn't have looked more relieved. He came over and hugged Joshua tightly. 'Man, I'm so pleased to see you.' He was trembling and his eyes were moist. Vaughan appeared behind Seb, and Jordan stepped quickly away from Joshua's embrace, wiping the tears from his eyes.

'Your friends here just might have helped us to solve this mystery,' Vaughan said. 'But first I need to tell you the little girl you attacked is going to be okay.'

Jordan stared at him and for a moment it didn't seem as if he was going to respond. Then he burst into tears. Joshua took him by the arm, guided him to the bench and sat down beside him with his arm around his friend's shoulders.

Vaughan handed him a handkerchief and gestured to Sebastian. 'I'll let Sebastian tell you what he believes happened.'

Blowing his nose, Jordan sat listening wide-eyed as Sebastian apologetically explained to him what must surely have led him to attack Daisy Baxter.

'We need to perform a little experiment if you're willing,' Vaughan said when Sebastian had finished. Jordan looked at him questioningly. 'The result will determine whether or not you get to go home tonight.'

'I'll do whatever you need,' Jordan said.

Vaughan looked at Sebastian. 'Tell me you're sure this isn't going to go wrong.'

'If this demonstration proves to you everything I've said, you'll have the answers you need. And I promise I can bring him out of it once and for all.'

Vaughan summoned Dorrington, who came in and handed Sebastian a clipboard. 'I pulled this off the notice board in reception,' she said.

Vaughan looked at Tilly. 'Can I ask you step out with Sergeant Dorrington for a moment please?'

When they'd gone Vaughan addressed Joshua. 'Okay, son, I need you to hold your friend by his shoulders as firmly as you can. Just for a few seconds.'

Joshua did as he was asked, gripping Jordan's shoulders tightly.

Vaughan looked at Sebastian. 'Okay, now.'

Sebastian held out the clipboard and flipped it round to face Jordan. There was a red sheet of A4-sized paper attached to it. As if someone had thrown a switch, Jordan's face turned to thunder. His nostrils flared and he snarled, squirming to break free of Joshua's grip.

Vaughan's eyes widened. He could hardly believe what he was seeing. 'Enough!' he exclaimed, and Sebastian dropped the clipboard face down on the floor.

As quickly as he had reacted to the red stimulant, Jordan slumped back against the wall and his expression returned to normal.

Vaughan looked at Sebastian. 'I'm not too proud to admit I didn't completely believe you,' he said. 'I'm sorry. Can you bring him out of it now? Permanently?'

'Yes,' Sebastian said confidently.

'Here, I don't suppose you do animals, do you?' Vaughan mused. 'I've got this Labrador, you see. Lovely dog but, my God, he barks for England. Drives me and the missus nuts.' He caught sight of the look on Sebastian's face. 'Yes, well, maybe you can just get on and deal with Mr King.'

*

When he lost his business as a restaurant owner during Covid, the last thing Jeff Morrison ever saw himself doing was deliveries. But with his wife unable to work due to health issues and a hefty mortgage to pay, he'd been given very little choice. The increasing demand for goods sold online meant there was a sudden abundance of vacancies for multi-drop drivers. The pay was meagre, but he was able to choose his own hours and on the whole the job really wasn't that bad.

The area he had been allocated left a lot to be desired though. His territory covered most of Slough and Windsor and it was a labourious drive at the best of times, but with the roads icy and visibility poor it was far from fun. It wasn't so much that he minded the conditions, indeed, he'd always considered himself an exemplary driver. It was just the other "muppets" – as he liked to refer to them – out on the road made the job less pleasurable than it might otherwise have been. The one saving grace as far as he was concerned was the top of the range sound system installed in the van and Planet Rock. Jeff loved music and however crappily the day might pan out, it could always be saved by guitar riffs and powerful vocals.

Roadworks on the South Lea Road were causing chaos and Jeff was currently sitting in a line of traffic that seemed to go on forever. He tapped his hands on the steering wheel, drumming along to the beat of Creedence Clearwater Revival's *I Put a Spell on You*. The van continued to crawl forward and he yawned as the cars in front ground to a halt once again. The endless red lights snaking off into the distance were making Jeff's eyes sore and he rubbed them with the back of his hand. He looked to the passenger seat where there was a clipboard detailing his delivery schedule. He had just two more drops to do and he could head for home – if he ever managed to get there.

The song finished and adverts began to play. Jeff tutted. He hated the adverts. The traffic started to move again and he could make out the temporary traffic lights that were causing the delay. Once he passed them, he'd be on the Windsor Road at last. The lights changed to green and the queue started to move.

Jeff let out a sigh of relief. 'Finally!'

As he drove through the lights, the adverts on the radio finished and the DJ announced the next song. 'And now folks an all time classic from 1977, Fleetwood Mac and *The Chain*.'

'Ah, tune!' Jeff rejoiced. He drummed along as his van cruised pleasingly down the Windsor Road. As the song reached the bridge, with the familiar *Formula 1* theme tune fading in, Jeff's hands tightened around the steering wheel. His knuckles turned white and, with his eyes fixed forward, he slammed his foot down hard on the accelerator.

*

Dorrington had managed to speak to a man at The Bloomsbury's box office and he had been more than accomodating, providing her with the name, home address and phone number of Sebastian's unexpected volunteer. She had immediately called the number and been told by Jeff Morrison's wife that he was at work.

'Sue, could you get onto this delivery company and see if we can track down Mr Morrison?' Vaughan asked.

'Yes, of course, sir, I'll do that straight away,' Dorrington replied.

Vaughan left the office whilst she made her call. He stepped out into the station staff car park for a breath of fresh air. It was dark, but the sky was full of thick grey cloud and there was sleet in the air. He sighed heavily. He had never really been a believer of magic or hypnotism; if anyone had asked, he'd have told them it was a load of mumbo jumbo. Yet here he was investigating the assault of a five-year-old girl by a man re-enacting the antics of a farmyard bull. He had no idea where to start when it came to filing his report.

Shivering, he stepped back inside, pulling the door shut behind him. As he made his way back to the office, he was met in the corridor by Dorrington. She was holding a black leather-bound notebook. 'Okay, sir, I've just got off the phone with a lady called Natalia. She's the planning manager for…' – she checked her notes – '…PDQ deliveries.' Vaughan opened the office door and gestured for her to go in. 'She confirmed that Mr Morrison does work there,' Dorrington continued, 'and that he's currently out delivering.'

Vaughan tapped a pen on his lip. 'Right.'

Dorrington consulted her notes again. 'Natalia said that Jeff – sorry, Mr Morrison – has worked for them since July 2021 and has a clean record. She also said that all their fleet is fitted with tracking so they can locate their vehicles at any time.'

Vaughan nodded. 'Okay, that's good. As I said, we have no reason to believe that Mr Morrison is going to commit any crimes and to be honest, despite what I've seen tonight, I'm still finding all this hypnotism malarkey a bit difficult to swallow. I think what we need to do now is…' he was interrupted by knocking on the office door. 'Come!'

The door opened and Bringsley entered, his face etched with concern. 'I'm sorry to disturb you, sir. But we've just had a call come in from traffic control.'

'Can't you deal with it?' Vaughan asked.

'Well yes, sir, normally I would. But it's our guy. Morrison.'

Vaughan's eyes widened and stood up. 'What's happening? Who called it in?'

'The mobile team picked him up doing 90 down the Windsor Road,' Bringsley said. 'ANPR traced the number plate back to the delivery company. We got straight on the phone to them and they're tracking him now. Goodman is on the phone right now with a woman called Natalia.'

Vaughan and Dorrington followed Bringsley through to the office where officer David Goodman was sat at a computer showing Google Maps. His phone was on the desk in loudspeaker mode.

'He's approaching the Edward VII bridge,' a voice reported from the phone.

Goodman tapped his pen on the computer screen. 'In a few minutes he's going to be driving right through Windsor.'

'Get onto Thames Valley,' Vaughan said. 'Tell them to send a chopper and as many cars as they can. They need to drop a stinger before Morrison hits the town!'

The voice on the phone spoke again. 'The vehicle has crossed the bridge. His speed has decreased slightly, but he's still moving.'

*

Traffic had started to build up and Jeff was forced to slow down. He revved his engine furiously, weaving through the narrow gaps between oncoming cars, oblivious to the sound of angry horns. As the road ahead cleared, he slammed his foot down on the accelerator again. The van shook as he took it up to 80. He could see orange flashing lights ahead, but his focus was on nothing more than driving as fast as he could until he reached the finish line.

*

'Sir, Thames Valley are sending cars now,' Bringsley said. 'They've just reported that Thames Street is closed for an event and the driver is heading straight for it.'

Dorrington gasped. 'Thames Street?'

'That's what they said,' Bringsley replied.

'My neighbour's daughter is there tonight!'

Bringsley and Vaughan looked at her, confused. 'What's the event?' Vaughan said.

'There's a big do on. The theatre there is putting on a tribute show in the square for the Queen. Little Maisie, she lives next door to me, she's in the dance troupe.' She put her hands to her mouth. 'Oh my God, there'll be *hundreds* of kids there!'

*

Jeff's arms relaxed on the wheel. The road ahead was clear and he smiled as he looked in his wing mirrors to see only the faint glimmer of headlights behind him. He was well in the lead with no clear challenger. He eased off the accelerator a bit until suddenly the lights seemed to be getting nearer.

It was a police car pulling up close, but to Jeff it was a rival; someone that wanted to take the trophy from him. The car sounded its siren twice, but Jeff paid no heed and pushed his foot down hard on the accelerator. As King

Edward VII Avenue met Dachet Road, Jeff spun the van around the bend.

A helicopter was circling above and three police cars joined the first and continued to chase the transit van. Jeff momentarily took his eyes off the road to look up at the helicopter, failing to see an orange and white plastic barrier positioned at the entrance to Thames Street just up ahead. The van hit it with incredible force and the two pieces fractured and separated. As sections of the barrier were sent flying across the road, the van ploughed onwards and straight into the closed-off road, where screaming spectators scattered in all directions.

The drum and trumpet corps dropped their instruments and ran as the van careered straight into a cluster of children carrying papier-machè models of the Queen.

*

The receiver on Bringsley's jacket crackled. 'Sir. This is Officer Baker. I'm at the scene. The van has hit the children. I repeat, the van has hit the children. Over.'

Vaughan's face drained of colour and Dorrington buried her face in her hands and started to sob.

Bringsley cleared his throat. 'Received. Over.'

CHAPTER 29

Tilly let out a huge sigh. 'You know, Grace, after losing Mum I never thought I'd ever feel a sadness as all consuming as that ever again. Grace moved her hand across the kitchen table and gently rested it on Tilly's. 'I just don't know what to do,' she continued.

'How is the counselling going?' Grace asked.

'I honestly don't know. He doesn't really talk about it. Truth be told, he doesn't really talk much at all.'

'It's going to take time. It's only been six weeks since it happened.' Grace was trying her best to sound encouraging, but she didn't really know what to say either.

Tilly sighed again. 'I know.'

Grace squeezed her hand tight. 'Everything will be alright.' Tilly started to sob and then, unable to hold it in any longer she burst into tears. Grace stood up and came round the table. She hugged Tilly tight. 'Oh, sis. I'm sorry. I wish I could make all this go away.'

Tilly's chest heaved in and out as she desperately tried to stop her tears. 'It's not just that,' she spluttered. 'I'm...' She managed to control her breathing. 'I'm pregnant.'

Grace pulled away and looked at her sister. 'Really?'

Tilly nodded. 'Yeah. About 12 weeks gone.'

'Oh my God!' Grace exclaimed. 'That's wonderful news. Does Seb know?'

'No. I only just found out myself. I mean, I skipped a couple of periods. But I just put it down to stress.' She took hold of Grace's hand. 'But look.' She guided it over her stomach and Grace beamed as she felt the small bump in Tilly's slender midriff. 'I did a test at the doctors last week.'

'I'm going to be an Aunty!' Grace squealed.

'You're going to be an Aunty!'

Grace kissed her sister on the head and returned to her seat. She leant forward. 'You *must* tell Seb. This might just be what he needs to bring him out of this quagmire.'

'I just don't know if it's the right time. I mean, you haven't seen him, Grace. He stays in bed most of the day, he doesn't bother to wash, he barely eats.' She started to well up again. 'Honestly, I feel helpless. But no matter what I say or do, he just looks at me with this absolute sadness in his eyes and all I want to do is hold him. But when I try, he just shrugs me away. The only time he leaves the house is to go to King George's for his counselling and I drive him there and back.'

Grace looked at her sister, trying to hide her own feelings of sadness. 'He needs something positive. Something to look forward to.'

'Yes. Maybe you're right. I spoke to Dr Hirsch – he's the counsellor – and he said that Seb has withdrawn because his brain can't process what has happened. He thinks that he has a form of PTSD.'

Grace frowned. 'Isn't that what soldiers get?'

'Yes, but it's not just soldiers. Anyone who has had a traumatic experience can suffer with it.'

'But Sebastian wasn't to blame. Surely he must know that.'

'He doesn't though. He says everything is his fault. What Jordan did to the little girl...'

'That was awful. But she was okay. And the mother never pressed charges in the end, did she?'

Tilly shook her head. 'No. But he blames himself for the death of that Jeff guy. And the injured kids and their

352

dance teacher at Windsor. He has nightmares about it almost every night.' She sighed. 'I wish Mum was here, she'd know what to do. It's all such a mess.'

There was a crunching of gravel from the driveway outside as a car pulled up. 'Oh, that's Jason home,' Grace said.

Tilly wiped her eyes. 'I'd better go.'

'You don't have to.'

'No, really. I need to get going, my shift starts at two.' Tilly stood up. 'And I think I *will* tell Seb. After work. I was going to make us a nice romantic dinner tonight anyway as it's Valentine's Day. It'll be the perfect time to make the announcement.'

'He'll be over the moon, I'm certain of it.' Grace stood up and hugged her sister. 'You take it easy at work, you've got a little one to think of now.' She squealed. 'Ooooh, I still can't believe it. I'm gonna have a little Niece or Nephew!'

Tilly kissed her sister and as she went to the front door it opened and Jason walked in holding something behind his back. He smiled when he saw Tilly. 'Hi! Not leaving on my account, I hope?'

'No, I've got to go to work.'

'How's Seb?'

Tilly smiled. 'He's okay. One day at a time, you know.'

'Well give him my best,' Jason said as Tilly stepped out the door.

'I will. Thank you.'

Grace looked at her husband and a single tear trickled down her cheek.

'Oh, sweetheart. What's up?' Jason asked softly.

'I'm going to be an Aunty,' Grace said croakily.

'Congratulations.' Jason stepped over and whipped out a big bunch of white roses from behind his back. 'And happy Valentine's Day.'

Grace beamed and threw her arms around him. 'And *you're* going to be an Uncle!'

*

Sebastian closed the front door and dropped his rucksack down on the kitchen table. Panting heavily, he sat down on the chair, his heart pounding and his body trembling. He had only been out for 20-minutes, just to the convenience store at the end of the road, but every step he took he felt as though people were looking at him. In the shop he was sure the cashier and another customer were talking about him. On the walk back, a neighbour was washing his car and Sebastian was convinced the man stopped what he was doing and watched him walk by.

As his breathing returned to normal, he reached for his rucksack and unzipped it. He pulled out three packets of paracetamol and laid them out in a row on the table. Dropping his rucksack onto the floor, he sat for a moment staring at the packets. Then he stood up and went upstairs to the bathroom. Opening the cabinet, he scanned inside amongst the various bottles and packets until he found one blister pack of tablets. He examined the tiny writing on the foil: Ibuprofen. Two had already been pressed out and there were four remaining. He went through the bedroom and opened the top drawer of Tilly's dressing table. Rummaging around, he found another blister pack with four more tablets in as well as an unopened box. Then he went back downstairs to the kitchen, where he filled a pint glass with water and took a small tumbler from the cupboard. He sat back down at the table, putting the two

354

glasses beside him. Moving the box so that it lined up with the others, he placed the blister packs on top and counted the tablets in his head: 72 in total. He sat in silence. The ticking of the clock on the wall was the only sound.

He didn't know how long he had been sitting there, but a cold draft down his spine suddenly made him shiver. He looked out through the kitchen door and across the hallway. He could see the sofa in the sitting room where his navy-blue fleecy blanket was laying, neatly folded up on the back of the settee. A lump formed in his throat as he thought of Tilly. He got up and walked through to the sitting room. Scooping up the blanket, he wrapped it around his shoulders and went back to the kitchen. The clock seemed to be ticking even more loudly now. He turned on the radio and raised the volume, then sat back down at the table. Picking up one of the blister packs, he slowly pressed the pills out into the small tumbler, then emptied the other one into the glass. He reached for one of the boxes and opened the flap. Struggling to remove the folded-up paper inside, he split the box to pull out the pills. As he pulled the contents out, the blanket slipped off his shoulders and onto the floor. He was about the bend the plastic inner to expel more of the tablets when a hand rested on his shoulder. With a start he turned around.

'Sebastian. What are you doing?' Tilly said softly. He looked at her; his eyes were sullen. 'My love. *What* are you doing?' she repeated. Sebastian dropped the pills and his head fell against her hip. She knelt down and took his head in her arms. 'Oh, my darling, please don't cry. I'm here.' Tilly held him and gently stroked his hair until he finally stopped crying. She reached for his hands. 'You're freezing!' Standing up, she took the blanket from the floor and draped it across his shoulders. 'Come on, let's go through to the living room.' She gently guided him to the sofa and sat him down, wrapping the blanket tightly around him. Stepping back into the hall, she turned the dial up on the thermostat, then went and sat down next to Sebastian. He was huddled in the blanket with his head down staring at the floor.

'Seb. Darling. Why did you have all those tablets out on the table?' Tilly asked softly.

Sebastian shook his head. 'I don't know,' he replied. His voice was croaky and he sounded exhausted.

Tilly felt under the blanket and took hold of his hand. 'Have you taken any?'

He lifted his head and looked at her. 'No,' he replied in a whisper. He started to sob again.

Tilly pulled him towards her and cradled him in her arms. 'It's okay. Let it all out,' she said, gently stroking his cheek.

After a few moments, Sebastian shuffled himself to sit up. Tilly handed him a tissue and he blew his nose. 'I'm sorry,' he said weakly.

'You've nothing to be sorry for,' Tilly replied, squeezing his hand.

He blew his nose again and unwrapped the blanket. 'I'm hot now.'

Tilly helped him pull the blanket off. 'I don't want to nag but can you tell me what happened today?' She took hold of his hand again.

Sebastian looked at her. His eyes were red and his brow furrowed. 'I just couldn't bare it any more.'

'Okay,' Tilly said.

'I... I just...' He exhaled a deep sigh.

'It's okay, my love. Take your time.'

'It's all the noises. You know, in my head. It never stops. I just wanted them to stop.' His head slumped. 'I just wanted them to stop,' he repeated.

356

Tilly stroked his hair. Her heart was breaking and her mind was racing. She was angry and sad and felt completely out of her depth. 'Seb. You know I love you,' she said softly.

'I love you too,' he replied without lifting his head.

Tilly cupped both of her hands around his face and gently lifted his head. 'So why would you leave me? Why would you take all those pills and leave me on my own?' She felt herself starting to cry.

'I'm sorry. I'm *so* sorry,' Sebastian replied. He closed his eyes.

Tilly put her arms around him. 'I don't want to lose you, Seb.'

'You won't. I'm sorry,' he said, bringing his arm up and around Tilly's shoulder. He held her tight. 'I love you so much.'

A couple of hours passed and Tilly carefully eased herself out from under Sebastian, who had fallen fast asleep on the sofa. She picked up the blanket and tenderly draped it over him. She went out to the kitchen and, shaking her head, scooped up the tablets. Pressing her foot on the pedal bin, the lid sprang open and she threw the packets inside and emptied the tumbler. She rested her palms on the worktop and looked out of the window into the darkness.

Sebastian appeared in the doorway. 'I'm *so* sorry,' he said. He walked over and wrapped his arms around Tilly. 'I promise I won't do anything like that ever again.'

Tilly smiled up at him. 'It's okay to feel the way you do, my love. But you need to try and move on. Put all this behind you.'

'I don't know if I can. I just can't get all those children out of my mind.'

'I know. But the liaison said they're all home from hospital now. Nothing more than a few broken bones and well on the mend. Kids bounce back. They'll be fine given time. And so will you.'

Sebastian sighed. 'I guess so.'

'I *know* so!' Tilly said firmly. 'Listen, I was going to make spaghetti bolognaise. Are you hungry?'

Sebastian shook his head. 'Not really.'

'You must eat something. Keep your strength up or it'll be *you* in hospital.'

'It's nothing less than I deserve,' he replied sorrowfully.

'Now come on. That's enough of that. You've got your whole life ahead of you. You've gotta start thinking about the future.'

'*What* future?'

Tilly felt the anger beginning to rise, but she stopped herself. She knew in her heart Sebastian couldn't help the way he was feeling, but it was difficult for her to see him wallowing. 'A future with me and...' She stopped.

Sebastian stared at her.

She took his hand and placed it on her stomach. 'We *do* have a future my love. You, me and our little baby.'

Sebastian's eyes widened. 'What?!' he said shakily.

'I'm pregnant. You're going to be a Dad!'

Sebastian's face lit up. It was the first time Tilly had seen him smile in weeks. He dropped to his knees and tilted his head, resting it on Tilly's stomach. 'I'm going to be a Dad.'

Acknowledgements:
The authors would like to thank Sue Hards and Sara Greaves.
They would also like to thank their loyal readers, whose support and
encouragement has got us this far.

Rebecca would especially like to thank Ray Frost for believing in her and
driving her to continue writing. You are my inspiration.

Cover design by TimBex.

Also from Rebecca Xibalba and Tim Greaves:
Misdial (2020)
The Break (2021)
The Well (2021)
Reset (2022)
Available from Amazon, for Kindle and in paperback.
All titles available in Audiobook format from Audible and iTunes.
3.2.1. coming to Audible and iTunes soon.

Printed in Great Britain
by Amazon

12400557R00207